COOL AMONG THE FLAMES

Third Edition January 2005   http://www.lulu.com/noel

First edition published June 2004

© Noel C Bailey: Sydney

All rights reserved: No part of this publication may be reproduced, copied in part or in whole or stored on any electronic retrieval system, on-site or remote, or transmitted by electronic, mechanical or other means, for any purpose, without the written consent of the publisher and author.

ISBN 1-4116-2414-9

General Retail: SIC Classification 5942

Non-Fiction

FORWARD

Do you play Chess? Wonderful pastime. So simple in concept, so complex in execution. I've been playing the same game with God now for fifty-eight years. I'm presently in 'check' but the game's far from over. Sure, he's sitting pretty having taken most of my pawns, one rook, a castle and both bishops, but while I'm on the board, the game lurches on. *"Cool Among the Flames"* is the story behind one man's rise to total obscurity, a lesson in skewed destiny or to put it more succinctly, life in the break-down lane.

You pick up an autobiography and would most certainly assume you must *know* the person, or at least be familiar with some of his or her finest achievements, be it in sports, science or the arts. In this case, my having achieved nothing of prominence, such assumption is sadly misplaced. What we have here are memories as opposed to memoirs, sustenance rather than substance and living as opposed to existing. My life has been a cruelly amusing pastiche of *"Every Which Way But Loose," "Fox On the Run." "Bad Moon Rising"* with perhaps a dash of *"Edelweiss."*

I would like to say that this book was inspired by some particular person or event in my life, but why lie? I have absolutely no definable reason for writing it, other than my daughter's constant harping as to "What DID you do over the past forty years daddy?" I must admit that it has provided free therapy during its compilation and serves if nothing else, as the surrogate diary that I vowed to maintain, but never did.

I would however like to dedicate this work to my five uniquely wonderful children, *Ghinda, Christopher, Kathryn, Jennifer* and *Lisa* (in order of appearance). Their names are real of course. Those of other friends and acquaintances who have made guest-appearances in my life at crucial, often comical times, have by necessity, occasionally been changed – purely to protect the guilty you understand.

But enough of this – I can hear my primary school teacher now….."Never start a sentence with a conjunction Noel." Whoever reads "forwards" anyway? Let's get on with it.

Baulkham Hills NSW   January 2005

Table of Contents:

	Page
Forward	3
Check-In	8
For the Term of His Natural Life	18
Winds of Change	30
Changing of The Guard	57
Worlds Apart	92
It's Hard Saying *"Orstraya"*	116
Marqued For Death	166
The Long and Winding Road	197
Becalmed	226
Nothing Succeeds Like Failure	251
Epilogue	292

FOR JOYCE AND COLIN

CHAPTER ONE

CHECK-IN

Mid afternoon December 12th 1945, just another day in the life of the 2.28 billion people then living on this strange little planet. I don't actually recall if it was raining or not. Let us for the sake of argument suppose it *was*, it bequeaths a rather more atmospheric feel to the events at hand. Careering along a near-deserted A449 in an army Humber Super Snipe which many years later, I learned my father had "borrowed" outside normal channels from his CO, loomed the mini-township of Raglan, midway between Usk and Monmouth inside the Welsh border. Whether of my own doing, natural causes or the Humber's dicky suspension, mother went into labour. It wasn't so much a case of "No room at the Inn" as "No Doctor in the house".....basically *no houses*. Remember this was backwoods Wales post-war, barely four months since the destruction of Hiroshima and barely seven following Germany's unconditional surrender. No cellphones, medical centres, only the occasional street light! The mystique of the birthing process to the average male in those days was such that most fathers still leaned toward the stork theory. If anyone had asked *me* at the time, I would probably have suggested heading south for Cardiff, but no one did and since the parents and families of the disaster-struck duo all lived in Watford, North London, it must have been quite a trip. Whilst without the benefit of modern motorways, "traffic jam" was a term yet to be coined and it is doubtful whether they encountered more than a dozen sets of traffic lights the entire trip, not that anyone would probably have noticed with the accelerator flat to the floor.

They tell me it was touch and go - for *both* of us! Evidently I did not appreciate the intrusion of forceps into my personal domain. I was quite content in the snug little room I had come to call home and proved quite a formidable adversary. Eventually, *forced* to vacate, I dragged certain things with me which were to ensure I would never have to cope with potential sibling rivalry. Perhaps the worst pain was suffered by my father (Colin) who was presented with a bill for fourteen pounds three shillings and sixpence, ten and sixpence of which was for circumcision (I could have saved them that one!)

Colin, one of four children, born just four years before the *Titanic* went down, taking with it the myth of class superiority, had a privileged childhood. Educated at prestigious Harrow University, he left in the early thirties with an architectural degree. Here was a man with an IQ well above one hundred and forty, a multi-talented dreamer equally at home playing the piano, re-building a gearbox, inventing household gadgets, composing poetry or cooking a four-course meal for six. He was also a keen sportsman, genes of which have filtered through to the current generation. Despite the foregoing, this highly educated twerp was content to sell eggs at a nearby farm until his father Harold seeing little return for his substantial educational investment, took stock of the situation and under the impression that the army might better channel his son's talents constructively, packed him off to boot camp.

My mother Joyce, was a curious pastiche of model femininity and stiff upper lipped Thatcheresque determination. The daughter of a successful insurance executive, she had the previous year, received unusually early promotion and high commendation in the Women's Land Army to which she had been billeted shortly before her nineteenth birthday. Demobbed in '43, she had obtained employment with a thriving grocery import/export business in her home town of Watford, owned by Harold Bailey unbeknowns to her, soon to be her Father-In-Law. As she explained to me years later, it was a case here of "love at third glance!"

"I was sitting at my desk filling out invoices when this strange army officer walked in, sat on my desk and started fiddling with my typewriter. I told him I was busy and had to finish my work but he wouldn't go away! Just then Harold walked in and said, "I see you've met my other son Colin!" He was still messing about with the keys when he told me that he had one more night before he had to go back to HQ and would I like to go to the cinema with him. I didn't go and wasn't even that keen on him, in fact I thought he was a bit odd but he was very persistent, and his next weekend off he asked me again and we went out for the first time."

Their courtship, like so many others at that time, was by necessity limited, being dependent on weekend passes and the occasional furlough. In time however, the wedding was set down for November 1944. Harold Bailey was delighted, he believed that he had found in Joyce the opportunity to safely pass-on the custodial keys to Colin's future safekeeping. Following the wedding, Colin still had three years of army duty to serve and found himself on transfer to a base in Kent, just south of London. Joyce remained with her parents in Watford working her old job.

Around the same time Hitler was taking both his own and girlfriend Eva Braun's life with a pistol in a bunker in Germany, Joyce would have been receiving confirmation from her doctor that she was "with child" no less and that my E.T.A. was pretty much expected to be Christmas day '45.

Sadly I was never to meet either my paternal grandfather or maternal grandmother. Just three months prior to my birth, Harold suffered an unexpected heart attack and died. He was just fifty-four. A fortnight later, Joyce's mother Louisa, already diagnosed with inoperable lung cancer, was unable to further repel the malignancy, and died herself, aged only forty-nine, the ages of both having particular significance later, all of which brings us back to the speeding Humber.

Following mum's discharge from Broxbourne nursing home in Watford that Christmas Eve, we were despatched to live with a distant Aunt Clara in Abbey Wood, relatively close to the army base. My clearest memory there is the early morning ritual wherein my rest period was disturbed when the milko would crane his head into my pram and perform his "goo-gooing" routine. I can still recall those approaching milk bottles! I retain too a clear impression of being trussed up in my small folding chair watching dad climb through the kitchen window on more than one occasion. Never did discover the story behind that one! Life at Abbey Wood was uneventful although there were pointers that my life ahead was unlikely to follow anything resembling simplicity. Legend has it that at eighteen months I wantonly emptied an entire can of treacle over a lounge suite ruining both the material and our welcome there. That Christmas, while chancing my arm with a ball I brought down a new chandelier. Surrounded by shards of glass, I was unhurt, a trend that was to continue unchecked through many life-threatening situations in later years.

In the summer of 1948, dad obtained his army discharge and we moved to Welling, a town on the main road south to Dover, just inside the Kent border. Only six minutes from Blackheath and little more than ten from the Greenwich Observatory or today the Millennium Dome, life at 88 Selwyn Crescent was idyllic and then some! Dad finally put his architectural skills to good use, taking up a position in the newly created Government department, The War Damage Commission. Here he was responsible for surveying and/or redesigning buildings, both commercial and private, that had suffered direct bomb damage or secondary shock during the war. Funny how some things remain lodged in your mind. I can still recall trips to London on the number 89 bus and the relatively few instancies of bombed and derelict buildings to be seen. I remember queuing up at our local grocers with ration cards (some food was still in restricted supply) waiting for the man to stamp that well-used little cardboard folder. We seemed to get more stamps than other people, which as I found out later was the result of dad using his army-officer status to arrange a few dodgy deals with other Government departments.

Then there were the Christmases! In 1949, I received my first gramophone record - *Rudolph The Red Nose Reindeer* by Gene Autrey, an old wax 78, for those whose memories stretch back that far. Also that year mum gave me a boxed 'Cussons' soap" *Bambi* from the 1942 Disney film. I still have it, being my most treasured possession. Every decade or so I treat myself to a few moments bliss by unwrapping the small figure and holding it up to my nose, the scent transporting me back to another period, another time. One that has no place or meaning in the dispassionate "make it happen" society of the new millennium.

Thus it was that the most coveted house in Welling, at least in terms of location, came to dad's attention by way of being listed for survey. Amazing just how "severe" the damage that house had sustained. Structural "faults" you'd never know were there and that were barely worth fixing! at least, as set out in the report dad filed. Within weeks the property was listed on the market for a song.

Whether or not the public ever got to know about it is a moot point, but dad had the house under contract within a week. It was Spring of 1950. To look at it, the house in Danson Lane was just another semi-detached home, one of hundreds in Welling and a common sight throughout the south of England. It wasn't *what* it was so much as *where* it was. At the very end of a row of semis, *Brookside* as it was called, shared a common boundary with the sprawling Danson Park. The irregular shaped garden was large, almost twice the size of most everyone else's in Welling. The rear fence was bordered by a dense forest, the palings and woodlands evidently jostling for dominance. Beyond neglect, the garden itself offered an impossible challenge to any but the most committed and talented of landscape architects. Apple, plum, peach and elderberry trees ruled the air-space, not just in close proximity, but in many places firmly entwined as if inseparable old friends. At ground level, blackberry, raspberry, redcurrant, gooseberry, rhubarb, strawberry and native bramble, grew in defiance of any master-plan, obviously with unchecked delight and having their own notions as to where they would next spring up. Amidst the chaos, grass grew where it was able, but to be realistic, it was hard to tell where a tuft ended and weeds began. For all its botanical dereliction, that first vista of wild magnificence is as clear to me now as that cool morning in 1950 we first saw it - an Aladdin's cave to a wide-eyed four year old with imagination.

The 'Wild Wood' as I called it, the absolute realisation of Kenneth Graham's fictional backdrop in *The Wind In The Willows* was home to a plethora of creatures great and small. Over the years to come, badgers, moles, hedgehogs, squirrels, even the odd fox dropped in, either for food, a chat or both. A few deer and wild goats also lived in the upper reaches of the forest, but were not sufficiently socially-orientated or disposed to breach our fenced perimeter. The two-way animal traffic was helped not a little, by dad cutting a gate for me in the rear fence and which gave us alone, access to the entire forest and park after closing time.

Besides friends with fur, hair or spines, the garden was filled with birdlife who had made the woodlands their enviable home. Robin redbreasts, thrushes, starlings, blue-wrens, sparrows, cuckoos, blackbirds, wood-pigeons, kestrels, finches, owls, ravens and woodpeckers all bore witness to *Brookside's* new owners and their shrill calls of vital communication were a lasting treasure. Each Spring I would watch the nests being built within the privet hedges which bordered each fence, wanting to climb up and look in, touch the eggs, but not doing so for knowledge that the birds would desert their home. Oh dear reader, if you could only understand - all the magic in the world was here. Peter Pan and Tinkerbell, Pooh Bear, Eeyore, Ratty, Mole, Merlin and even during those silent snowfalls, The Little Match Girl.....I knew them all. Whilst all of us must grow and develop as we experience the best and worst life has to offer, in many ways I had the misfortune to be cast amongst utter perfection to begin with, an ultimately extended ladder on the topmost rung - there *was* no way up.

The house itself was drastically short on magic however! Dark, desolate and cobwebbed to such a degree it could well have been mistaken for a film-set left over from *The House on Haunted Hill*. How long since anyone had lived there was open to speculation and the first weekend we moved in, everyone pitched-in stripping stained unsightly wallpaper and dingy brown paint which had unaesthetically been introduced to every portion of exposed woodwork in the house. Even by daylight, you needed a torch to see your way round the house. In fact, dad's assessment of localised war damage wasn't a complete fabrication.

Less than quarter of a mile east of the house, in Danson Park itself, had been located an active gun-site, one of the largest in Kent. In daily use up until five years earlier, repelling nightly raids by the German

Luftwaffe, shock-waves from the guns had caused substantial cracking and stress fractures in *Brookside's* eastern and northern walls. As a highly competent builder however (as were all the Bailey clan), the damage was minimised and rectified within months. Vast amounts of building materials and supplies found their way to Danson Lane from Government stores, that something tells me were officially "lost in transit."

Up until September 1950 then was seen unprecedented activity on the home-renovation front. Room by room the house was handed a new identity. Bedrooms became livable, mine becoming a haven for forest artifacts, stones of interest, fossils, last year's bird's nests, etc. Somewhere we found a lounge-room, with rotting carpet, dipping floorboards and bile-green ceiling, but it did offer twin French-doors which opened proudly onto the rear garden. All-up, barely a challenge to dad's wizardry with plaster, a paintbrush and electrical re-wiring skills. *Brookside* was back!

We come now to the nerve-centre, the very *pulse* if you will, of my existence - Danson Park itself. What words to describe this unequalled slice of childhood wonderment? What is a park? A piece of grass with a few benches? A memorial to some forgotten politician or local identity? Something the size of New York's Central Park?... perhaps, but Danson Park was something else. A timeless tribute to happiness, freedom and innocence. Here somehow, man and nature had worked together with inspired ability to conjure up a place that stood as an epitaph to each's full potential. Maybe only I can see it. Maybe only I ever *had* to! Walking through it today, it isn't the largest, best equipped, most historic, visually stunning piece of recreational reserve to be found, but in my childhood it was "The Pyramids," "Mount Rushmore," "The Colosseum," "The Taj Mahal," "The Grand Canyon," and "The Hanging Gardens of Babylon!" Just some thirty or forty yards from the rear fence, a gentle brook wound its way east to the Lake, a man-made landmark built long pre-war which had originally been water-cress beds. Legends abounded of buried treasure from the middle ages which some years later beckoned my own involvement as I will detail a little later. The Lake being marginally less than a mile in length was a third of that at its widest point. A miniature railway ran its full length on both sides, doing brisk business on Sundays especially, with six open carriages packed with excited and expectant young children, often accompanied by parents who looked thirty years older than today's equivalent and smelt of tobacco and home-baked pastries. I never heard the "f" word! The cost of the ride? - threepence (return!). Those kids without the necessary funds, had as good a time running along the small-gauge track behind the rear carriage or, waiting around a bend, the bravest hanging back until the last second to jump off the line before a close encounter with the engine.

The driver spent hours each Sunday morning polishing the three engines in their steel sheds right at the water's edge having lit the boilers and waiting for a full head of steam. This was life! Barely anyone had television, even less had a car, everyone rode a bike. With no coffee-bars, 'Game Boys,' 'Play Stations,' rave parties, or even a 'Shopping Mall,' the park was always looking good as an entertainment venue. People of course were always willing to *talk* in those days. Families *spoke* with one another, children wanted to be with their parents who in turn wanted to spend time with their children. If anyone was "gay" they were just happy! When did the wheels fall off?

Beyond the north-eastern border of the forest the park grounds rose rather majestically towards their highest point, providing a commanding view down across the lake. Twice a year, at Easter and the August (Summer) holidays, the fairground came to Danson Park. As the first of the semi-trailers loaded up with the disassembled Octopus, Cha-Cha, Bumper Cars and Big Wheel rolled through the huge gates, further up Danson Lane I and my best friend Peter, would high-tail it through the gate in the fence, following our well-worn trail through the forest to come out at the top of the rise. There we would stand for hours watching the rides being put together so expertly. The Big Wheel particularly was an eye-opener. What appeared to be a truck full of girders, seats and nuts and bolts, became a fully recognisable entity within hours. The ultimate jigsaw! Hand in hand with the advent of the summer fair was the traditional firework display alongside the lake which due to the fact dusk in England is so late mid-summer, could not commence until complete darkness had fallen, right on the stroke of 10.00 p.m. The Baileys of course had the shortest of trips home - down the hill, alongside the river and through the gate, which was totally undetectable from the outside.

To the south east of the Lake over towards the park's southern gate, lay Danson swimming pool, a Mecca for sun-worshippers who would take up residence along the many grassy verges or tiled areas bordering the wading pools and the children's play-centre- a pastel blue scalloped fountain, down which water cascaded in ever-widening circles and under which a child might crouch, watching sheets of water crashing down and drowning out his mother's shouts to be careful there. Where now are those young girls in their one-piece, tanning themselves unmercifully and taking care not to actually get wet, thereby ruining the whole illusion? Looming imposingly over the whole complex was the refreshment kiosk, an impossibly huge building, some twenty feet to its domed ceiling with wooden floor and an interior large enough for a ballroom. Still I smell the sun cream and chlorine cocktail wafting across the room as both children and adults queued up at the counter, so dwarfed by the architecture surrounding it, to buy their *Wall's* Ice Cream, *Mountain Maid* ice blocks or cheese and cress sandwiches, which by mid afternoon were usually suffering from advanced *rigor-mortis*! the water dripping off the eager little customers and invariably turning the floor into a skating rink. At the far end of the main pool, an Olympic-size diving board where the young men could be seen contorting their bodies every which way in an effort to impress their young companions, laughing off the occasional belly-flop with some difficulty considering the agony coursing through their bodies.

Directly opposite, across the Lake, perhaps some three-quarters of a mile from the pool was to be found the Mansion House, a Gentleman's residence built in the eighteenth century long before the zoning of the park itself. The second storey was, in my earliest recollection, given over to a private museum of weaponry from the middle ages - lances, armour, shields, picks and swords. It was home undoubtedly to many a spectral ancestor, as indeed I later discovered. Long since given over to the Local Council for maintenance, the ground floor was a pleasant enough tea-room where older couples would sit at carved tables staring out across the acres of clipped grass sloping down to the Lake and look at a world passing them by, perhaps regretting the children they never had, the places they never visited, while young couples with all their hopes and dreams ahead of them passed by, sometimes nodding pleasantries, others so caught up in their own emotional distractions that they didn't see anyone there. It remains such a paradox - youth, with so much promise but not the knowledge to forge the way and old-age, all the *knowledge*, but not the youth to see it through.

Immediately to the rear of the Mansion stood (and still stand) the Olde English Gardens, a veritable monument to the best of British gardening expertise. Fully surrounded by high brick wall, the gardens in the summertime begat a riot of glorious colour. Azaleas, Delphiniums, Salvias and Hollyhocks competed for attention, gently swaying to the cross-breezes and nodding to their compatriots in flower beds across the way from the crazy-paving pathway that circumnavigated the walled enclosure. Towards the centre, a shallow fish-pond filled with carp and goldfish, mostly covered by water lilies yet presided over by an elegant fountain that sent sprays of water skywards at regular intervals. In this place, the full spectrum of nature's talents were on aromatic show. Could anything possibly have interrupted this life of new experiences and discoveries? Indeed it could - school! What were my parents thinking? surely I knew all I needed to know already? The best and quickest way through the forest, the difference between a blackbird and a starling, how to tie my shoelaces....what else was there? Unfortunately, come the new term in September 1950 I found out - they sent me to primary school - *Danson County* Primary to be precise.

CHAPTER TWO

FOR THE TERM OF HIS NATURAL LIFE

It wasn't that I resented authority particularly, I simply could not condone the rude interruption to my daily routine. Getting up when I felt like it, playing with my train set, jumping off the garage roof into the sand pit by which time, all things being hunky dory, breakfast should be just about ready. Fried tomatoes, three strips of bacon (middle rashers) and two pieces of fried-bread cut diagonally, never down the middle, sitting in their regular spot on the right hand side of the plate. One glass of orange juice at room temperature, slightly away to the left of the cutlery, right alongside my HP sauce! "What? Is he for *real?*" I hear you say. "Spoilt little bastard, should have been on his way to reform school!" Well dear reader, I make no apologies, think about it? I was an only child, they loved me - wanted to spoil me no doubt, who was I to shatter their delicate psyche and knock back their attentions? Besides my come-uppance was at hand - school, remember? Precisely three hundred and thirty-seven footsteps, after crossing Danson Lane, and turning left, brought us to the main entry-gate of Danson County Primary School (DCPS), another bummer, living closer to the school than anyone else, I never had any decent excuse in subsequent years for being late! That first morning, mum left me at the entrance and walked off. Halfway home, she recognised the footsteps and carted me back. Not usually given to crying, I didn't, I began *screaming!* This was murder, straight-up neglect, child abuse if not dereliction of duty. This time she saw me into the playground and into the care of Miss Attorano, who if I'd been twelve years older, would have had no problem holding my attention, I'd have gone in early! As it was though, watching mum retreat through the gate and my wrist in the vice-like grip of my teacher - I was history!

Speaking of history, American forces in the Korean War, pulled off the daring Inchon landing on September the 15th and just seven weeks later on Nov 2nd playwright George Bernard Shaw died at his home in Lawrence, Hertfordshire.

Thus, the new recruits were paraded before the School Principal, a towering, humourless woman, the type memory can only recall in black and white. Probably an ex-marine, she had me pegged from the word go as "the one to watch."

"My name is Mrs Gunson.....Mrs *D. H.* Gunson," she intoned, looking directly at me, "I welcome you all to Danson Primary, (now, she was definitely looking at everyone but me!) Work hard, behave (she was back fixing me with a death stare) and we'll get on just fine. Go to your classrooms now with your teachers."

Like, what else were we going to do? snort a joint? start up a game of touch footy - prison rules?

It was embarrassing enough having to take sandwiches and an apple, but at least they were mine. Wrong again! "Now children," said the rather daintily constructed Miss Attorano, "Some of you I know, don't have any lunch, so we're going to put everyone's sandwiches and fruit into this bin which we'll share out at recess," she indicated an enormous metal drum behind her that would have done World Vision proud. All the children traipsed over and dropped their food in - God knows what it did to some of the apples.

"Noel," she said, smiling sweetly, "Yours too!" She sat there expectantly. Now, there is no way anyone and I mean *anyone*, was having my sandwiches. It wasn't a case of hygiene, although thinking back, who knows where some of their grotty little hands had been? This was basic civil rights! I returned her stare. For a moment she looked bemused but quickly clicked into "take-charge" mode. "Is there something wrong Noel?" she asked in her best little-girl voice.

"Yes Miss," I answered truthfully, "I want to keep my own lunch."

"We have to think of *others* Noel, don't we?" *Big* mistake, appealing to my sense of fair-play on this issue. I didn't say "Do we?", but I thought it.

"Now come on Noel, just drop the sandwiches into the bin." So saying, she had moved to within striking distance. Both our hands darted into my satchel at the same time - hers were unfortunately stronger. I bid a silent farewell to my brown paper package as it fell into the abyss, feeling a sense of loss one tends to associate with a family funeral.

Victorious before her new assembly, Miss Attorano sat all of us at our newly appointed desks and proceeded to outline school policy and what we would be studying in Year one. I wasn't listening by then, wondering instead if they'd finished taking down the Big Wheel yet. She was on about English now, how important it was to spell properly and had we noticed all the hard words spelt out for us hanging round the walls? yada, yada, yada!

I wondered if it was lunch yet. Glancing around at the clock, I noticed it was barely a quarter to ten. I looked at Miss Attorano, she *was* pretty, no doubt about that. Then I thought about Mrs Gunson, Mrs *D.H.* Gunson. There had to be better things to think about.

Suddenly from way left-field, "Can you spell 'should' Noel?" I was jolted out of my reverie, but composed myself quickly... "S-H-O-U-L-D" I replied.

"Well, isn't *he* a good little boy? He didn't even look at the wall." She beamed at me. I was beginning to like her a lot.

"Barry," she asked, "Can you spell the number 'eight' please?" Poor old Barry, I doubt he could have counted that far! Summoning up all his mental resources, he shifted awkwardly in his chair. "A....'em, T- E?" He sat there, pleased with himself.

Miss Attorano looked disappointed, then turned to the class.

"Who knows what's wrong with that?" she asked demurely. I put up my hand.

"*Yes* Noel," she inclined her head. "It's E-I-G-H-T Miss." I sat back, resting my case.

I don't think Barry and I spoke the rest of that week. No big loss from my viewpoint. Thus the morning wound its inevitable way down and Miss Attorano, true to her word began to dispense the lunches. I saw my beloved cheese sandwich passed to Milly, a small and very shy coloured girl, my apple to Gordon, the class fatty, while into my hands was shoved some disgusting mayonnaise creation which was last seen heading skywards behind Miss Attorano's desk. Though decades ahead of diagnosably potential food allergies, vitamin supplements, special food requirements and such like, I was not about to embark on a course of stuffing someone else's culinary trash down my throat to please anybody. I walked out to the playground. While the others were holding hands, playing hopscotch and making new friends, I walked down to the southern boundary of the well-grassed playing fields, and with my face pressed up against the mesh stared at my distant home, the furthest I'd ever been from it. I remember so clearly wave after wave of hot tears coursing down my face. My world was just shattered. I remained there sobbing and staring into the distance until some twenty or thirty minutes later when I felt a hand on my shoulder. It was Miss Attorano. I couldn't talk to her and pushing her away, I just ran. Not yet five hours at school and it was my first face-to-face with the dreaded D.H. Gunson (Years later, I called her *'De Havilland'* after the fighter aircraft!)

She waved away her subordinates and I was alone - with Satan!

"What appears to be the problem Noel?" she asked imperiously. "Don't you like it here?"

"I want to go home," was all I could stammer.

She looked at me for a moment with about as much compassion as the head of a firing squad. Probably in her case however, the extent of her maternal capability.

"Nonsense boy, now grow up and get back to class."

Such was her unique understanding! I should comment in my defence, I was only just over four and a half, by far the youngest in the school, having only made selection by a matter of weeks, else I would have had to wait until the following summer. Many in my class were almost eighteen months older.

I made my way back to class and sat out the afternoon. I recall when Mum came to take me home that night, she and Miss Attorano exchanged words with Mrs Gunson. It hadn't been my finest hour. That night Mum suggested I try to make friends with some of the other children, my seemingly anti-social tendencies having been noticed.

The second day was much better. I only lasted three hours before falling off a low brick wall and exposing my knee-cap almost to the bone. I actually got to ride in Mrs Gunson's blue Morris Minor as she had to drive me home after the First Aid room had patched me up. Hopefully I bled all over the upholstery.

Gradually things fell into a routine. Though for days I stared out from that wire mesh, eventually I found something better than misery - *marbles!* The mini championships that went on in the playground knew no limits, they had to drag us back to class when the bell went.

Just one other incident a fortnight later earned me a few more demerit points and a trip to the Headmistress. Gordon, the class fatty you will recall, was not only a full-time slob, but also an oversized racist pig. During Craft, he would take delight in picking-on and insulting little Milly, the Jamaican girl. The day in question he had twisted the neck of the little camel she was making out of a framework of wire, and broken it. Milly just sat there crying. I lost it and shoved him headfirst into the nearby drum of papier-mache, which unfortunately for him, was over half full. Had not Miss Attorano knocked over the drum and dragged him out by the legs, he may have been "glued to death," a fitting end in many ways. Back in "The Oval Office" Mrs Gunson let me have it from both barrels. She was going to "note this on my report card," "speak to my parents," and "keep a sharp eye on me." We really weren't close!

In America, Charles M. Schulz had just published his first "Peanuts." Who would have guessed that Linus, Lucy and Charlie Brown would become the most successful comic-strip characters of all time, still going strong December 11ᵗʰ 2000 when Schulz died, just hours before his last strip was published?

On the academic front I must have seemed such a smart-ass! This wasn't the case at all but I had been given such a huge advantage over most my age. Mum had read to me since my second birthday. Noddy and Big Ears to start with, then advanced Enid Blyton. I went on every adventure with The Secret Seven, knew where half the buried treasure in England was. I was an honorary member of The Lost Boys, backed up Peter Pan during the final showdown with Captain Hook, and flew over so many lost reefs I've forgotten. I could draw a map of Pooh Corner, knew where Piglet, Kanga, Baby Roo, Tigger and Eeyore lived, not to mention Tom Sawyer and Huck. By four I knew every nook and cranny of Toad Hall, had cried my eyes out with Mole when he reclaimed his old home in "The Wind in The Willows," one of the all-time emotional and moving episodes in English literature.

There could be no stopping now. All those nights I lay there, mum's voice bringing to life the very essence of centuries of literary magic. Hans Christian Anderson, Grimm's fairy tales. I walked alongside every famous character that was ever conceived, the good, the bad and the ugly! The Grecian heroes - Perseus, Heracles and the whims of the Gods on Mount Olympus itself. Invariably she would ask me questions on what we had just read. Words and phrases were explained, key points emphasised. I came to know other cities, other ages. Modern New York to Ancient Egypt, Venice to Carpathia. *Queen Hatsepshut* to *Count Dracula*. By six we were into detective novels, Agatha Christie, Rex Stout, Ngaio Marsh, John Dickson Carr, Edgar Wallace etc. While other kids were doing Blinky Bill, I was studying up on all the available evidence to figure out "whodunnit" before Mum would hit me with the final chapter. Fact is, she wouldn't read it until I'd at least come up with some logical suspect, based on what had gone before. Sometimes I was right, sometimes not but I was getting better. This was not a normal childhood, albeit the only one I ever had.

From dad I learned to use my brain cells. Whilst in less concentration than his own, my formative years were spent poring over a multitude of puzzles and mind-twisters. At one stage I recall, he designed and built a pair of portable battery-operated morse-code receivers enabling us to send messages from one room to another upstairs. Amazing how fast you can build-up from "Hi dad" to "Is mum cooking chicken again?" The rudiments of mathematics he taught me, such that I could comprehend at least, even before I went to school. How many 4 year olds know the formula for the circumference of a circle or how to find the area of a rectangle, pre-school? How many *should?* There is a time and a place for all things and I remain unconvinced that knowing what I did, *when* I did, was ultimately a good thing. Eventually Miss Attorano phased out my existence altogether. It began with "Not you Noel, you answered the last question," moved on to, "Can anyone think of six words ending in 'ough' - *except* Noel," and finally "Put your hand down Noel, we all know you know the answer!"

All this rejection may otherwise have set me up for a serious childhood complex, but fate had been unusually kind in other ways. It had orchestrated events such that I was sitting next to Gillian Cooper, which totally distracted me from feeling neglected or in any way sorry for myself. I may only have been six or so at the time, but I knew quality when I saw it! Somehow we were to stay together pretty much through Primary school. Gillian was an appealing mix of intellect and fun - we shared a common wavelength and played together during many warm summers and long winters. I can still see her standing by the steps leading up to the sports lock-up, laughing herself stupid after a snowball I threw at her, lodged in her hair somehow - you had to be there! Her pretty light-blue eyes lit up when she was happy and if there was ever a more perfect example of youthful innocence then I never saw it! Gill's personality was matched only by her immaculate presentation and my memory of our times together are tinged with a sadness that they couldn't just go on *ad infinitum.*

As the early fifties rolled on ever thus perceptively, *Brookside* became a haven of unparalleled charm. The garden's wild nature was tamed, surrendering its years of autocratic rule, in the face of subtle brickwork, concrete paths, flowered borders, rockeries but more significantly, design and planning. New turf was laid, perennials planted, new fences and clipped trees became part of the new order. The air was rent by multiple replays of Dean Martin's *That's Amore,* Rosemary Clooney's *This Ole House* (Poor old nephew George wasn't even yet in the planning stages), Patti Page's *How Much is That Doggie in The Window*? and Guy Mitchell's *Pittsburgh, Pennsylvania* to name but four heavy metal head-banging classics of the period.

From my earliest youth, weekends spent up at *Raymead*, Dad's family home in Park Road, North Watford, were a treat to savour, as was the steam-train journey to get there. Just standing on the platform at Kings Cross station, watching the approach of the platform-shaking clanking steel dinosaur as it drew alongside its ten coaches of corridored wood and leather, far exceeded the joy to be had travelling in today's coldly impersonal though efficient electric or diesel train. Where now are the sliding doors that one may shut off the rest of the world from your own compartment? the steel-framed photographs of yesteryear above the seats? the card/games tables? the water decanters (always filled) with their cluster of glasses on hand? It was my privilege to have known such things, gone from all but the keenest of memories.

Following Harold's death a decade earlier, the mansion, for such it was, had fallen into disrepair, Granny Bailey, being anything but an astute business person, had allowed herself to be taken advantage of and the family fortune had been frittered away in the cause of others. Even in its dying agonies though, *Raymead* was magnificent. A stone and brick, three story edifice built at the turn of the century, with ornate slate roof and gables, one could have organised a family barbecue on the front porch alone! The upper floors converted now to grotty little self-contained flats, containing for the most part, grotty little tenants, the majority of which might once have inhabited 10 Rillington Place. Only the ground floor retained its tarnished grandeur. Much like the British Empire itself, its best was behind it now.

Entering the cavernous hallway, a visitor would be struck immediately by the prolific woodwork, not unlike some gothic cathedral in solidarity. The high ceilings and oversize doors bespoke a period long gone. The first set of double-doors on the left, opened into the smoking room, fully forty feet long and twenty wide. Two full-size billiard tables in parallel were dwarfed by the intricate archwork, wood panelling and the enormous bay windows hung with faded velvet curtains. Cigar smoke from another generation hung about the room and implored the casual observer to be seated in one of the high-backed leather chairs, close their eyes and let the multitude of stories floating in that room be whispered aloud.

Glass display cases, such as you would see in a national museum, stood equi-distant along opposite walls. Diverse war mementos, rare silverware, medallions, marine treasures, personal items and souvenirs from multiple lifetimes sat proudly in their respective cases desperately trying to draw attention to themselves and willing the newcomer to at least glance their way before leaving again. The room's centrepiece however was the hearth and open fireplace, midway between the billiard tables on the far wall. Large enough to step inside, Arthur, Lancelot...in fact the entire members of the Round Table would have been right at home there, carving up some roast venison before battle. These days however, the great hearth was partially boarded up in an effort to conserve heat when the winter chill began seeping down the chimneys in

November. Temporary beds set up around the billiard tables provided weekend accommodation for mum dad and myself when we were to visit, which in my memory was far too infrequent. Further along the hallway was a series of rooms, Granny's parlour being nothing less than awesome with an enormous dome mid-centre of the ceiling.

Well into her late sixties now, Granny was everything a Grandmother should be. A fine lady in every sense of the word, she was generous, cuddly and selfless in all respects. Having children around her she glowed, holding their little hands, showing them the hidden cookie-jar, reading to them and none ever left at least five shillings better off than when they arrived. Even later when well into her seventies, and far from well, she would be down on the floor studying a doll or train or some other special toy belonging to one of the eleven grandchildren. Both Granny and her lodgings smelt of bakery treats, roast dinners, happy days long gone, safety, sincerity and welcomeness. She had no favourites, loving all equally. No-one was judged, hurt or embarrassed. By the same token, no family member ever treated her with anything but utter respect.

More often than not Granny would be seated reading, in the huge glass conservatory that opened on to the garden - "grounds" might be a better word! "Brookside" in its entirety would have fitted snugly into one far corner! Dominated by a colossal Cedar of Lebanon that stood mid-centre of the grounds which but for the low branches, one could have erected a marquee beneath, the garden in no way reflected the disintegrating condition of the host building. Lawns remained clipped and edged, flowers in expertly designed and manicured beds flourished and gave the impression of a giant test-pattern one might see on a television screen. Park-like lawns shimmered with an emerald hue, some set aside for croquet which visitors, the children in particular would take great delight in attempting. What child could resist trying to knock a wooden ball through a hoop? Well over an acre in size, a hedged off crazy-paving pathway wound its way around the high-walled perimeter of the grounds, and it was here that the real wonder was to be found. Set sometimes within their own little tableaux, occasionally recessed within the hedgerow itself, and further along, elevated in a tree-walk, dwelt the main characters from Alice in Wonderland, hand built in plaster. They had been the creation of dad's brother, Uncle Bill, arguably the most talented of the clan, a poet, mechanic, artist, writer, builder and raconteur extraordinaire, with degrees in mechanical engineering and architecture. He spent the majority of his life living in a broken-down bus on the south coast of England, dying probably alone, unknown and unfulfilled in the mid seventies. As it was though, Alice herself, the Cheshire Cat, the

Queen of Hearts, the Mad Hatter and the whole assembly brought to life in full colour and movement, cavorted along that walkway when I was a child. Caterpillars, mushrooms, gnomes and all manner of creatures waylaid the visitor at strategically placed gaps in the pathway and from each of which views of the great garden were presented. Two thirds along, the path rose up to tree level and wending its way through higher and higher branches, came eventually to a multi-roomed wooden teahouse built within the trees itself, huge boughs rearing up through the floors and through the ceilings and around which seats had been built. Here, one might rest and contemplate the beauty of the place with light refreshment, before continuing on, the suspended walkway descending finally to ground level once more. At night, the entire "theatre" could be floodlit.

Christmases were invented for Raymead. Few families ever gathered in such splendour, a condition unaffected by worn carpets, dusty crevices and sagging downpipes, besides, what children would ever notice these things? The tree was huge, the blinking lights reflecting their yuletide message off the long strands of tinsel that enveloped its girth. More importantly, it was always stacked with presents beneath it. All the better, since the family assemblage was always set down for Boxing Day which meant for the eager children, this was their second bite of the cherry.

Year 3 was memorable mostly for the hot day in June '53 (2nd) when the entire school was shepherded up to Buckingham Palace in a fleet of buses to stand behind barricades and wave to Queen Elizabeth after her coronation. Seasons came and went. Summer would invariably see everyone making a regular trek to the Swimming Pool, bike riding and many leisurely hours spent in Danson Park. Winter saw the onset of freezing weather, darkness falling before 4 o'clock each afternoon and regular fog-banks that limited vision to a matter of feet.

Walking up the road to Welling shops was a slow process. In the densest of these fogs, it became a case literally of *feeling* your way along the sidewalk. Fun for children, but deadly for many older residents. The "smogs" as they came to be known - fog mixed with smoke from industrial chimneys, were responsible for many deaths amongst the elderly.

Aside from Christmas, the high point of each Winter was Guy Fawkes Night: *"Remember Remember the fifth of November, Gunpowder, Treason and Plot."* What English child of the 50's could forget those words? Most shops would begin stocking fireworks in October and to watch your little pile of crackers, Roman candles, Mount Etnas, catherine wheels, aeroplanes, rockets and sparklers, grow, was the next best thing to eating. We bought most of ours from a unique little shop called "The Orange Library" in Welling High Street. Somewhat of a misnomer really since it was neither orange nor a library, but a remarkably well-stocked little stationery outlet. Eventually the great night would roll around. Always cold, foggy, often with friends over, that long wooden bench would be dragged out beneath the giant oak tree and dad would light the huge bonfire before igniting the first firework - traditionally a catherine wheel. As Mary Hopkins sang so many years later, *"Those were the days my friends!"*

Miss Attorano's tenure had long since come to an end and we had a succession of new teachers - none of whom liked me. The feeling was mutual! Miss Gunson's eye was beginning to turn inwards perceptibly, doubtless the result of fixing it upon me at every opportunity. I think I was winning, because she was starting to look so old. We still sang *"All things Bright and Beautiful"* and *"Land of Hope and Glory"* most mornings at Assembly but most significant of all, I still sat with Gillian.

Round about this time, I met Peter Dawson. In a grade above me, Peter and I drifted together, both being loners of sorts. From as different a pair of homes as could be imagined, we became absolute best friends, a relationship that was to last through most of our childhood. This entire book could be devoted to our many adventures as we roamed at first the forest and park, then when older, further afield. Peter didn't so much stay over as "live over." Homework played a very small role in my life when Peter was with me - actually, it played a very small role in my life altogether. In the next chapter we shall revisit one or two of our joint experiences but for now, let us return to the winter of 1954. It was the weekend following the marriage of Marilyn Monroe and Joe DiMaggio (January 14th). Cold enough for the most discriminating polar bear, snow having fallen steadily all night, it took a degree of will-power to get up at all. Peering through a frosted window, the back garden was a re-sculptured masterpiece. Trees bowing under the weight of their white splendour, the most remote of their twigs host now to a delicate frosting of newly formed ice-crystals. Flower beds, lawns, concrete, now a common finish, crests and valleys where snow flurries had smoothed over the differing surfaces in an attempt to bring conformity to bear. The forest beyond gave the impression of a mountain range - on loan for the day, the close knit canopy of tree tops now angling upwards as if multiple ski-ramps. All this I see now in my mind's eye, *then*, as an eight year old, all I saw was - fun! Grabbing my anorak ("parka" elsewhere in the world) I was out of the back door faster than you could say "Noel, where are you going?" I believe someone *did* actually say that, but I was gone.

It required considerable exertion to push open the rear door in the fence, snow having drifted up against it during the night, but I was in no hurry. The main trail had long since been covered up, but I could have navigated my way blindfold and fairly bowled along, at least as fast as deep snow permits. Emerging at the rise, I headed for the 'swings,' actually a combination playground containing two sets of swings (junior and advanced), a large roundabout, horse, huge slippery dip, twin see-saw and a rotating monstrosity called the *umbrella* that could seat at a pinch sixteen children. Only the bravest of the brave rode the *umbrella* - it was never full.

Except for an old man who appeared to be asleep on one of the long benches where the mothers usually sat, relaying their mostly plebeian experiences of the previous week, there was no one around. I headed for my favourite. It was always a challenge grabbing hold of the rail and running around until the roundabout was well up to speed and then attempting to jump aboard where the centrifugal force was such that even if you *could* get on, there was no guarantee you'd be able to stay on! Many were the kids, showing off to their mothers or younger siblings who ended up airborne rather than seated, usually copping a grazed arm or leg. Had any enterprising person set up a band-aid stall, they'd have made a fortune at the weekends. After a few whirls, I realised that this was my problem, no-one to show-off to. The old man certainly wasn't too interested in my performance, in fact he didn't look quite right somehow. I climbed down from the roundabout and slowly approached the bench where he was propped up at one end. He was very old, and I remember wondering why there was so much snow on his shoes - they were almost covered. His face now a frosted blue, his wispy hair was stirring perceptibly, blown by the gentlest of breezes that had sprung up. He looked peaceful enough, one hand clutching a newspaper to his old coat as if he had decided to try and keep his tummy warm. Something told me the man was dead and I sat beside him for a while as tears came to my eyes- I couldn't stop them nor did I really want to, as all manner of emotions crowded in upon me. It was my first encounter with death. A short time later, I returned home and told mum. Dad went up there straight away. When he came back, he was quiet but said to me, "He's alright now son." whatever that meant. Mum knew what I needed - to be left alone. She was always right!

CHAPTER THREE

WINDS OF CHANGE

School was getting on my nerves. Surely someone could have come up with something better than this? Perhaps surgery at birth to insert a microchip within the brain, an implant of all the stored knowledge of mankind up to that day, for instant recall as required. All that would then be necessary would be to supplement it as we write our own history, both personally and communally. As if to reinforce the many years of drudgery ahead, bulldozers, caterpillars and pile drivers moved on to the gun-site directly opposite the school gates early '54, to lay foundations for what was promised to be the last word in educational excellence - Bexley Grammar School. Personally I was sad to see the gun-site go, having spent many happy hours wading through the mud over the years, picking up spent shells and the odd rifle part. Even a couple of the old gun carriages themselves had been left for children to clamber over - blissfully unaware of the true horrors of war and many of the fatalities these old weapons undoubtedly must have wreaked, some might consider deservedly, upon the enemy, less than a decade earlier.

If then I had to partake of a secondary education, *this* was where I wanted to go for several reasons. Firstly, it was on the same side of the road as *Brookside,* probably only 329 steps - a total education just up the road! Secondly, in those days, anything but a Grammar School condemned one to a 'secondary' education in every sense of the word. No problem if you'd planned on being a builders' labourer but the only possible avenue for any student wishing to pursue his or her professional career or perhaps a higher education at University. Thirdly, I knew that Gillian would be going there.

Nothing is simple however and there was a catch. A big one! The only way of gaining admission to a Grammar school back then, was from success in the 'Eleven-Plus,' an unpleasant exam sat by every student in the country at the conclusion of Primary school and which sifted the "brains" from the "drains." Thus one day late July '55, just days away from the start of the summer holidays, I was standing near the gates, watching the men put the final touches to BGS, as it was called already. I didn't hear the footsteps behind me.

"Don't waste your time *thinking* about going there Noel, you won't pass your Eleven-Plus. You'll never make anything of yourself."

It was Mrs Gunson, looking younger with the passage of every syllable. Today she would probably be up on charges of verbal assault, discrimination or psychological abuse. I just remember standing there looking up at her and thinking "What a twisted and nasty old woman - but I wonder if she's right?" Exactly half a century later, I'm still wondering!

But hey, the day of reckoning was a year away and this was no time to dwell on such things - the summer vacation was here, seven weeks of freedom and time for self-indulgent excesses. I was out of there!

Rock'n roll was in its infancy, Chuck Berry was riding high with *Maybellene*, Little Richard was shaking his bon-bon with *Tutti Frutti*, Dean Martin was crooning all the way to the bank with *Memories Are Made of This* and newcomer Pat Boone had hit number two on the charts with *Ain't That a shame?*

Two things happened that summer which changed our lives. We subscribed to television and the telephone was connected (Bexleyheath (BEX) 2434 as I fondly recall - all 'timed' calls too!) As far as the TV was concerned it was a genuine case of "Nice cabinet, shame about the screen!" A discard from a neighbour, dad had been tinkering with it for days, finally isolating the bum valve which he replaced. Even so, we had always to poke another valve with a ruler, around the back of the set before it would come on. In time, we all became expert at avoiding full-time electrocution. Set within a quite magnificent walnut frame, the smallish twelve inch screen was not exactly digital entertainment in full blown Dolby sound! True, the picture was only black and white, grainy and with a dicey vertical hold that in time induced severe eye-trauma, but it was still high-tech entertainment with a capital 'E.' Thousands still did not have it, preferring to stick with the old radio shows ("The Archers," "Peter Brough & Archie Andrews," "Journey Into Space,") and quiz shows. This old friend sat in its appointed spot in the dining room and never once let us down for our remaining years in England. In those early days, TV audiences howled their way through *I Love Lucy, Hancock's Half Hour* and cowered in fear from the BBC's *The Quatermass Experiment, Quatermass II* and *Quatermass and the Pit* - the most frightening sci-fi trilogy ever screened and inarguably decades ahead of their time. At the conclusion of the third it was estimated well over three-quarters of Britain were tuned in.

This narrative has unintentionally bypassed up until now a significant influence on my life, the holidays spent up in Yorkshire. Most years,

Mum and I would retrace our steps to a small stone cottage on a farm in the "blink and you'll miss it" micro-township of Wilsill, population less than fifty, itself six minutes from the larger and beautifully preserved centre of Pateley Bridge - a village frozen in time some thirty-five minutes from Harrogate itself. Owned for generations by the Bentley family of which mum's late mother Louise had been a member. My earliest recollections are of being greeted by Aunt Janie and Uncle Reg and whisked into the kitchen for hot bread and freshly cooked rhubarb pie. Still without electricity, sewage or any other modern convenience, this was as far away from modern England as you could get and I let myself be lulled into a world of tranquility, beauty and folklore. Uncle Reg would wake me at 5.00am. to help him round up the cows for milking. I'd mutter something about breakfast to which he'd invariably reply, *"By gum lad, you get now't t'eat wi breakfast 'till them cows yonder be milk'd 'n fed."*

I loved it, frequently unable to understand a word he said. Still, we got those cows milked, the fresh-laid eggs collected, fresh straw in the boxes and cow pats all over my Wellington boots. You couldn't walk but half a dozen yards in any direction in some of the fields without stepping in them. The farm itself was not large, though it rates a mention in King William's "Doomsday Book" of 1086 - the two-volume index drawn up that year by Royal survey covering the length and breadth of England, showing tax and revenue liabilities of landowners and feudal estates. Five or six main fields connected principally by gate or stile, the property sloped at its southern boundary down to the beautiful river Nidd, where even in summer the crystal clear water was always icy cool. A wooden 'swing bridge' that permitted only one abreast at a time, gave access to adjoining properties the far side of the river. Anyone with river frontage was free to issue a fishing licence and a common sight back then was to see interminably old men hunched up over their fishing gear, whiling away the hours in peaceful contemplation. As far as one could see in all directions, typical Yorkshire stone walls separated field from field, property from property, legend from legend. Nights would find us all snugged up in the tiny lounge, not twelve foot square, reading by gaslight and well fed after some freshly baked treats. An ultimately narrow stone staircase led to two upper bedrooms, host to little more than a bed and solitary cupboard, nothing else having room to fit. From the deeply recessed windows of each, a view across the farm and down to the river imparted such untainted beauty, perhaps an inkling of Utopia itself, Nature bidding its gentle goodnight with an assurance it would keep an eye on things while you slept. This was a world so far removed from bitterness, racial prejudice, politics or even crime, you could well understand the locals' disinterest in world news, the latest fads, fashion or even strangers. So long as those stone walls sat there, there was nothing much to worry about. The 20th century has had little impact on Pateley Bridge, probably no more so than the 21st will! If and when Jesus returns, it won't cause much fuss up in Wilsill.

With no car or bike, and buses running every two hours or so, invariably anywhere but where you're headed, it is a good idea to use the transport God gave you - your size nines! How far mum and I walked in those distant days is anyone's guess, however and I'm sure my feet will back me up here, it was a long long way! Starting straight after breakfast, we would head across field, navigating the gates and ancient stiles heading towards Middlesmoor where grazing sheep, disinterested cows and the occasional horse would be the only evidence of life. We would refresh ourselves at various natural springs, mum, having spent the greater part of her childhood there, knew of course where they were located. The things we saw! "Two-Stoops" - a Norman 'folly' - an unfinished building project, commenced to give the unemployed of the time something to do, of which now only two sides of an archway remain, visible atop the moor from the farm and indeed twenty or thirty miles from multiple directions. "Brimham Rocks" a unique collection of natural outcropping rock formations, wind-eroded over countless centuries into fantastic shapes - *'The Boat Rocking Stone,' 'The Cradle'* and *'The Lancing Bear'* who will still be waltzing long after humanity has moved on. "Stump Cross Caverns," an underground limestone cave wonderland. Then of course there is Fountains Abbey, the best preserved of its type in the world and nearby Bolton Abbey - haunted as it is reputed to be.

To the west we walked to Hawarth, where the Bronte family are buried in the tiny church there and where the ghost of Heathcliff walks his windswept *Wuthering Heights* still, the ever present heather still being caressed by the breeze. We walked and walked, across the valleys near Ripon even to the very ends of time it seemed. Only problem was, we had to walk back! The Yorkshire moors are the most beautiful spot on earth - they can also be the most dangerous. Mists sweep down unheralded, blanketing what was just moments before a view to near infinity. Visibility is cut to just a few feet and all sense of direction is plucked from the unwary. Locals can predict such events and know when such rambling is unwise. Not only visibility is denied, the dense mists bring with them an unnatural silence and to the uninitiated, the numbing of the senses can be a frightening experience. No way of knowing what direction you are taking, where the break in the wall is and worse, what may be lurking the other side - either weighing several hundred pounds with horns or wet and several feet deep. The fog can lie at ground level for many hours and in winter with the onset of darkness so early, the moors are not the most hospitable of environments at such times. Many is the legend of tiger or wild beast up on the moors. Again, the locals will not be drawn into such argument, you either heed the warnings or you laugh at superstition - it's your throat! Once, many years later when walking with what was actually my first girlfriend (second, if you count Gillian) we found ourselves trapped in just such a situation and at the precise moment the silence was broken by an uncomfortably close splashing sound at the nearside of the field we were crouched in, followed by a loud 'roar' for lack of a better word, that surely emanated from no local animal I was familiar with. Something large passed us by in the mist at close quarters and we were off, over the wall uncaring as to what might have been the other side - it would have had to be better!

Thus the second week of those summer holidays we all (dad came with us this time) boarded the Pullman steam train at Kings Cross station for the long haul to Harrogate, after which we caught the local bus to Wilsill. From memory, it was raining - a not uncommon occurrence during an English summer. We stayed for a week. It was not enough, it was never enough!

As I intimated in the last chapter, most of my waking time outside school and holidays away, was spent with my best friend Peter. Sharing a common yearning for adventure, the forests and the park provided the perfect counter for our rampant imaginations. When reality would sometimes bring an unwelcome halt to current proceedings, we were able to cross-over to a world of fantasy and keep the dream alive, whatever it may have been. The tree-houses we constructed way up high in the branches of the sycamore tree at the extreme north eastern point of the garden, and which we stocked with "essentials," tins of food, lollies and even a few pennies, to survive with, when the great flood came - we were sure it was just a matter of weeks. The "time machine" we constructed from some packing crates, fence wire, bicycle parts and bits off an old car dashboard, was in my memory at least the equal of anything Steven Spielberg could come up with. Sitting in it, with levers and dials you'd be wasting your time now telling us we didn't go anywhere. We saw dinosaurs, visited ancient Egypt, the Great Circus in Rome and witnessed the Great Fire of London. We even watched them raising the great uprights at Stonehenge and all through the safety of the wire mesh.

That summer of '55 however, we really thought we had stumbled across the real mccoy. Mum had sent me up the road on an errand and I had taken Peter with me. Some quarter of a mile or so up the road, workman had been laying a new pavement and had roped off an area of sidewalk to be upgraded next. Thus, boys being the halfwits they tend to be, we cleared the rope with a flying leap and hop-scotched the next half a dozen squares. Peter, slightly ahead of me, appeared to slip and he went sprawling. On closer inspection it could be seen that the square he landed on was unbalanced and had tipped slightly when he struck it with his feet. Although most of the paving squares had been loosened by the workmen ready to be replaced in the next day or so, this one was so loose we were easily able to drag it to one side - halfwits remember? The vaguest of shiny edges glinted in the sun and bending down we flicked away some muddy soil and retrieved what looked like a very old coin. Smaller than a penny, Its edges were corroded away and only a vague imprint of a head was visible on one side. Hoping to find more, we scrabbled away at the surface until we had unearthed to almost a foot deep. I couldn't see much use in wasting further time, besides we had nothing to dig with and already both of us looked like we'd been given coloured-hand transplants.

"Just a bit further," Peter said, and turned back to our handiwork.

I let him amuse himself for a few minutes and was somewhat surprised to hear him call out, "Hey Noel look - there's something here!...it's metal I think."

I knelt down and looked closer. A flattish edge could just be made out beneath the dirt and tapping it, it was obviously metal of some sort. Gradually we loosened the clay and dirt around the object, and some ten minutes later were able to pull the thing free. For our trouble, we were now the proud owners of what appeared to be an old and very heavy metal box, about eight inches square.

We filled in the hole and replaced the paving stone. Where at one time there looked to have been a lock of some sort, the metal had all but rusted away, but in doing so had also rusted together! Thus, completing mum's errand, we returned home and took the box in to the garage. With a screwdriver, it took but a few moments to prise the lid open. Hoping (and half expecting) to find more coins, perhaps wrapped up - after all the box was quite sturdy and may well have contained treasure of sorts. All we could see however, was a folded piece of parchment, greatly yellowed and obviously very old. Unfolding it, we could see a vague outline of something hand-drawn, a map of sorts. Symbols for trees were fairly recognisable as were three distinct crosses. Such wording as could just be seen was indecipherable and didn't appear to be in English. Two or three arrows might have indicated the points of the compass but nothing more.

I suggested to Peter that we take the box and the coin to the Park Warden and Gatekeeper, who was something of a historical expert. He was also custodian of the museum at the mansion and also happened from memory, to be the father of one of the boys in my class, Martin Eul. We then headed into the park and climbed the rise to the Mansion House where we found Mr Eul in the rear grounds. He looked first at the coin and told us it was some coinage from the sixteenth century - he asked where we found it. The box appeared to greatly interest him. He turned it over inspecting every feature before declaring it to be of about the same vintage.

He then took us inside the Mansion, upstairs to rooms where items from hundreds of years past, sat on shelves, in glass cases, hanging on walls even crammed into desk drawers. Books, coins, weapons, trinkets, silverware littered the place. The dust had shown no preferences. Any antique dealer would probably have passed-out with excitement just walking in there.

After studying the parchment for a good two minutes, Mr Eul handed it back to us and sat back.

"Do you two not recognise this?" he asked, fully aware obviously of something we weren't. We looked again, no seed of understanding coming to us.

"It's the park lads, or at least the area where the park is now! When this was drawn it would have been open fields for miles, probably right the way to Blackheath."

He took the map and laid it out on his desk.

"Here," he said, pointing with his fingers, "These symbols - you knew they were trees didn't you?" we nodded. "They represent the forest right behind Noel's house, It were much bigger in those days, but that's it alright. See here?" he pointed to a wavy line, "there's the stream that runs across the park into the Lake. 'Course there were no lake there either hundreds of years ago....and this," he went on, "That there, be some building where the Mansion stands now, most likely some great Feudal estate, there were several round these parts in the fourteenth and fifteenth centuries."

I looked at Peter as if to say, "Told you he was pretty knowledgeable!" He hadn't finished.

"You see that arrow here with the writing underneath it?" we peered at where he was pointing, "That's the old way of writing "Dover" - it's showing the direction the road ran then, same as it does now, the old

Roman A2. That's it running along behind the swimming pool up yonder." He waved a hand, indicating the far side of the Lake.

"Now where exactly did you find this box lads?" he asked in earnest. I told him again and he thought for a moment, studying the map. He looked up. "Yes, well there you are then....If this here is the forest," he pointed to the shaded area with the symbols, "this spot here would be Noel's house, well approximate like, and this cross is more or less where you say you found it ...way up the far end of Danson Lane?"

He was right! Allowing for distance, rather than any recognisable feature, it was pretty much *exactly* where we dug it out. This was coming along nicely, an adventure the 'Secret Seven' would have liked to unravel! We asked him about the old stories of buried treasure in the park that had been going around for years He smiled, "Aye lads, heard that story myself. Fact is, some fifty or sixty years ago, a group of historian folk did actually come to Welling and spent weeks so it's said, researching these stories. Actually came to the park as well, but nothing came of it. 'Course they didn't have this box, but there again, what does the map mean? Could be anything, couldn't it?"

I looked hard at the other two crosses. "Where would you say these were?" I asked. Mr Eul frowned.

"Well, the lower one looks to be pretty much centre of where the Lake is now. Even if there *was* anything there still, it'd be under twelve to fifteen foot of water. I think we can forget that one lads. The other? it's hard to say. It could be somewhere close to that old storehouse, way over the western border where they used to keep the old boats. Hasn't been used for years now. Problem is, there's acres of grass there now. Where would you start? even assuming you could get permission to dig up the fields which you can't. Sorry boys but looks like this is as far as you're going. I'll pass this on to the local historical society, if you leave it with me for a while, but that's all I can do."

I looked at Peter, he shrugged and we departed the Mansion, leaving the map with Mr Eul. On the way home we took the western route and walked the half-mile or so to the old boat house. Mr Eul was right, nothing but flat grass for as far as the eye could see and even if by chance the building covered the marked spot, there was no way in. Peter still has the coin I imagine, it was his discovery and was therefore rightly his. So, the adventure ended and the 'buried treasure?'...well, just a tale still, passed down through generations of local children. Maybe one day, they'll drain the Lake! We never did see the map again. Mr Eul died I believe, from a recurring heart condition and vagrants are alleged to have been responsible for a fire which destroyed the boathouse not long after. The collapsed rubble was an eyesore for months.

The remainder of the holidays saw to it that not a day, nary an hour was wasted in anything but enjoying to the full the temporary freedom afforded us by the seven week sojourn from the clutches of D. H. Gunson and Co. A film buff from way back, since sitting in awe of my first movie, *Mickey Mouse* in the late forties, 1955 saw many movies destined to be classics of their genre, come to the local Odeon and Granada cinemas. Among them, *The Ladykillers,* Disney's *Lady and the Tramp,* and *Mister Roberts.* Even Clint Eastwood got his first break with a bit part in *The Creature Walks Among Us.* July 18th of that year saw the opening of Walt Disney's $17 million dollar "Disneyland," the ultimate fantasy theme park for children the world over.

Time has no respect for high living however and despite our prayers, that third week of September rolled around right on clockwork. New blazer, new badge, new shoes, new tie. Same teachers!

"I would like to welcome you newcomers to Year six, a special year as you all know (Mrs Gunson had so far managed to avoid eye-contact with me). We must work and study very hard the next three terms, as we head towards our Eleven-Plus in July." Did I detect a wicked sneer in my direction at this juncture? Why do teachers always use the terms "we" and "our" at such times? Are *they* going through hell the next twelve months perched on spine-challenging wooden chairs, writing essays, singing daft songs like *"Who is Sylvia?"* simply to end up twelve months later losing their breakfast as those exam papers are placed face down on the desk. So small yet so deadly!

Mrs Gunson was continuing her "message to the people" speech.

"And I say to each and every one of you, what you do this year and the results you obtain next, may well shape your entire future. I can remember when I was a child...("Oh *God,*" we thought, "we're all going to be here till recess")...my father was a very strict man (from the looks of her now, I'd say he tied her to the table and branded her with a hot poker if she got her sums wrong!)...he made me understand that study comes first - fun later." All the pointers were that she must still have been waiting to get to that one.

Eventually she ran down, and we were able to return to classes. In all honesty, I don't think I knew a single thing more at that point, than I had the day I started school. Whether that was an indictment of the education system or my own disinclination to pay attention, I couldn't say. Even during her speech, I was far more interested in Gillian's attentive little face with its high cheekbones, neatly turned cuffs and let's be honest, her *physical* attractiveness, than Ms Gunson's pre-programmed monologue. You study what you *like* I always say.

Conkers! Now what sort of a time-tripping revelation would this be without reference to that most British of playground traditions? Late September, early October each year the Chestnut tree bore its wondrous fruit across the land. All we cared about though is where it bore its fruit, specifically in the park! It so happened that to the immediate rear of the Mansion, a corridor of chestnuts fronted the road to the south-eastern gate, and here could be found each year, groups of young boys, armed with heavy sticks, hoping to dislodge the best of the best from the higher branches. Most of them were wasting their time poor buggers, Peter and I having taken first option a few nights previously after the park's closing time. Yep, that rear gate sure did come in useful.

Encased in its pure green spiked seed-case, inside would nestle a fresh chestnut, looking as snug as an astronaut in a space capsule. Mind you it was still to be many years before even *they* existed! The "professional" conker exponent would naturally select the freshest, and largest, having regard also to the shape. Wide and thin you didn't need, well-rounded and having some weight - those you kept. Having maybe a dozen specimens the average player would kill for, the next step was to very lightly bake the chestnuts, drill a hole through the centre, pull a piece of string through about eight to ten inches long and hold the chestnut in place with a knot. Then a coating of linseed oil and let it dry, the more coats the better. Armed and ready you then swaggered to school with that "Guess what I've got in my pocket?" look. At recess one boy would challenge another - one alternate strike each, one chestnut 'conked' against the other. By lunch you could have a 'twoser' or even a 'sixer', depending on the number of (witnessed) victories. A few of the 'super-bakes' hit 'twentier' status. It was always sad to see a tournament-winning conker finally brought down (probably having sustained so many cracks and fractures in battle) by a fresher conker of half its potential, wielded by a novice, neither of whom would ever make the big time.

September bade farewell to 1955 when, with only hours to go on the 30th, James Dean wrote both himself and his Porsche Spider into history, on his way to a car rally in Los Angeles. He was just 24.

In hindsight, Year 6 was like any other year. Emerging from a cold winter, the prospect of a return to cricket, baseball and all that good stuff, was of greater prominence than worrying about the 'big one' just around the corner. That 'corner' came around mighty fast though and the fact is,

I don't remember the slightest thing about it. There was a general consensus that it had been 'one of the most difficult' ever, a belief given some credence by the fact that only four people at the school passed, as opposed to the yearly average of twenty five to thirty, some ninety odd sitting for it. The trend was evidenced in Primary Schools across the country as it turned out, incurring the wrath of many parents and eventually finding its way into the Press who conducted a soon-to-be-forgotten "what happened?" expose. Unfortunately for Mrs Gunson - I was one of the four! Doubtless she heaved her Tarot card collection and dumped her astrologer. Probably also did herself some serious dental damage, gnashing her teeth in fury when she read the names of the successful candidates. The only outward sign of her troubled soul was at Assembly the day after the results were published. She congratulated the other three (of which Gillian was one), never once mentioning me and afterwards staring my way, daring me to speak. We never exchanged a solitary word again and our paths never re-crossed.

Feted for a brief period as I did the rounds of the family - the kid who beat the odds, a case-study of hard work and application. All I could think of was, some *money* would be nice! Even dragged around the shops on Saturday mornings, I was doing everything but signing autographs. Talk about everyone's "fifteen minutes of fame" I was your genuine suburban celebrity there for a while. Then came the Bexley Grammar School interviews, and entrance test - which from memory was worse than the Eleven Plus. Seemed to me, I had sat through a tough exam and passed, simply to earn the right to sit for a more difficult one. The story of my life as it turns out!

B.G.S. as we will refer to it, had technically opened for business the previous year with just a couple of trial year-eleven classes (England actually refers to them as Year five of High School) we however were the first *official* intake. The entire building was brand new, all but two of the classrooms never having been even unlocked. The Biology, Physics and Chemistry Labs would have been the envy of every school in South East England, being fitted out with every hi-tech piece of equipment of its day. The auditorium and gymnasium were colossal even by today's standards while the kitchen/canteen areas would seem to be a case of overkill in all but the largest aircraft carriers.

Outside was another story, huge playgrounds, tennis and netball courts and literally acres of grass, housing multiple football fields, cricket pitches and field and track areas. To achieve this the designers had actually resumed acres of Danson Park itself. The southern fence was no more than two hundred yards from *Brookside*, while the western

40

boundary reached almost one-third of the way to the Swimming Pool. Ironically, the furthest of the football pitches was now sited where families would once have spread their rugs and picnic baskets.

All good things come at a price though, in this case Mr Edward LeFeuvre, the School Headmaster. His reputation preceded him. This man saw no schoolchildren before him, merely "recruits." He ran a tight ship, with the staff as well as the students. Humour was not part of his make-up and not surprisingly, neither was I. Mid-way through that first Assembly I was wondering if he and Mrs Gunson were ever related in a former life? Of the "old school," it wasn't just a case of addressing him as *Sir*, you didn't address him *at all*. No-one spoke in his presence, the school would rise when he swept into the auditorium, all gowns, mortarboard and malevolence. His ability to smile had long since passed, the muscles around his mouth probably having lost their elasticity due to lack of use.

In his world of black and white, divide and conquer, perform or leave, there was no place for smiling - only succeeding! Perhaps the only time he ever came close to looking pleased was Monday morning Assemblies when he would announce the weekend sports results - usually that BGS had trashed every school in the district in everything from cricket to tiddleywinks. In his study, an opulent set of rooms in fact, at the furthest recess of a labyrinthine maze of corridored offices, was squired away the cane! His own personal nuclear weapon. Rumours abounded that two wayward young lads from the previous year twelve test-run, had been on the receiving end of this little beauty, having been overheard by teachers uttering less than flattering remarks about the school's place in their lives. Not only could they not walk it was whispered, their parents were summoned on the spot and instructed to remove their low-lives from the school grounds. You could *do* things like that in those days. Long before the do-gooding lobbyists were to condemn respect and discipline to becoming totally extinct virtues, there was a time back then when teachers were just that, students looked up to them, for what they *were* as much as what they knew. Sure, the odd paper plane cruised the rear desks, a rubber might be seen on target for some girl's shoulders (if not worse) and the phantom whisperer occasionally struck, but we were there to learn and we all knew it.

Poor old "Bails," first on the register, first-up in any class work, first one to have to tackle any task set *and* I was the youngest in the grade. While half the class was pushing twelve, I was still ten, one of only half a dozen in short pants, all the rest wore long trousers. It was highly embarrassing. Still, I made my mark. *No-one* could play my in-swinging yorker! Cricket in fact, became my one claim to fame. Having practised long hours at *Brookside* with dad, on a full-size pitch he had turfed specially, he had taught me many fast-bowling crafts, having been a very accomplished player himself in his youth. With space left in the back yard for only a limited run-up, dad showed me how to develop speed from my shoulders rather than the traditional 100 yard sprint used by most aspiring young quicks. Thus when playing at school later and with the benefit of a longer approach, I was able to bowl well above my grade. Much to the chagrin of Mr E. LeFeuvre of which more will be disclosed later, I took an extended hat-trick (four wickets - all bowled - in four balls!) in my first match for the school, against Crown Woods too, who had fancied themselves as the team to beat in the South East Kent Schools Comp. It was a home match, and I recall both fondly and sadly, dad watching from home through binoculars, at the upper landing windows, I was bursting with pride......for *him!* In those days, parents were not invited to school matches in any sport. Mr LeFeuvre would probably have had him arrested for 'spying' if he'd known. Interestingly, the following Monday at Assembly, when he announced the "Under Twelve" victory against Crown Woods he praised the team's performance, singled out two batsmen and the Captain, but made no mention of a certain bowler taking eight for twenty-two (eight of which the wicket-keeper had let go to the boundary). This however was almost nine months after I had first taken up residence in 1A. A lot had happened in that time.

Hard to say where I initially went wrong. Certainly, I first came to prominence on day one when I refused to drink my milk. I *hated* milk, had never drunk it and was not about to set myself heaving just to please the teacher on duty.

"You'll be put in detention." I was told.

I think I said "Go for it," or words to that effect. The score at that point was "Days-One, Detentions-One." Dad, a champion of equal rights, fair play and the like, refused to sign the slip and was up at the school the next day. I don't know what happened, but I never drank milk there again - the only one. Either everyone else liked it or no-one felt strongly enough about the issue to argue the point. I think I had my own "file" even at this early stage.

Teachers either liked me or hated me on sight. It ran both ways of course and was pretty much a 50-50 proposition in the upshot. Mr John Collins, the pick of the school, was my Maths teacher. An educated and smart man, he knew his subject, understood the psychology of teaching -

and could strike any desk from any angle with the board rubber when the situation demanded. Acting Deputy Principal on occasions, he had the respect of staff and pupils alike. It was said that he had tackled, overcome and restrained two male intruders in their twenties during a botched robbery one weekend, when he had been driving past the school and had noticed movement in one of the science labs. No-one messed with Mr Collins.

Welsh baritone Mr (*Percy*, as he was affectionately known) Prothero was the English teacher, also doubling as the cricket coach.

"C'mon boyo," he would call to me at the nets, "The Welling Express is up next!"

What he didn't know about English Literature wasn't worth knowing. He could have made the Lord's Prayer an interesting case-study! A kindly little (Welsh) leprechaun, he was nevertheless very strict but scrupulously fair. No favourites for him.

Mr Kelly taught Biology. Looking rather like some distant relative of David Attenborough, he dressed in smart casual clothes, tan jacket and exuded somewhat the English air of actor Kenneth More. For him, I worked well.

Miss Johnson - Deputy Principal. Taught Chemistry and was never out of her black robes. Well into her late forties and very much with the imposing manner of Mrs Gunson although greatly more of a humanitarian. Work well with her, you did OK. Screw up and you'd find her totally the wrong person to get on the flip side of. She wielded great power throughout the staff room and it was said even Mr LeFeuvre took in confidence her advice in most matters.

Many more there were but few are the fond memories. Basically B.G.S. had the same problem as Primary school. It was radically interfering with my home life.

Maths was fine - dad was still coaching me, roughly a grade ahead of where we were at. I learned the basics of algebra while everyone else was trying to figure out fractions. Mr Collins was suspicious, stopping me in the corridor one day and asking me what occupation my father followed. When I told him he said, "That figures - tell him he's doing a good job. Has he taught you any algebra yet?" I nodded, then he smiled at me and swung into the staff room.

Sport, now that was more like it! Except perhaps the cross country jogs in mid-winter. More like a work-out for trainee Marines. We would depart the school gates, throw a right and head for the park's main gate just up from my house. Heading west along the school boundary we would run up to the pools, across the lake, which would be frozen solid, then up the rise to the Mansion turning east towards the playground then down the steep hill back towards the main gate and back up Danson Lane to B.G.S. Sounds OK? ...It wasn't. You try running, wearing just light shorts and a vest in temperatures around zero! Even a cold shower seemed invigorating when you got back.

Under the self-induced belief that the park was my own, I usually led the team, which in 1957 proved my ultimate undoing. Having accelerated away from the rest (including the PE teacher Mr. Jacques) just past the pools, I sprinted to the lake seeking to consolidate my lead. Twenty feet from the shoreline, an ominous cracking! Looking down like the Coyote, I saw a network of fractures spreading outwards in all directions. Before I could decide whether to remain motionless or to try to get back, the whole surface gave-way and I plunged in up to my neck - luckily it was only four feet or so deep at that point. For fully five minutes the class was shrieking with laughter, even the PE master having to control himself as he helped me out. Later, I was first in the shower but that was small consolation for the overall embarrassment. I never lived that down.

Shortly after this I earned my first major demerit points and an unscheduled appointment with the big man behind the desk. No-one ever bothered me at school, not because I was particularly adept with my fists or because I kept in with the 'in crowd.' I think I was just considered too right wing and basically too wrapped up in my own thought-processes to be worth provoking. That isn't to say though that others didn't bother me! One in particular, a rotund and unappealing loud-mouth, had a habit of pestering the girls - probably a power thing, since no member of his own sex could be bothered giving him the time of day. One of the girls, Daphne I think she was called, was the primary target of his unwelcome advances. It so happened that this particular day - it was morning recess - I came upon him with Daphne squashed up against the wall trying to 'kiss her,' giving him the benefit of the doubt on this point. It was one of the best kidney punches I ever delivered...and he must have had pretty big kidneys! Daphne took off, macho man hit the deck, *just* as the teacher on playground duty made her brilliantly timed appearance.

I didn't even get to make my one phone call. Guilty without trial, I was served with a detention and then paraded before Mr LeFeuvre. His methods never varied. Keep them waiting for five to ten minutes outside the office, fling the door wide open, robes fluttering, moustache a-quiver and then in the most menacing of tones, "Come in."

Inside everything was just so. Desk perfectly tidy, pictures level, chairs symmetrically placed and the cupboard door open just sufficiently to permit the prisoner a searing view of......the cane!

"I believe you were caught, involved in 'fighting' in the playground Bailey, is that correct?" He was at the window, peering out at the main road.

"Yes Sir," I replied warily.

"Why is that? - you know the rules here."

"I was helping a girl in my class sir, she..." he cut me off.

"You were fighting Bailey, *fighting!* You struck another boy!"

"Yes Sir, but he...." He was in no mood to hear the whys and wherefores.

"Normally you would be caned for this Bailey, but you have not been here long, perhaps this will serve as a warning. If you are sent here again, it will be the cane, do you understand?" I nodded. Justice was dead! "Now go back to your class!" He stood at the door closing it all but on my departing ankle. Doubtless further notations were made in my file after I left.

Even as the seasons were changing batons, Buddy Holly was proclaiming the virtues of his *Peggy Sue*, Marty Robbins was wailing about his *White Sports Coat and a Pink Carnation,* and Elvis hit town with *All Shook Up.*

With the advent of summer, down came the soccer nets and laid-out were the cricket practice strips. Perhaps the season's highlight was the ultimate grudge match....teachers versus students. Following my earlier eight for twenty-two, I won a place in the school eleven and took Mr Kelly's wicket to polite applause. Mr LeFeuvre observing from the spectator area merely smoothed his moustache. In later years when I was able to generate substantial pace, the match took on new meaning.

End of Year exams, a couple of farewell hymns and the holidays were back. Of course there was the small matter of my school report to get over. Sealed in a foolscap envelope with what must have been some early type of super-glue, there was no way you could pry or even steam it open! The report itself was presented in a thin, stiff-covered book, so far just the first page filled out with many ominous blank pages following, awaiting the whims and fancies of teachers yet to come, subjects yet to trash, exams still to crucify!

My first report reflected my developing split personality.

"Works well in class, excellent knowledge of basics and very good exam results - keep it up" - Maths.

"Solid work throughout the term. Attentive (she was, very pretty!) and homework is of a high standard. Exam results pleasing." - French.

"Disturbing influence, short attention span and below average results." - Physics.

"Excellent grasp of sentence structure. His spelling is the best in the class. Impressive exam results. Very pleasant member of the class." – English

"Totally unsatisfactory! Noel is capable of far better work. Homework erratic and exam results reflect his inattention during the year." - Geography.

"Noel's only interest in this subject appears to be when the bell rings for recess. Although not given to working with his hands naturally, he should put in more of an effort. Class work poor, exam results to match. In the class practical test to forge a three-pronged toasting fork, his alone had *two* prongs! - Metalwork.

"Very high standard of work. Understands chemical structures and has the best knowledge of the element table in the class. Homework on time and class work excellent. Pleasing exam results. - Chemistry.

"Unsatisfactory in the extreme. Disturbing member of the class who shows no interest in his work. Homework rarely finished and very poor exam results." – Music

"Noel's work during the term has been consistently of the highest standard. Excels at Cricket, Tennis and Gym work. A pleasure to instruct. - P.E.

"Very unsatisfactory. Does not appear to take this subject seriously and can be very disruptive. Although exam results were better than expected, he must learn to pay attention. - Art.

Headmaster's comments: "Most curious report! Noel must understand that he cannot simply work hard at the subjects he likes and ignore the others. He must also realise that he is a member of a class and must act in a more mature fashion at all times." - E. LeFeuvre.

Mum and dad dissected the above and I was fed all the appropriate advice. Basically, if I still wanted that bike at Christmas - shape up! I promised the world, before taking off up the road to Peter's house. The status quo was returned, the three "f's" were back in style - fun, fantasy and freedom!

That summer of '57 brought to realism the greatest thrill of my life to date. It also ushered in my life-long association with difficulty, misfortune and mishap. (Though perhaps that started with my 'ice-show' on the lake the previous winter.) Unbeknown to me, Mum had earlier bought two tickets for a day-trip to France on one of the Eagle Steamers that plied their trade between various English Ports and the French coast. Overseas travel in those days was something most dreamed of rather than had the opportunity to do. Costs were prohibitive and usually only the very well-heeled could take advantage of air-travel. So what if it was only for one day? it was still France and I was so excited, I walked, slept and played, dwelling on nothing else for weeks.

The trip itself was booked for the second week of August, all I had to do was count the days. It had been a bleak and wet summer and the day mum answered the phone late one afternoon was not a good one. The shipping company had been forced to cancel the trip due to bad weather, and had deferred the sailing to the following week. Could I wait that long? - I had to. Lightning does strike twice! Came next Friday - a similar message. Another week. I had a bad feeling about this! The day came however without another telephone call and dressed and packed, we caught the train to Southend, a major resort on the south coast - home to the largest funfair in Europe - *The Kursall*. Cold wet and overcast, I didn't care, all I could see was *HMS Royal Daffodil* moored at the end of the mile-long algae-stained Southend Pier. Of course when we had walked the green mile, past all the stalls, fairy floss stands, steak, chips and onion eateries and endless souvenir shops to be met by a representative of Eagle Steamers who said "Sorry, the sailing's cancelled due to rough seas," then I *did* mind! Shattered doesn't adequately cover it. Mum asked why they hadn't rung of course and they said it was because they had only minutes before decided to cancel it with weather forecasts just in, predicting impossible berthing conditions in Boulogne Sur Mer, the port of Calais. "Next week," they promised.

"You're just so unlucky dear," mum had volunteered - shepherding me back to the train platform.

Next week came, it was still drizzling. Mechanically I re-boarded the train, Mum having rung first to make sure of no impending cancellation, and back we were at Southend Pier. As the Eagle Steamers' rep approached, I feared the worst but no, all was A-OK. Boarding took well over an hour. The *Royal Daffodil* was no *Queen Mary,* but as far as ferries go, it was pretty lavish and a fair size steamer. A very rough crossing they told me - although I had nothing to compare it with, but three and a half hours later the French coast was in sight. Foreign soil, you can never know the utter excitement that coursed through me, the adrenaline had free rein.

With more inclement weather rolling into the channel, the "day trip" became a "two hour visit," as the re-boarding time was brought forward by four hours. Still though, I was there standing in France, counting my francs and centimes, Armageddon could have been on its way for all I cared! The time was well spent, walking around the main streets of

Boulogne, many of them cobbled still, peering in quaint little shops and buying drinks and ice-cream. Shortly before we had to be back at the departure gate, we went into a minuscule souvenir shop so old and stooped it appeared to have grown out of the sidewalk in the narrow little street wherein it resided. What sights and pages from history had it witnessed? what famous or yet-to-be-famous persons had crossed that tiny threshold ahead of us? One of the Louis' perhaps? maybe even Admiral Nelson himself had graced this tiny conclave with his presence. Nothing "Made in China or Thailand" in those days...the oldest of old wares and quality-made souvenirs looked out hopefully from glass cabinets and the front display case. The old proprietor, wrapped in shawls and a voluminous tweed skirt, got to her feet whence she had been reading and fixed me with a kindly stare.

"You English student no? Your first visit to France?" I nodded, continuing to look at the treasures crowding in upon me from all sides, I only had a few francs.

"I think Madame," she was addressing mum, "Your son - perhaps he like something special? - he is not, how you say, the *average* type of boy - yes? He has I think an awareness, a liking for unusual things?" Her English was in fact though heavily accented, very clear, doubtless from decades of usage.

Mum said something to the effect that we didn't have much money, to which the old lady replied, "Money, she is nothing - memories - they are everything Madame." So saying, she pointed to the rear of the top shelf of a small glass case atop the counter and said. "You like - yes?"

Perched behind some ornate glassware were two tiny animals - a tiger and an ostrich. I obviously looked interested as she opened the rear door, lifted them out and set them down on the counter. Tiny hand-carved figures, the lady read me well. I asked her how much they were and she mentioned an amount. They weren't cheap - nothing of quality ever is! I laid my money on the counter, it was more than two francs short. She looked up smiling, her wrinkled old hands scooping up the money.

"Just exactly right mon petite. I see you 'ave an understanding of our money, tres bon!"

She began to wrap each with tissue paper carefully and with the patience of the very old. I still have these two treasures - they sit on the shelf above "Bambi." They're not for sale!

We made it back to the ship with minutes to spare. Already rain was falling quite heavily and the skies appeared intimidating. It was far more pleasant within the main cabin, snug in fact, seated comfortably by the huge windows taking in the last sights of Boulogne. Guide-lines and mooring ropes were tossed aboard and the ship gave a shudder as the enormous pistons kicked in and HMS *Royal Daffodil* pulled away from the dock. I unwrapped the two animals and examined them in detail, they looked pleased to have been chosen and were probably wondering what life in England would be like. Little did they know the travels ahead of them, as if any of us knew!

Twenty minutes out from France and the waves were beginning to launch a major offensive. The ship was sadly disadvantaged in this one-sided contest, the Atlantic in full control. What began as a noticeable 'roll' was progressing now to a full-scale assault. Waves began crashing over the bow and crew members hastily moved everyone into the main cabin and sealed all exits. This was frightening stuff - mum lit a cigarette.....a dead give-away that she was rattled. Through the spray-battered windows the view was alternately grey-black skies or a wall of water. Cresting enormous waves, the ship would drop unmercifully into the next trough heeling over to one side and then the other. Passengers were throwing-up every which way, by which time the bridge was issuing instructions for everyone to hold on to some part of the super-structure until conditions improved. They didn't however - they worsened!

Two hours out and things were grim. The swell was now so bad that the Captain had given orders to abandon course directly for Southend and to head up-channel, lessening the wave impacts. He also advised that the trip would by necessity be lengthened by an hour or so. Many on board I'm sure had no expectation of even *seeing* England again! Conditions remained fearful, the largest of the waves tossed the ship like a rag doll, loose chairs and tables were hurled across the cabins, thousands of dollars of liquor were dislodged from shelves behind the bar and smashed all over the floor, hot food and snacks formed an ever spreading pool of unappetising sludge, mixed now with vomit from passengers. I remember thinking, the ship would be in need of refitters rather than cleaners if and when it ever berthed. Rain and spray was pounding the glass, truly the ultimate ride from Hell!

As we finally neared the English coast, six hours later, the storm had abated to a degree but the waves were still such, that berthing at Southend was not an option. The message from the Captain was that we would have to hold our position for a while until conditions improved...another hour or so in limbo. Finally the gale force winds dropped, light improved and we turned in towards shore. Passengers were finally allowed outside, where it smelt considerably better, and mum and I headed towards the bow. It wasn't exactly a case of "I'm flying mum," but it was progress all right.

The Pier was in sight - not hard when it reaches a mile out into the ocean! As we pulled alongside, mum returned to the cabin to retrieve some bags. Still near the bow, it occurred to me we were approaching the wharfside at not quite the right angle. Less than thirty seconds later the ship struck the wooden wharf not twenty feet from where I stood, the impact threw me down and I grabbed hold of a steel bollard. Heeling inwards, the hull impacted with the side of the pier, the collision was deafening, Wooden supports, planking, rear shop-windows, retaining walls and railings were ripped out for almost eighty feet, everything collapsing into the sea before the ship slowly swung outwards. The damage to the pier itself was enormous, the side of the ship where one disembarks was slightly caved in and pieces of jagged steel had been torn loose. There was panic aboard as many people had been thrown to the floor - following the trip there wasn't too much else on board left to damage. Mum hurried outside to check that I was still a passenger, and not yet a resident of Davey Jones's locker.

The ship made a three hundred and sixty degree turn making its approach to the eastern (and as yet undamaged) wharf, where it finally managed to be tethered without further incident. Steering failure was later cited as the cause of the collision. By the time we disembarked, the damaged areas of the pier were already roped off and the potentially unsafe shops closed. From memory we made the late night news. Sleep wasn't a problem that night.

Brookside was at the height of its glory in the mid to late 50's. Summer saw a veritable kaleidoscope of living colour as the flower beds competed with one another for brightness, variation and rich scents. No sooner had the delphiniums closed their petals for the season when the variegated phlox, antirrhinums and chrysanthemums made a play for the top horticultural honours with an unbridled performance of well-choreographed splendour. Each plant knew its role, from the lowliest alyssum patrolling the rockery borders to the statuesque hollyhocks in perfect formation along the western fence, standing to attention like Royal Guardsmen - a grand "Trouping of the Colour" if ever there was one.

The fruit trees now produced their finest offerings in gratitude for the years of attention bestowed upon them, by way of trimming, shaping, pruning and constant nourishing. The apples, both *Granny Smiths* and *Jonathans* put to shame in size, texture and taste, anything you might find at the greengrocer's. The *Victorian* plums were firm and juicy as were the succulent peaches. Many was the caller over the years asking for 'windfalls.' None ever left empty-handed even if the odd shake was called for. You couldn't call it an 'orchard' but it wasn't far off Paradise.

As late autumn drew-in the long evenings, the plants, tired after so many months on stage, wilted as they nodded themselves off to sleep, fully prepared for the long hibernation until next Spring. The entire forest shedding its greenery was a symphony composed of many movements. The restless breezes urging and directing the leaves where to fall until a sepia-tinged carpet covered the landscape crackling underfoot and yielding up comforting images of red-ochre sunsets and approaching cold nights with roaring open fires.

In world news, Russia staged a scientific first on October 6th when it launched the first man-made satellite into space - Sputnik 1, following this up just a month later when *Laika* became the first dog to orbit the earth. Meanwhile America had conducted a launch of its own - what proved to be the greatest automotive turkey in history - The Ford Edsel.

Christmases in my youth were not simply ritual observances, they were the embodiment of childhood wonder, family togetherness, smells, tastes and sounds quite impossible to duplicate in later life but which live on through one's children, assuming one is so blessed or of a mind to thus procreate. Only six weeks or so after Guy Fawkes night, most families would be making preparations from then on. Whilst the world's image of an English Christmas as such, generated by works such as Dickens' *"A Christmas Carol," "Miracle on 34th Street,"* and seasonal rhymes such as *"The Night Before Christmas"* would seem to be rosy red faced children tripping through snow, the fact is I think I only ever saw three genuine White Christmases in my life, I seem to recall reading that there have been only nine since 1900. Only a technicality of course, it was usually so cold and frosty anyway, it didn't make much difference. Christmas trees back then were real - full growing trees, not some sawn-off branch to stick unceremoniously in a stand, hoping it will last for a week or two before its demise in the back yard. Sometimes they would live for a few years other times not, but they felt different, looked different and inarguably *smelt* different. Besides the traditional room decorations, both parents expended much creativity on the presentation of the Christmas tree itself. Long strands of silvery tinsel would be individually hung, complementing the fairy lights and glass balls, many of which having been passed-down for generations.

The festive centrepiece however was always the great sideboard. Hewn of oak, polished and treasured since the turn of the century, having at one time served its apprenticeship in "Raymead" during dad's childhood, this grand old lady took up pretty much one entire wall of the dining room. The high-backed sculptured rear section supported two smaller shelves where-on sat two brass candelabras. Each December would be laid out a silver runner - the full length of the top, tasselled extremties draping gracefully at either end. By Christmas Eve, each jostling for space, could be seen boxes of Tunisian dates, figs, mandarin slices, bowls of fresh fruit surrounding a central wicker basket containing the choicest apples, bananas, pears and mixed berries. Fresh sultanas, glace fruits, milk chocolates, shortbread and bakery treats enticingly set out in small shell-shaped pieces of bone china, formed a guard of honour around the other items. Clusters of grapes hung from the upper shelves. Taking up rear spot was a row of bottled liquor: *Gilbey's* Gin, *Taragona Port*, *Johnny Walker* Whisky, *Harvey's Bristol Cream*, *Tio Pepe*, *Tia Maria*, *Orange Curacao* and always, half a dozen bottles of *Babycham*. Except for the Port, it was 'adults only' unfortunately. To the left of this yuletide tribute always sat the revolving Swiss-cheese musical box that played a medley of tunes while offering the onlooker at every turn, individually foil-wrapped processed spreads. To the right would sit the illuminated church - a winter's scene in relief, with snow-overed fir trees set at its base. Last thing before bed, we would sit there by the fire, all lights off except for the little church, allowing its glow to permeate the room, the light dancing off the silver foil, as the simple strains of "Silent Night" issued forth from its tiny windows. Had you perhaps drawn up close and looked in, you would have surely seen the families huddled in their pews, the eager children rugged up against the bitter cold trying to pay attention for their father's sake to the words of the Minister, valiantly but futilely trying to compete with the dreams of pillow-cases overflowing with promise, now just hours away.

    The great morning arrived. Down the staircase, careful of the goldfish bowl at the turn into the hallway, past the lounge and a tight left straight into the dining room. And what to my wondering eyes should appear?....but a pillow case. Where though was the bike? Not liking to say anything, I started on the goodies to hand. Puzzle - that's good, box of Cadbury's chocolates - get to them later, some more railway track - need that, Guinness Book of Records - *Yes!* Airfix model plane kit - hope dad enjoys putting that together! Soccer boots, games, more books, some glass animals and what's this? a box of handkerchiefs? - Santa must have been really scraping for stock this year! I looked around, mum and dad were in their chairs watching intently.

    "Good presents?" asked mum.
    "Nice boots!" volunteered dad. I looked at them both.
    "Something wrong son?" he said, "You look bothered."

"No dad.....it's nothing," I lied.

"Well then, I'd better get the turkey on," he said, getting up to go to the kitchen.

"Oh son, would you fetch the milk in from out the front please?" Mechanically I ambled to the front door, opened it and picked up the bottles sitting on the step. Something blue glinted in the corner of my eye. Odd, since here was usually nothing blue out there. I lifted my head.

Lord help me! I'd dreamed of a bike, but this? This couldn't be happening. There, up against the porch stood the ultimate dream machine. An iridescent metallic blue Chrysler New Yorker. Named by Chrysler after their top-selling luxury hardtop, this was the top of the line two-wheeled transport to blow anything and anyone else off the road. Full U.S. Import, 10-speed Sturmey Archer gears, flashing right/left indicators, speedo, hub-dynamo kit, quartz headlight, stainless steel rims, rear rack, white wall tyres, pedal-straps, kick-down stand, twin drink bottles, power-pump, lots of chrome and looks to kill. The "Goldwing" of its day!

Would have set them back not much less than a clapped-out second hand car! I think I screamed. Leaving mum and dad holding the milk, I was in the saddle and on fire, pedalling north-west to Peter's. They didn't see me again till lunch. I was hardly going to pass up Christmas dinner.

Now, there are dinners and there are *dinners.* No-one cooked like my father. Had he been so inclined, he could have carved out a career (I just *had* to say it....sorry!) as Head Chef in any five-star eatery world-wide. He had the *talent* you see. Fried bread done his way, was a mouth-watering treat! His roast turkey, basted with herbs and stuffed with home-made seasoning, piled up with roast potatoes, Yorkshire pudding, two strips of bacon, sprouts, and peas with self-recipied gravy on the side together with a small hill of cranberry sauce - was an experience the world has never known and if anyone believes they have partaken of a better meal in their lives, they are deluding themselves. Less than fifteen people in the million or so years since pre-history have had this awesome experience by my reckoning.

And still to come – dessert. His piece-de-resistance, the Christmas pudding! Maturing in the bread-bin since early December, loaded with brandy and containing that most vital of traditional touches....the elusive sixpence! Find *that* and your luck was supposed to change for the better. Naturally if you swallowed it you might not see it that way! To be sure, it never helped us any.

Fit for little in the way of activity following *La Grand Bouffe*, the afternoon was spent in quiet contemplation - of which side of the

Cadbury Box to start on! Deciding to see out the day "in the saddle," the Chrysler and I headed up past the Grammar School for one last ride down Wendover Way. Darkness had long fallen of course but this particular street was the nearest thing you'd find to a roller coaster with its angled bends and gradient steep enough to sort the wimps from the winners. Had it been a main thoroughfare it would have borne signs "Warning - Trucks use low gear!" With dull street-lights only at eight-house intervals, it was a lonely climb to the top. Square in the saddle, headlight on, scarf wrapped across my mouth, I kicked off....you didn't need to pedal, simply steer. First turn, expertly done, wheel starting to vibrate with the speed - hang on tight, next bend approaching - the big one! What the hell was that? Someone's tabby just shed eight of its nine lives in one dash. Corner right up ahead.....looking good....except perhaps for that looming dark shape no more than two milliseconds ahead. The noise of the collision was rapidly receding, left far behind with the wreckage. Still travelling at an unimpeded twenty to twenty-five mph, I was afforded a remarkably clear view of the shape beneath me as I began my descent. I remember thinking, "What degree of insanity would you need to register, to use a black car-cover on an unlit corner of a steep hill at night time?" I can still see the aerial, a lone sentry, passing by on my left as I came down, no more than a foot or so past the front fender. Touchdown was not good - multiple bounces, a series of forward rolls and sliding.....a lot of sliding! Finally coming to rest, ripped clothing and fresh blood making each other's acquaintance, I got to my feet, albeit gingerly and shaking uncontrollably returned for my bike. Hurt and bruised as I was, the 'New Yorker' was waiting for a Priest! The front wheel was no longer round, bent completely out of shape now with a huge "V" dent at the front. Brake calipers hung loose like dancers without partners, the handlebar was now at a right angle as if willing someone to pull it to its feet.

The frame itself was buckled beyond help and the headlight, a chrome shell with its former occupants strewn all over the road. The pedals faced different directions and even the seat had suffered whip-lash and was pointing skywards, perhaps indicating where I could well have found myself with a new address! The pain was nothing to what I would face when I got home with my scrap metal! Dragging the bike from the back, I somehow managed to get home. Skin was hanging from one knee, something wet and sticky was running down my neck and neither leg seemed to remember how once they coordinated when we all used to walk normally. Mum answered the front door, looked at what I had with me, took one long glance at the clothing rejects, the blood flow and generally poor presentation, before uttering simply, "I see!....you'd better come in!"

No anger, no pity, just the eternal composure.

The bath was hot, the pain in a class of its own. From memory, only a small section of my left foot didn't hurt! It was fortunate there was no need to perform skin grafts, there being not too many large areas remaining undamaged. The heat was soothing, mum's medical skills remarkable and dad's self-control absolutely commendable. Whilst mum was into her second tube of antiseptic cream, dad was conducting a post-mortem on the bike. To be friends for life, we'd been separated after just ten and a half hours bonding. The verdict was that in the unlikely event the frame could be straightened, the rest was fixable. Patched and bandaged I went to bed early, Dad went out - I never knew where but I've always had a sneaking suspicion that someone in Wendover Way that cold Christmas night had a visitor remarkably short on Ho-Ho-Ho's.

The next morning brought such discomfort I was in two minds as to whether I even wanted the bike back! Every internal organ I possessed had its own tale of misery, most I suspect were in totally different locations from the original blueprint and were jostling between themselves to get back on site. If I hadn't been in such pain I would have laughed whenever they played Presley's "All Shook Up!"...but all things pass, as did 1957.

CHAPTER FOUR

CHANGING OF THE GUARD

Doubtless the more romantically-inclined reader out there will be wondering what *did* become of Gillian? I've often wondered myself! In 1958 we found ourselves literally, separated by a brick wall. Gillian was now in 2A (Year eight!) and I had been relegated to 2B in payback for my perceived anarchy in certain subjects. At the time I was heartbroken and not a little concerned. Resident in 2A was one Danny Ross, an immaculately turned-out little boofhead, only son of the wealthiest parents on the P & C association. Dropped off at school in his mother's new Rover each morning, Danny had all the right accreditation. Teachers held him in high esteem, he had all the appropriate pre-programmed responses. His books were never creased, his homework never late, even his damned tie never crooked! *and*...he fancied Gillian. Worse still, she seemed to respond to the little twerp. Physically, Danny would have been at long odds to have gone three rounds with any of the girls. Perhaps Gillian could see something no-one else could. Maybe she just liked Rovers!

I still saw her at recess and the occasional lunch-hour but it was never the same again and I knew that my memories of her at Primary School and the times we had shared together were consigned now to the past. It was about this time I decided not to grow up - Peter Pan had managed it, so too would I. I promised myself that even if my body should eventually age - I would hide within it, secure in a world of my own making, one that no adult would be invited to or would even have an interest in visiting - I still live there - with all my memories, my conkers, the sights and experiences of childhood. I knew the *Sounds of Silence* long before Simon and Garfunkel wrote about them. There are those who speak of "searching for the truth - spiritual enlightenment, etc." So few realise - we *have* all this at birth and fritter it away growing up!

Early Spring and mum suffered the first of many subsequent bouts of pleurisy, a rampant infection of the lungs and thorax. In her case, particularly debilitating since a near-fatal bout of diphtheria when just six years old, had left her with only one functional lung. Her respiratory system had received little help either from years of smoking, which in those days had only once before been nominated as a potential link with cancer in a scientific report leaked to the U.S. Press in February 1954 and which had received little in the way of follow-up.

Just as she was recovering, a 23 year-old Elvis was inducted into the U.S. army and the following day (March 25) Sugar Ray Robinson recaptured his middle-weight boxing title for a record-breaking fifth time.

The biggest change wrought in our lives occurred in July of that year. With the closure of the War Damage Commission - their job complete mid-year, my father found himself without a job, but the possessor of some six thousand pounds by way of retrenchment monies, a not inconsiderable sum in those days. The following week dad swung the surprise of the decade when he returned from London one afternoon with not only an unused train ticket, but a 1955 Ford Consul. Black with red leather upholstery, the car was in true showroom condition and life was never the same again. Weekends meant new places, discoveries, a freedom never before envisaged. Every country lane between Welling and the South Coast were ours to scour. Out-of-the-way tea-rooms, lunch at quaint little thatched pubs, all brass and class, the aroma of fresh shepherds' pie wafting across the threshold. Lots of cider....dad always his pint of bitter and mum her gin and tonic. From Sevenoaks to Bexhill we roamed like motorised gypsies navigating on a whim and a prayer. All manner of unpublicised places of interest we came upon. Ancient frigates tied up at inland waterways, Roman ruins strewn across desolate fields long since having given up hope of ever attracting their share of visitors. Disused airfields with *Spitfires* now sad abandoned hulks, their insides exposed as the rivets corroded beyond service, had let slip the steel plating protecting their modesty. The Consul drove on. Villages of unparalleled beauty, forests with no name, secluded Tudor mansions whose owners probably never even knew there had been a war in progress and coastal hideaways where the narrowest of roads reined in the few dwellings like a good mother, fearful of the lure of the sheer cliffs just across the way.

Neither parent being given to overt emotional behaviour, it would not have been apparent to the casual onlooker the pride with which my father handled the car. A very skilled driver with a keen awareness of others, he blended with his new-found soulmate and man and machine combined to operate in perfect harmony. If there *was* a downside, it was that "presentation" was a long way down his list of "need to's." I don't think he ever cleaned the car once! That befell yours truly, who expended so many hours polishing, waxing, vacuuming and dusting that on more than one occasion dad was heard to comment, "You've got a real problem there son!"

Dad's best friend and sometime drinking buddy whenever he was in the country was Ernie Thom, an absolute dead-ringer for actor Hugh O'Brien for whom he was mistaken the length and breadth of Europe. Ernie was a born adventurer and had swung a big-time job opportunity in Africa. His daughter Kitty had boarded with us frequently over the years and many was the time I yearned to have been just a few years older...though with my luck, she most likely wouldn't have been able to stay then. Shortly after the War Damage Commission folded, Ernie was in London and came over to see us. Dad and he had often pondered about going in to business together and the timing appeared to be right. Dad had his severance pay and Ernie had the equivalent in African earnings. Timing is one thing, choice is another! Against mum's better judgment they invested just on ten thousand pounds, most everything they had, in a US company - which manufactured vending equipment - ball gum machines to be precise. At a time when the average wage was barely twelve pounds a week, the fifty machines already acquired and sited around East and South-East London were demonstrated to be generating on average, four pounds a week each in pennies, just needing to be bagged, and the machines refilled with swap-cards and ball-gum. On paper, a can't lose deal......even if half the machines broke down, an income of one hundred pounds a week meant a pretty easy life-style even after tax. Ernie returned to Africa, Kitty was on her way to Welling for a month or so and dad was up and running.

The "new face" of pop was making its mark. Duane Eddy's *Rebel Rouser* was blasting the ears off conservative old fogies like my father, Connie Francis was sobbing herself to her first million with *Who's Sorry Now?* and Don Gibson's *Oh Lonesome Me* was the most requested song of the month. Buddy Holly, The Big Bopper and Richie Valens having "signed off" prematurely when their plane crashed near Fargo in North Dakota a few months earlier.

Early days yet, but from dad's viewpoint it was a case of so far so good! The machines *did* bring in the predicted four pounds or so each, although driving around many of the less salubrious districts of East London to refill the machines was hardly the style of work dad had been trained for. Within a month, ten machines were either broken or barely functioning while dad awaited replacement parts from the States. This was still insufficient to cause panic with well over one hundred and fifty pounds a week coming in for what amounted to less than a twenty hour a week job. Things really started to unravel when shop-keepers, sick of complaints began requesting that we remove the machines altogether. I say "we" as I had usually accompanied dad on his weekend sojourns and became as expert at dismantling, refilling and fixing the machines as he was. Our home had become a haven for broken machines, out-dated cards and dysfunctional coin-slots....an aroma of stale gum settled throughout the house. It didn't feel right!

Re-siting machines was not the formality dad had expected. Their fame preceded them and no-one wanted the hassle. It wasn't long before just twenty of the original fifty were operating. Income was down to barely sixty pounds a week, half of which was technically Ernie Thom's. Still waiting for parts from the US the first rumblings of real trouble were felt. The vending company was named in the evening tabloids in connection with alleged fraudulent misrepresentation and various other unsavoury business dealings. Mum was never one to say "I told you so dear!" but the despair on dad's face was inescapable.

That summer we were invited to Wilsill and for the first time we drove up to the farm, perceiving this to be a most welcome break from the gathering storm-clouds at home. Mum and dad may have been troubled but they didn't show it. This time however I encountered substantially more than the stone walls and time-honoured life on the moors. Staying at the farm opposite for a week was a family from the south-west county of Cornwall and accompanying them was their extremely pretty fourteen-year old daughter Ruth. To say we spent "some time" together during that week would be an understatement in the extreme - I never left her side. We walked the near moors, to Brimham Rocks, Pateley Bridge and spent hours sitting atop the walls talking about our homes, our lives and our hopes. The day before she left we were up in the hay loft...she was talking and I was just looking at her. I remember telling her softly that I loved her (and with all that I knew of life at that juncture - I did!). She blushed I think but came over to me and kissed me. We remained there for maybe three hours or so and what was awakened in me all those years ago has not been dimmed by the passage of time. We were ageless, sharing the purity of the moment and for me at least the full impact of her presence was nothing less than emotionally confronting. The next morning her parents were looking at me rather oddly but promises were made that she would come and stay with us in Welling the last week of the holidays. That's all I heard, I couldn't bear to see her leave so I climbed back up to the loft and stayed there for hours re-playing scene by scene.....some in slow-motion!

Time slipped by - with a car now, we were able to see so much more than was possible on previous visits. Knaresborough, York itself, Leicester, Leeds, Peterborough, before, merely names on a map but now with their own evidenced identity. We returned home via the Leicester township of Melton Mowbray to see mum's sister Peggy and my two cousins Peter and Michael. Aunty Peggy had married well...into the Easom family who produced the world famous Melton pork pies and Stilton Cheese. We received a hamper well stocked with both, each Christmas. Peter and Michael were common visitors to Welling in those early summers but again, nothing lasts and tragedy many years later was to strike at the heart of this family.

The "New Yorker" had been given a second lease of life, and Peter and I began to explore further afield, often riding ten or twenty miles away, maybe more. We would stock the saddle-bags with snacks and make a day of it. Thus it was, that towards the end of the holidays we decided to go in search of the fabled "Dean holes." Legend had it that somewhere in Borstall Woods, an enormous untamed expanse of woodland, some forty minutes or so ride from Welling, existed these "bottomless pits" dug for obscure reasons by totally unknown agencies. Just why they were called Dean Holes was equally unclear. Supposedly they had been there for many hundreds of years, if not of Roman origin or earlier. Where they were and how many of them, no-one knew - it had just always been an unwritten law to keep away from Borstall Woods! The area had long had a sinister reputation which over the years had taken on a "Blair Witch" level of folklore. The name "Borstall" of course being synonymous with the area's infamous detention centre for juveniles from the wrong side of the tracks, did little to offset the negative reputation of the locality.

Telling mum that we were "just going for a long ride" we headed off along Wickham road which led ultimately to Plumstead and Woolwich. Within half an hour the dark mass of Borstall Woods could be seen on the western horizon rising high above the residential areas below. Turning off, it was merely a case of following one's vision. Gradually the road's elevation increased as the density of housing lessened, giving way finally to fields which heralded the fringe of the forest itself - a dark and forbidding front which reared up behind a rusting fence that had long since given up any pretence at serving some purpose. Just a single worn path indicated an entrance of sorts to the brooding leviathan. A faded and weather-beaten sign declaring simply "Borstall Woods" hung sideways on one surviving nail on a steel post, itself considerably out of alignment either the result of natural causes or by human intervention....possibly a little of both.

Chaining the bikes to a solid portion of the fence, we retrieved our sandwiches and headed for the entrance.

"You sure this is a good idea?" Peter asked. He was far more practical than me. Unfazed by anything, Peter would have accompanied me into Hell itself but now, I detected his reluctance.

"Probably not," I answered, "but we've come this far and don't you want to see if these holes exist or not?"

"I suppose," he replied, "let's go then."

We breached the perimeter and took off wherever the track was of a mind to lead us. Not five minutes into the forest and the natural light was struggling to penetrate the gloom. The trees had grown so closely together in places that the entwining branches had formed a dense canopy, a wickerwork at tree-top level. Creepers and bramble bushes limited any swift progress and the pathway itself was fighting a losing battle for dominance amongst the encroaching undergrowth. Here, one's sense of direction was challenged with no clear feature from which to take bearings. It was exciting though and there being just the one path to follow, becoming lost was hardly likely. Perhaps twenty minutes on however, the pathway, substantially less worn at this point suggesting rather infrequent use, appeared to diverge into two forks. We took the left and moved on. More of a track now than anything else, progress slowed as the way was frequently blocked by rampant bramble and knee-high thorn. At intervals small pockets of grassy areas appeared on either side, miniature glades, owing their existence to a break in the overhead canopy and the admittance of uninterrupted sunlight. Occasionally a young rabbit would dart across one of these, startled by the sudden appearance of creatures our size, having most likely never encountered such a thing in their short lives. Some twenty minutes or so later, the track wound out to what can only be described as one of the forest's nerve-centres. Before us was an area some fifty yards across devoid of anything but trees, themselves reasonably well spaced with patchy grass between. Multiple tracks ran off at approximately the four points of the compass all of which appeared to be much like that we had just navigated, bramble and thorn encroaching right up to the edge of this central "clearing." Before deciding which option to take, we sat down and had our sandwiches and drinks. Certainly nothing even vaguely ominous here, the woods reflected much the same serenity and peacefulness as our own "Wild Wood" back home, only on a gigantic scale. The air was rent with bird-life communicating the call of the wild, one species to another of its kind, the constancy of it all a measure of comfort somehow.

After some discussion we decided to take the trail virtually opposite, first tying our paper bags to the bushes where we had emerged, simply as a reminder of the way back should we lose our bearings by chance. The track here followed many twists and turns, often opening into small glades, such as we had seen earlier - some being large enough to fit a reasonable size house. How far we were into the forest by now was anyone's guess and at length it all appeared to be a waste of time, nothing remotely like a "Dean hole" was seen, no signs, no warnings ....nothing but one unending vista of unseasoned wood. Peter was all for returning, but humoured my suggestion of "Just another ten minutes." We veered onwards where shortly two subtle changes seemed to come about. Firstly, the light was noticeably in restricted supply, not because of a lateness in the hour but due to the denseness of the overhanging canopy of branches. This also contributed to a distinctly sharp drop in the temperature at ground level. The second change was not immediately obvious but was somewhat disturbing on realisation. There was no bird noise and but for our own footfalls, a disquieting silence - the very air was still. The natural beauty and tranquility of the forest had evaporated in the space of a few minutes to be replaced by an unnatural quiet and air of intimidating disharmony. Neither of us spoke, there was no need, we simply turned around and began retracing our steps.

Simple as it had been following the trail inwards, it looked quite different trekking back. Several times, the path appeared to offer alternate routes which on a couple of occasions we took before having to back up and realign our direction. At the precise moment I glanced backwards to make sure Peter was still right behind me, my foot caught in a creeper, and I fell forward. Unhurt, it came to me something was radically wrong. An ice-cold draught was buffeting my face which should have been resting on hard ground instead of tilting downwards somehow on a bed of pliant fronds. I called out to Peter who pulling up now behind me simply said.

"God Noel, don't move!.......you're right on the edge."

Raising myself up to my elbows I could see it - the rim of the hole. Surely twenty feet in diameter, the blackness of its depths concealed by the advance of undergrowth covering inwards to at least two to three feet around its circumference. My hands were within inches of the ingress, my head well over the drop zone. Backing up slowly and with every limb trembling uncontrollably I got to my feet. Even at close-range, the hole was hard to see, camouflaged as it was by natural growth and deprivation of light. The thing was horrific, no two ways about that, exuding a chilling atmosphere of absolute evil. That nothing good had ever happened in this place was a foregone conclusion! The existence of other such holes in the immediate proximity could not be in doubt, though we had no wish to find them. Before leaving, we tossed several large rocks into the abyss and I tell you with absolute conviction - we did not hear any of them hit bottom. Whatever was down there, did not bear contemplation.

Finding that we had in fact strayed from the original trail slightly we retraced our steps and found our way back to our bikes waiting dutifully where we had left them. We spoke little on the way home and the subject of Dean holes was never raised again, the day's experiences being consigned to the furthest recesses of our joint memories.

The holidays took a turn for the better when Ruth was deposited on our doorstep for the final week....her parents still looking somewhat askance at me as they left, making arrangements to pick her up the following weekend. The personal nature of that week is by preference best left unspoken, remaining forever - a small but prominent memory-chip inscribed July 1958, a time of carefree adolescence bordered with an encroaching awareness that my childhood was making preparations to move on, despite our pact that this would never be. I saw Ruth on three other occasions, I spent a week with her family, and she returned to Welling twice. The following year her family moved to the South of France and I never saw her again.....but in my mind - she has never left and remains now even forty-six years on, the most beautiful girl on the threshold of maturity, untouched by the ravages of time and wearing still her cotton print dress, her rich auburn hair framing those exquisite features, smiling as she always was and pleading with me to row her around the lake "just one last time."

The change of seasons brought with it the onset of a winter of discontent. Pressure was building on dad to keep what machines he could in service. Battling as he was, with faulty mechanisms and disgruntled shopkeepers, weekly earnings were down to less than fifty pounds and the time spent on the road was on the increase. On many such trips I accompanied him, it seemed we spoke increasingly less. At each location the same old story. "If you can't get this thing to work properly Mr Bailey, take it away, it's not worth the trouble." ..and all *this,* for the privilege of sitting in the car, parked in some grimy little rabbit-warren, counting out and bagging three or four pounds worth of pennies, which being the large clunkers they were, was an opportunity to be missed, believe me. This of course was not to mention the now weekend routine – unjamming coin-slots, freeing up seized card-stackers, re-filling, cleaning and whatever, at least, those machines that were *able* to be fixed. A steadily decreasing population! Christmas came and went. It wasn't the same!

3B was no more conducive to fun-times than 2B had been. School and I had now a healthy disrespect for one another. Mum and dad had taken on roles in the developing P & C Association where dad's views on procedure generally, were received with no greater relish than my own presence. Where he came into his own however, was in his ability to coordinate the activities and operational functionality of the school fete each summer. His design specifications for many of the stalls, such as *"Slosh the rat," "Hook-a-bottle"* and *"Sink the Battleship,"* were nothing short of creative genius. They earned the school a fortune. Even his own painstakingly constructed *"Wheel of Fortune"* was a hand-painted six-foot high piece of mechanical wizardry that brought the crowds in. Only Mr LeFeuvre remained aloof, parading as he did on the day of the Fete in his tweeds and shooting cap, attempting the impossible - to smile at parents, before sidling up to me suggesting I "move away" from the *"Hook-a-bottle"* as I had an unfair advantage, having been able to practice at home. He had a point there, I *had* been monopolising the stall and what *did* I need with sixteen goldfish, ten chocolate bars and all those Smarties?

Wafting across from the fairground that year, visitors to the Fete were assailed by *Lipstick on Your Collar,* Bobby Darin's *Dream Lover, Red River Rock,* from Johnny and The Hurricanes and for every screaming teenage girl of the period, newcomer Cliff Richard with *Living Doll......*and Justin Timberlake thought *he* was big?

While the ever-deteriorating saga of the ball-gum machines played itself out, my father faced a crisis of unprecedented proportions. A picture of abject despair, he was a broken man late that summer when circumstances forced him to dispose of the one symbol he so cherished personally - the Ford Consul. I stood with him in the upstairs bedroom watching, the day it's new owner drove out of sight along Danson Lane. He lost far more than the car in those fleeting seconds!

As the year and the decade closed out, Hawaii was proclaimed the 50th State of America on August 21st. Barbie hit the world's toy-stores, albeit without Ken, for whom she would have to wait another two years. The Soviet-built spacecraft Lunik II crashed on to the Moon's surface, *Ben Hur* hit the movie screens in November and *The Sound of Music* opened on Broadway just before Christmas.

1960 - it sounded at the time so futuristic, a door opening to accelerated hope and discovery. The "forties" seemed as dated then as they appear now in the new millennium. *Brookside* remained its picturesque self, yet beneath the vibrancy both inside and out, began now to seep a hint of a new influence.....uncertainty! As if suffering from the same malaise which afflicted Dorian Gray, everything *looked* as it always had, but a change had come about. Tension infiltrated our lives. The dinners somehow lost their edge, conversation was less urgent, jokes less funny, it seemed even that the clock ticked louder.

Dad had been able to replace the Consul with an old and very cheap 1950 Vanguard which although loved, could not compete with the memory or functionality of its predecessor, though we had agreed never to mention such in the newcomer's presence. It did what it could and in fact what it *had* to, but not without much cajoling and nurturing on dad's part. Many was the hour I helped him as he bequeathed remarkable time and effort in his endeavours to keep it going. The gearbox, starter motor and clutch were facing imminent retirement, if not burial but somehow he coaxed the very last gasp from each vital organ. The period was not without humour. Dad and I having to sit on a headlight each for twenty minutes one night as we crossed the River Thames by car ferry, an electrical short preventing them from being turned off. Our predicament mid London when all four gears came apart and by changing down, you had no way of knowing whether you were likely to engage first, third or even reverse! (Mum worked her way through several cigarettes that night!) My personal favourite, dangerous as it was in hindsight, was during the last ten minutes of one trip to *Raymead* when dad announced to no-one in particular....."We've got no brakes." Mum, little mechanically minded, suggested, "Then why don't you *stop* Colin and check them?" Ever-resourceful and with undeniable quickness of thought....noticing a local bus up ahead travelling at roughly the same speed, dad steered to within a couple of feet of its rear bumper. As it slowed for the stop ahead, the Vanguard very gently nudged its rear and was brought to a halt by the bus itself - no damage to either vehicle. It proved a source of great amusement to the row of schoolkids in the rear of the bus, less so to the driver who leant out of his window and let fly with some choice phraseography before he was made aware of the situation. The laughs though were few and far between. Barely fifteen machines were functioning at any one time now and with even the kids showing less and less interest in them, weekly income dropped to below twenty pounds. Deduct from that the costs incurred servicing the business and it didn't take a genius to see that the future posed a challenge roughly equal to that facing David when Goliath made his unscheduled appearance. Thus dad did the only thing left for him to do - he had a heart attack! The prognosis was not good. High blood-pressure, poor family medical history, overweight and unfit. Over the next three weeks or so's hospitalisation, two of which were spent in intensive care, he gradually recovered physically but the scars from his decimated investment were never to leave him. Having only ever had a wish to give his family a prosperous and comfortable life, seeking absolutely nothing personally, he showered himself with blame, declaring in his misery, his perceived failure as a father, provider and husband....the three things for which, no one on this planet could ever have been his equal.

On his release he was under strict instructions to rest-up and the business was ultimately phased-out by necessity. For a while, I did what I could to keep a few machines on site, but at fourteen and being able to commute only by bike with the nearest of them some fifty minutes ride from home, it was never going to be a realistic proposition. His partner Ernie Thom fared little better, dying the same year in Africa. He never saw a penny on his investment. The US Company was finally bankrupted and the only remaining evidence of the entire distressing interlude sat stored away upstairs in our attic. A rusting pile of useless machine parts, broken stands and rotting swap cards.

Late March came and with it, mum's second bout of pleurisy. Her respiratory system already overloaded, was at near meltdown and the doctor was by necessity summoned. His stern pallor gave away that which he tried to conceal. She had developed pneumonia additionally and there was now no option but for immediate hospitalisation. Despite the great pain she must have been in, mum merely said to me between laboured breaths. "Make sure you wash up properly Noel, hang the washing out and do your homework.....I'll be back in a few days."

At that juncture, there looked to be little likelihood of her even coming back, let alone soon....but I had reckoned without this great and brave woman's resolve and iron will, one that later was to carry her through impossible physical adversity and hardship. No one called the shots for Joyce!

Dad meanwhile was looking for work, but even with his qualifications, positions for someone the wrong side of fifty were about as elusive as a responsible teenager. He took mum's illness hard and without her presence there, appeared unmotivated and directionless. She was his life and despite my assurances that it would take a lot more than pneumonia to get the better of her, he remained unconvinced and inconsolable.

True to her word however, not six days had elapsed when we were able to bundle her into the Vanguard and head off towards the only street in this world that led where I ever wanted to go - Danson Lane.

With all that was going on, I had almost forgotten that this was year four at school (Year 10).....only the most important year of my academic life. The G.C.E. (General Certificate of Education). Stuff up your 'O' levels and you could kiss any sort of decent career goodbye. The stigma of failing your GCE would be worse than not sitting for it! Aside from the assembly-line trials and mock exams, in preparation for the moment of truth in July, 4B was no worse than other years. Homework still ruined my nights and weekends...at least that which Dad wasn't able to complete for me. The year was notable only for my getting the cane for refusing to nominate a friend who had spilt concentrated sulphuric acid, albeit accidentally, over a work bench after school one night. Three of us having been present we weren't about to dob in a friend. Mr LeFeuvre's solution was simple, cane all the little bastards! In my case, he finally had his wish. I watched him lovingly caressing his little instrument of torture ahead of a couple of practice swishes - I'll swear he was smiling. It hurt like hell but I didn't utter a sound....I simply slammed the door on the way out, tears trying to make their way to the surface but no match for my will-power. In those few moments of extreme discomfort I lost all fear and respect for him. He was just an old soldier with no regiment left to command. My greatest achievement was that he saw my recognition momentarily before I left. He never came near me again.

As it happened, Mum found employment first or at least, work found her. A small private commercial college nestled in north Welling. Cottingham's was looking for an experienced Shorthand/English teacher. Mum's name came up for nomination as she had maintained a few private students in and around Welling over the years. She was appointed swiftly and took up duties early April. While dad was pleased for her, and of course the money was life-saving, it was obvious that the ease with which she had been accepted reflected in his mind, his *own* inability to make ends meet. His body language defined his inner thought processes and he took to long periods out walking. It was a time he so needed me to love him, to re-assure him and to be a supporting son.......and God-help-me I failed him. I had taken all that he had to give and more, yet now when my turn came, to give that which he needed, I was but a *shell*....a son by default! Why this should be, what caused my inexcusable remoteness and seemingly uncaring disposition, I have absolutely no recollection. In all the years since, I have never been able to formulate any possible motive for my apparent disdain and cruel intentions such as they must have seemed. I was however in line for my own rude awakening! The day came mid-June, barely a month before the exams when I walked home to find our next door neighbour waiting for me on the front porch. Clearly agitated, she informed me that both mum and dad had been taken to hospital and that I had to ring the College. The Principal there told me that mum had suffered some sort of relapse and they had called an ambulance which had taken her to Woolwich Hospital. Dad, so the neighbour informed me had been taken away also by ambulance, only twenty minutes or so before I had arrived home.....she couldn't say to which hospital. Ringing first our own doctor's surgery I found that dad had been taken back to Plumstead Hospital, suffering from what sounded like a further heart attack. He had just managed to call the doctor himself before collapsing. Having rung Woolwich hospital, staff there said that mum was "serious" and that I should come in. Plumstead was on the way, so hastily grabbing my bike I headed off.

Dad was unconscious and with tubes criss-crossing his body like a broken piece of trellis it didn't look encouraging. The doctor-in-charge took me aside and asked where my mother was - I told him and he simply looked at me. I suppose in hindsight, what *could* you say?

"Well Noel," he said, not sure of how to proceed. "Your dad's very ill, he has had a severe heart attack and, well...we don't yet know how he will respond to treatment."

I remember clearly asking almost casually, "Will he die?" Again the specialist's look of "How do I handle this?"

"It is possible, yes son, I'm afraid that is a likelihood. His heart has already been weakened by the last attack. Better you go now and see your mother, we will call you at home - I'm so sorry lad!" he said as an afterthought. Then he turned and walked off, leaving me looking down at dad's creased and perspiring face.

Woolwich Hospital was some twenty minutes further on, a rather sombre and depressing edifice which had been stretched to its limits during war-time. The old corridors would, if you had stopped and allowed them to, have unburdened their stories of loved ones who were never to see their thirties, families wrenched by tragedy, young men with bodies torn asunder but who clung to life, all of whom had been wheeled, carried or otherwise propelled along those soulless walkways. Not a place a fifteen-year-old would willingly wish to find himself by any circumstance. Checking with information, I found the ward where mum had been admitted. Her doctor was quite candid. "Your mother has severe emphysema," she told me, "Her condition is most serious." Having no idea what emphysema was, I had no intention of showing my ignorance and merely asked what were her chances of recovery. She looked at me but said nothing.

"Could she die?" I asked for the second time that night. The doctor, showing at last some compassion, took my arm and led me to a nearby waiting room. She asked where my father was and I told her. Quite unable to make a satisfactory reply, as if anyone could, she just took me to mum's bedside and said quietly, "Try not to mention anything about your father, you understand?...it wouldn't do her any good right now!" I recall wondering what exactly was going to do *me* any good on this particular night.

She tried explaining to me the technicalities of emphysema, most of which were in such pseudo-medical terms I could do little but nod wisely. From what I could understand, her one surviving lung was able to generate less and less breathable oxygen as the emphysema, much like lung-cancer, spread from capillary to capillary, shutting down options for any quality of life.

Mum at least was conscious, although in no condition to sustain a full-on conversation. She held my hand and I found myself somehow at peace with the situation despite its seeming hopelessness. Her breathing was aided by machine and I looked down at this great fighter, wracked with pain, her arms limply at her side, the left wrist host to a taped drip. I took it all in, the damp hair plastered around her forehead - in places now little ringlets, her neck and upper chest sunken and straining even with mechanical aid. But it was the eyes that betrayed the full impact of her predicament....ringed as they were and slightly bloodshot. Mercifully sleep came and I bent down to kiss her. She whispered to me just as I turned to leave, "Look after your father." I made it outside and just broke down, unending waves of worry, guilt and sheer desolation. No one to help, nowhere to go but home, I rode and rode, finally getting back at almost ten o'clock.

I was wrong about no-one to help. *Brookside* was there, it had *always* been there for me! Even as I unbolted the back gate, put the bike in the garage and took out my latch key, something took me under its protective care. I sensed it and before going inside I walked around the garden - perfectly still on a warm summer's night, the forest a dark silhouette against the back fence. A solitary hedgehog taking its time crossing the far lawn. The mixed scents from the many flower beds, predominantly though the roses alongside my bowling strip, had never been as powerful - perhaps I had never been so needful of ingesting them.

I walked inside and through every room in the house. The kitchen, with its own pantry off to one side where dad always left his used razor-blades on the little window sill. The window propped open with the cat's 'run-up' as we used to call it, a ten foot piece of wood that gave "Tigger" access all night. My HP sauce was still sitting on the table where I'd left it at breakfast and one odd plate was sitting forlornly on the sink, waiting for someone to kindly dry it and return it to its friends. The dining room was waiting expectantly for me, as if to hear some news of its occupants which for the first time in memory were strangely absent. Dad's chair looked particularly sad....mum's, hopeful! The small pouffe that dad had made from rags then covered so professionally with spare curtaining and which had gladly supported his feet through so many episodes of *Perry Mason* and *Rawhide*, sat now idly by, waiting for an explanation. The lounge was quiet and having always fancied itself as a cut above the other rooms, wasn't about to betray too much emotion. Upstairs, my bedroom simply took charge. All those years of books, treasures and collectibles drew every last bit of distress and anxiety from me. I knew I would be OK whatever happened and I nodded to the shelves and cabinets in acknowledgment of their support. Mum and dad's room was unchanged, still reeking of dad's leg and shoulder liniment that he used to relieve muscular soreness. The spare bedroom, the biggest room in the house, and somewhat proud of that status remained undisturbed, its five windows providing an uninterrupted view across the moonlit garden. Life could put together no lasting threat to me in this place - not in *this* house!

I can't say I retired to bed fully at ease, but I was mentally on track and in far better shape than when leaving the hospital. Tigger was in shortly after and as if divining the problems at hand, came and slept on my bed, purring on all cylinders. Waking up the next morning I summarised my position. Sleeping upstairs in an empty house, the possibility of being an orphan at fifteen, if not by lunch time. No food in the house, no money to buy any and my final exams due in just under four weeks. Surely this gave new meaning to the term *home alone*? With this devastating realisation, my childhood left me without even packing. No child could have handled this situation and thus I could no longer be one.

I rang the only person outside my immediate family who, it occurred to me, would be remotely interested in my predicament - Mr Collins. He was down in less than five minutes having made arrangements with the school over my absence.

He and dad had always gotten on well and it was obvious his actions were not solely motivated by civic duty. He even left some money for me (so I found hours later) on the kitchen table. As it has often been said....."Many are called - but few answer."

A little after eight-thirty, a phone call from Plumstead Hospital conveyed the news that dad had gotten through the night and was making some progress. While still serious, he would be able to receive visitors later in the morning. I then called Woolwich Hospital and determined that mum's condition though unchanged was at least stable. Shortly after eleven I swung into the saddle of the New Yorker and headed off uptown.

Dad, by whatever criteria you judged, was a resounding improvement on the previous night. With some vestige of colour restored to his features and the intra-venous tubes removed, his appearance gave rise it must be said, to some hope. Although groggy, he was able to talk and predictably one of his first questions was "Where's Joyce?" With what I hoped was pre-rehearsed credibility, I said that she was "really tied up" with work at the college but would try and get down later by bus. This I knew, was only a very short-term solution. Fortunately, patients did not have their own telephones in those days else he would have expected a call I imagine. He seemed satisfied with this explanation and we sat and talked for a while.....probably more than we had for some time. In answer to his query as to why I wasn't at school I told him that they had said I could stay home 'for a few days' as long as I kept up my study. Before I left, the doctor took me aside and said that he had gotten through the most critical phase and depending on his continued improvement, they would re-assess his chances of returning home next weekend. Something positive at least.

Leaving him propped up and reading the *Daily Telegraph*, I rode on to Woolwich Hospital. Mum also appeared a vastly different proposition from the night before. Her face was far less creased with pain, and her breathing though not what one could call regular, was at least of her own issue, the mechanical aid having been disconnected. Propped up also, she smiled at me as I entered, her entire demeanour registering an attitude of "There's not much wrong with me lad, let's wrap this up and get out of here!" Unfortunately, her blood pressure, respiratory monitor, and vital signs told a somewhat different story.

Whether my body language gave anything away, my eyes were averted at the wrong time, or simply her sixth sense was working overtime, I don't know, but she asked simply, "Where's your father?" I held her gaze and said that he had been out until rather late last night and when he called the hospital they had said she was sleeping and that it was better she rest now. I compounded the lies by adding that he would 'be down later.' It was a stunning performance, actors have picked up an Oscar for less. Still it was totally wasted - she simply repeated, "*Where* is your father Noel?" I took her hand which she hastily extricated.

"*Well?*" she demanded, " I'm waiting!"

I told her, there was no other way. Her inevitable response of "I see," was followed by a period of intense thought. Her mind was running the numbers, working the permutations, evaluating the bottom line. No dramatics, no hand-to-the mouth stuff....just the usual 'cool runnings.'

She asked if he knew of her own hospitalisation to which I assured her he didn't......yet. *Now* she took my hand.

"You've had to cope with this all on your own you poor kid," she looked up at me somewhat pained.

I was moved to say that since ten o'clock last night I wasn't a kid any more, but thought better of it.

"I'd best be getting better then," she was saying, as the doctor came in to oversee the morning's administrations. Promising to get back that evening, I left and returned to Welling.

Trying to study under the circumstances ranked somewhere between foolhardy and straight-out impossible. Instead of "equations" I was reading "prescriptions," and "acceleration rates" were immediately replaced in my mind by "heart rates." The shortest distance between two points, far from being a straight line - was my bicycle! I turned on the radio instead and listened to *Cathy's Clown, Good Timin', Rubber Ball, Only The Lonely, Wooden Heart, Poetry in Motion, Will You Still Love Me Tomorrow?* and *Because They're Young*....all of which, with the possible exception of *Wooden Heart*, were far better therapy!

Later, after cooking one of my all-time-great fried bacon, egg, sausage and tomato culinary masterpieces, I returned to see dad at Plumstead. His condition was yet improved and when the subject of mum finally could be deferred no longer he asked logically enough, how she was and would she be coming that evening. I was fresh out of ideas and could prolong the charade no further. I had no need to. At 7.30 pm, by what miracle I have never known, she walked into the ward herself, sat down at his bedside and simply said, "Sorry I'm late dear, I missed the earlier bus."

History has recorded the deeds of many heroes from Achilles to Rob Roy, Marcus Aurelius to Joan of Arc, Davy Crockett to Scott of the Antarctic.....all of whom were in the peak of health. Standing five foot one in bare feet, slight of build and with just one partially functional lung to her credit, Joyce would have seen them all out in any test of endurance. Only the occasional sharp intake of breath betrayed any hint of a problem...and I was looking for it. Dad was so pleased to see her he wouldn't have noticed if she was still wearing a hospital gown.

Afterwards we returned home by bus, which afforded the bike a well-earned rest after the last two day's extended travel. I took then the opportunity of asking her how she had managed to sign herself out. "Mind over matter my boy," was her typically evasive answer.

Over the next two days mum somehow coerced her body to recover and the news from St Nicholas' at Plumstead was promising, barring any set-back, Dad would be eligible for discharge at the weekend. The one down-side - I had to return to school.

If you don't know your subjects three weeks before an exam you've had ten years to prepare for, last minute cramming won't solve your problem. I've always maintained the theory that the best option just ahead of the 'big one' is to relax....do anything but study. Lie on the beach (or stones, if you happen to live in England's south east!) or rest-up in the Cumbrian Lake District (where two years earlier on a school excursion I had tried running down Mount Helvelyn only to find I couldn't, before tripping and rolling some hundred and fifty feet into a tree trunk!)

It was here! a week of unmitigated brain-drain. Amazing how many questions they seem to concoct involving items you'd swear were never covered in the syllabus. Aside from the fact my answers included a bus averaging 350 miles per hour, a rambling discourse on King Henry V, when the question I realised later was about Henry IV. A beautifully drawn map of the Rhine river that should have been the *Rhone* and perhaps my greatest accomplishment - my chemical analysis of a "compound" that confirmed the presence of several rare metals - none of which are found in Britain!......it wasn't too bad.

This of course still left the end-of-year formal where the boys were traditionally presented with their one chance to press their claims for the "ultimate jerk of the year" award. The girls, would-be little sophisticates, trilling and cooing in small groups along one wall, watching the more adventurous (and usually least talented) pairs jive themselves into a frenzy centre-floor. That year, it was all Adam Faith, Cliff Richard and Elvis. God, life was so simple then.....

"What do you want if you don't want money?"

What do you want if you don't want pearls?

Say what you want and I'll give it you darlin'[1]

'Wish you wanted my love baby[1]*......."*

---

1 © 1959 (J Worth) *"What Do You Want?"* **Adam Faith: Parlophone records**

Playing the 'waiting game' was never fun. if you *knew* you'd passed you could swagger round with that "was it ever in doubt?" look, whereas a resounding "fail" mark meant at least you could go and put your name down with the Council for the tree-lopping apprenticeship.

For half the summer holidays, I had on exhibit my best "really doesn't matter to me" attitude whilst inside, the stomach acid was beginning to dissolve my principal organs. Dad was home and remarkably improved, mum seemed well enough to be teaching martial arts and most every little thing was on track.

I was "in love" again! Dad's fault this time - he kept offering to drive me over to her place. Maybe it was just an early case of *American Beauty!* Actually I think I was more in love with Susan's father. He owned this stunning Jaguar dealership in Bexleyheath, just two miles south of Welling and every second weekend he took Susan and I down to Brighton on the south coast, to the family's palatial little home-away-from-home in just about the entire Jaguar range. Cruising down the highway in the latest 3.4 auto, Mark 10 saloon and on rare occasions, an E-Type convertible (it was worth being wedged half on the floor), did have its attractions.

The day came however when the familiar "thwack" of the letter box in the front door, bore admittance to "the letter" or rather, the envelope identified simply as "Department of Education." Thank God I got to it first. I needed to be in a position to hit the porch running if the worst came to the worst! "O Level" passes in English, Maths, French, Biology, Chemistry, History, and English Literature were all I saw - stuff Physics and Art! Where was Mrs Gunson? - I wanted to see her cry. The results meant at least that I would be able to move on to year five and study three "A Levels"....most likely Chemistry, Zoology and Botany, required for entry to University.

The park was never greener, the air fresher or life more worth living. The last week of the summer holidays, a school excursion had been planned by Mr Kelly and the Biology department to Whitstable, a south-eastern coastal resort right at the mouth of the river Thames, where it opens into the English Channel. Thus in company with Susan and half a dozen other members of (then) year four plus Mr Kelly, we all boarded a train at Welling and within two hours were ensconced in rented digs just across from the beach and main strip of Whitstable. The term "beach" may have inappropriate connotations here. Comparisons with Miami or other stretches of golden sands, common to the South Pacific region, may perhaps lead to subtle disappointment in this case. The beach at this point of the Thames' estuary, is marked by the predictable stony entry giving way to a composite of muddy sand....perhaps sandy mud would be a more accurate description! The tide here recedes at a remarkable rate, the water-line withdrawing at least half a mile or so. At low tide are exposed acres of mud flats, as far removed from picture postcard status as can be imagined. The area is however home to a wide range of marine life and a well-equipped marine biology and research laboratory built nearby was placed at our (and other schools') disposal at this time each year.

Unfortunately the girls and boys were housed in separate lodgings but were allowed at least to fraternise after work. Most everybody would hang-out at the one coffee-bar in town, where historically I first developed my life-long appreciation for a capucchino. Susan and I would have a coffee together then go and sit on the beach-front for hours talking about that which teenagers do at such times. It may not have been communally purposeful but remains a distinct comforting memory notwithstanding. Work? now that was something else again! In essence, each student was asked to mark out his/her "quadrat" of the beach, an area some five foot square, where all specimens of marine life, from the tiniest mollusc to the largest crab, would be identified, marked by location and studied. This task would be performed at mid-tide and low-tide (High tide of course, it would be under water!) Other specimens would be collected and returned to the lab for further analysis, leaving simply the task of writing up all reports, remembering that this was still a quarter of a century ahead of the first laptop. Most days the research would be completed by four o'clock leaving us hours of quality swimming time. Some of the boys on this particular day suggested we see who if anyone, could swim out to the old wreck. More of a "dare" really as the thing was so far out and only partially uncovered even at low tide. Protruding from the sand and in a semi-fossilised state now, no more than twenty to twenty-five feet of the bow remained visible arching upwards. Totally staved in, it gave at close hand the appearance of a dinosaur's skeletal remains, disturbing beyond question as water could be heard dripping off the crossbeams in the recesses of the old ship. No one ever ventured inside for fear of collapse or even being trapped by the turn of the tide - besides, it smelt of death with seaweed and crustacean life its only adornment now. At high tide, just the merest two or three feet of its foremost beam extended out of the water, just visible from shore yet enough to register its eerie presence. With no known history the ship was estimated to be several hundred years old and had most likely been there since the great fire of London, the tide pounding its sides and buffeting the solid cross-members far back down our historical time-line.....and today we were going to swim out to it! Nothing like a challenge to set the adrenaline on stand-by! Four of us kicked off from the shallows, watched by two disinterested girls, three other classmates and an elderly local, a crusty old Negro who looked more than likely to have been wedged into his old deck-chair there against the sea-wall, the day the old schooner itself ran aground. Being a strong swimmer in the local pools, doesn't count for much when you're being battered by waves fifty or sixty yards from shore. By now, the onlookers were mere specks....the wreck was seemingly no nearer. Two of the boys had given up and were dog-paddling their way in-shore. Myself and the other lad were pretty much together, neither wanting to voice the other's true feelings that this had not been a great idea and that our arms were feeling like pieces of lead already.

"You OK?" he said,

"Sure," I replied, wondering when the hell he was going to turn around.

In all sports, indeed as is the case with any major physical exertion, one reaches a level of such exquisite agony that if you can overcome it and keep going, a stage is reached that there is no longer any pain and you can switch to automatic. I hadn't yet reached that point as my arms, back and legs were on the brink of collapse, I had swallowed so much water the salt was making me heave, and I was feeling the onset of cramp - a big worry at this distance! The only good news was that the ship's mast, well clear of the water now, was suddenly not far off. Looking around I found myself alone, my partner having turned around at least twenty yards back it seemed. The beach was so distant it didn't bear contemplation. Just a fraction more effort now and I was there...the mast was within twenty feet, ten, five - I touched it.! The sea at this distance was quite smooth and I could clearly see the dark mass fanning out just below the surface. My foot struck wood and the feeling was one of repulsion - it felt dead, an alien thing that having drawn me thus far would keep me here if it could. I turned and half-panicking started to swim away, again my foot touched something hard way down, as the swell momentarily carried me backwards towards the ancient mast and I had nightmarish visions of sinking, being trapped in the debris far below.....then as a surge of inner strength, borne out of fear and trepidation I suspect, coursed through me, I began to swim strongly with no backward glance. Not twenty yards further I crossed-over to that next level and with the aid of the tide additionally, made the shoreline infinitely faster than the outbound trip had been.

"Damn fine swim son!" extolled the old Negro, "Best thing I ever did see," he added, offering me his gnarled old hand....I took it.

"You idiot!" said Susan, evidently less impressed and turning now walked back to the lodge.

Year five was a minor achievement in the peer-ranking stakes. A small common room where you could mingle with your equals, leaving the door open to watch all the poor year 1- 4 plebs walk by. "Sorry suckers!" would be hanging off your lips as they stared in, envious of the half-a-dozen chairs arranged around the single desk trying vainly to look like an up-market board-room the decanter of water with a handful of glasses in attendance and the small but personal notice-board on the far wall, where the more desperate year fives would advertise social bulletins - usually upcoming parties for which up until now, they had been unsuccessful in attracting a partner of the opposite sex either through restricted physical appeal or total lack of any charisma....strictly the "dogs" and "dorks" set! Though far smaller than the year-six common room, it was a start, the lowest rung on the upwardly mobile ladder.

It was with the onset of an early and cold winter that the year wound down, not uneventfully as it turned out. Harper Lee's To Kill a Mockingbird was published, Alfred Hitchcock's ultimately controversial *Psycho* premiered in London at the Odeon Leicester Square and had audiences gasping with fear while amassing what was then a record for opening-weekend takings. John F. Kennedy became the US President on November 9th and Clark Gable died just one week later. America announced the imminent launch of "The Pill" and just one week into the Christmas holidays I had a diabolically close encounter of the worst kind. Susan and I had planned a picnic in a St James Park in London, some thirty-five minutes by bus, for which we boarded the regular number 73 route. Road works that morning, just east of the rail overpass, necessitated a diversion through the Eastside, along a few back-streets. We hogged the upstairs front window seats as kids always were prone to do. It was somewhat of a status thing, quite apart from it being the best view on board, this particular day it was almost empty but for an elderly couple at the very back (equally sought-after by the geriatric set!) The conductor had just been up to collect the fares and I was snugged up with Susan pointing out landmarks and features with which she was probably as familiar as I. Immediately ahead lay the overhead railway line with the timely reminder "Warning - Low Bridge" which was unfortunate as we were riding in a *high* bus! There were but two or three seconds perhaps to react. I screamed out to the old couple to get down, then grabbed Susan and pulled her to the floor. Bad as the impact was, the noise was worse!

We must have struck it travelling at well over 30 mph as steel girders cut into the bus just above seat level. Lying across Susan (and with absolutely *nothing* else on my mind, I assure you.) I can see now the roof being peeled back straight over our heads like a sardine can. Lights, windows, and even the conductor's cord, decimated amidst a deafening rending and grinding of bizarrely telescoped metal. Talk about an "instant convertible." The sudden deceleration caused us to slide somewhat forcefully into the forward bulkhead, such that was left of it and but for pieces of the side windows still falling inwards, all was now still. To say we were 'frosted' in glass would be to state the obvious. Covering my entire prostrate form including my hair, I "crinkled" as I got to my knees - it looked to be quite a nice day outside! Several people were gathering now and pointing upwards. I waved back at a couple of them. With a clearance now of no more than three feet, we were forced to crawl towards the rear section of the bus. We watched as the conductor came racing up the rear and undamaged stairway. I wondered for a minute whether or not he was about to refund our money. The two elderly passengers had been thrown forward but appeared unhurt. As for the bus itself, it was securely wedged more than one third its length beneath the overhead railway and we had now a temporary roof - the blackened underside of the bridge itself. You notice the oddest things at times like this! Just away and up to our left, strategically sited where two steel girders intersected, a pigeon, to judge by its size, had built a nest for itself - anticipating doubtless a little privacy. Hopefully it wasn't in residence when we dropped in. As it was I'm sure this would have dampened its enthusiasm for dark places. The peeled-back metal, some six or seven seats forward from the rear seat, was dangling precariously from the left hand side of the bus and onlookers were being moved back for their own safety. Susan was more concerned for her new coat which was in substantial need of an experienced dry-cleaner. Mine was a riot of glitter, seemingly the work of some insane seamstress. How I managed to avoid being cut by the inbound glass remains a mystery, but so much more was to happen in future years, this was merely an entrée.

By now every local resident was converging on the scene, doubtless the most exciting event to befall south London in that generation's experience. No one paid much heed to the dozen or so passengers on board, or the driver, out of his cab now and sitting in the gutter, hands to his head and shaking like an inmate after excessive shock therapy. The bus itself remained the focal point of most every sight-seer, looking from the back like some distant relative of "Henry the Green Engine," still refusing to come out of the tunnel. Sirens heralded the arrival of a couple of Police Wolseleys - shiny black 6/99's.

Walking among the passengers I heard the constables asking in the most accentuated of British tones, "I say sir, are you alright?" and, "Let me help you there madam - nasty little incident I don't mind saying."

God bless them! If and when Armageddon arrives in my lifetime, I want to go out surrounded by the "Best of British"....."Looks like we're in for it now chaps, anyone for a last brandy?"

Dad's birthday was December 21st and this year he was to receive his most welcome and best-timed present. The mail that morning brought confirmation of his successful appointment as Assistant Store Manager at The Civil Service Stores, a popular four level shopping complex in London's Strand almost opposite Charing Cross Station and some thirty seconds from Nelson's Column itself. He had been short-listed for two interviews but had held out little hope of success, being up against other applicants twenty years younger. Someone at last, obviously knew talent when they saw it. His salary at sixteen pounds ten shillings a week was above average and his spirit so restored it was really quite an emotional morning.

"Brookside" glowed that Christmas. Dad's brother Uncle Don, came over Christmas afternoon in his beloved 1946 Rover and despite the freezing cold, in company with my cousins Rupert, Elizabeth and Ghinda, with whom I shared a special bond. We roamed and ragged the entire park, boundary to boundary. Next day we all headed off in convoy to the traditional Boxing day family gathering at *Raymead*. Life was back on an even keel.....for now.

After some deliberation and educational research, we decided to complete my Years five and six at a newly opened centre of learning, The North West Kent College of Technology in Dartford Kent, another ten minutes on from Susan's home in Bexleyheath. Not that there was anything wrong with Bexley Grammar, but the facilities at this new college were said to be the best in Britain. The size of an average University, the college offered a much wider syllabus and smaller classes with more individual tuition. "Civvies" instead of a school uniform was a major attraction additionally. Certainly I missed initially the familiarity and utter convenience of Bexley Grammar, but the sheer size and equipment level of the College far outweighed any other consideration.

Weeks and months sped past in a blur of flashing scalpels and neatly dissected frogs, mice and cuttlefish. The nervous, digestive and reproductive systems of many a deceased animal came to be displayed (in my case at least) with various levels of professionalism. Some copybook, some testing the patience of our Zoology lecturer, missing as they sometimes were, vital pieces of anatomy. E.R. this wasn't!

Chemistry was a cinch. Advanced compound analysis, atomic structures and weights, inorganic theory and the like. No chance of losing a kidney here or sneezing at the wrong time and cutting through some rodent's spinal chord by accident. Botany? well just how exciting can it be studying up on the root system of a crocus? We didn't even get to run over any mountains singing "The Hills are Alive."

Just a week or so after Russia's Yuri Gagarin became the first man in space on April 12th 1961, my father was summoned to the Managing Director's Office and told he was now General Manager of the entire store with an appropriate pay-rise. Things like this just didn't happen to him and he came home early that day really pumped. In his new capacity, he was responsible for basically the running of the entire store including a multi-million dollar re-design and refurbishment that had just received boardroom approval. Saturday nights, a new tradition was set in motion. We would drive to London very late evening, making use of a 24 hour reserved parking spot in The Strand. With the doors closed, dad was able to walk through floor by floor drawing up preliminary architectural plans and sketches, in peace and quiet. For me, an entire store at my disposal. I usually headed straight for the record department where I had access to many of the latest recordings by Cliff Richard, Elvis, Del Shannon, Roy Orbison, The Shadows, Ike and Tina Turner, Connie Francis, The Everly Brothers, etc. pretty much a who's who of the early 60's. Records not due for release until late the following week, many not having yet even received air-play. I'd give each a whirl on the store's stereo system and *groove* baby. The original Saturday Night Fever....and Travolta still barely out of nappies. Then, on to Menswear. An entire floor of pants and tops to try on. No waiting to be served, no-one in the changing rooms, come to that no need for changing rooms. Want to see the latest stereo gear? portable record-players etc? No problem, Radio and Television, second floor folks and hey, we'll road-test those express lifts on the way. No delays as the crowds jam up and jelly tight, no waiting for the old ladies to drag their squeaking carts across the elevator entry. I must have spent at least half an hour each of these nights riding lift number one (the biggest and fastest) up and down the four floors. Somewhat pathetic now when you come to think of it! There weren't too many occasions I didn't front-up home with multiple items - records, clothes, etc that would have hit dad's expense account later that week, albeit with his own mega-discount plan. I suspect not a few were ultimately listed as "stock losses" somewhere down the line.

The old Vanguard that had seen us through such dark times, deserved a better farewell. Mid-June, dad called home one evening and asked Joyce, "I *did* take the car today didn't I?"

Whilst seemingly a dumb question, he had taken recently to walking to the train every few days. Parked as it had been, on the ramp leading up to Welling station, in the company of thirty or so of the latest model Austins, Zephyrs, Vauxhalls, Humbers and Rovers, .all pretty much ten years newer and infinitely more valuable.....someone had stolen 'old faithful.' As luck (or providence) would have it, I had actually ridden-up to the station after college not an hour and a half earlier and cleaned it for him. Obviously I did too good a job! Car-theft in and around Welling in those days was virtually an unrecorded event, and as the constable at Welling Police station muttered to dad while filling out the report, as he subconsciously smoothed out his moustache, "A *Vanguard* you say Sir?" as if this would have to be the work of either a rank amateur or a certifiably deranged madman.

We never saw it again, nor the soft and exquisitely-made yellow lion that had sat on the rear shelf since 1959. All the sights it had seen, the highs and lows as the pendulum of destiny swung unchecked at times. We were as distressed at losing *that* as the car, though in an obscure way we always hoped that one would have comforted the other during their enforced exile. Ads were placed in both local and city papers offering a substantial reward for the lion's return - no questions asked, but to no avail.

The Insurance money finally came through and having had such good service from the marque, dad bought another Vanguard, albeit a more modern and immaculately preserved 1956 model, once again, black. It should be remembered that British cars pre-sixties were offered almost exclusively in only black, white or grey. Twenty years earlier the choice had been even easier - black or black!

The next twelve months was one of stability and consolidation or in today's parlance, "right up there," "shaking loose," "getting it on," "putting it all together" or simply "on-line baby." Mum was teaching up a storm at Cottingham's, my new-found dissectional ability should have had me on stand-by with the next heart-transplant team and dad's re-design of the Civil Service Stores had brought hugely increased patronage, the board's gratitude and more immediately, another pay-rise. Life was most definitely on the upper. Susan's family had moved way out of the district, but hey, three out of four's not bad!

And so it was one night mid year '62, just a few weeks away from the finals. I was up late studying, and listening to Radio Luxembourg, the "hip" station of its day, broadcasting from a vessel moored somewhere in the English Channel. I heard the DJ announce.

"And now, a recording by an English group who are pretty big up in their home town of Liverpool - they call themselves "The Beatles!" This is *"Love Me Do."*

Didn't make me want to rush out and buy it - but it *was* different. Still the song faced rather formidable competition up against the likes of Freddy Cannon's *Palisades Park*, Bobby Darin's *Things*, Gene Pitney's *The Man Who Shot Liberty Valance* and the original *The Loco-Motion* by Little Eva....thirty years before Kylie Minogue earned her title of the "singing budgerigar" with the song's re-hash. The "A Levels" weren't the trauma of the "O's," probably on account of the fact there were only three of them. The results were not what I had expected. Passes in Chemistry and Zoology, the former with an unheralded distinction, but Botany took a dive unfortunately. I should have shown more interest in that damned crocus! Still, I was better off than Marilyn Monroe who on August 4th was found dead in her Los Angeles home having apparently od'd once too often. Needing that third "A level" to make Uni without complications I signed up for a re-run and still younger than most of the students. As it happened, almost half the class were back for that first semester. It must have been an unusually hard exam, not that I had anything to compare it with.

That summer, dad found me full-time work at the Store right throughout the holiday. This was more like it! A suit, a copy of *"The Times"* and I looked like any other smart-ass yuppie winging it to the big city. Shame the job description didn't match the image.

"First floor, Ladies wear, whitegoods....electrical? - just around the corner madam!"

"Second floor - Menswear, soft furnishings, haberdashery."

Was I being punished for all those night-time rides in lift number one? I lasted two weeks before begging for a departmental transfer. They sent me to see the General Manager.

"What's up son?"

"I can't take it any more dad. I'm opening and closing doors in my sleep now. If we just had *one* more floor...something different for once! You need any cleaners?"

"You want *my* job son?" he asked, "Everyone starts at the bottom and works their way up!"

"*Dad*," I implored, "You've just described my job. I start at the basement and go up - all day long."

On the train to Charing Cross the following Monday morning, dad lowered his *Daily Telegraph*.

"Found you something different son," he said.

I raised my eyes from *The First Pan Book of Horror Stories* (which by the early 80's had reached volume twenty-seven!)

"Different from *what* dad?" I asked, half listening, half pondering still the predicament of the young girl chained up in the dungeon, and about to be eaten alive, by a pack of marauding rats.

"Different from what you're doing - a *new* job son!" I forgot about the wench in the cellar! Dad was continuing.

"Sales assistant in the Electrical Department if you're interested." Had the train not been crowded, I'd have leapt up and hugged him. As it was I just said, "Thanks dad, I'll do it." We both carried on reading.

How difficult could it be? "A blender madam? - certainly, I'll wrap it for you. "Here's your change, have a nice day."......"Next please?"

Very first up, one enormous heavily mascara'd aggressive bulldog of a housewife.

"I want sixteen light bulbs. All 100 watts and make sure they're clear!" she barked. I looked at her, "*Sixteen?* - what happened madam - a major blow-out?" I think I was frozen with shock.

"I can buy sixteen light bulbs if I want sonny, I don't have to give *you* an explanation." she retorted, laying one imposingly fat hand on the counter. light reflecting off the jewels set into the enormous gold band encircling her ring finger. Game, set and match!

In Britain all globes have to be tested before sale, for which a socket is provided behind the counter. Who in the history of electrical salespeople has ever had to test sixteen globes while an increasingly restless queue of customers looks on, especially on their first day?

First four, no problem. Globe five didn't work, neither did two others. Final score: fourteen clear, and by necessity, two pearl.....that's all we had! She wasn't to be deterred.

"I don't want two *pearl* sonny. Are you deaf? I said sixteen *clear.*"

"I'm sorry madam," I replied, "We only have fourteen at the moment, we can get them in for you this afternoon if you....." she cut me off.

"I want them *now,*" she demanded, "Go and get me the Manager."

84

"Dad, I mean, The Manager, won't be able to help you either Madam. We *have* no more here right now." The head salesman hearing the kerfuffle, walked over to me.

"Is there a problem here?" he asked, looking not unlike Rowan Atkinson on a bad day.

"Too right, there's a problem." She turned her attentions to the newcomer.

"I asked for sixteen *clear* light bulbs, and I'm not leaving here without them." Cyril or whatever his name was, visibly wilted under her onslaught. I pointed out that we only had fourteen "clear" left.

"Don't give the lad a hard time lady," said a voice at the back, "You're holding everyone up." Music to her ears!

"So?" she said, "When I get my sixteen light bulbs, I'll leave."

For at least ten seconds nobody moved, then seeing the futility of her stand she glowered at me,

"All right then, I'll *take* the sixteen - but I'm never shopping here again!"

Ever tried to wrap sixteen light bulbs?.....especially with a crowd watching. In shapes ranging from a collapsed pyramid to a dodgy rectangle, I tried them all.

She was last seen huffing her way out to The Strand with the misshapen package under her arm. Even today the mere sight of any light-globe brings back nightmarish recall of that morning.

One bonus of having my father as *numero uno*, was that instead of mixing it with the masses in the staff canteen, I was able to while away my lunch-hours up in the executive offices on the top floor. Dad would sit there planning the new-look Travel Department, I would relax in his plush leather chair across from his desk, wondering how the hell I was going to tolerate going back to College after this buzz! One lunchtime, as if reading my thoughts, he asked me,

"Noel, (that was serious to start with!) what plans do you have after Uni?"

Was that ever thinking ahead! I hadn't even figured out yet how to handle the repeating of the "crocus" foul-up!......not that he would have wanted to hear about that! "Not sure yet dad," I choked on my ham sandwich, "Most likely medicine, just depends on my grades I guess."

"You *guess*?" he replied, "Guessing isn't going to get you an Internship son. Set your mind to what you want, put in the work and you'll do it!"

I was going to ask him if that was the psychology he used on himself to pull off that job selling eggs at the farm but something stopped me. Fear of getting a smack in the mouth most likely. Besides he was continuing.

"Last thing I want is for you to end up a failure like your dad son."

I looked across at his polished walnut desk, wide enough for a decent game of table tennis. The mahogany shelves around the wall, his own high-backed leather chair, parked-up against those magnificently carved recessed windows, themselves looking down on to one of the most famous and historical streets in the modern world.

"This is *failure?*" I thought to myself. Then it all came to me. The hitherto unseen scarring and self-inflicted pain brought to bear by his error of judgement with the ball-gum machines. Evidently he could not or *would* not, see the man all his staff, as well as his own family could see.

"If you're a failure dad, then what does that make the two hundred people who work for you?" was all I could think to say. He made no further comment and I returned to my globe-testing duties.

During that summer holiday, I first entered a radically new world...one that was to try its best to take me out lock, stock and barrel, so many times in the years ahead - the world of driving! Although just sixteen, dad decided it was time to teach me the basics of motoring. No highway patrols in those days....most local Police had only the use of their trusty bike...used for transport only - there was nothing to chase! I don't recall anyone being robbed or a single act of violence in Welling, my entire life (aside from Mr LeFeuvre's chosen punishments). So there was really no risk hitting the streets under-age, though mum, a stickler for law and order was heard to mutter.

"I don't think you should be doing this Colin."

My first day, my first drive. My very first *traffic light*, not five minutes from home and but a few hundred yards from the scene of the New Yorker's destruction years earlier....and I had my first accident.

Sitting there in the left-hand lane, waiting to turn left, a woman in a small Morris Minor (notorious for shall we say, the less predictable drivers) beside me in the right hand lane, decided she had some urgent shopping on the left and turned straight in front of me, our car remaining stationary. In any altercation between a seriously heavy-duty car such as a Vanguard and a wimpy piece of transport as is the Morris Minor, the outcome is predictable. On this occasion she caught the front of her left-hand mudguard on the Vanguard's bumper bar and continuing to drive, opened up a gash the entire car's length, seemingly the work of a feral can-opener. Her rear bumper fell off in the street. We hadn't moved! Dad leapt from the car and checked the Vanguard - not the slightest scratch. The Morris would have been not far from a write-off. The old lady climbed out of her car and I left them to it. Last I saw, dad pushed the wreck off to the side of the street and we continued onwards.

"Don't let this deter you son," he said. It didn't.

October 28 of that year saw the onset of the event later known as the "Seven days that shook the world," The *Cuban Missile Crisis*, in which President Kennedy and Premier Krushchev had the world on the brink of a push-button nuclear war. These were somewhat dynamic political times to be living through, "living" being the predominant aim.

On the science front, America's Mariner 2 spacecraft beamed the first historic pictures of the cloud-shrouded surface of Venus, 32 million miles back to earth on December 14th after a 109 day journey. The following morning, one of England's greatest actors, Charles Laughton, died at his home in Britain.....forever to be remembered as the defining Captain Bligh in the 1935 version of *Mutiny on The Bounty*.

1962 was such a happy Christmas, hopes and prospects had never been higher. Typified in many ways by the ultra-splendour of the Christmas lights along Oxford Street in London that year, the most dazzling yet presented, and the enormous Christmas Tree shipped over from Norway that was erected in Trafalgar Square, where thousands upon thousands of bright-eyed children muffled up to the ears, dragged their weary parents in the days leading up to Christmas Eve. Nelson himself had only to reach out slightly to touch the great tree. The Civil Service Stores even had their brightest Christmas display ever so it was said. Who could possibly have known it was to be our last Christmas in England?

At the height of winter, mid January '63. Mum suffered another severe attack of emphysema and was again hospitalised. Mention was made of the fact that the English climate was less than ideal for her worsening condition and that a drier and more equable environment may be of benefit. In the mid fifties, there had been discussed at length the possibility of both dad and his brother uncle Don, taking their respective families to Vancouver, where many of Granny's relatives had settled in the late forties. The time was right, both being highly qualified architects, their services would have been in great demand during that particular period of Canadian economic development. Neither dad or Uncle Don were natural adventurists however and being British to the back teeth, the colonial experience was not ultimately something they were prepared to take on, and the opportunity passed.

Mum was home again in a week or so, but certainly weaker and her recovery slower this time. However she was back at work the same week The Beatle's *Please Please Me* became their first chart-topping release.

Dad was at this stage the fittest and healthiest of his married life. Deriving enormous work satisfaction and recognised as the most progressive and successful General Manager in the store's history, he was shown great respect by staff and directors alike. Financially, the distress of the ball-gum era was almost erased and the next year would undoubtedly see the rewards of his endeavours. March 24th saw the closure of Alcatraz and the next day, Dad was summoned to *Raymead* where Granny had been taken not unexpectedly, ill...with multiple complications. With her family around her, she died and the funeral was set down for a few days later. Dad took her loss very heavily and the grand-children lost one of the greatest and kindest influences on their young lives.

As a family, over the past year or so we had taken to playing cards with a passion, Solo Whist being the most popular game. No-one could lose tricks better than dad. Had he turned his talents to it, he could have been a world-class card-sharp. So it was that late Sunday night April 21st, having watched an extended episode of *Z Cars,* the three of us were dealing away, oblivious to all else but winning that last hand. Tigger was prostrate on the mat in front of the fire, though it wasn't that cold. The aroma of a late roast beef dinner was fading and in the background The New Christy Minstrels were singing so prophetically, *Green Green (It's green they say, on the far side of the hill.)*

It was dad's call. Without warning, he dropped his cards and holding his head in evidently great pain, fell back against the couch.

"Joyce, Joyce," he managed and began to shake violently still clutching his head tightly. The pain was obviously increasing and his eyes were beginning to roll in his head. Somehow we managed to get him up lying full-length on the couch before mum dialled the emergency 999 for an ambulance. Dreadful beads of perspiration were breaking out on his forehead and barely conscious, his body was at the mercy now of whatever gripped him - it didn't appear to be a heart attack as such.

The ambulance was very quick but by then he was fully unconscious and not seemingly responding to the paramedics administrations. They carried him out by stretcher and took him back to St Nicholas' Hospital at Plumstead once again. After the ambulance departed I turned and looked at mum. Sitting unmoving in her own chair I knew instinctively that conversation was uncalled for, in fact quite the inappropriate thing right then. There were no tears, no fears, really no expression of any

kind......but tellingly, no cigarette either! That she was shattered was beyond question. She was still sitting there thirty minutes later when the phone rang and it was suggested we come down to the hospital. I sensed she wouldn't be going, *couldn't* go, and thus I merely told her that I would be back whenever. She simply looked up and smiling in a way that betrayed the true agony of her feelings, said to me,
"Say goodbye for me Noel."

It took twenty five minutes or so to cycle there. Poor dad was face-down on a bed in a lonely cubicle in the emergency ward. The Doctors had performed am earlier lumbar-puncture and were standing around dispassionately discussing his condition. Lying there deeply unconscious still, tubes to all points of the compass, he looked so desperately sad and it reminded me just how alone we all really are in this life. What need for the friends, the back-slappers, the back-stabbers, the nosy neighbours, the shopkeepers out to squeeze that extra half ounce of meat you hadn't ordered, the shonky salesmen, the children never there when you need them, the Police there when you don't...when you're dying? I just wanted them to turn him over to restore some final vestige of dignity. I knew instinctively he would never be coming home. *Home*, the only place he ever really cared about.
"I'm afraid your father is critically ill son," said a doctor walking across to me. "He has suffered a cerebral haemorrhage - a blood clot in the brain. We have no way of knowing yet the extent of the damage."
"He's going to die this time isn't he?" I asked mechanically. The doctor looked at me kindly.
"It would probably be the best thing son, Even if he were to recover, he would have suffered irreversible brain damage and could not expect any quality of life beyond that a nursing home could offer."
I knew then that not only *must* he die, but that whatever portion of his great brain was still working, it too would have arrived at this conclusion. The doctors then faded away one by one and I was left alone with him. All the things I wanted now to say, the apologies to make, the thanks to give him, for my marvellous life and great start that he had given to me.....all too late! He died while I was with him not long after midnight, and I whispered Joyce's goodbye.
They gave me his few clothes which I put in my saddle-bag and set off for home. Half-way incredibly, I was pulled up by what must have been the only Police car on the road at that time of night. Wanting to know what I was doing on the streets riding around at this time of the morning

they searched the saddle-bag and finding dad's clothes demanded to know where they had come from. I told them my father had just died and that I was on my way home. With no ID and far from believing me, I was taken to the local Police Station where they insisted on calling Joyce to confirm my story. Surely not an experience many have had to contend with at such times?

That dad had followed his own mother to a new life within just a three week period was a sobering thought. Like his father, he too was just fifty-four.

CHAPTER FIVE

WORLDS APART

The devastating loss to Joyce was measured not by her actions, her demeanour or even her conversation - it was in what she *didn't* say. She continued on at Cottinghams and I'm sure no-one there ever perceived any change in her countenance, she would have seen to that. If only she could have cried, showed some demonstrable anger at her loss, screamed at God for his utter selfishness, anything but her control, her unwavering ability to handle anything dished up. Her great inner strength on this occasion was no ally to be sure.

Brookside itself openly missed dad's presence. Something had gone out of the place that couldn't return. His old moth-eaten chair displayed no zest for life any more. The television, taking longer than usual to come on now, refused to screen any decent programs suddenly and the kitchen curtains, for so long privileged witnesses to his great cooking exploits, leant inwards, despairing of his absence. Outside it was the same story. Edges were harder to control, flowers - their colours and scents less acute. Even the woodlands perceived his absence and the birds seemed to flutter by, anxiously looking for some trace of the hand that used to feed them so patiently.

Having already given up my childhood voluntarily I now found myself cast in the role of surrogate husband. Dad, having no Life Insurance and back then, no superannuation equivalent, we suddenly found ourselves once again in dire financial circumstances. Only a couple of months before I re-sat my Botany "A" level, we faced an uncertain future. That I would be unable to attend full-time University was obvious, the money simply wasn't there and I needed to find employment if saving the house was to be a realistic option. Long before "Equal pay for women" was adopted in the work-place, Mum's salary alone would barely have kept us in cappuccinos for a year!

We struggled by for a couple of months before mum was levelled by her worst attack of emphysema yet. How much was due to her deteriorating physical condition and how much was catalysed by inner-stress can never be known. What *was* diagnosed however....another year or so in Britain and her chances of survival ranked between slim and none. It was time for a chat.

Where the fifties had failed to instil a change in our lives, the sixties would triumph. We decided with great reluctance to put *Brookside* on the market, a house that would undoubtedly sell within days....and move to Canada for better or for worse. The climate of British Columbia being far milder (so long as one stays west of The Rockies!) than London, it was a case from mum's viewpoint at least, of nothing to lose. Having relatives in both Toronto and Vancouver it would be a flight of discovery.

A decision to turn your back on everything you've ever known, for the totally unknown, is one tinged equally with sadness and excitement. Bidding farewell to every familiar street, shop, bus-route, train station, signpost, relative, television program...even the accents you've heard from birth, takes considerable resolve. Naturally though where the alternative is a likely trip to the undertaker in the short-term, the decision is rendered simpler.

Both of us having nurtured a dream like so many, to one-day seeing the great sights of the world, we planned a globe-hopping itinerary towards our final destination. Preliminary inquiries showed that under the guidelines of the (then) economy round-the-world air tickets, so long as one progressed in a "forward" direction, there were no restrictions on the number of stop-off points selected, merely a case of how long your cash reserves could hold out - and ours would be limited given the funds remaining after the sale of *Brookside* and the deduction of several outstanding debts. The ticket would also be valid logically, within a twelve month period of original departure, for a return flight to England should such prove necessary.

Perhaps unwisely now in hindsight, I failed to sit for that last "A Level," caught-up as we were with planning and preparations....guess I never did have much interest in crocus' anyway.

Letters were exchanged with various newly acquainted relatives in Canada and arrangements made for introductions and assistance in settling-in when we finally arrived some time close to Christmas.

Brookside would never forgive us. That the house knew of our plans to desert it and worse, to bequeath it new owners was beyond question. As if marshalling its own feeble attempts to force us to re-consider, several inexplicable incidents occurred. On one occasion the front door refused to open, from either inside or out, we tried everything - the key simply would not turn the lock, nor the inner latch engage. Duly calling a locksmith, he could find no problem, the door opened as it had always done. In weeks to come, the same thing was to occur regularly. Lights, especially in the dining room, had taken to dimming and flashing on and off at irregular intervals. Wiring problems? ...perhaps! Outside, an entire lawn, that which we had all played "clock golf" on for years, suddenly turned brown virtually overnight, dying from no apparent cause and pointedly, just that one area. But perhaps the most significant event occurred late July of that year. Returning home from shopping, a pall of smoke could be seen rising up far behind the house.

Throwing the latch on the side gate, I ran to the back garden. Crackling furiously, a fire was raging mid forest, less than thirty yards from the rear fence. Even as I watched, an enormous tongue of flame leapt skywards engulfing a tree that bent and swayed in the agony of its predicament. A sudden pealing of bells and sirens announced the arrival of the fire brigade, pulling up in Danson Lane outside the house. Men in uniforms scampered through the side gate, hoses laid with cool efficiency. Several palings of the rear fence were knocked down with strategic precision and the firefighters crowded through, dragging their hoses alongside. The inferno was making its point. The firemen were forced quickly backwards, finally retreating to our boundary, now their sole aim being to save our fence and garden. Reinforcements were summoned urgently from Blackheath, Blackfen, even Dartford. The forest was dying. The heat of the blaze was scorching now as the fire moved ever mercilessly into the heart of the forest itself......burning trails, rendering homeless so many animals, chewing and spitting out memories in its unstoppable fury. "You wouldn't listen, You wouldn't listen!" could be heard as each new sapling exploded in flame, to join its incinerated companions. I was on my knees by the fence, uncaring who saw me, pleading with it to stop, trying to explain that we had to go. I was drowned out by the roar of nature, its fury in full vent.

Whether the firemen were ultimately successful in containing it, or that simply the point had been made and the fire burned out of its own accord, really didn't matter afterwards. I was left with the impression that in desperation the forest had given us the message, "If you don't want us any longer, no one else will ever be given the opportunity".....and so it was. Never again did the forest regenerate and years later when we returned temporarily, it appeared little more than an ill-defined area, a shell of its former redolent self, far smaller than was contained within its original boundaries with simply a few token trees in attendance with here and there, sporadic grassy glades.

Summer was reaching the end of the line, Ronnie Biggs and his cohorts had just pulled off the Great Train Robbery in Britain and it was nearing time to put the house on the market. We had already decided that we would sell only to a family we felt deserved *Brookside* or were otherwise of 'the right stuff'. Perhaps the only complication and one entirely of my own doing was in the form of a most beautiful young Turkish-Cypriot girl - a student at mum's college that I had been seeing steadily since before dad's passing. A year older than me, we had met during the week or so I had "filled in" for mum at Cottingham's while she was hospitalised. Able to do this as I had been taught shorthand myself when twelve, and besides having used it throughout school and college for note-taking, I had maintained a few part-time students also at weekends. Sabiha's family were based in Famagusta on the island of Cypress, barely 150 miles by boat from Beirut. Many were the days we had each taken off from college and I had picked her up in the Vanguard (after Mum had gone to work) for a few meaningful and tender hours in Blackheath, Greenwich Park and even Danson Park. The deception worked well, for months in fact, before I went down to the garage one morning having waved Joyce off, only to find the mother of all padlocks across the rear doors with a note attached, "You need to get up earlier than this to put one over your mother. No licence - no car.....and tell Sabi she has an exam tomorrow!"

Emotions run high in your late teens and that I wanted to marry her was simply the way it was. The fact that we were of different backgrounds, skin colour, religion, cultures and language, besides the fact I was going to Canada and she, following completion of her college stay, back to her family in Cypress, were minor, glossed-over points. Sabi as it happened, returned home in September and we exchanged letters on a weekly basis right up until our departure.

Brookside was sold, as expected within a week. Several willing purchasers were shelved on sight - truckies, childless couples, elder dorks. It was finally agreed to be sold to a respectable middle class family who had lived in Welling for years. As Mr Waters commented, he had been driving past the house for years, waiting for it to come on the market. Looking at his two small children running around the paths and playing hide and seek in one corner, I hoped the house could live again and weave its magic for a different generation, one that if they could ever retain half the memories I'd had, would be able to look back on a childhood with great affection. There was now barely seven weeks remaining of the countdown. Packing and cataloguing of a lifetime's possessions for shipment halfway across the world is not the work of a few hours. For insurance purposes, every item, from a rolling pin to queen size bed must be notated. Every glass, book, piece of cutlery, clothing, not to mention tools, records (there were almost two thousand), pieces of jewellery and utensils had to be listed. Many thousands of items all up! Realising the need to be able to drive, mum embarked on a driving course, securing the services of one Ernie Moore from the local Blue Star Garage. He was a patient man. "A fish out of water" doesn't adequately describe Joyce seated behind a steering wheel. Just everything about her "looked" wrong.

"What's this pedal for?" she asked Ernie after several minutes in motion.

"Er, it's the brake Mrs Bailey. You'll be needing that shortly," he is alleged to have replied.

Following an inordinate number of lessons, mum went for her driving test in the Blue Star's Ford Cortina. She passed first time and never once drove again the rest of her life. Early November, also under Ernie Moore's tutelage, I became a legal driver, paying the somewhat paltry fee of two and sixpence (twenty-five cents) for a three year licence.

In the few weeks left and mobile now, mum and I indulged our appreciation of movies and could be found up in London two and sometimes three nights a week seeing just about everything on release. From *Lawrence of Arabia* to *How The West was Won*. We also had to go and say goodbye to her father up in Watford.

Grandpa like Granny was the quintessential grandparent. Many were the hours I had spent peering out of the lounge-room window throughout my childhood, waiting to catch a first glimpse of he and Nanna when they came to visit. The thrill of sitting on his knee as he would read to me, much as mum had done, was matched only by the magic of his surreptitious whipping-out of his gold watch and chain which he kept secure within his waistcoat pocket. A self-made and refined man of impeccably high standards, he was now into his late sixties and none too pleased at the prospect of his daughter hightailing it to the colonies, although he was fully aware of the causes.

40 Munden Grove was Cecil Bavin in still life, from symmetrical rose-garden to immaculately presented lounge. Clock, dead centre of the mantle-piece as reliably accurate as the Greenwich meridian itself. Chairs measurably equidistant around the polished dinner table, one that I had never seen used all my life. Dining room and kitchen a shrine to cleanliness and precision. Inside, not a dust mote given a moment's rest - outside, not a weed permitted even temporary residence. Then there was Nanna. Formerly Grandpa's secretary for many years, they were married a year after Louisa died. Ranking right up there with dad, Nanna was mistress of her kitchen. Breakfasts were her specialty. Mum and I would wake up, aware of the pain we would cause later upon discovery of the sheets now hopelessly out of alignment and the eiderdowns not only

crooked, but *creased*, while drifting up from the kitchen would be....that smell, Oh God, what bliss when I think of it! Pork sausages like no other, gammon rashers just about done, none of those streaky pretenders! On the front gas-ring, fried eggs coming along nicely with a fried tomato or three skulking around the inside of the frying pan. Over to the left, the coup-de-grace.....fried-bread approaching its golden perfection. Nothing on this earth smells or tastes like a traditional English breakfast. It is to die for. You can keep your continental offerings. Snobby little croissants and pastries, oafish little pots of unidentifiable jams and spreads, a bowl of fruit you can barely see and a newspaper in a language you passed-up early in year-seven. Incidentally, for those who seek the ultimate in breakfasting in this world at least, you may like to pay a visit to the John Betcheman room at the Charing Cross Hotel in London. If any can afterwards nominate the location of a more memorable, hospitable or atmospheric breakfast eatery worldwide, either they were born without taste-buds or they have failed to complete the prescribed course with their therapist. To have eaten there is to have partaken of a full life.

Thus it was, on this day in November 1963, that we had the opportunity to enjoy what was in the nature of a "last supper." To the observer probably a rather low-key little affair, neither Cecil or Joyce being prone to showing much emotion but I knew what it meant to both of them. Returning home, we had now but seven days left to share with *Brookside*.

Mum had been working at Cottingham's right up until this last week and her departure there caused great sadness amongst both staff and students alike. The Principal gave a highly moving speech and presented her with some exquisite pewterware in appreciation of her personal contribution, also a substantial cheque which she hadn't been expecting. Dry eyes were few and far between it must be said.

Final packing was achieved with the assistance of the removalists - Bonners of Welling, whose services we had used since the late 40's. All week, furniture and effects were crated-up and sent to storage until the day might arrive that we would have a home again. The gradual emptying of the house created a scene of utter desolation, The house was being stripped of its dignity as surely as a soldier after court-martial, having his buttons cut from his uniform by the sword of his superior officer. It was now Friday November 22nd - the last day. A dreadful awareness could be felt in the garden, the flowers straining to catch a last glimpse of their carers, unsure now as to their own future. It remains for me one of the saddest moments of my life - my very childhood being shredded with each of the last few items being carried out. The wisdom of our decision was being challenged and my every fibre wanted to run out to the vans and drag everything back to its rightful place. Mum saw my misery and simply put a hand on my shoulder. "We can't go back Noel, we have to move on," she said, as upset as me but with so much more control.

I didn't *want* to move on, and I ran out of the room, out of the house and through the gate in the side-fence into the park. Not pausing for breath I followed the stream along to my beloved lake. Surely it would have some words of wisdom for me, something to hold on to? Flat and with barely a ripple, there was no salvation here either. Trees on the distant island turned their back on me as I stood on the shoreline, a lone and wretched figure. I raced on up to the Mansion which only seemed to confirm my own dreadful reflection...."No one asked you to go?"....But they *did*. God himself forced this untenable situation when he left mum with one lung. It was just too much and I sank to the ground numb with grief.

I arrived home just as the final crate was being carried out. Other than our travel suitcases, we were alone, waiting for that last taxi. Nothing but bare floorboards throughout, I looked at the "clean" areas along the walls where once had stood our treasured furniture as a breeze blowing now through the open French doors removed the last traces of a lifetime's intimacies. The phone rang suddenly, a forgotten link with normality. It was Ernie Moore.

"President Kennedy's been shot." was all that he said.

The impact of that particular moment was forever seared on my memory, like so many others worldwide who will recall their exact circumstances as that news sped around the world like none before it.

The taxi arrived and we walked straight out to it. As we drove up Danson Lane that one last time, neither of us turned around. I couldn't speak until we were almost at Heathrow. I remember nothing of the ride, merely the last record I ever played in *Brookside* .... *"It's My Party"* (*and I'll cry if I want to*)

Inside the terminal and far removed from Welling, excitement quickly replaced depression. Through check-in and passport control and finally the departure lounge itself. All the collective experiences and disparate tales that must have contributed to those two hundred or so people being gathered there in that lounge that day and ours was just one of them.

"Ladies and gentleman, Gate 28 is now boarding."

After all those years, the total experiences of my lifetime, those eight words heralded a new beginning, an unknown future. Somewhere in the recesses of my mind, I heard a book slam shut.

A Boeing 707 was, in the early 60's, the ultimate air transport. As we boarded via the rear steps - no air-bridges in those days, the plane seemed inconceivably huge. Hustling up the centre aisle, we took possession of our window seats and stared out at a bleak and icy-cold runway. So many unformulated thoughts jostling for space - all of which had to take a backseat as the 707's giant engines set the aircraft hurtling down the runway. Nothing can ever replicate that first experience of take-off, the thrust of those mighty Rolls Royce engines forcing a deeper acquaintance between passenger and seat. Rain was sleeting down now and the lights of Heathrow were soon nothing but memory as the great plane climbed into low-level cloud.

With lift-off had come the final realisation of physical separation from English soil. Everything we had ever known left behind on the rapidly receding wet tarmac. However, giving due attention to our immediate environment now, a stewardess was pushing a hand trolley along the aisle up ahead, handing out what appeared to be drinks and snacks. Very obliging of her I thought, hope she keeps coming. The seats were comfy, we hadn't hit anything yet. Things could have been worse.

Rome was our first port of call and having completed the disembarkation routine, we found ourselves at the mercy of the craziest driver I had ever encountered up to that time, as we sped towards the Hotel Minerva, itself, within walking distance of most of the city landmarks. Sleep was no problem that night.

Waking next morning it was significantly warmer than I would have expected, but first things first......breakfast! The Minerva was very *olde world*. They even appeared to have a hiring policy of only those encroaching upon retirement. The waiter who bore our room-service must surely have once himself, thrilled crowds in the Circus Maximus. We left him a larger tip....something to put towards his wheelchair.

To read about the Colosseum is one thing, to *stand* in it and sense the spectacle, smell the fear and having no more than to close your eyes, to hear the penultimate roar of the crowd, is another. Together with the Forum the Trajan Baths and just about every other historical site within commutable distance of the hotel, I learned more Roman history that day than an accumulation of four years' history lessons had made possible.

The Vatican was a day's indulgence in itself. Far bigger than I had imagined, we spent hours in the Cistine Chapel and its environs alone, taking in the awesome detail and intricacies of an age so rich in history.

As was to become a tradition wherever we travelled in years to come, we hired a car, whereupon I was soon to discover a latent talent - the ability to find anything anywhere. Possessed of an in-built "compass" of sorts, I appear to be able to find my way around any city with little difficulty and with a minimum of map reference. Thus early the next day, ahead of the approaching dawn, we headed north in the Fiat 1500, still years before motorways were to criss-cross Europe with such sterile efficiency. Later, diverging at Orvieto, we back-tracked to catch the magnificence of Lake Bolsena before rejoining the Via Darno en-route to Florence some 200 miles or so north of Rome. After a cursory although totally insufficient inspection of the Renaissance splendour that is Florence, we headed due east, close to the coastal town of Massarosa then south, the fifteen miles or so to Pisa.

First impressions of the "Leaning Tower" echoed that of every tourist for the last few centuries...."It's *that* small?" It isn't that photographs lie or that any legends have sprung up as to its great height (181 feet) It just sits there looking abjectly sorry for itself and in many ways less remarkable than the ornate Romanesque Cathedral built of white marble alongside, for which in the late 1370's it was originally the bell-tower. Following a cappuccino or two in the Piazza Del Duomo, we returned to Rome via the coast road having but a fleeting acquaintance with Livorno, Cecina, San Vincenzo, Grosseto, Orbetello and Civitavecchia. From Rome we flew to Beirut, principally to link up with Egypt-Air the following day. An ancient city, dating back to the 15th century BC, many of the great mosques built by the Druzes sect, when Beirut (Beyrouth) remained part of the Ottoman Empire, are well worth visiting. We also took the opportunity to drive out to see Damascus in Syria, only some fifty three miles due west, where much of the outer fringes appear so little changed from biblical times.

Arriving in Cairo, one is struck not only by the oppressive heat but by the noise. An incessant wailing can be heard almost twenty four hours a day and staying as we were at the Cairo Hilton it seemed such an incongruous mix of East and West. Cairo retains too its own unique smell, part desert, part alleyway cooking, part camel......together, as identifiable with Egypt as Omar Sharif. With camel milk as the basis for most Egyptian dairy products, eating was a distinct challenge - thus we consumed a lot of salad! We weren't there to eat however but to visit what is arguably the greatest sight this world has to offer - The Pyramids of Giza. The first morning in Cairo however was otherwise memorable.

Having taken a guided tour of the ornate Mohammed-Aly mosque, pretty much in the city centre, mum had decided to return to the hotel for a rest, the heat having a detrimental effect on her understandably. I lit-out for the Cairo Zoo, a short trip by bus - one that would have been consigned to the wreckers in any other country. Dressed as I was in an all white outfit, I had to choose carefully where exactly I sat in the bus. By world standards, this particular zoo would not have featured in the top ten, however it beat sitting in a hotel room listening to that deranged snake-charmer outside. Peering at a particularly moth-eaten antelope I was suddenly aware of being surrounded by several prostrate locals and one robed enquirer who addressed me directly. His English was excellent.

"You are enjoying our humble zoo young sir?"

I nodded, pleased that he appreciated my patronage, but there was more.

"You come please, meet our Zoo Director - he have some things to show you."

He gestured with his hand that I should follow. Seeing no reason *not* to and being in no particular hurry I did as he asked. He led the way between several exhibits, turning now and then to ensure my presence still. Four or five of his group keeping a respectful distance behind me, followed, careful to make no eye contact. We came to a larger whitewashed building with a solitary door set into the ancient brickwork. My new-found acquaintance knocked twice and stood back, head bowed. A tall man, evidently of Egyptian extraction yet dressed in European clothes emerged. The two spoke in the local dialect for some seconds, hands being gestured towards me. The tall man then approached and mopping his head with an enormous handkerchief, shook my hand. "So pleased to make your acquaintance," he said...."Come, come..." I was now following *two* people, the convoy behind still, tagging along.

We came to the reptile house and I was amazed to see the few patrons, all of eastern appearance ushered out of the rear door. Two "guards" from the group in attendance stood silently at the entry and exit doors while the Director indicated I should follow him through a third door behind the exhibits. A glass panel was removed and I was standing not three foot from a green python. Fortunately I have always been fascinated by snakes which is just as well as the Director leant in, pulled the snake out and handed it to me.

"Here, our latest specimen! You like?" He was glowing with pride.

Wishing not to cause insult or disrespect, I allowed the reptile to make itself comfortable on my arm. In no way slimy or unpleasant to hold, I was only vaguely concerned that any increased pressure would render my left arm permanently useless. The python was squired away. I subsequently played host to a variety of snakes including a cobra that they assured me had been "milked" of its venom just a half-hour earlier. Didn't overstay my welcome with *that* one! Last, but definitely not least amongst the reptiles was my introduction to half a dozen baby crocodiles. I passed-up on some quality time with their mother.

Thus it went on. I was privileged to see them all "behind the scenes,".on each occasion the paying public being first turfed-out.

"And lastly young Sir," beamed the director, "You must see our most prized new additions." He and my original contact exchanged smiles. We walked between several cages and coming to a rear door, the Director unlocked it and leaning-in called out various instructions in Egyptian. He turned and stepping inside bade me follow him. The smell was stifling, but I didn't notice, all I saw was what he handed me - the most exquisite lion cub that couldn't have been more than a few days old.

Even today one of my life's highlights, the little thing was so remarkably heavy and just sat there letting me hold it, as content as could be, looking up with the most soulful little eyes as if to say, "Well haven't you seen a lion cub before?"

I wouldn't have cared if it had chewed my suit to pieces, anything was worth this! They took him off me and his sister was brought over. She was more playful and was snapping about until I found the right spot behind her ears, which settled her right down. Handing them back was difficult, though an impulsive roaring close by, suggested that at least one of the parents would like them returned.

Back outside, the Director was bowing and thanking me for gracing his Zoo with my presence which I thought overdoing it somewhat, if not a tad unusual, there was yet a further surprise. Leading me to the main exit gate I was by no means expecting to see my original guide holding open the rear door of a stretch limo, still it looked a better option than the bone-rattling monstrosity that had conveyed me there earlier. Sinking into the plush leather, the limo pulled away from the kerb, bound presumably for the Hilton. Wrong again, the car pulled up in what was obviously one of the main (if not the main) streets of Cairo. The driver got out and walked into the building outside which we were parked. I noticed the sign "Embassy of The United States." Shortly, he and another man emerged - European by appearance. He was communicating with the driver in his own language before indicating I should lower the window.

"Sorry son, " the accent was unmistakably American. "There's been kind of an embarrassing mix-up here. The guys down at the Zoo took you for the son of the US Ambassador ...the white outfit most likely, although you do look quite like him I gotta say, 'bout the same age and all, what are you - 18?" I nodded, it was near enough. He was continuing. Anyhow, they're *real* sorry about the inconvenience and hope you enjoyed what you saw at the Zoo. The car will drop you off at your hotel now, just tell him which one. Have a nice day!"

Walking back into our hotel suite, mum was reading USA Today. She looked up as I entered, sniffing.

"I thought you were just *going* to the Zoo Noel, not cleaning the cages out!"

I relayed the whole story to which she simply nodded.

"Be a good boy and call up for a gin and tonic for me would you please?"

The next morning we took a hire-car out to Memphis and Giza to see the great Pyramids. No amount of presupposition can prepare one for the actuality of seeing and touching these awesome pieces of history. Disappointing to many who expect to see perfectly smooth sides, their highly eroded surfaces, requiring the talents of an experienced rock-climber in places, only adds to the wonder of their survival all these centuries. What is the Empire State Building going to look like in the year 7,350? Close-to, their size is breathtaking, Khufu/Cheops' particularly. With far less restrictions then, than are placed on tourists today we were able to walk up and touch the Sphinx and walk unescorted into some open chambers within the pyramids themselves. At nearby Saqqara I attempted to climb part of the so called "Step" Pyramid (no disrespect to Djoser or Imhotep intended) with ultimately little success. Right there on the fringe of the Sahara, time has stood still - so evident when you realise little will be different by the time your own great-great-grandchildren may stand in those same shadows staring up at the life-draining work of more than one hundred thousand slaves over a thirty year period.

The following day we took an overnight Nile cruise to Luxor, in the Valley of The Kings where we explored the Tomb of Tutankhamen, from which many of the major treasures discovered by archaeologist Howard Carter are now displayed in the Cairo Museum itself. In 1963 construction on the enormous Aswan Dam was in its early stages and the Egyptian Government was in the process of moving the enormous statues of Ramses II at Abu Simbel, as well as the temples themselves, stone by stone, to higher ground to avoid flooding, upon the dam's completion.

Our stay in Egypt was rounded off by a day's shopping in the famed Bazaar where anything and everything is geared to extort as many US dollars or British Pounds as possible from the unwary tourist. The long standing suggestion of dividing all asking prices by two before bartering downwards remains to this day, good advice.

The heat of Cairo was but a memory as we shivered, crossing to the Terminal building at Tehran International Airport the following evening. A magnificent city of some four million people, we had come at the invitation of the parents of two students from Cottingham College, who had lived with us at Welling for three months in 1962. We stayed at the family's palatial home not fifteen minutes from the city centre and were treated to a few days of unparalleled luxury. Amongst the many sights and wonders of the Iranian Capital, we were taken on tours of the outrageously extravagant Shah Abdol Azim Mosque, the tomb of Riza Shah Pahlavi, and the Shah's Palace itself, which houses the famed Peacock Throne.

The crown jewels of Iran, displayed in the National Treasury Building would probably edge those of Queen Elizabeth in monetary value. A highlight of our visit was a tour of the ruins of the ancient city of Rhages a few miles south of Tehran itself.

Emerging from the 707 at New Delhi, the air was still and warm. Having secured our baggage we put our lives unknowingly at risk climbing into the battered old Mercedes at the head of the taxi rank. This turbaned death-cheater was evidently familiar only with the accelerator as he negotiated street corners, traffic lights and pedestrians with the same suicidal ineptitude. Notable were the clutchless gear changes and the tortuous grind of metal on metal on the rare occasions he used the brake. As we were to discover, India's drivers are in a class of their own. Obviously the taxi industry there, had in those days, no controlling body monitoring acceptable driving standards or levels of mechanical safety. If the wheels turn and the engine starts – you had yourself a taxi!

The Swiss Hotel in New Delhi, reflected its 'British colonialism' pedigree from its pukka lounge to the impeccable dining room, hung as it was with brassware and faded pictures of members of the British Military at the turn of the century. The superbly appointed bedroom suites were built around a rectangular grassed courtyard where immaculately turned-out and proudly turbaned waiters would serve iced tea, lemonade or anything else that might take a guest's fancy.

New Delhi remains a tourist's enigma. A confronting mix of wealth and poverty as is typified by most great Indian cities. We shopped at roadside stalls as well as several well-appointed department stores in the sprawling city's centre. Like Cairo, India has its own unique smell and noise, both of which once experienced are never forgotten.

However, we came to India and New Delhi particularly, for one purpose only, that being to see the Taj Mahal.

Thus late the following morning after a full and most satisfying breakfast, we ordered a Taxi and climbing in to a dust-enveloped Chev of mid 50's vintage, requested the driver to take us to The Taj. The young driver looked stunned.

"The Taj Mahal sahib?" he asked rather incredulously.

"Indeed, " I said. "Is there a problem?"

"But the Taj Mahal is near Agra sahib!"

We stared at each other, mum was becoming agitated.

"Well then," I replied, "Let us be on our way to Agra."

"One hundred and fifty *miles* sahib," his turban was coming loose in his anxiety, "It will take almost three hours....cost *many* rupees!" He looked hopeful!

We agreed on a pre-arranged sum, including his waiting for us at the Taj and bringing us back to the hotel. The prospect of what was probably the biggest fare he had ever pulled in, saw him galvanised into mad action. Racing around from the driver's side, he flung open the rear passenger door, "Please madam," Mum flicked a layer of dust off the seat and climbed in - I followed." Our host positively scampered back to his cabin, and we hightailed it south in a cloud of dust.

Give the man his due, Agra was no outer suburb. Passing through a multitude of mud-bricked villages, an eye-opening panorama of poverty in transit....this was the real India. The tiniest of children, some barely having mastered the art of walking, would clamour alongside the (once) yellow Chevvy, their palms extended upwards and pleading for a few rupees. Drive-through tourists more than likely providing these amazingly happy-looking people with their only means of survival, we probably parted with more local currency along the way than the entire pledged contract-fee. Our driver, obviously familiar with many of these tiny villages, slowed at several to walking speed to allow the children to crush themselves up against the car - quite possibly one such village was his own!

At Agra, it was perhaps a further half an hour to the Taj itself. Mere words cannot do this most majestic of sights the beginnings of justice. The aura of the great building humbles the spirit and raises an awareness that all things possessed are just transient. Built in 1648 by Shah Jahan as the ultimate tomb for his wife Arjumand Banu, the cenotaphs and four slender minarets stand guard, possibly for all time, overlooking the tranquil pool and to the rear of the marble dome, the exquisite gardens.

Our Taxi driver accompanied us to the viewing areas. "Proud" of such heritage, I could understand now why those children were smiling. Never did the words "What doth it prosper a man to gain the whole world and lose his own soul?" have a clearer meaning.

"You *will* be staying to see the Taj at moonlight?" he asked expectantly. I recalled then hearing somewhere, comments that the "only time to witness the Taj Mahal is at midnight under a full moon." .....which left us some five hours to wait at that juncture. It wasn't a case of "shall we?" we simply chose ourselves a comfy spot. The taxi driver was already seated, deep in contemplation of his beloved surroundings.

Many places in India breed a 'silence' quite unlike any other place on Earth. It is a quiet borne of peace and mysticism. At the Taj itself, the silence is deafening. With absolutely no background hum, no vehicular noise....where even nature has learned to hold its breath, you can hear the rhythmic breathing of fellow tourists and even your own heartbeat.

Sitting beside me was a sprightly lone American tourist, somewhere in her late fifties to judge by her clothes and manner. She whispered to me of her life the past ten years or so, a period of constant travel, her husband having died in Minnesota and leaving her "very comfortably off" to use her own words. As she set up her camera tripod with practised efficiency around 11.30pm, she asked suddenly, "How old do you think I am?" It wasn't said in any manner of boastfulness or with any trace of self-indulgence.

Thinking perhaps very late fifties, maybe even early sixties, I erred on the side of gentility and volunteered, "Fifty-five?"

She smiled and said, "I will be eighty-four next birthday young man." Now, if you consider Gloria Stuart made a well preserved centenarian in *Titanic*, this lady could have been her grand-daughter. Unwrinkled, strong of voice and with a confidence indicative of someone not much beyond middle-age, she was surely a reminder of what is possible when your mind is right.

Shortly before midnight the moon, a full one at that, was rising and shortly after the dawn of the new day, the worth of that long wait could not be in question. The Taj was bathed in a virginal moonlight, the smallest feature discernible, and as the party of some fifty or sixty persons arose and walked across to the great mausoleum - no one spoke, there was no need, and entirely nothing that could be uttered which would achieve anything except to lower the dignity of the moment. It remains the singular, most profound and moving experience of my life to date.

Flying on to Calcutta, we had available the greater part of a day there, ahead of our scheduled link-up with the Qantas flight that was to take us on to Singapore. Whilst not denying the fact a few hours is insufficient time to quantitatively profile *any* city....it was more than enough to witness much of the third-world lifestyle experienced by the teeming masses of this sprawling metropolis. Where hustle is survival and lunch - a pot-pourri of questionable meats cooked along many kerbsides, the visitor is assailed by sights, odours and living standards that quite defy western expectations. Eternally restless like a vast cauldron coming to the boil, Calcutta was then, a window into a world where even the likes of Roald Dahl and Edgar Allan Poe could draw renewed inspiration.

In Singapore during the 60's, there was only one place to stay - *Raffles Hotel!* One of the world's greatest hotel experiences, the ultimate in British colonial comfort, charm and character. Named after the great British administrator and social reformer Sir Thomas Stamford Raffles, who founded the settlement in Singapore in 1819, Raffles Hotel has played host to a who's who of historical figures during its existence. It is said that "If one sits in the lounge at Raffles long enough anyone will meet up with an old acquaintance in time." Absolutely the last word in good-taste, fine food and plush surroundings, a stay at Raffles was a holiday in itself.

During our second night there and having expended many hours in somewhat oppressive heat on local sight-seeing, Mum was feeling less than invigorated. I left her resting in our suite and headed off downtown to see *McClintock* at a city theatre. It must be said that until one has seen John Wayne mouthing off in Mandarin, with English sub-titles no less, any would-be film buff's experience is sadly lacking. So it was, that as I gazed upon John Wayne copping an earful from an irate Maureen O'Hara...in Chinese....just ahead of their first big clinch, I was, probably in company with the rest of the audience, somewhat surprised to see the screen go black and a message flash up... *"Would Mr Noel Bailey please return to his hotel immediately."* Naturally, followed suddenly by the eyes of hundreds of patrons in the theatre as I stood up to leave, amidst growing whispers fanning outwards like a verbal Mexican wave.... "Who *is* he?.....another drug-dealer, look at his suit, you can tell!"..."Bet he skipped without paying his bill!".....I left rather quicker than I had entered. Anxious staff met me at Reception. Mum had suffered a severe breathing attack and had been taken to Singapore General Hospital.

By necessity, somewhat familiar with the inside of a hospital, I had never seen anything like Singapore General. Between the information desk and mum's ward, I counted at least half a dozen rats on scouting missions. Conditions were worse than Scarlett O'Hara had ever had to put up with in *Gone With The Wind*, I felt ill myself! Mum was holed-up in a private ward though "cubicle" might be a more apt term, and was surrounded by a team of doctors. How she smiled, given her obvious inability to breathe satisfactorily I don't know. I looked down at her and took her hand, just then one of the doctors took my arm and pulled me to one side.

"Your mother very ill," he said, "Very ill - it is emphysema - you know this, yes?" I acknowledged this fact. "We can stabilise her condition, but she need urgent treatment - *professional* treatment in better equipped hospital," he looked around and indicated the general ward... "You understand?...this not right place for her - we cannot do much here. I'm sorry!"

I wondered what fate was in store for most Singaporeans should they fall ill, if this was the best available centre for medical care in the country at that time. It was archaic, dirty, ill-equipped and who knows what qualifications secured one an internship there. The doctor was continuing.

"Sydney, Australia has the best facilities for dealing with your mother's illness. It is the nearest place and the only advice we can give you." I told him that we were travelling to Canada to live. He shrugged, "Your mother cannot make that journey now, you *must* go to Australia to help her." He turned back to her and whispered something I couldn't make out. She was drifting mercifully into unconsciousness now from the drugs they had administered and I told them I would return in the morning.

The trip of a lifetime was now the nightmare of a lifetime. Difficult enough to be stranded alone in your own house in your own country at a time like this, but with the added complication of being the far side of the world in an alien landscape, this wouldn't rank high on anyone's list of "fun-experiences."

The next day with only one potentially relevant fact to my credit - that Grandad's cousin, one Thomas Bavin, had been Premier of NSW in 1926, I sent a cable to the then Premier - Mr Hefferon, outlining our predicament and asking whether or not any relatives still existed in New South Wales. Within hours, information was telexed to the British Embassy....names and addresses of those who might help. Shortly after, a cable arrived from one John Bavin, Thomas' son, who had already pre-arranged for Mum to be admitted to a Hospital in East Sydney and that his cousin, Thelma, would meet us at Sydney on arrival. Help doesn't usually arrive with more dramatic flair than this.....though we still had to *get* there! True to their word, the medical staff were able to stabilise mum's condition and within two days she was fit to travel..."fit" though, being little more than able to be moved.

And so we found ourselves winging it to Oz, the home of Rolf Harris, who once I watched in company with half the kids in England on BBC TV on the five o'clock children's program straight after school. *Tie me Kangaroo Down* had been a bigger hit in Britain than Australia and Rolf and his wobbleboard had scored an appearance on variety shows the length and breadth of the country. What I knew about Australia was confined to the river systems of New South Wales, that had been my best geography project ever; The exploits of Ned Kelly and the fact that Murray Rose was one hell of a swimmer.

I like to think I remain the only person in the history of recorded emigration to have landed at Darwin Airport in 42 degrees (107 Fahrenheit), wearing a heavy suede coat, and carrying on one arm, a portable typewriter and a three foot high stuffed camel, on the other - my mother! Our first impression of Australia was not good. Darwin International Airport apparently consisted of a large shed in front of which appeared to be an an outsize desk, jealously guarded by two uniformed officials set forth on the tarmac some forty yards or so from where the plane pulled up. At the desk sat a further two Customs Officers one wielding a stamp with which he was ferociously bequeathing entry permits to startled passengers. We were next up.

"You bloody mad son?" were the first words of welcome I ever heard in Australia "Too bloody hot for a bloody fur coat. What's that you've got there?" he indicated towards my arm.

"That's my mother," I replied, offside with the Continent already.

"The *other* arm mate!" he gestured with his stamp.

"It's a camel," I said.. "We bought it in Cairo last week."

"Cairo mate? sorry you're going to have to leave that with us. Quarantine don't permit no stuffed animals from the Middle East - too risky." He indicated to one of the stooges behind the desk who moved forward and seized the camel. Before I could drop Mum and make a grab for it, the camel and our quite significant investment, disappeared into a large crate behind his desk.

"That cost twenty-five dollars.....*mate,*" I said....he wasn't moved.

"Passports please," He tapped the desk in front of him.

With some difficulty I shifted mum's weight, put down the typewriter and handed him both passports. Flipping through them, he came to the photographs and took his time lining us up.

"Your mother doesn't look too good son, what's the problem?"

I told him of the Singapore experience and her being expected in Sydney for treatment. Shrugging and lacking any sort of sympathy he was about to stamp mine, but pulled up abruptly.

"This is no good son, we can't accept *this*?".....he was tapping a page in my passport. "Can't see the doctor's initials here." Turned out it was the international health stamp certifying I had been given Cholera, Yellow Fever and Smallpox vaccinations. Mum and I had received them the same day in Welling and both stamps affixed to the passports.

"My son has had them," Mum interjected, holding the desk for support, "They were done together."

"Don't doubt that madam, but rules is rules. Yours has initials, your son's doesn't. He'll have to have the shots again - now!" Thus with some one hundred and eighty people queued up behind us in a visibly ugly mood over this worsening hold-up in stifling heat on a desolate stretch of airport concrete, I had to put everything down, remove my coat and basically strip to the waist so the medical officer summoned, could successively puncture my right arm.....

"Can't do the left one," he said smirking, "Looks like you've had recent vaccinations there!

More than two hours later, the complement of passengers were back on board and we were taxiing for the five hour flight to Sydney, less than impressed with Aussie hospitality and etiquette so far on display. Mum was hanging on...just, and was able to sleep for a large portion of the flight.

Sydney Airport December 12th 1963.....bigger than Darwin, but not much more than a *series* of sheds. Made contact with John Bavin's cousin Thelma, and was given the address of a guest-house at Cremorne Point - wherever that may have been. Piling our baggage into the first Holden Taxi we had ever laid eyes on, we set out for the elusive destination. Formative impressions of a country can be deceptive and should such impressions include first-up suburbs such as Marrickville, Alexandria, Newtown and Redfern, after one has just visited The Colosseum, The Pyramids, and The Taj Mahal, to name but three sights, a certain degree of scepticism must be understandable. Aware that Cremorne Point was somewhere to the immediate north of the Harbour, by the time our taxi-driver had crossed the bridge *twice* it was obvious we were being ripped-off. It was ultimately no problem as we simply paid half the total fare on arrival at "The Laurels" guesthouse.

Now, this was more like it. Cremorne Point - one of the choicest pieces of real estate on any harbour foreshore worldwide. If this was typical of Sydney generally then things were looking up. Guided mum to our lodgings, a most gracious set of rooms overlooking Cremorne inlet, where private boats starting at the base salary of a Prime Minister.....were moored in colourful clusters. A note handed us by the proprietors, was a kind message of welcome from John Bavin and advised that St Vincents Hospital in Darlinghurst, East Sydney was on standby and ready to admit mum at the first opportunity. Within the hour mum had been admitted, together with her full medical history from England. St Vincents it appeared, was the country's leader in heart, lung and respiratory treatment. Certainly they had never experienced a bigger challenge than was on its way.

Having little else to do but to return to Cremorne Point, I reassessed the position. Once again, holed up in a strange country, at least they spoke English here, of a sort at least....future unclear - totally insufficient data to draw up any game plan.

Mid-contemplation, I heard my name paged for the phone. It was Thelma, John's cousin and Grandad's second cousin. She introduced herself and enquired as to Joyce's circumstances, before asking if she could meet me at "Wynyard" in an hour or so. I said I would be delighted to, having only the slightest problem in that I had no idea what "Wynyard" was. Having established its existence as a mid-city underground station, and its location from Circular Quay where all ferries from Cremorne Point terminated, I thanked her and made ready.

Harbour travel in Sydney in those days was sedate and un-rushed, ferries were clean, ran demonstrably on time and were idyllic transport. They were also insanely cheap. The trip itself took little more than quarter of an hour and as I disembarked at Circular Quay that first time, I stared up at the AMP Centre right on the foreshore, just twenty-six storeys, but towering over the remainder of the city with nothing else on the skyline much over half its height. With a viewing platform on the top floor, it was promoted to be the tallest building in the southern hemisphere at that time.

Sydney itself could best be described as *quaint* rather than dynamic in the early 60's. Despite its sprawling suburbs, the city itself, at least the central business district, was quite small by International standards - certainly more American influenced than English, although some of the older buildings in Martin Place and lower Pitt Street reflected British turn-of-the-century facades. The streets, as they remain even today, appeared so narrow, following as they did the early settlers' horse and cart tracks.....pretty much back to the founding 1700's. George Street being the main thoroughfare, was also where I found Wynyard, and the ramp leading down to the subway. The other thing I found was Thelma.

A twinkling, highly refined and educated *elf* would best describe this uniquely charismatic lady whose presence simply commanded attention. Standing in "comfy shoes" a less-than-towering 4 foot ten inches, Thelma spoke with an assuredness and authority indicative of an upper-class breeding yet despite her obvious worldliness and social accomplishments, she maintained a camaraderie that set her equally at ease in the least gracious environment. The Bavin traits were all there. Impeccable presentation, dry wit, clinical selectiveness and the natural raconteur. She would have been at home at 40 Munden Grove alright. Into her late fifties now, she had worked in the travel industry since the war having never married, following the death of her fiancee at Normandy...a part of her history that was never to be alluded to or elaborated upon.

Formalities exchanged, we got down to the serious issues at hand - finding a coffee bar and dredging up a couple of sandwiches. If that's what one has in mind, Wynyard is certainly the place to be, such locales being in somewhat distinct proliferation. Within half an hour, I had known Thelma for at least twelve years and taking leave of our second excellent cappuccino, she invited me back to her rooms at Neutral Bay, which as it transpired was but five minutes from Cremorne Point itself.

Did I say "rooms?" Thelma's ground-floor apartment in Wycombe Road was the ultimate in turn-of-the-century splendour. More a penthouse at street level, the magnificent old building housed I think, three residences, one atop the other though in different configuration. The front-door connected by short hallway, to a magnificent oak panelled ante-room off which led a variety of doors to kitchen, bedrooms and study. The room itself was pentagon-shaped and large enough to double as dining room and lounge. The lofty dimensions contrasted sharply with its diminutive resident who pottered about, the very image of Agatha Christie's Miss Marple, ushering me into the most comfortable of high-backed leather chairs while she poured me a glass of inarguably Australia's finest sherry - Mildara Chestnut Teal, a bottle of which Thelma retained on hand until the very last days of her allotted time here.....at least, in this incarnation. Never having partaken of such liquid splendour since my last encounter with the remnants of the final bottle of Harvey's Bristol Cream to ever grace *Brookside's* antique dresser, I took my time with each sip, ensuring the warmth of the subtly distilled liquor reached the furthest recesses of my appreciative palate.

Thelma's life to date, was revealed in faded photographs and framed studies around the old room. The most exquisitely pretty young girl beamed down at me through the years, as she stood beside her pony in fields long forgotten. Beside this, hung a picture of a strong-featured and sincere looking man in cleric collar, so obviously Thelma's father with the same propensity to twinkle around the eyes. Her mother, a fine-looking Victorian lady, stood guard still over her daughter on the far wall, accompanied by photographs during Thelma's early education and later at finishing school, picnics - everything but "Hanging Rock" itself. The room reflected such grace and tranquility. In the late seventies, the building like so many of its contemporaries, was pulled down to make way for soul-less but infinitely more profitable high-rise units for developers, alert enough to the lure of the dollar, less so the lure of the past.

Later I accompanied Thelma to St Vincents where we found Joyce in somewhat improved condition. The two had much to talk about, not the least of which being Grandad, who despite her several trips to England and Europe in previous decades she had never met. We left together and I saw her home before returning to "The Laurels" on The Point. I remember standing on one of those great rocky ledges extending as it was, as far out over the blue waters of the harbour as gravity would permit, the wake of passing ferries washing up against the Point far below, musing that this was a unique if not rather solitary way of celebrating one's eighteenth birthday.

Recovery was slower this time and Joyce was confined to St Vincents for almost two weeks and only days before Christmas was she able to come home. "Home?"...it was anything but, the mercury nudging 100 degrees, bloated Christmas beetles flying in the window, sweat glands at war with the best of deodorants, while outside, Good King Wenceslas was out with his mates, heading down to the beach with a six-pack! In almost forty years, I was never able to come to terms with this travesty of yuletide celebration, Santa and surfboards not being the most harmonious of seasonal icons in my experience. So there we were Christmas Eve, seated in plastic chairs at a formica table looking down on the narrow pathway that wound its convoluted yet inevitable way to the small white lighthouse at the very tip of the Point.

"Well, happy Christmas Noel," said Mum, ever striving for an acceptable slant in any given situation, "Warm old night isn't it?"

Watching perspiration trickle slowly down her forehead as she spoke, I had to admire her complete mastery of the understatement. We clinked glasses and quaffed the remainder of the wine before it could heat up any further. Straining my ears, I knew I was going to be pushing it to catch any sleighbells on my account that night.

As it turned out, I fully underestimated the man in red. I should have known better. For one able to unload well over seven hundred million presents to expectant children worldwide in the one night - how difficult was it ever going to be to drop off a surprise or two to one of his greatest believers, notwithstanding his circumstantial relocation and a few inconvenient extra degrees? Did ice stop Sir Edmund Hillary? fire worry Shadrack Meshack and Abednego? or wind bother the Wright brothers? I think not. Santa found me alright!

CHAPTER SIX

IT'S HARD SAYING "ORSTRAYA"

Christmas morning, mum called home to Grandad in Watford - a tradition she was to maintain the rest of her life. Cooler than the previous day, having nothing else to do and nowhere else to go, our "Christmas Dinner" comprised a rather spartan picnic down at the Point. The day brought with it a sensation of mixed realities. Not only were we displaced persons as such, the immediate future was unplanned and far from obvious. In the coming days, given the enormous help and support we had received from such as Thelma, we decided we owed it to their efforts to at least stay a while before moving on to Canada. This then required that we seek employment early in the new year as funds were dissipating now with an unhealthy rapidity with no prospect of short-term replenishment. The one positive financially speaking, being that in those days, the British Pound carried a very favourable exchange rate of just over two and a half Australian Pounds.

Before anything though we needed transport and the following Monday morning, the 30th of December, we answered the prayers of one anxious car salesman on Parramatta Road, which even today is the city's used-car Mecca, by relieving him of a 1960 Vauxhall Victor, a vehicle he had doubtless long given up hopes of ever selling. No one in their right mind bought a Vauxhall Victor, the earlier models having been Britain's answer to the Ford Edsel. For the next two years that car upheld its end of the bargain and never once let us down.

Even as we exited the car yard we were in accordance that we should firstly check out that world-famous and best-known of all Aussie tourist spots - Bondi Beach. These were also the last weeks that double-decker tramcars were ever to run in Sydney's eastern suburbs. The days were numbered even then, when locals would drop the old phrase "He shot through like a Bondi tram," when referring to someone "doing a bunk" or just plain in a hurry.

Disappointments don't come any bigger! With the anticipation of a golden sandy beach stretching as far as the eye could see, white tipped waves rolling in from a blue-hued ocean, where the sea-front is separated from a Florida-like backdrop of magnificent residential buildings and shop fronts, by a coastal highway.....what we encountered was numbingly different.

Now admittedly, it was overcast that morning, but emerging from a depressingly underwhelming approach via Bondi Road itself as it swings left just short of the coast, into Campbell Street which runs along the face of the beach, mum and I just looked at each other. One tenth the size of expectations, the flat grey ocean rolled into the bay of dismay. As far as the eye could see, dismal and squalid little cottages and apartment blocks, relics from the worst of the twenties and thirties, if not earlier. The 'concourse' as such was a cracked and non-descript little concrete affair termed Queen Elizabeth Drive, presumably an attempt to bequeath it an air of importance....an exercise in total failure. Such shops as existed were old, run-down and the last word in repugnancy. Retro-architecture was in evidence everywhere. Unattractive and under-nourished alleyways ran amok between decrepit flats, doubtless the haunt of the shadier society come nightfall. *This* was the fabled Bondi Beach? - Cremorne Point was multiple rungs up the ladder by comparison! It was to be months before we were to discover that in fact Bondi would be one of Sydney's least attractive beaches, all those on the northern coastal suburbs - Manly, Harbord, Mona Vale, Dee Why and Palm Beach offering much of what Bondi had promised.

"Drive, she said,".......and that's precisely what we did in those early weeks. If there was a road there, we found it. From glorious Cronulla beach to the south of the harbour to affluent Palm Beach in the north, we logged up many miles of coastal investigation. By international comparison, driving was an unbridled pleasure with traffic lights a pleasurable rarity, parking no problem and gridlock - a term destined to have no meaning for a decade or so. It was a time of freedom and discovery. Significantly, Joyce's constitution and well-being was, at least for now, on the up and up.

Each bank statement brought further bad news and ultimately the low-warning light began flashing. Early February the Sydney Morning Herald advertised for the services of a Shorthand and English teacher for their cadet trainees. Not even bothering to short-list applicants, Mum was offered the position the same day and without hesitation accepted. It was to be a lengthy union. From my viewpoint, things were less cut and dried. Unqualified for anything particular except perhaps to be able to perform an exploratory on a cuttlefish or ailing lobster, I scanned the positions-vacant column looking for my big break. "Fifty pounds a week guaranteed - no experience necessary, immediate start!" stared back at me from the neat boxed ad in the employment pages.....and mum thought she had hit it big on twenty pounds a week! Following a quick shower and on the offchance I was to be confronted by a female interviewer, I ladled on the after-shave. I most probably od'd on the *Brut* as my co-travellers on the ferry seemed to keep a respectable distance the entire trip. Finding the advertised address was absurdly easy and locating the appropriate suite I entered - to find a motley array of personnel seated ahead of me. Several my own age if not younger, middle-aged professional-looking types, even a few who may or may not have spent the previous night in a shelter for the homeless.

Of concern, nowhere did it say what the company was! Neither at the point of entry, across any wall, or in the vicinity of the reception area. Perhaps "reception" being an exaggerated term, there being a solitary girl seated behind a rather plain desk littered with messages, empty "in-trays" and from all appearances, the greater part of the contents of her hand-bag. Assailed by something remarkably akin to "Haveyousecomeboutourad?" I immediately regretted leaving my English-Australian dictionary at home. At close range she was worse! Dandruff the size of snowflakes and eye-liner which almost met over her nose, giving the vague impression of a Police identikit picture.

"What does this company *do* actually?" I asked. That rocked her.

"Mike'll tellya," she answered, chipping away at the one bit of nail left growing.

"Don't you *know?*" I persisted, aware that it was annoying the hell out of her.

She backed off from the nail temporarily.

"Books of some type," she fired back, not a break in the chewing. The answer was of no great help, there being nothing to indicate whether they published them, imported them, sold them....or hired people to steal them. She gave me a number which being seventeen, corresponded roughly to the number of desperates billeted around the room. Allowing say five to eight minutes each, I wasn't going to be up for almost two hours - more than time for a cappuccino. I gauged it well, upon my return "sixteen" was on his dishevelled way in. Lasting but a few minutes, my predecessor emerged. Definitely not short-listed!

"You're next," cooed Miss dandruff, looking my way.

Mike's room at least conveyed one previously withheld fact - the company! *Grolier Encyclopaedias*, both in the flesh and in multiple full colour A2 blow-ups, that adorned each wall. Two sets of *Grolier '64* sat impressively behind my new host's desk in custom-built walnut cabinets. Mike was all flash and glitz. Trendy dark two-piece with open neck, home-base to a chunky gold chain that was undoubtedly the parent of the smaller one hanging off his left wrist. To have gone swimming with them still on, would consign the wearer straight to the bottom.

Mike had developed a singular interviewing technique- a rapid-fire spiel that gave no opportunity for questions. An American hot-shot presumably, he had obviously been sent to this Australian outpost to kick-start the company Down Under. As for the "guaranteed fifty pounds a week," this *was* partially true, so long as you could sell a minimum of two sets a week....the actual basic retainer being only eight pounds ten shillings. Sell nothing and that's all you got...plus the opportunity to look for a new job!

He asked me one or two questions, looked me up and down a couple of times, then sank back in his chair musing.

"You wanna give it a try son?" he enquired.

What was there to lose? We shook hands and I was on my way back to Miss dandruff to fill out a couple of employment forms. Then having been booked into a base "training session" the following Monday I returned home. *Fait accompli!*

Now, if you have never at some stage in your life tried door-to-door selling, then you have missed an opportunity to be belittled, threatened and insulted in many different languages. Basically the "training" session was intended to equip the novice with ways of handling and overcoming *objections*, as the company liked to refer to them. Where was the insightful advice however when you really needed it?.....just yards away from the snapping jaws of a Rottweiller or when the man of the house happens to be president of the local bikie chapter and with less than an interest in family education.

Having been accorded a 'sales territory' close to home, I figured at least I was in the right locale - upper middle class suburbia in an enviable disposable-income bracket. I figured wrong. Either they all already had an encyclopaedia or my sales technique was sadly lacking. Whatever, having offloaded two sets in three weeks Grolier and I mutually called it a day. Less running costs for the car, I could only describe the experience as a non-profit learning curve.

Unemployed again, another ad caught my eye.

"Unusual position available - preferred age 18-22. Experience in customs and shipping procedures essential. Current NSW Driving licence required and thorough knowledge of Sydney metropolitan road system mandatory."

Could be worse! I held a licence, albeit International. I knew what a ship looked like and surely I'd spent time enough in customs to be familiar with *that* little aspect. As for an in-built map of Sydney, I knew where Cremorne Point, The Airport and all the beaches were - it was a start! At *least* I was eighteen!

One of twelve applicants as it turned out, the company was looking for an outrider who could clear major shipments including car-parts from the States, machinery from Europe and rolls of paper from Sweden and organise their transportation to various parts of the city. In hindsight, it doesn't say much for the other eleven applicants but they gave me the job....and a new Holden ute with which to accomplish my task. A starting salary of almost nineteen pounds weekly was nothing to sneeze at and Australia was looking good! Just one week's training, then being introduced to all the customs-clearing houses and an indoctrination into the Sydney Wharf system and I was up and running with my first set of paperwork.

Looking back at the period now I remember it with fondness. Climbing down into the holds of those rust-streaked steel leviathans tied up at Parbury Millers Point, Cowper's Wharf, Walsh Bay and their oil-stained companions, checking product codes and other import identification. Where now I wonder lie the *Mariposa, Arafura, Sea Princess* and *Tokyo Maru*?.....rusting hulks in some distant maritime graveyard or already broken up and beyond all but the most distant of memories?

In coming months my acquired knowledge of the Sydney road system would have outstripped the majority of Sydney's taxi drivers. Despatched by necessity to the four points of the compass, I learned the quickest and most expeditious way to any suburb (of which there were even then, five hundred plus) landmark, or feature you might have cared to mention.

With now two incomes, we were able to finally look for a home of our own. Since early January, we had moved into a small but eminently serviceable cottage in Claude Avenue, Cremorne where those hot nights we would sit on the front porch, looking directly across the harbour at the city skyline and watching the ferries ply their leisurely marine duties with tranquil efficiency.

The early sixties afforded the home-buyer in Sydney a smorgasboard of choice. In yet-to-be trendy areas such as Paddington, where you couldn't give-away homes, semis were on offer as low as a few hundred pounds - we actually looked at one needing somewhat more than "tlc" admittedly, for five hundred and ninety pounds. Given mum's potentially limited ability to commute any great distance should her condition likely worsen, we were by good fortune introduced to the most charming of homes that had just that very week been listed in Greenwich, an inner north-shore suburb, (then) not six minutes from the harbour bridge itself, a feature itself visible from the small but well-treed rear garden. Following the usual haggling attendant on any real estate purchase, a price was settled on... just three thousand two hundred and fifty pounds. Even with the very limited funds we had left as deposit, finance was quite easily arranged....a far cry from the "show cause why we should give you any money" attitude so prevalent these days. The home today would fetch well over half a million dollars.

"*South Pacific,*" as 6 Greenwich Road was known, had much to commend it. A solidly built detached brick cottage, typical of Sydney's inner north, yet quite unlike a lifetime's experience in such as Welling, where most every home in the area is much like the next. We were able to move-in within a month and telegrams were sent to the removalists in Welling to arrange for the prompt shipping-out of our entire effects now languishing in storage somewhere.

As it happened, working for a transport company as I did, came in remarkably useful when advice came through that the container had been landed quayside. I was able to clear the paperwork through customs myself and two of our own drivers were more than happy to unload the contents at Greenwich when the day came. Even though it had been barely five months since they so abruptly exited *Brookside*.

Each item as it was unpacked was a new discovery, one to savor as a new 'home' was found for it. Having purposely acquired a residence that offered comparable living-space to *Brookside*, most everything was eventually accorded its own spot. This of course still left multiple packing crates of personal effects stacked floor to ceiling that over the next week or so were gradually unpacked and checked-off against the original master-list. In the final analysis, all was not without heartbreak. The large walnut dresser that had spent my lifetime at least, reclining elegantly against the wall at the foot of my bed, was now A.W.O.L. as was my entire *Hornby Dublo* electric train set...still packed piece by piece in the original boxes somewhere. Worse was to come. Of twelve suitcases packed with clothes and personal effects, one was missing - that containing all Joyce's personal diaries that she had religiously compiled day by day since 1935, close to thirty year's observations and inner thoughts, these then being the most irreplaceable items of all. The case had also contained the few valuable items of jewellery mum had ever owned, their having value to her. Rounding off the devastation were the now missing lifetime of photos, mementos and wedding memorabilia - this was the cruellest of losses. Urgent telegrams were despatched to Bonners Removalists in Welling who promised an "immediate investigation," being unable to explain how these possessions had become separated from the remainder of the effects. Within a week or so we heard that the missing items had been traced but had "somehow been included in another consignment" and were believed to be en-route to Cape Town. Hopes and expectations raised temporarily, received their last rites a month later when a letter received from England relayed the incredible news that the cargo ship carrying the missing articles had reportedly sunk in high seas off the South African coast The letter contained a draft for two hundred pounds as consolation for the loss. Two Hundred Pounds....for *thirty* years of the most personal reflections? not to mention all the other items. Mum took the news very hard, but in her inimitable fashion, commented practically, "It could have been everything!" She never spoke of the matter again.

Now we entered a period of stability and contentment in our adopted country. Mum's debilitating asthmatic turns were becoming a rarity, seemingly confirming doctor's diagnosis' that in the short term at least, a warmer climate would prove beneficial. We were content in our respective employment.....and the Beatles were conquering all before them! Being regular customers at the local drive-in movie at North Ryde, I recall so clearly the Saturday night late February '64 we sat parked in the queue for the entry lane to the 12.30 am. session of Cary Grant's *Charade* waiting for Radio 2SM to play for the first time, the Beatles latest single *"I Want To Hold Your Hand"* right on the stroke of midnight.....it was already number one in the charts on advance orders alone! Such were the early sixties. The world saw a twenty two year old Cassius Clay (who in 1967 changed his name to Muhummad Ali) take out convincingly, the presumed-to-be-invincible Sonny Liston, for the Heavyweight Boxing Championship of the world. Australia that same month, witnessed its worst sea disaster in peace-time, when *H.M.A.S. Voyager* was sliced in two and sank with the loss of eighty two lives after a collision with the aircraft-carrier *Melbourne* off Jervis Bay. In March, King Constantine ascended to the Greek throne at just twenty-three and civil rights activist Malcolm X split with the Black Muslim movement to form his own "Black Nationalist Party."

The middle of June saw Beatle hysteria at flashpoint (in some cases, fleshpoint!) when the mop-top quartet hit town for their series of concerts at the old Sydney Stadium, a decrepit but much loved circular steel shed at Rushcutters Bay in the city's east, home-base for the boxing fraternity and the only venue capable of staging anything the size of a major pop concert. Uncomfortable, draughty and with no acoustics to speak of, *concert* might be the wrong term for what the Beatles actually delivered. For as much as anyone could hear anything, above the screaming, the Fab Four may as well have been screeching "Please Tease Me," "I Wanna Throw Some Sand" or "From Me, The Flu." Lyrics such as,

> "If there's any germ that you want,
> Any malady old or new,
> Just call on me and I'll bring it along,
> With love from me, the flu'....."

would have sold equally as many copies! In the upshot though, it was simply a case of *being there*. No-one had turned up expecting a sedate musical recital. If they had simply harmonised the *Lord's Prayer*, everyone would have gone home happy.

Seasons came and withdrew with clinical efficiency, though it should be said, Spring and Autumn in Sydney exist realistically in name only. Summer invariably loiters well into mid April in the harbour city, reluctantly handing over the baton to Winter in May. By late August, warmer days are already queued up just over the horizon and narrow indeed is the corridor between skiing and tanning.

Mum's emphysema reared its head during the colder months but generally speaking, it remained a controllable event. Able to celebrate Christmas '64 in our own home again was a cause for some satisfaction. *Brookside* could never return of course, but equally relevantly, neither could my childhood. Whilst not aspiring to dad's league, my roast turkey platter could hardly be discounted as a worthy first-attempt. With temperatures again nudging the high 30's (Celsius) outside, it was line-ball as to which was the hotter - the food or the dining room?

As we moved into the mid-sixties, farewelling our first twelve months in Australia, we sat at the crossroads of an uncertain future. For all its free-spirited and uncomplicated nature, there existed for us at least in Australia, an ever-present undercurrent of isolation. Absolutely no fault of a Continent that offered so much and demanded so little in return. A standard of living the envy of many nations and a genuinely extended hand of friendship. But always there, a limitation born of geographic restriction. In Canada and North America...adventure by road is limited only by funds or inclination. Alaska to Tierre Del Fuego. Countries, landscapes, histories, cultures on tap - a lifetime's adventure for those with the desire and passion to seek out the real Americas. Europe, a multiple gateway'd leviathan - Britain to Italy, France to Switzerland, Spain to Norway. Further afield, Greece to Russia, even India to Africa, quite the ultimate "Road Movie!" One highway with infinite permutations, all you need - transport, time and your American Express gold card. In Sydney, what are your options? ten hours or so to Melbourne or Brisbane and essentially what's different - except the weather? Certainly parts of Tropical Queensland, The Red Centre,

Kakadu, The Tasmanian Wilderness and the glorious South Australian countryside to name but five, offer uniquely breathtaking sights the equal of any but at its nucleus, the same old song - only the words vary.

Admittedly, Australia's very location does itself, favour those keen to explore the far east, with the Philippines, Thailand, Singapore, Hong Kong and even Japan as relatively commutable neighbours! Thus with Canada still very much on the periphery of an agenda too far away, we paid the incoming 1965 its dues and in the long-established seasonal tradition of the local populace - we headed off for the beach.

In January 30th, the world lost an elder Statesman when Sir Winston Churchill 90, died in Britain. A man larger than life, who single handedly rallied the British cause during World War Two and who will forever be remembered for his political wit as much as his two-fingered victory salute.

Weekends we would spend in pursuit of adventure and discovery. Seeking out places of interest, some well publicised, some less so. To the north we scoured the Central Coast and beyond. Long before the first freeway, the Pacific Highway was the major route north being little more than a two-laned road the entire way to Brisbane. Negotiating this often curvy track that did not always have the driver's best interests at heart, necessitated a high degree of concentration - especially at night. Back then, the Australian road system was a decade behind the rest of the world.

The Great Western Highway, also a misnomer in terms of motoring expectations, ferried the road traveller to the sleepy village of Penrith at the base of the Blue Mountains - so named by virtue of the bluish hue of the eucalyptus trees that covered the landscape as far as the eye can see, as the flat plains gave way to the steep slopes of the ranges themselves. The Highway followed closely the original tracks forged by the first explorers Blaxland and Lawson, after which two of the local townships were named. Thus our first journey westwards, led to the discovery of a radically new world. The Blue Mountains has an obliquely different climate from Sydney, a drier and more temperate heat in summer and it is significantly colder in winter, with snowfalls a not uncommon occurrence, and this less than a hundred miles from Bondi Beach! Demarcation of the seasons is far clearer here with a highly visible springtime awakening of the local flora and traditional autumn hues make their appearance in April and May which for the most part, pass unnoticed in the metropolitan area. The Mountains have attracted many foreign settlers, at ease with the colder conditions....thus British, German and other south European accents are no rarity. The Blue Mountains, especially the main towns of Leura and Katoomba exerted a major appeal to the well-heeled Victorian traveller and were a favourite holiday spot for those willing to put up with the four to five-hour horse and buggy journey in the late 1800's. Hotels dot the landscape, many of which reflect an early British architecture, although sadly, many now being in need of some serious restorative touches. Perhaps the grandest of them all, The Hydro Majestic, fronts the highway at Medlow Bath for some two to three hundred yards at its eastern border. Built right on the edge of a cliff face, the huge edifice looks down hundreds of feet to The Megalong Valley below. Upon entering, one is confronted by a cavernous reception area where the check-in is set apart from clusters of chairs and lounges where guests and their visitors relax with a drink before an open fire of awesome proportions. Perpetually fed by wooden logs requiring at least two people to lift, the thermal output warms the furthest visitor, some twenty yards distant. Labyrinthine panelled corridors link the vast domed ballroom (with orchestra pit) and the dining rooms further along, which with their floor-to-ceiling double-glazed windows, open on to the great balcony which looks directly down into the valley spreading below like an aeronautic "Constable." For years, the Blue Mountains premier stop-over, The "Hydro" as it is affectionately known, stands as an epitaph to the charms and extravagancies of a bygone era.

At the highest point of the Blue Mountains, some four and a half thousand feet above sea level, is situated the major township of Katoomba which in the mid seventies was officially recognised by dual ceremony, as the "sister city" of Flagstaff, Arizona. Both share a common link as guardians of two of the most wondrous "lookouts" one could hope to see. Follow the main street of Katoomba west to its furthest-most point and the first-time visitor experiences the sight that once assailed Blaxland and Lawson as they emerged from seemingly unending bushland - *Echo Point!* A jaw-dropping vista directly across the Jamieson Valley. Several hundred feet sheer drop to the valley floor and millions of acres expanse of dense forest to the limits of vision...here and there cleared areas at great distance, indicating sporadic farmland. Some four hundred yards to the left are sited the magnificent *"Three Sisters"* a triple outcrop of rock which stand as silent sentinels hundreds of feet in height and which for the Aboriginal people who once lived here, hold great religious significance. In time, it is predicted, all three will crumble under natural erosion and collapse into the Jamieson Valley. Unlike the Grand Canyon which is far deeper and more stark in contrast, *Echo Point* is a place of utter peace and tranquility. Less confronting, it is perhaps at its most appealing late at night with no distraction and the *"Three*

Sisters" floodlit. The visitor will appreciate it is a different type of silence, one that brings to bear man's mortality in a sobering yet dignified manner. With the possible exception of *Ayer's Rock* (now referred to as *Uluru*, in deference to indigenous Australians) in Central Australia, *Echo Point* must be at the top of any prospective tourists' "must see" list.

Just to the east of *Echo Point*, as we discovered on that first visit, stands the Skyway, a cable-car ride directly across the valley floor and the world's steepest railway, according to the Guinness Book of Records. Operating on a cable-pulley system, the six-car train drops stunned passengers to the valley floor at a descent fifty-eight degrees at its steepest point. The reality is far worse, most would swear it was nearer eighty-five degrees! In today's parlance.....Xtreme tourism!

But I digress, thirty five years ago as the Vauxhall struggled to make the gradient up towards Lapstone, the first township of the lower Blue Mountains, we were an odd couple indeed. At nineteen, I looked and probably acted, twenty four. Joyce, despite her illness and just into her forties, appeared nearer thirty-two or three and I was frequently asked "What would your wife like to drink Sir?" This was to be the case for some years. In our relationship I would have to say we were more akin to brother and sister. So much passed between us that had no need of words there was undoubtedly a degree of telepathy at times as was later amply demonstrated.

Since arriving in Australia, I had kept in regular touch with Sabi who having returned to London from Cypress early in 1964, had found well-paid secretarial work there. Not an entirely satisfactory courtship, exchanging pleasantries by way of air-mail alone, yet still I dredged up hope, however unrealistically, that future circumstances would one day prevail, that might engender a return to our former close relationship. The day then that I learned she was to be married late Spring and was returning to Nicosia to prepare for the wedding was the day I heaved my English-Cypriot dictionary, tore up some fifty letters of young love unplugged and swore an oath never again to eat a bar of Turkish Delight! Had it been thirty years later, I would have set up a website - http://www.cypriotssuck.com. in the hope of forestalling any such eventuality descending upon some other poor wretch! Of course in the light of rational thought days later, I realised that this was all undoubtedly for the best - I could hardly have expected her to hang around chastefully, twelve thousand miles away....her biological clock ever ticking, waiting for some move my end! I wrote back, thanked her for some wonderful memories and wished her well come Spring.

Long has it been said "One door closes and another door opens"....and so it proved to be. Mum's position as Cadet Trainer at the *Sydney Morning Herald* newspaper office, had distinct advantages - for me at least. Regular visitors to our house at Greenwich were media personalities and young journalists and their friends, many of whom were to attain fame in later years in many aspects of the entertainment industry from radio and television to film. Presented then with a veritable line-up of available female consorts, the Turkish connection was soon relegated to ancient history. Eyed with considerable suspicion by Joyce and doubtless seen as a threat to her own security, even her most favourite of cadet reporters were accorded minimal warmth whenever the subject of our socialising was mooted. Yvonne, one of the first girls I ever seriously dated in Australia, the acutely attractive daughter of high profile 60's race-caller and sports journalist Des Corless, eventually found the track "heavy going" and quit while she was ahead. She wasn't alone!

Mid '65 and mum received an unexpected phone call from Nanna relaying the news that her Father was seriously ill in a Bournemouth Hospital. Having little option, she was booked on the weekend's flight to London, where arrangements were made for a family friend to convey her to Bournemouth, some two hours or so distant on the south coast. Neither funds or work commitments allowed me to accompany her at such short notice. The following week, the worst-case scenario was evidenced by phone call. Grandad had shown a significant recovery however Joyce had been placed in intensive care just two wards away. With absolutely no cash to speak of, or funds of any significance, it is amazing what use you can put an American Express Card to! Finding myself in Bournemouth then, rather than hotfooting my way around the Sydney waterfront, I listened patiently while the Doctors explained the cause and effects of emphysema....and to *me*, one of the few people could actually spell the word!

"You really should consider moving her to a warmer climate," said one earnest intern. I didn't have the heart to show him my NSW driver's license.

It wasn't a critical attack as it transpired and within three days she was able to be discharged. Grandad, home several days ahead of her, was more distressed by his daughter's condition than his own coronarial diagnosis. As for me, I guess I enjoyed the most expensive weeks' bacon and eggs on record.

It was a long drive, pretty much half a day I'd recall, but as I passed under that so welcomingly familiar railway bridge and into Welling High Street itself, I wondered how Danson Park would receive me? The reluctant prodigal, or Judas, back looking for one more piece of silver? Turning left into Danson Crescent, the main gates a distant speck, symmetrically the centre of a kaleidoscope of unchanged front yards of uniform size and appeal, my emotions ran riot! Here was my life, looming now just thirty yards distant. I pulled up, switched off the engine and gazed upon those great steel sentinels. With tears in my eyes, I saw a small boy scamper through the entrance, his parents in tow. In his hand, a small balsa wood aeroplane that he began to throw in the air wildly until his father knelt down and showed him the rudiments of aerodynamics. The scene was so familiar somehow, the players following a script penned long ago. The man turned around and I saw what I already knew. Even as I leaped from the car, the three phantoms faded into the ether, but on the gentle wind of their passing I felt, rather than heard, the words....."Life's like that plane son, you've got to learn how to use it!"

In the next hour or so, I retraced my steps across the entire park. Nothing had changed in almost two years...with the exception of the forest which was now simply a pitiful shadow of its former self, having never re-generated following the conflagration. The lake was as prominent as ever, host currently to a veritable flotilla of small craft, mainly row-boats, commandeered by the least-skilled oarsmen. The Mansion was doing brisk business in its tea rooms and a steady trek of couples were making their way to the swimming pool. Here in this place of unchanging solidarity my new life in Australia was surely but an extended dream. I would wake up shortly back in my old bed, hearing that fourth stair creak as dad would bring up that steaming hot plate of fried bread and fried tomatoes, hoping to avoid Joyce's keen hearing.

"You spoiling that child again Colin?"

Then I looked down. Almost twenty now, I wished only to shed this mature body and climb back through the gate in the fence...back to the security over which time had been so cruelly victorious.

I could not bear the agony of looking upon my home and with no backward glance, drove south-east to Bournemouth.

The following Monday we returned to Australia with a brief stopover in Hawaii, principally to allow mum a further two days recuperation beachside in Honolulu. While there, we took the opportunity of exploring Oahu itself, taking the scenic route along the east coast, driving beneath the shadow of the volcanic Koolau Ranges, from Kailua north to Kahuku Point. By the time we had also climbed up to Diamond Head and inspected the Pearl Harbor monument - there wasn't exactly "time on our hands" left for a lengthy stint on the beach. The plan was good and by the time we boarded our return flight, Joyce had never looked better!

Turning twenty brought me nothing except an awareness that time was slipping into fifth, and that the gas tank was no longer full! I recall a party at "South Pacific" where I drank substantially more than I ate and wondering the next day if it had all been worth it - washing up more plates, glasses and utensils than I knew we had and sponging carpets between chairs, under tables and along skirting boards to counter the staining effects of food, drink and vomit respectively.

'1966' seemed to have a nice ring to it. On February 14th however, it had even more - the day Australia converted to decimal currency, forever immortalised by some-time singer and (in decades to come) game-show host Ian Turpie's jaunty little ditty "The Decimal Song." Overnight, my twenty-five pounds-a-week salary, became fifty dollars a week. I was rich, rich, rich! Shame that everything else suddenly cost "twice" as much the same day. Pounds and ounces became kilos and grammes, yards became metres, miles - kilometres. All those years spent working out the cost of four tons, three hundredweight, two quarters and eighty six pounds of coal at one pound, four and sixpence three farthings per quarter - wasted! Years spent scrawling calculations on scraps of paper, the ruler....your hand! and now this - everything just multiples of ten. Where was the challenge in that? Worst of all, the demise of the sturdy and time-honoured one, five, ten and twenty pound notes...all gone, and in their place, wussy little play-money. In fact, the change-over took time and remnants of the old currency were in circulation for more than a year before the last of it disappeared into people's treasure chests, keepsakes, coin albums or dust-filled jars on shelves - some beyond reach, others beyond memory.

By degrees, mum's emphysema was taking its toll. Attacks became marginally more acute and their frequency measurably greater. Quarterly check-ups at St Vincents Hospital were now a bi-monthly occurrence and through it all I never heard a word of complaint or discomfort. Financially it delivered a crippling broadside, since being a pre-existing condition, no health-fund would cover her for medical expenses. By arrangement with my own employers, I took increasing time off to fill in for her at the Sydney Morning Herald where I found myself teaching cadets much my own age, often having to return to my own work desk in the very late evening to catch up on essential paperwork that could not be deferred. I became an expert at time-management by necessity.

Mid year and Australia was being drawn further and further into the rapidly escalating Vietnam conflict, following Prime Minister Menzies' announcement last year that Australian troops including conscripts would be sent out to reinforce the US presence. Understandably highly unpopular with the Australian people, three detachments of young troops had already been sent over. Selections, so it was leaked to the Press earlier, were being made randomly by 21st birthdates.

A watershed for pop classics, 1966 was the year of *Good Vibrations* by the Beach Boys, *Yesterday* and *Paperback Writer* from The Beatles, *Monday Monday* by the Mamas and Papas, *Paint It Black* by The Rolling Stones, *Friday on My Mind* - arguably Australia's greatest ever pop song, from The Easybeats, *Strangers in The Night* from Frank Sinatra, *Wild Thing* by The Troggs and *You Keep Me Hangin' On* - Diana Ross and The Supremes, to name but ten releases that year which pop historians will be analysing decades after Christine Aguilera draws her first pension cheque.

Something was missing from my life - aside from money! My former ambitions of a medical career had long since disappeared, mainly through circumstance, but still something nagged at my subconscious. The truth is, having long harboured a desire for some involvement in the entertainment industry, I was beginning to realise that cavorting around Sydney town, either in the dank holds of some marine relic, or express-delivering an engine part to some far-western destination, was indeed at the wrong end of the adrenaline-pumping scale. Thus it was, late in September that I chanced upon an ad in the classifieds: "Film and TV work – screen tests being held first week of October." Probably overkill to order my own trailer at this stage I pondered, but called and made an appointment with the company. This had to be it! A couple of bit parts in local dramas, maybe an ad or two, then on to Pinewood studios for a guest appearance in *You Only Live Twice,* currently in early production - I was quite looking forward to my climactic fight with Sean Connery.

"The London Academy of Modelling," proclaimed the bronze plaque over the doorway to the suite in Kent Street, mid city. Inside, high level activity wall to wall. The receptionist, duly attending to some eight or nine people ahead of me, was of the right stuff. Fully made-over, mid London accent, barely dressed and with shimmering red nail-polish to match the candy-apple red lipstick which most everyone in the queue I'm sure would have been pleased to sample - she was actually quite pretty! Cyrils, Bruces, Eugenes and Cedrics tripped in and out of doors carrying cameras, film-cans and other paraphernalia......suddenly I was up.

According to the dolly-bird, registration and initial film test were $55 after which they would call you back to discuss options. "I think you'll do pretty well," she smiled up at me through fake eyelashes that somehow defied gravity. I would have stayed on for more, but there were many queued up behind me by now and I took a seat after handing over my $55.

A screen-test? now that's something different again. Glamorous as it may sound, they don't have you standing decked out in full costume, scowling up a flight of stairs, emoting "Frankly Scarlett, I don't give a damn!"....You're asked generally to make a complete fool of yourself by improvising upon the instructions given you. It shows (a) If you have even the beginnings of being photogenic - useful if you really can't act, but can look good, or (b) If you can perform on cue and convey to those who judge such things - realism, spontaneity and charisma. First up, I was daubed with some light make-up, hi-lighter and a smidgeon of lippy (that I suspect was the remnants of the tube which dolly-bird had near emptied across her tooth-covers earlier in the day) then made to stand in front of a bank of high-powered arc lamps and simply "laugh" - beginning with a creased smile, rounding out into a light chuckle and with no break in continuity, developing into full-on hysterical laughter. By the third take, it *was* funny and I had no problem. Next I had to read a letter (a blank piece of paper) informing me of the death of my brother, and "communicate" my loss to the camera. Couldn't do it for two reasons.

Firstly I didn't *have* a brother, secondly how distressing could a blank piece of paper be?

"But that's the point, they insisted, "You have to *imagine* the loss, feel the hurt."

Well, with all the will in the world - just nothing was happening. *You Only live Twice* was not looking a goer at this point! I asked for one further prop - a pen! Hastily scribbling the following, "We are writing to convey the news to you that Danson Park is to be resumed next month by the local council for development as a housing estate. The Lake has been drained and the Mansion House subject to demolition. Furthermore, houses in Danson Lane are to be pulled down to accommodate a proposed Nursing Home complex."

My next performance drew praise as I recall.

Finally a girl my own age was brought in, we were each handed a cup of coffee and sitting opposite one another at a small table were told simply to chatter normally for five minutes or so. This was more like it. By the time they halted filming, I'd forgotten there was anyone out there. Wrapped and in the can.....all I had to do now was wait for the call! Having heard nothing in a month, I called *them*.

"Yeah, these things take time - you just gotta be patient," was the response. "Your screen test was great, we've sent copies to several casting agencies. Cadburys are about to shoot a new ad and they're looking at your tape now. You could get a call any day."

"*Cadburys?* - well, its a start," I thought to myself. A hop, skip and a semi-trailer ride from Pinewood, but a start nevertheless. But no call eventuated - the following week or the next three! Thus, during an extended lunchtime break shortly after, I called in to the offices of the London Academy. No dolly-bird, no 'Cedrics' - barely any activity of note. Addressing the new receptionist, a rather dour young lady with mousy hair, freckles and poor command of the English language, I asked to speak with the Manager who, she related was "out" and would not be back until tomorrow. No, she *couldn't* help me with my queries, didn't know where my original screen-test film was, and had no knowledge of what was happening much beyond her "in" tray. I left her to it and with something less than an outlook of unshakeable confidence, re-joined the lunchbreak junkies.

Two nights later, all my chickens came home to roost, plus a few ring-ins. The evening paper ran a small story about a company being investigated for alleged mis-dealings. There it was damn it, confirmation that an English-based advertising company *The London Academy of Modelling* was believed to have been placed in liquidation subsequent to complaints from more than three hundred people that following the payment of registration fees, no further contact was made by them.

Investigations suggest that similar scams have been perpetrated in other countries. The directors of the company were not available for comment. They were never seen again.

Of course I, like many others, returned to Kent Street the following day. It was of no surprise to anyone I imagine, to find an empty suite. Even the sign had been squirrelled away. I never *did* get to say "The name's Bailey, Bond!"

August 19th and Australian troops in Vietnam fought their toughest battle since the Korean War. In Phuoc Tuy Province, just forty-eight miles from Saigon, Delta Command, a division of the sixth Australian Battalion, comprising just one hundred and fifty troops in all, defeated a Viet Cong force of over one thousand men with the loss of just seventeen lives. Most were conscripts.

In November, Ronald Reagan made it as the duly elected Governor of California and I swung a handsome pay-rise, the decade was looking good. It was time now to trade in the Vauxhall that had served us so well and in its honour we acquired a '64 update of the same car. It too served its time with distinction until brought down by circumstances which will be detailed in the next chapter. Twenty-One, according to my birth certificate....*forty*-one might be nearer the mark by way of experience! The celebration was duly marked by another round of sponging the carpet, walls and skirting boards. Even found a few people still unconscious in various parts of the house and garden - remembering of course that journalists do have a legendary capacity for alcohol - *drinking* it, rather than holding on to it.

The year of Mary Quant, the mini-skirt and Carnaby Street was bowing out and the Christmas tree had never looked brighter. Looking at mum across from my roast turkey, it struck me just how much strength of purpose it would take to present such an uncomplaining and serene exterior to the world with such biological chaos on the inside.

Early '67 and I won the lottery, but not one that I had voluntarily entered. The message on Government letterhead was quite straightforward. "Would the recipient kindly present himself at Puckapunyal Army Boot Camp mid February for immediate induction into the Australian Army," the only time my numbers have ever come up! As it happened, this particular recipient did have a slight problem -a sole and critically unwell parent fully dependent on him. Driving her to and from work door-to-door and pretty much full-on housekeeping, everything from cooking to the twin-tub, didn't exactly leave much time for bayonet practice. The fact is, I had no objections to the draft and in other circumstances would have undertaken a tour of duty without complaint. By electing to live here, however temporarily, I had as much right to be called-up as the next guy. There was only one course of action - Right of appeal by Court, based on "undue hardship" and that was the avenue selected. With a plethora of evidence, both medical and by witness, together with John Bavin's offer to defend the issue himself, having forty eminent years experience at the Bar, the result was expected to be a foregone conclusion. But we had reckoned without the prejudicial eye of this particular magistrate.

At the hearing mid year, despite evidence of Joyce's condition from such as leading Specialists at St Vincent's, and the confirmation of his own eyes, as she gave, with difficulty, evidence in the witness stand on my (and her own) behalf, complete details of the degree of aid she required domestically, Magistrate Murray Farquhar made it clear in his decision to over-rule the application, that he disliked "those who shirked their duty" and that the country came first. My mother's condition though "potentially serious," was a totally secondary issue and he suggested we bring in some "home help" while I was away being killed in Saigon.

When asked if I had anything to say, I was fortunate to avoid being held in "Contempt of Court." I did mention that this left us with no alternative but to leave the country to which he commented, "That is your prerogative of course, but you can expect to be met by two MP's at the airport should you ever return!" He was still smirking as we left the court. Once in a while, justice *does* turn full circle! The same Murray Farquhar, almost two decades later in March 1985, was himself in court over motoring offences, later charged with "Perverting the Course of Justice" for which he was jailed for several years, the first Australian magistrate in fact to ever be thus convicted. Further allegations of involvement with a major drug-importing ring years later, rounded off his C/V quite delightfully. Where he is now, is a question few would be asking.

How quickly can circumstance turn your life on its ear! One day just winging into Court, the next - back on the "starting" square, trying to throw a six! Like *Brookside*, there was never any doubt we'd sell *South Pacific* in days and in fact this proved to be the case. Back having to pack everything once again was barely credible but at least this time the destination was a known quantity. Mum contacted her father, explained the situation and made tentative arrangements to be there in September. Unsure again of what the immediate future held or for that matter where it might be, we didn't quit our jobs as such but sought a "leave of absence," being careful not to qualify the duration of such leave.

With all possessions in storage, the Vauxhall was entrusted to the care of Ernie Moore, who having followed us out to Australia the previous year, had once again taken up a position as a local Driving Instructor, he and his family living in a nearby suburb.

Thanking *South Pacific* for its gracious hospitality for three years, we found ourselves pushing the replay button, in a taxi heading for an airport with as much knowledge of the future as John Lennon at Art School.

Our first port of call on an open-ended itinerary, fully bereft of logical planning and progression, was Hong Kong. Still a full thirty years before the English hand-over, it was then a colourful and vibrant centre of cosmopolitan mayhem. Holed up in the magnificent Mandarin Hotel, rampant modern colonialism at its most gregarious, Greenwich NSW, seemed an orderly and structured world in a galaxy far far away.

The Mandarin on Gloucester, being sited on Hong Kong Island itself rather than Kowloon was a gateway to many wondrous discoveries. Barely fifteen minutes by bus to the south east, the awesome Tiger Balm Gardens stand as a celebration of Chinese mythology. Built in 1935 at a cost of HK$16 million, here was colour at the furthest extremes of the spectrum. Flamboyant, if not grotesque statues residing in grottoes, adorning pavilions and lurking in wait for the unwary photographer down to his last roll of film. Clinically dead would be the only phrase possible to describe the sight-seer who could find nothing to admire within these thirty-two thousand square feet of sculptured and pigmented wizardry.

The sweeping vista bequeathed the tourist riding the cable-car to the apex of Victoria Peak could leave no doubt as to why property values on the Peak rival if not surpass other real estate property world-wide. These you inherit, win at the casino or acquire with the help of *Powerball*. Unless your surname is Gates, you don't waste your Bank Manager's time.

Courtesy of the Star Ferries, a full day was spent on the mainland at Kowloon running the gamut of shops and cinemas....an American Express "black-hole." The fishing quarters of Aberdeen, the walled village of Kam Tin in the New Territories, Lantau Island, Macau...sights of historical and oriental splendour. Transportation in '67, being twelve years before construction of the Harbor Tunnel and the opening of the MTR Rail system was vastly simpler - bus, ferry or hire-car! These were sights and sounds to last a lifetime.

Heading north-east, we flew into Tokyo on a hot summer's day. A sprawling metropolis of some (then) nineteen million people and most of them seemingly on the road that day between the airport and the International Okura Hotel. Little was done the first day or so with mum endeavouring to simply breathe and being restricted to our hotel room. Having said that, if you are going to be limited to one place in Tokyo, the Okura is certainly the one to chose.

Day three and with increased mobility, mum was fired up for some serious sight-seeing. There was plenty to accommodate her. Scanning the hotel directory, Hertz were offering a three-day car-hire package for peanuts. You had to pick the car up but so what? I found out what! Their car-rental offices were at a place called Shibuya, way out in the western suburbs, necessitating a highly unwelcome experience on the Japanese rail system. Alighting at Shibuya, groggy from lack of oxygen....the carriages in peak hour (which this was) being so crammed with bodies, air could not find a foothold, I eventually located Hertz. The receptionist (I'll swear she was smiling in Japanese) handed me the key to my car - a pint-sized Bellett. Moderately larger externally than a Mini, but totally re-defining the term cramped, I wedged myself in, then had the un-nerving experience of having to drive the twenty-five odd miles back to the Okura - with no road map!

Motoring in Tokyo, one of the few right-hand-drive nations, was a remarkably uncomplicated affair. Zero knowledge of Japanese proved no hindrance to understanding street signs. Other drivers appeared absurdly polite and deliberate, when compared to their western counterparts - Australians in particular, which any impartial study will confirm, lead the world in aggressive and inconsiderate driving attitudes. After a cursory tour of the central business district, littered as it is with tunnels and overpasses, we took some rudimentary bearings from a hotel map and ventured further afield. Having located Tokyo Zoo, we spent many hours negotiating the expertly laid out exhibits, a credit to the Zoo's director. In time, we located The Emperor's Palace, The National Museum and the great Science Museum in Ueno Park. A major highlight was Tokyo Tower itself, some hundred or so feet higher than the Eiffel Tower and with a view to match.

Night time and there is only one place to be in Tokyo – Ginza! The central commerce and theatre district. Tokyo's own Times Square. By day - packed, by night - kerb to kerb humanity, an undulating sea of serial shoppers. Ginza is not the suggested haunt of bargain-hunters as credit-limits mean nothing in this madhouse of frenetic spending.

Atop the wedge-shape designed Hotel Okura was to be found the Starlight Lounge, the last word in tasteful eateries. Being accorded favoured status for reasons fully obscure at the time, but which came to light long after, we were reserved a particularly fine table directly beneath the starlight dome itself. Here, my father's culinary talents could have been fully exploited. The food was inspirational, the service ridiculous in the extreme. Any delay, no matter how minor, galvanised the Maitre-de into pre-scripted apologetic mode. Ensconced in a strategically-placed corner near the service area, this delightfully costumed oriental penguin, with seemingly independent eye movement, surveyed his kingdom from afar. There came then the night we had been waiting - perhaps ten minutes tops - for dessert. Apple crumble as I recall. Mid conversation and the "road runner" stood at my side.

"*Sir* has been waiting eleven minutes for his dessert - the management apologises." He was mortified, though not an oiled hair out of alignment, and no apparent increase in respiration...the embodiment of suave correctness.

"*Sir* is fine, thank you," I replied, "Following that excellent steak, the break was most welcome." I quite truthfully appended.

"*Sir* is most kind," he bowed, "There will of course be no charge for tonight's meal and I shall speak with the kitchen." after which he formally withdrew, still bowing. Following the repast, mum retired for the evening to our suite while I spent a pre-arranged hour or so in the main lounge with Mio, a girl I had met two days earlier, and who managed one of the hotel-lobby duty-free shops. About my age, highly refined and educated in California where she had lived for several years, she was still a traditional Japanese doll, imbued with life. I found her company refreshingly different and we had no shortage of topics, calling to mind the myriad factors in our respective lives which had come into play, to bring us to that particular evening at the Okura. Seeing her to her car, I returned to the lobby, intent on sleep myself.

Entering the main lift, I was aware of another person there but my mind was on other things. Between the fourth and fifth floors, the elevator lurched to a sudden halt and the lights flickered off. But for the merest localised glow from a tiny red security light on the control panel, we were in total darkness. I heard my companion close the book she had been reading and sigh audibly.

"This is not one of the Hotel's advertised features is it?" she said. The voice was unmistakably of Indian extraction, at once educated and dignified. Totally unable to make out any features, something about her presence marked her as a person of grace and civility.

"*No*, it certainly isn't." I replied, "But I imagine they will rectify the problem pretty quickly....at least I trust so. This isn't the place to spend a night."

"There are worse!" she said, somewhat with a sorrowful edge to it, then added, "One should always see the best in any situation you know."

Shades of Joyce Bailey here! Actually, she was right, it could have been six thirty, and crammed with fifteen or more people on their way up to dinner, or even worse, nine to ten thirty, stacked full of business men overflowing with saki, on their way down.

After five minutes, a voice of unmitigated remorse, muffled but audible, called from somewhere above, informing us of a power failure (though our collective pooled intellects had hit on that eventuality) and that it would be "just a few more minutes."

My companion was smiling I think, though of course I could not see.

"I understand the Japanese way," she remarked, "Had this been India, it would reflect badly on our standard of hospitality. It is interesting how the various cultures react to given situations do you not think? You yourself are British I believe?"

I told her that I should by rights have been Welsh, but given the circumstances in attendance at the time - there being no available medical assistance on hand, I was put on hold for several hours and eventually logged in as "English."

"Perhaps then, your destiny will be equally lacking in simplicity," she said.

The "few more minutes" had long passed and neither movement or light had yet been induced into our current domain.

"Tell me about yourself," she asked.

"Not a great deal to tell," I replied, but felt constrained nevertheless to comply with her request. I re-visited so much in those minutes, including my experiences in India, and at no time did she interrupt my words - I knew she was listening attentively. When I had finished, she did not speak for a few moments and then with quite some deliberation, said, "You have undoubtedly an ultimate purpose in this life Noel - of course we all have, but perhaps yours is to be found more so by searching, than the straight path afforded to many others. Difficulty and obstacles are invariably placed in the way of those able to overcome them by resourcefulness. Do not lose sight of goals and become distracted by side issues. I speak from experience."

Her words struck a chord in me and from then on we spoke on many widespread topics. Her knowledge was prodigious and her opinions an object lesson in tactical thinking.

It was my turn. I asked her about her early life and experiences.

She told me she was born in Allahabad - a city almost midway between New Delhi and Calcutta.

"The day you drove to The Taj Mahal," she said, "You were barely more than two hundred miles north from my home-town." The eloquent voice detailed her childhood, her upbringing in what was obviously a very privileged family of high social standing. She spoke of her years at the University of Bengal and at Oxford University in the late thirties.

A sudden jolt, and the elevator was on the move - jerky in the extreme and obviously being winched up manually. Stationery once more, sudden audible activity at close range suggested outer doors being forced open.

"Salvation is at hand," my companion whispered.

The doors were flung aside and the sudden brightness a rude assault on the retinas! I turned to my fellow traveller just as a uniformed and turbaned Indian national called out anxiously, "Are you alright Prime Minister?"

Indira Gandhi, the daughter of former Prime Minister Nehru and just one year into office herself, nodded.

"We are fine," she replied, then turning to me, "For myself I have enjoyed greatly the time spent with you Noel, perhaps we shall meet again in different circumstances."

I had no idea what to say...or do. Whether appropriate or not, I merely took her hand and kissed it. She smiled and left with her escort. History was to show that this great lady would be assassinated on October 31st 1984 when she was gunned down by two of her personal bodyguards as she walked from her home in New Delhi.

Later, unlocking the door and entering the suite, mum was still up watching some late late show.

"Have a good evening?" she asked.

"Pretty much," I replied, "Spent half an hour or so with Mrs Gandhi in the lift, between the fourth and fifth floors while they tried to fix it."

"That's nice dear," she called out, "Why don't you get some sleep now?"

Fully rested up, the next day had been pre-booked on the Bullet-train to Osaka, a service unequalled in most countries three decades on. Just three and a quarter hours from Tokyo and travelling at a whisper-quiet one hundred and twenty-five mph, the service is perhaps the train experience to be reckoned with, world-wide. Osaka, once the capital of Japan, is impossible to scour thoroughly in just one day - we saw what time permitted. A major commercial and financial centre, Osaka is also the cultural home of Bunraku - better known as "Puppet Theatre." A day in itself could be spent doing the rounds of Toyotomi Castle in the central part of the city - we covered it in little more than an hour and a half. The many canals spanning the city gave the impression of an oriental Venice but for the modern architectural backdrop. Impressively re-built from the ruins of the 1891 earthquake and the 1912 fires, Osaka presented it seemed, a time-tunnel linking modern and traditional Japan with seamless efficiency. Having an understandably inate love of parkland, our last port of call while there, was Tennoji Park in central Osaka, home to the city's magnificent botanical gardens. These were times to cherish.

Farewelling The Okura (and Mio, who assured me that she would come to Australia in the new year, a promise she was to keep) we headed for the airport, but not before I had the dubious pleasure of returning the rental car to Hertz at Shibuya and the sardine-trip back to the city - again it being rush hour.

Due to board an *Aeroflot* flight to Moscow, we were met at the check-in by a highly agitated flight manager who, apologising profusely, told us that an urgent Trade delegation of Japanese officials had commandeered all available economy seats and the airline had been forced to give up additionally, several pre-booked seats - ours included. There being no further flight for several days - Moscow in the sixties being unavailable to western tourists except by special arrangement, which I had earlier gone to great trouble to organise with the Russian Embassy in Sydney - I suggested he re-evaluate the situation swiftly. A few 'phone calls later, he turned and asked if we would be prepared to accept two first-class seats on the same flight instead? Big decision! Given that this was at the time, the longest non-stop flight anywhere at twenty two hours, the offer was swiftly accepted.

The colossal four-engined Tupelov was substantially larger than a 707 and the best appointed aircraft in International service. First-class was nothing less than sumptuous. It even was assigned the best-looking hostesses. Twin reclining seats that could be laid almost horizontal, in-flight entertainment, champagne and whatever else you wanted on tap and a-la-carte meals to kill for. Some forty years ahead of any Gold-Class cinema-ticket experience, this was a close-encounter of the very best kind! The twenty two hours sped by and in terms of pampered luxury, I have not experienced the like since.

The honeymoon however was very soon over upon touch-down in Moscow. To say that familiarity with tourists was not a Russian strong-point would be to understate the obvious. In fact, the degree of disapproval reserved for westerners generally was something I was yet to experience. All bookings had by necessity been made through Orbit Travel in Sydney the only Russian appointed agency permitted to negotiate with the Russian Consulate direct. I had been warned, "Keep a very low profile and do not stray from agency guidelines."

Met in the customs area by officials of some kind whose English was at best, barely comprehensible, our suitcases were subjected to a lengthy search, as were the clothes we wore and all hand-luggage. Stony expressions of disinterest met any attempts to spark some degree of civility between us. Finally we were "released" and accompanied to a hire-car obviously the property of the hotel at which we were booked. The driver, a throwback to the Russian revolution, spoke fragmentary English and appeared to exude a degree of cordiality - all that we ever saw at least! The streets of Moscow, the architecture and even the people visible on the sidewalks were trapped in an 1800's time-capsule. Had Doctor Zhivago and Lara crossed the road ahead of us it would have been no cause for surprise.

The hotel when we reached it that freezing night was something out of a *Dario Argento* horror film. Gothic, heavily draped in red curtaining and with columns left over from the Tsar's Palace. Accompanied to the reception area we were thrust a form to be filled out which was a no-go on both sides. I didn't read Russian and no one spoke English. Eventually an elderly porter, to judge by his faded uniform, was introduced into the stand-off. With his translation, the form was completed and handed back across the desk. Words were exchanged and the porter relayed with difficulty, "Please, no cameras...your passports stay here until you leave - yes?"

I had been told absolutely no photography would be permitted anywhere in Russia, thus I nodded and handed over our two passports.

Two keys were produced from beneath the counter but were handed to the concierge who motioned to us to follow him. No attempt was made to assist with our luggage which I managed myself - with difficulty. We entered what must have been the oldest lift in regular service worldwide, little more than an iron cage.

Making a point of slamming the outer grilles, our host swung the handle to his left and the apparatus creaked upwards. In the time express lifts in the Empire State Building would have clocked upwards of fifty floors, we had ascended five, slow enough at times to have scrawled "Boris loves Yana" on the concrete walls as we passed! At the sixth, the concierge flung open the doors and ignoring the most basic of social niceties emerged first himself. Catching the grille before it slammed into my face, I ushered mum out and we followed "Serge" as I had named him, along a dank and doubtless little-used corridor of lofty proportions. If there were other guests there, we never saw them, either in the corridor or in the lift. Serge was striding ahead, never once looking back, either to see if we were following or had in fact even managed to get out of the lift! Heavy red drapes graced much of the interior, blending well with the ancient red carpet that must have been laid years before Tsar Nicholas came to power. Serge had stopped and was unlocking two adjoining doors. I hadn't realised how much he looked like a KGB operative in "Get Smart." Motioning us to enter, mum's quarters were to the left, mine next to hers, but on the corner of the building. Holding my hand out for the keys, Serge's expression drew a blank. He then withdrew, keys residing in his clutch. Bemused, I turned to mum who had entered her "apartment."

"Different dear, isn't it?" she was saying.

"Different" doesn't adequately describe the immediacy of the moment. The room, surely thirty or forty foot square was best described as...."empty!" Not expecting a mini-fridge, colour television, telephone handset or lavish menu, expectations *did* run to finding a bed! Obviously, Serge had stuffed-up. I had a quick look in my room - none there either! Returning to mum's quarters, she was standing over towards the far left of the room beneath a faded oil-painting of monstrous proportions, a Tsar to judge by his bearing. Beneath this was a huge plain-wooden object, some six foot square with a semi-circular indentation at the top. For all the world, a giant paper-clip receptacle.

"What is this?" she enquired of no one in particular. I studied the alien carving. Polished to a high degree and seemingly quite without purpose.

"I believe it's the bed," I answered, approaching what apart from an appropriately massive table and solitary chair, was the only other item of furniture in the room – a solid double-wardrobe. Speculation became fact as upon opening the door I found heaped there, a veritable pile of blankets and cushions, together with a single sheet. An inspection of my own room delivered the same result.

Ever tried to make a bed in a curved block of wood? It's the type of poser you could expect to find in a Mensa book of mind-games! Ultimately, the best you can hope for is a nest of sorts! "Better House and Garden" has never really zero'd in on this aspect of modern living. After experimenting wildly, I came up with a winning combination. Layers of cushions filling the deep curve followed by the sheet folded under and the blankets strata'd in order of texture. Skin-bearable first - mammoth hide last! Of course, *getting in* to it was another thing! Passed on the formula to mum and we retired for the night, it being late by then and food the last thing on the agenda following the pigging-out courtesy of *Aeroflot*.

Waking at 8.30, I thought I would look-in on mum, something which wasn't to be easily accomplished as my door was securely locked - from the outside. Were these people paranoid or what? Call me old-fashioned, but having my most basic liberty - freedom - withheld from me, did tend to grate on my sense of civil rights. First up however I had to see if mum was OK. Hopefully she had not yet discovered her state of imprisonment. How then to contact her? The doors would have withstood a shoulder charge from *The Hulk* and knocking on the walls, much the same effect as an ant tap-dancing. That left the windows! Peering out, it appeared that a balcony, at least four foot wide ran the width of the building on each floor....all I had to do was circumnavigate the corner. Throwing up the sash, I climbed out - to be met by air that could only be described as super-chilled. Although four foot would seem to leave a healthy margin for error, six floors up doesn't and progress was not rapid. Negotiating the corner was easier than expected and I was on the home straight - mum's window being next on the left, some ten or twelve feet away. As the room slid into view I could see she was up - the "nest" being empty. I knocked on the glass and she emerged from the bathroom. Mouthing something inaudible but which was doubtless along the lines of, "Why are you out there cleaning the windows?" she walked over and opened the sash. I told her of the Hotel's door-locking policy and was about to climb in when I became aware of a major commotion below.

Looking down, a hammer and sickle emblazoned army truck had backed up to the entrance, disgorging four soldiers in full dress uniform. I wasn't impressed so much by their immaculate turnout as the four high-power rifles trained on my good self. Commands were shouted up to me in Russian which could have been anything from "move and we'll shoot" to "kindly explain." I fell back on the only international response that seemed appropriate - I raised my hands!

Russian with attitude, was still being directed up at me as mum peered down from the safety of her polished floor. "I think you'd better come in dear!" she said. "Easy for you to say," I replied, "What if they shoot first, ask questions later?"

"They *won't,*" was all she said.

Either she was right or wrong. Pretty good odds when you think about it! I turned and climbed in. Plenty more yelling - but no bullets!

They must have used the same lift as us as it took five minutes before the door was thrown open. At close range, the trenchcoat mafia were even bigger, the guns just as real though. We were both escorted downstairs where we all had a real problem. Neither party could understand the other.

From what I could deduce from their body language, the soldiers wanted to take me away and have me shot - no questions asked. The hotel manager, not wanting to create an "incident" seemed more conciliatory. I could have been wrong! Eventually an English-speaking member of staff was located and we were able to make progress. I explained that my mother was unwell, requiring my care, and that the Hotel, having locked me in my room had created a major problem. There was I said, no other way of reaching her. All this was relayed to the others. The uniformed C/O shook his head.

"*Nyet, nyet,*" ....now that was the one word I *did* understand; "No!"

"He thinks you are spy" tendered the translator.

"Spies don't travel with their mothers," I suggested. "We are tourists."

The C/O levelled something or other in my direction.

"He wants to know why you were outside building? It is serious security breach."

"I re-hashed the locked-door scenario - to no avail. We were getting nowhere!

This was a case for the British Embassy, plain and simple. Eventually I managed to convey my wish to make a phone call and the number was found. Fortunately it was a weekday and someone answered. Outlining my predicament I emphasised the point that we needed consular intervention sooner rather than later. Give them their due, an attache was at the hotel within a quarter of an hour.

"So we're in a spot of bother are we?" said "Basil," an old Etonian by the sound of it. "These Ruskies are deuced difficult chappies you know, need to handle them *softly softly*, if you know what I mean!"

I relayed the full facts leading up to the confrontation. Evidently fluent in Russian, our man for the moment played up the public relations and played down the Cold War threat. The tension eased and the military took their leave with many a backward glance in my direction. The crisis averted, the management formally apologised (via translation), for the earlier door-locking fiasco, and mum just about emptied her *Ventolin* inhaler.

After the simplest of breakfasts - cornflakes and fruit, we were escorted back to the hire-car for a pre-arranged tour, being no more and no less than that which Russian authorities considered it 'appropriate' we should see.

Even modern high-rises cannot disguise Moscow's antiquity, but that after all is what we came to see - living history! and Red Square and the Kremlin, certainly delivered on that point. The size of the latter is stunning to the casual observer. The seat of Government, The Kremlin is in reality a triangular complex of palaces, monuments and ecclesiastical buildings, surrounded by an impenetrable stone wall, seventy feet high in places. Nineteen towers reach skywards, the most visually striking being that of Ivan The Great, which is more than three hundred and twenty feet in height.

Nearby is the two hundred ton Czar's Bell, the largest in the world. Red Square is to Moscow what *The Statue of Liberty* is to New York. An awesome sight with the uniquely domed St Basil's Cathedral at its far end. Beneath the Kremlin Wall and facing Red Square is Lenin's Tomb, the founder of the Soviet State. Our guide then conveyed us to the gigantic Lenin Stadium and the new seventeen hundred and fifty foot Ostankino Tower, then the world's tallest structure. The remainder of the day was spent perusing exhibits in the Tretyakov Art Gallery, the AS Pushkin Fine Arts Museum and (with special permission) The Lenin Library. Sleep came easy - even in the nest, which with a few more days practice might have become a hard habit to break.

The next day we flew to Leningrad, this being part of our "cultural learning curve." Just over 400 miles north west of Moscow, the former St Petersburg is by far the most westernised of the Russian cities, it is also the second largest. A magnificent seaport by any accounts, Leningrad could have been the sister-city of Canberra, many of the buildings along the Neva river recalling the clinical and capitalistic aura of that to be found in the Australian city. Temperate indeed when we were there, Leningrad's harbour freezes over from November to April during which time sales of vodka no doubt skyrocket. Following a tour of myriad baroque buildings, that which is best remembered is the great Winter Palace, home to a succession of Tsars and which was finally completed in 1762. Saint Peter's Cathedral and The Summer Palace of Peter 1st were also high spots of a day's exceptional sightseeing. Lastly we had permission to visit the quite incredible Saltykov-Schcedrin Library which contains more than twenty five million books and artefacts. We cannot claim to have seen them all! Returned to Moscow for one last night.

In possession of our passports once again, we were taken next morning, or to be more accurate - *escorted*, back to Moscow Airport. The customs experience this time was even more up close and personal. Every item, including a hundred or so slides we were carrying, were individually checked to ensure no rogue picture of the USSR had crept in there. Three times they asked if we had been to any railway station and three times I replied that not knowing where any were, somewhat ruled against that likelihood. Humour wasn't their strong point!

Within minutes the Air France 707 had placed many miles between us and the recent socialist soil. Probably a little known fact that Paris is but two and a half hours flight from Moscow, barely half the distance between Kennedy and Heathrow. Paris itself, being much the same distance from London as is Blackpool, and although far nearer to the English Capital than even Ireland, comparatively few English families had ever been there back in the sixties, ourselves included. We had two days there and probably saw less than twenty percent of what we would have liked. Having returned several times since, the percentage is improving but back in '67 that initial acquaintance was much like a first date - you sense you like the girl, but you want to get to know her better....not a situation you can (or should) hurry.

The subway is by far the easiest way of getting around, and we knocked over the Eiffel Tower, Notre Dame and The Louvre with almost indecent haste. As so many before us and multitudes after, have commented, The Mona Lisa must be one of the least attractive paintings in the history of art. Smaller and darker than normally imagined, yet worth more than some countries! The Louvre alone requires a full day to take in and you still would have seen but half of it.

Quasimodo, Piaf, Du Maurier, Boyer, D'Artagnon.....fact or fiction, it makes no difference, all are here in spirit, you just have to look in the right places. Paris is for romantics, historians, poets, writers, dreamers and those looking for that elusive yet undefined quality in life. It is a special place and one with no charismatic equal.

For the fourth time in as many years, we found ourselves back at Heathrow, seemingly in the company of half of Europe, with interminably long queues for both baggage and customs.
"Welcome to Britain!"
"Thanks, but I've only just left!"
"Anything to declare?"
"Just my mother."
"Excuse me?"
"Little in-flight joke there, sorry.....no, nothing to declare. If the Soviet Customs couldn't find anything - I don't fancy *your* chances!"
"I see sir, you've recently been in Russia? - would you kindly step over here please?"
Mum fixed me with a look just short of a white-hot laser beam!
"You simply don't know when to hold it, do you Noel?" I felt the heat! Somewhere in my mind, I could hear Oliver Hardy at the Saturday morning matinee, "Another fine mess you've got us into Stan?"
Far less thorough than the Russian authorities, they nevertheless rooted out every square inch of baggage, desperately hoping to find something, *anything*, to make their day - and our misery.
Freed eventually, we wheeled our possessions over to Avis, and rented a smart new Mini. With the likelihood of running up thousands of miles in the coming weeks, this was the type of fuel-economy our finances were geared towards.
Ahead of anything, we needed breakfast having flown Paris pre-dawn. That left but one choice - The John Betcheman room at the Charing Cross Hotel. Beyond superlatives, we ate most everything on offer. At $500 it would have been a bargain!
Afterwards, strolled across the Strand, almost directly opposite The Charing Cross Hotel, and walked through The Civil Service Stores, little changed from dad's tenure. *There* was the lift from Hell. Further on, the travel department he had so eye-catchingly re-designed and now packed with mini-skirted young things ooh-ing and ah-ing over foreign destinations with the promise of overflowing passions, yet for most of them undoubtedly, a more likely trip to Blackpool or Southend, where at best they might rumble beneath the seawalls with their pimpled lap-dogs, sharing a bag of cold and greasy fish and chips. Ah, perchance to dream!

The electrical department looked unchanged. Cyril was gone, but there beneath the counter *it* lay.....the socket I used to test those sixteen light bulbs. Could this be the same life? It was to be the last time I ever walked through the Store.

Over Vauxhall Bridge, past the Elephant and Castle, through Greenwich, not forgetting a nod to the Cutty Sark, across the green expanse of Blackheath and straight up Shooters Hill. From the clock tower at the summit, Welling lay spread out below like a time-immune welcome mat. Mum I know shed a silent tear, just one, then with an instant emotional re-grouping, announced, "Nothing's changed, has it dear?"

Descending the hill down which Peter and I had free-wheeled so many times, past the "Sun in the Sands," the cosy little pub where dad had occasionally shared a pint of *Watneys* with the locals including Roger Moore, whose stocks then were fast rising with the success of *The Saint*. Straight down Welling High Street, past Barclays Bank whose manager had dashed any hope of assistance during the last months of the fading ball-gum era, parking directly opposite the Orange Library. I had to have a Ferrara's ice-cream wafer. Nothing like it before or since. I'd grown up with them....the ice-cream wafers that is, not the Ferraras, although their daughter Maria had been in my class at Primary School. As smooth and as bodaciously slurpy as ever - the wafer, not Maria. I had three!

While there, mum decided to call-in to Cottingham's College as much to catch up on four years' gossip as to let the Principal know she was back in Britain for who knew how long, should a position become available. She was shattered to find the old building boarded up, overgrown and a likely target for imminent demolition. The Principal, we learned from the neighbouring Blue Star Garage (that where Ernie Moore had once plied his trade), had died in 1965 and the college closed down shortly after.

Returning to Danson Lane at my insistence, mum had nothing to say as we parked outside *Brookside*. I held her hand - or was she holding mine? She stared at the house for fully five minutes.

The gloss was fading, memories being cruelly tortured. The front garden was not how we left it. Edges were indistinct, hedges unkempt and the hydrangers and rhododendrons gone. One gate hung crookedly from a rotting post no longer on speaking terms with its partner. The beautiful bay windows had been replaced with one-piece glass which sat awkwardly, trying to bridge the gap between good-taste and modern living. A Rolls Royce with Daffy-Duck seat covers! Much of the fencing was buckled and in need of replacement and if I had had more sense I wouldn't have walked around the back and looked over the fence.

Dad wasn't home! Just able to see where the flower beds had been, time had taken care of the least attempts by the garden to engender its own self-preservation. Neglected in the extreme, grass and weeds were reclaiming paths, walkways and brick walls. Why did they buy this house? Was the prospect of undoing a family's pride and affection that big an enticement? Could satisfaction actually be derived watching the destruction of a thing of beauty? It is an enigma I could never fathom, but came to witness more than half a dozen times in the next three decades seeing former homes turned to waste following our departure.

Mum walked through the park with me however and this served to invigorate our spirits somewhat. Here, nothing was different and sitting in the Mansion cafe hosted by a devonshire tea, looking down towards the ageless lake, I saw for a moment the living aura, a halo of indescribable colours hovering around the shoreline, concentrated above the trees, landlocked as they were on the tiny island, the smallest of self-contained ecosystems and for which the terms bitterness, violence, greed, racism, war and resentment could never have any meaning! Wherever Eden was, it ran a disappointing second place!

That first night back, we stayed in Watford with dad's brother, Uncle Don and my cousins Ghinda, Elizabeth and Rupert. Much was there to talk about and catch up on, as you would expect following a four-year hiatus.

The next day we drove to Bournemouth where Nanna had prepared rooms for us, the standard of any five-star hotel, not to mention those bacon and eggs! Grandad was delighted to have his daughter back of course, but by degrees the reality of it all hit home. We had to fend for ourselves and make a stand somewhere. Perhaps now was as good a time as ever to seek out Canada, thus to this end, we made contact with relatives in Vancouver and organised our arrival for late September. With time in hand therefore, we put to good use our freedom and drove the length and breadth of England, beginning with the South East. Lands End, Dartmoor, Torquay, Exeter, Plymouth and only forty miles or so from Bournemouth, Bath and Bristol.

Places within a relatively few hours drive of London, but which we had never considered going to - like so many British families - stagnant in terms of wander-lust. For the first time in my life, the wonders of Stonehenge were revealed, the only real challenge to the Pyramids in terms of our links with pre-history. Midway between Amesbury and Warminster right at the intersection of the A303 and the A344,

Stonehenge simply loomed there at the side of the road, awesome in its stark singularity. No fences, kiosk or any hint of the 20th century. Visitors were then free to wander up to the monument and touch the great stones, which to those with a higher awareness, made an instant and direct contact with nerve endings at the base of the spine. One could not stand in that inner circle, look up at those ancient monoliths and not feel the enormous magnetic power and majesty of the place. Today, you can no longer approach the circle, much less stand in it. Fencing and heavy security prevents any approach nearer than several yards from the ring of outer stones. Commercialism has taken over and much of the immediacy of Stonehenge is denied the modern tourist.

We then shifted our base up to the farm in Yorkshire, having covered Wales, from Swansea in the south to Mount Snowdon, Rhyl and Carnarvon in the north, not forgetting to reacquaint ourselves with the legendary Welsh Rail station on the Isle of Anglesea with the stunning name "LLlanfairpwllgywngyllgogerychwyrndrobwllllantysiliogogogoch"

We spent a week or so as favoured guests of Uncle Reg, in reality Joyce's Uncle by birth, though only some eighteen years older than her. During this time, we fulfilled his greatest wish - that being to see *The Sound of Music,* allegedly the only time he ever went to a cinema in his life! That week, making contact with my employers in Sydney, Bruna, the company receptionist, an Italian girl a couple of years younger than me and in whom it must be said, I was not disinterested, mentioned that she was flying home to Turin for two weeks the next day and that if I could make it there, the family had ample room in their villa for a short stay. I recall the ensuing conversation with mum.

"Look, I'm just going to Italy for a few days."

"Why?"

"Er, to see Milan....always had this urge to see Milan Cathedral," then adding casually, "and I might just drop in and see Bruna at Turin for a day or so while I'm there."

"Bruna....that girl from your office? What's she doing in Italy and why does she want to see *you?*"

I desperately wanted to say "For a few nights of unbridled passion mum. Girls *do* find me irresistible if you did but know it!" but thought better of it. I simply answered, "Nothing serious, just an opportunity to see her family and check out the local sights. You could use the break yourself mum, catch-up on things with Reg."

Suspecting everything, but keeping it suppressed, she merely said, "Well just a couple of days then. Her family *will* be there the whole time won't they?" She really couldn't help herself!

Hastily booking a flight to Turin, via Milan, this left three days which were fully maximised, traversing the historically-enriched Scottish highlands. A cursory tour of Edinburgh and Glasgow, then north to Loch Ness stopping at Urquhart Castle, which like Stonehenge, was in those days unhampered by kiosks, fences, entrance fees and the like, sheep being the sole guardians of the area. At the widest part of the Loch and famed as the locale of several sightings of the serpentine creature said to inhabit the depths, it was highly disappointing to come away having monitored not even a solitary rogue bubble...and we gave it at least thirty minutes. Continuing up to Inverness, Bonarbridge, Helmsdale and Wick, there was left but eighteen or so miles to John O'Groats - the very tip of Northern Scotland. Cool as it was in early Autumn, this would obviously be the place to hold a mid-winter ice-sculpture contest.

Staying overnight at a couple of B & B's, we returned to the farm via Leicester, where we called in at Melton Mowbray to see mum's sister and my two cousins Peter and Michael. The youth of the world at that time was experiencing the height of flower power and Michael particularly was smoking vastly different cigarettes from those you bought in a regular packet. I don't know how successful he was on the "love" front, but the "peace" he found most certainly wasn't that they were singing about! A gentle soul, with no ill-feeling toward man or beast, just three weeks after we had a few drinks together at the "local" that evening, he took a shotgun, loaded it up with broken pieces of pawns from his chess set, and ended his life at eighteen, with a gruesome re-decoration of his bedroom wall. Auntie P. later sought refuge from the horror of the moment in all the wrong places, and all the wrong bottles, and a family with so much, became just another dysfunctional statistic. Looking back at photographs now of our families together at *Brookside* and Melton in the idyllic 50's, such an eventuality would appear unthinkable. Many families worldwide will regrettably be able to identify with this scenario to be sure. I have missed Michael over the years, and to the question "why?" can contribute nothing. The answer most probably lies with the significance of the chess pieces, but he alone knows the answer, and I tend to think that's good enough!

The following Monday saw the Mini at full throttle (no speed limits in force then) blindly on track for Mach 1 as it scampered its way back down the M1 to Heathrow. The Alitalia flight to Milan was brief and without incident. In terms of "Wonders of the Modern World," Milan Cathedral is right up there with the best of them. Ornate beyond belief, this incredible marble edifice, that was commenced in 1386, yet only completed in 1965, is Gothic architecture at its most unrestrained. Three hundred spires (I exaggerate not) adorn the roof and more than three thousand statues inhabit the interior and exterior niches. A gilded statue of the Madonna looks down on visitors to the Piazza Del Duomo from the topmost spire. Beside this, The Leaning Tower of Pisa would appear to be a "no frills" Pizza-hut!

Later that afternoon, flew on to Turin where Bruna's family awaited in the disembarkation lounge. The drive to their villa, some thirty miles or so out in the country was accomplished in less than an hour. Mainly a vineyard, the property was tended by several workers - none of whom spoke English, as was the case with every member of Bruna's family. I became very proficient at nodding. She was an excellent translator however and it's amazing the degree of in-depth conversation two parties can have when neither has the slightest idea what the other is talking about. I ate well, drank even better and slept like a baby. This situation had distinct possibilities, even if I *would* have to master Italian.

The following day we drove north to Arona and Verbama along the northern shores of Lake Maggiore, the most picturesque of scenery right on the Swiss- Italian border and in the shade of the snow-capped Alps, real *"Sound of Music"* stuff. The family's obvious life-long familiarity with the area ensured that we covered points of interest, many of which would never have seen the inside of a tourist guide.

Bruna was quite the perfect hostess, gracious, accommodating and dignity personified. I don't recall that we once mentioned Australia all the time I was there. Despite two nights when we sat up to the early hours talking about that which young people find stimulating at such times, the limited time-factor precluded the possibility of any meaningful romantic exchange. Well, always assuming such options existed.

The last day we pulled out all stops and the big Fiat was called upon to perform well above and beyond the call of duty. In a ten hour drive'n munch-fest, we sought out the attractions of Asti, Allesandria, Novi Ligure, Genoa, Savona, Cairo and Rossano en route back to Turin. You'd see less in a lifetime's membership with Club Med.

Thanking her parents and Bruna herself for three days hospitality I could never forget in back-to-back lifetimes, I boarded a British Airways flight to London via Frankfurt. Barely seventy minutes flight, the plane no sooner reaches maximum altitude than it is obliged to commence its descent. Having circled Frankfurt Airport suspiciously once too often, the captain announced to a restless complement of travellers.

"British Airways regrets the slight delay ladies and gentleman. We appear to be having a spot of bother lowering the undercarriage, please bear with us while we continue to circle the airport - a purely precautionery measure. Thank you!"

Purely precautionery? How much precaution can you take sitting in a metal cylinder, scudding along at three to four hundred miles an hour with no means of landing? Suddenly a flight attendant appeared at the forward door.

"No panic ladies and gentleman," It must have been Captain Lightoller's younger brother. "This is just routine procedure while the Captain obtains confirmation from the control tower that the landing gear *is* in place. Our light indicator appears to have a slight technical fault." Great news. If *one* indicator had a technical problem, what was to say the wing flaps weren't on the blink and the auto-pilot locked on "self-destruct?"

"Ladies and Gentleman," Captain America was back, "We have a visual OK for landing, simply in the interests of safety we ask you to assume crash positions. I stress however, there is no cause for alarm!"

Like everyone bought that! The girl beside me began sobbing, the lady across the aisle was just this side of screaming. A middle aged man behind me was cursing the woman in the window-seat as she wanted to retrieve a bag from the overhead locker to get her "lucky" rabbit's foot. Catholics up and down the cabin began crossing themselves and reciting Hail Marys. One mega-dumb blonde a few seats in front of me and who obviously passed-over Geography as an elective in year eight, was asking where the life-jackets were. For myself, I opted not to take up the traditional "heads down" position, firstly because I wanted to see what was happening and secondly because with any compacting of the fuselage, there would be rows of passengers with broken necks! In any event I sensed my time wasn't up and have always liked nothing better than the spectacle of people making fools of themselves.

The landing was copy-book. The front tyres blowing-out weren't. How many were shredded I couldn't say, but the pilot was having inordinate difficulty keeping a straight line. A lot more Hail Mary's as a jolting vibration filled the cabin. The reverse thrusters quickly slowed the plane to manageable speed but the pilot was coming off second best in his quest to control direction. Reaching the end of the runway finally, the aircraft had slowed to perhaps thirty miles an hour and life was fun again. The people cheered a hero. Turning east towards the terminal building, the tyre damage was distinctly more obvious, a clunk, clunk, clunk accompanying the drone of the jets. Within sight of the terminal and travelling at not much more than walking speed, the plane suddenly lurched to the right amidst the sound of tearing metal and listed over to one side. She was going no further! Mobile stairs were brought in and the passengers disembarked with a somewhat longer than usual walk to the arrival lounge. Looking back at the plane, well down at the nose now, the damage to the landing gear was revealed. Most likely under stress from the blown tyres, it had crumpled at strategic points obviously. Perhaps it had not been correctly locked into position in the first place which would account for the lack of instrument confirmation - also the blowouts! Either way, had the undercarriage collapsed on touch-down, at least one hundred people would have found themselves with an allotted fifteen minutes of fame they hadn't counted on!

With four hours to kill, I caught a cab downtown to have a quick look at Frankfurt, or as it is known locally, Frankfurt-Am-Main, being sited across both banks of the River Main, just over eighty miles south of Bonn. Even after two decades or so since the armistice, many Europeans still think of Germany only in black and white. The result most likely of its association with wartime news-reels, black and white movies, newspaper articles. One may be quite unprepared to be confronted by a Germany in full colour! Frankfurt was an interesting stopover. Basically two cities in one, the older and traditional *Alstadt* which borders the river and which is home to the tradesmen and craftsmen, and *Neustadt*, which as the name implies is the "new" city - the business quarter and political hub. The cluster of Gothic buildings known as the Romer, for five-hundred years the city's town hall, is a must-see for tourists as is the Cathedral of Saint Bartholomew that was built in the 13th century. Walking through the main shopping thoroughfares it seemed quite incongruous to hear songs such as *Judy in Disguise, All you Need is Love, Green Tambourine, Happy Together* and *Incense and Peppermints*, wafting through record stores.

Another hour or so and we were back on the ground at Heathrow. The Mini was waiting impatiently and I was more than happy to let it work off its frustrations scurrying back up north on the M1 motorway. Many hours later, pulling alongside the farm, I wound down the window and listened....to the sound of stone walls, smoke rising from chimneys, the spectre of the moors and the approaching dawn. When you can hear *these* things, you are at peace with your environment, more significantly however, at peace with yourself! Squeezing into my bedroom, only marginally larger than the single bed it contained, I fell asleep, what must have been only half an hour or so before Reg would be embarking on his milking, feed and egg-collection duties. As routine to him as night following day, cats chasing birds or more depressing news articles on the front page.

The following afternoon, I journeyed all the way back to the south coast so Joyce could farewell her father. Just as well I had rented the mini on an "unlimited mileage" basis.....it was near collapse! She was strangely quiet as we edged on to the motorway, an ultimately fast and efficient, though arguably hypnotic concrete and bitumen desert, mile after disappearing mile in a straight line. Some thirty minutes into our journey south, probably in the vicinity of the twenty-fifth emergency telephone, mum turned to me and said, "You know, Reg told me again last night that he would leave the farm to me one day.....funny, but he used to say that when I was staying up there during the war."

Following this statement and quite unsolicited, she then told me what was obviously a situation a quarter of a century earlier, where Reg must have been besotted with the winsome seventeen/eighteen year old, and realising that nothing could ever come of his affection, pretty much hid himself away up on the moors, never once in all that time, seeking out female companionship and probably carrying his torch right through the years. She told me how Reg would take her on his motor bike to Pateley Bridge and Harrogate, shopping, his feelings towards her obvious but the words unspoken. In later years, after Joyce returned to Watford, he became she said, a familiar sight up and down the moors chugging along with his Siamese cat riding pillion. The old cat was still there when I first saw the farm in the fifties although well past its Harley Davidson days. Now that I think of it, it *did* seem to have trouble walking a straight line on top of those stone walls!

With *Itchycoo Park* by The Small faces being played on demand by just about every radio station, a song destined to become one of the defining anthems of the flower-power era, we hung a left, and were once again back in Heathrow's main terminal. Getting to be on a first-name basis with the boys in Customs, we were in possession of boarding passes and ensconced in the departure lounge before you could say "It's all too beautiful."

Probably not first-up on anyone's proposed travel itinerary, yet Iceland is a wily treasure-trove, a virtual smorgasboard, of unseen sights and rarely experienced natural wonders. Take it from one who came to this northern Utopia unsuspecting, when planning the big get-away, forget the traditional stop-off points in Asia, Europe and the Americas - all major touristy habitations to be sure but to have never clapped eyes on the geographical splendour of Iceland is to be handed a Lamborghini without the ignition key.

The final descent into Reykjavik the Capital, is as unearthly as it is fascinating! Little more than five hundred miles north west of Scotland, at times almost moonscape in appearance, the volcanic nature of the area affords a panorama without equal. More than one hundred glaciers have eroded the uplands with an artist's original touch, creating in many places, lakes in parallel and in the proximity of which, thermal springs and geysers spout forth their reminder of the warring geological forces beneath the surface. Iceland's many volcanoes, of which twenty five have been active in modern times, Mt Hekla being the principal culprit, have spewed forth massive lava fields which to the incoming visitor appear now as an erratic bordered shoreline of fancifully baked clay, one that an errant child might have walked through while it was still setting.

Perhaps they cornered the market for singular display at the airport, but I was struck by the uncommon beauty and similarity of the girls at the International terminal at Keflavik, a few miles south of the city-centre. Another interesting item of social trivia, illiteracy in this country of some three hundred and twenty two thousand population, is listed as being non-existent.

With little time at our disposal, we took a hire-car out to see the most dramatic of the hot springs, appropriately named *Geysir* and which incredibly was mid eruption as we arrived. This, according to guides was sheer good fortune as eruptions are irregular and anything from four to thirty-four hours apart. The boiling mud pools there were somewhat reminiscent of the thermal springs in New Zealand's famed Rotorua. Many homes and commercial establishments in Iceland are heated by water piped from accessible hot springs much along the lines of the Roman example in Bath. Other points of interest included the Reykjavik Museum of Natural History and the Einar Jonsson Art Gallery.

Not an hour out of New York and I became increasingly aware that some vestige of long-lost emotion was tugging at my subconscious. With regard to what, I had no idea, yet the nearer we approached US air-space the more pronounced the feeling became. As we commenced our final descent into Kennedy, my pulse rate had greatly increased, and an overwhelming sense of longing and expectation pervaded my whole being. Mum, aware that some undefined influence was at work here, asked if I was OK? I assured her quite truthfully that I had never felt better.

Could any two places be more dissimilar? Welling and New York? I had never set foot on American soil, yet as we crossed The George Washington Bridge that day, heading up towards mid-town Manhattan, I couldn't suppress a tear of utter exhiliaration for knowledge that I was back after so long away. Mum, as dumbfounded as myself at the current turn of events, simply asked,

"Noel, what is it?"

I just shook my head and replied, "I don't know mum, but this is my home, I have been here before, lived here - everything is so familiar to me." And so it proved to be. After we had checked into Lowes Summit Hotel at the corner of 51st and Lexington on the east side, I left mum unpacking and took off. I knew it all. St Patricks, just a stone's throw away on Park Avenue, Radio City, Times Square, Grand Central, The Empire State, even the street corners were old friends, patiently waiting to make my re-acquaintance. Many of the shops I knew I had been in before, though my impression was that they were somehow younger then. Taking the nearest subway station I had no need of a map. From The Battery to Queens and New Jersey, uptown, cross town - all was as familiar to me as the lake in Danson Park. Perhaps the oddest experience awaited me on 34th street.

Directly across from the Empire State building, sits Macy's Department Store said to be the world's largest. Having but a hazy memory of some "abnormality" is the only word I can think to describe it, with one of the escalators, I joined the morning shoppers huddling through the entrance. Past the perfumery counters, behind which the immaculately coiffed and uniformed girls were, as I knew they would be, applying their make-up artistry to those seeking in many cases, to artificially heighten their visual appeal, and straight up to the central escalator.

Somewhat disappointingly, nothing vaguely "abnormal" presented itself always remembering that I had no idea what I was looking for. The old stairway creaked upwards, ever narrowing like a tired river, towards the upper levels. Some floor on Macy's is forever being renovated - in '67 it was the turn of Womens and Childrens' Wear with displays and serving staff (relics of an era long-passed!) impossibly cramped up on one half of the floor while painters and shop-fitters scurried about their business in roped-off sections. Alighting at "Toys" on the seventh or eighth floor, I walked through the endless aisles of childhood magic, able to sense still the generations of excited children who seasonally dragged their exhausted parents through the maze of Christmas delights on show and then years later, were themselves the victim of their own offsprings' demands.

I had by necessity now to be getting back to 51st street, there being nothing here in the way of paranormal or precognitive suggestion. Glancing back at the shelves of new toys, many of which had yet to find their way into other stores worldwide, I stepped back on to the down-escalator. Almost at the bottom of level six now - Home Furnishings or some such thing, and the escalator shuddered just for a moment as it levelled off. Turning to take the next descent, I looked back....my spinal chord having involuntarily iced-up and my legs taking orders from no-one. I stared down at the travelling wooden floor, just inches before it disappeared beneath the metal grille, watching the slight kink as it passed over the same spot.

Disseminate to your heart's content. Belabour the theories of inherited memory, write it off as coincidence if it pleases you but explain to me if you will, how I could possibly have had knowledge ahead of time of this most incidental of phenomena?

Back at The Summit, I had little to say. Mum had even less to ask. Fully accepting of events and situations that defied logical explanation, she was content the next day or so, to scour Manhattan with me from top to bottom having but one life-long yearning, to see the old brownstone houses along west thirty-fifth street, the fictional home of US author Rex Stout's greatest of detectives- Nero Wolfe. This I think, moved even her, close to tears. Besides a love of the genre and in fact of all things American, Colin used to buy her every new Rex Stout novel as it was published, bringing them home from work religiously as he had done since their courtship. She had them all, from *"Fer-de-Lance"* onwards, the first Nero Wolfe novel published in 1934. The many evenings I had laid in bed as a child while she read aloud from *"More Deaths Than One," "Murder By the Book," "Bad for Business," "The Silent Speaker"* and Rex Stout's masterpiece, *"Even in the Best Families."*

I mentioned Central Park in the first chapter of this book. I have long wondered whether my childhood, if not lifelong intimacy with Danson Park has had at its core some other prevailing factor. Walking through Central Park that day came close to addressing that possibility. Again, the famous landmark was so familiar to me. The walkways, the zoo, the pond just across from the Plaza Hotel. The magnificent lake with its small bridge where couples have met and exchanged their most intimate of thoughts over the years. Everywhere I looked, a crushing awareness of both my *belonging* here, as well as an unavoidable feeling of separation. Where had I once been? and with whom? Near the lake, a small boy's ball thrown to him by his mother, well overshot its mark and rolled towards me. The little de Niro-featured youngster sidled over and retrieved his possession, fixing me with a long stare as he did so. A recognition well outside either of our understandings was acknowledged and smiling he returned to his recreational pursuits.

Much more was there to recount then but this is neither the time nor place to do so. Suffice to say that upon leaving New York after three days, I took away with me emotionally, far more than I had brought - at least knowingly!

We sped on to Chicago, which though historically interesting, well planned and offering a uniquely efficient transportation system, appeared staid in many ways, somewhat greyish in aura and entirely too conservative for my taste. Certainly it awakened no spectre of a forgotten past in me and standing on the sidewalk downtown with the wind gusting off Lake Michigan, I had no interest in checking local real estate values.

In Los Angeles, we were fortunate to be the house guests of Sue Chandler, one of Joyce's former students with whom she had kept in touch since '63 shortly before her marriage to an electrical engineer employed at Disneyland. The latter fact proved decidedly beneficial as we had a privileged behind-the-scenes tour of the Anaheim resort and free access to every ride in the theme park. In three days we covered every "A-list" highlight LA had to offer, from Sunset Boulevard to Bel Air, The La Brea tar pits to Long Beach, Hollywood to San Jose. Sue's old Dodge Phoenix was a mechanically dysfunctional wreck by that third day! The same day I found myself in the lock-up of the LA County Police Precinct.

Having been dropped off downtown by Sue's husband that morning, I had bought a few shirts in a small shop just off Wilshire. Exiting the boutique, I had taken barely twenty paces along the sidewalk when I noticed a large grey Chev Impala shadowing me. I stopped, it stopped - I moved, it followed. I was about to accost the driver and enquire what the problem was, when the car swung directly across the sidewalk and its two excessively large occupants spreadeagled me across the hood.

Flashing LA Police badges, one wrenched the shopping bag from my grasp while the other produced handcuffs. "Nice shirt," said the plainclothes officer, pulling one from the bag. The handcuffs were no restriction to my opening the rear door - they did it for me, before bundling me into the back seat.

"How'd you find 'Frisco this time of year?" said the driver, the other chuckled. "As a matter of fact," I replied, "When we sort this out, I'll be going there tomorrow."

"Tricky little accent you got there," said my co-passenger, "What is it - Limey?"

"Look guys," I started to say, but was cut off.

"Just shut the hell up son, you can talk yourself stupid when we get back to the station!" he paused...possibly looking for inspiration, "We don't want to hear none of your crap!"

Nothing further was spoken until we pulled into the precinct where I was escorted to a holding cell after some inaudible exchange with the sergeant on duty. Other detainees with me included a bald-headed John Malkovich look-alike, a couple of probable crack dealers and someone looked like Dennis Rodman's brother. This was right off the conventional tourist track to be sure - something to tell your kids during a dull evening! Just then the cell door was unlocked and I was escorted back to the front desk, behind which the uniformed sergeant was sizing me up.

" You got anything to say son?" He began making some entry in a book before him.

"Only that you've made a major mistake here, I don't know who you think I am, but I'm a tourist, I've never been to San Francisco and I'd like to know what the hell's going on - if that's OK with you guys. You know? my rights, and all that? Which reminds me - my one phone call? this would be a real good time to make it, before you all get yourselves in any deeper!"

Something in my tone must have cut some ice with the cop who'd brought me in. He looked in my bag they had in the "evidence tray" and found the receipt from the boutique. No-one spoke. They were just staring at me.

"Christ Almighty" said Dirty Harry behind the desk, "It's *not* him either!"

"I'm really missing something here," I said, "Just what *is* the problem?"

"You got any ID son?" said the other, motioning to have the 'cuffs removed. Having nothing on me, I gave them the name and address of our friends where we were staying, and while the sergeant checked the number and called the house, getting through to Sue eventually, I filled in the missing "history" for them.

Their story was equally of interest. It seems they had been on the look-out for a thief, specialising in articles from small clothing shops. His modus-operendi never varied. He would first buy something minor - a shirt or similar item, then return a short time later under the pretext of looking for something else, only to relieve the shop of multiple new garments, stashed in their original bag. Having a preference for the west coast, he had the previous week, robbed several small boutiques in San Francisco. The Police knew his identity apparently and were on alert in the LA area. What was incredible and certainly, in my mind at least, cleared the Police of any wrong-doing was that they had a photo of the felon which the sergeant then handed me. I just stared at the picture. It *was* me! Not even someone very similar. it *was* yours truly. Same age, same hair, identical features and in this particular shot, even wearing clothes that were virtually the twins of those I had on. "Eerie" doesn't adequately cover it! If the doppelganger theory was right, I was looking at mine!

I'm real sorry Mr Bailey," said the arresting officer, "You can see now why we had little doubt there?" He extended his hand which I shook. From behind us in the holding cell, the "Rodman" clone called out, "Hey man, when you're done shakin' white boy's hand there, I still gotta call me a lawyer. Maybe the same as got him a ride outta here?" he flashed me a smile.

"Good luck brother," Those three words alone conveyed more sincerity and intimacy than Ms Gunson and Mr LeFeuvre had been able to dredge up in twelve years between them!

"Least you can do is buy the kid some lunch," The desk sergeant winked at the two who had brought me in. In that respect, they certainly acquitted themselves superbly and in a hot-steak eatery nearby I was treated to the works. Their genuine regret for the incident was obvious, their apologies limitless. Shortly after, they dropped me off at Sue's place in their highway patrol car. I've had a soft spot for Chevvies ever since.

"Just can't keep out of trouble can you?" said mum giving me the once-over, "I don't know Noel, I just don't know."

Deciding to put San Francisco on hold for a few days, we flew east to Las Vegas having first organised a suite at the Hilton. The world's capital of sleaze and an enduring monument to bad taste, everyone should see Las Vegas just once.

Crassness gone feral! Poker machines wall-to-wall in the airport terminal itself - jaded fiscal sentries with a solitary mission. To ensure the visitor leaves the city with as little cash as possible. Acres of blue-rinsed middle-aged women pouring their husband's earnings through the eager slots, squeals of delight as the machines return occasionally their encouragement to keep feeding them. Still, we saw what we came to see. The crude, the mad and the hungry! I have to say one thing in its defence, Las Vegas is most certainly alive and not half-bad when it comes to pulling on the feed-bag! Day two, we hired a brand new Mustang, a midnight blue drop-top which was advertised at an insanely cheap two-day rental. With gas at that time something like thirty-five cents a gallon (near enough to fourteen cents a litre) fuel consumption was not a consideration, nor was distance! Thus we lit out on the Great Boulder Highway heading south east, having just one destination in mind - The Grand Canyon. Some eighty to ninety miles from Vegas and just past

Boulder City itself, we stopped at the colossal Hoover Dam a feat of engineering with few equals in the modern world.

Between here and the next township was pretty much a hundred miles of dead-straight highway through desert and the Black Mountain ranges. Other than serving as a fuel-stop, Kingman looked for all the world like a setting from a Stephen King novel. This day however, it sticks in my mind! Having re-fuelled, we had reached the town limits when an older model Chev, a '61 Impala hardtop, flashed past headed north. Nothing unusual except for the fact the underside of the car appeared to be well alight, flames streaming from beneath the rear doors. The driver, evidently unaware of his imminent demise, was cruising unconcernedly. Taking off after him, there being no-one else on the road, we could see the fire spreading rapidly, flames belching out beneath the rear tail-pipe now. Pulling alongside we yelled out to the driver, pointing to the roadway. Glancing down, he saw his predicament. No-one *ever* uttered the words "Oh shit!" with more meaning or sincerity. As he braked, the flames increased and skidding right off the shoulder into the brush he leaped from the vehicle. Less than six seconds later the car erupted in a ball of flames, the heat intense even at the safe distance we were. The driver lived in Kingman and we dropped him home still in shock, before continuing on. Five will get you ten, that guy has never owned a Chevvy since!

Near enough to three hundred miles from Las Vegas, Flagstaff, the sister city of Katoomba in New South Wales, sits close to the southern rim of the Grand Canyon, the hotels there giving new meaning to the term "A Room with a View!" Whatever preconceived notion one has of the Grand Canyon, seeing it is quite something else. For me, the over-riding impression to be gained looking down at that timeless river-eroded masterpiece of natural wonder is just how unimportant our individual lives are. What relevance, that new car, a pay-rise, smart new clothes, that first kiss, your new home? when centuries after your forgotten funeral, standing there on that same rim everything looks much the same. More than two hundred miles long and varying in width from four to eighteen miles, at no one point can you see all of the canyon. The Colorado River has cut its way to a depth of more than one mile in the main gorge, now preserved as the Grand Canyon National Park. There is no more a spectacular sight on this planet!

"If you're going to San Francisco,

Be sure to wear some flowers in your hair,

In the streets of San Francisco,

You're going to meet, some gentle people there"

So sang Scott McKenzie on behalf of every hippie along the American west coast and in 1967 flower power was at its most aromatic. Any musician worth his beads was bedded down somewhere in walking distance of the Golden Gate and the strains of McKenzie's great anthem, penned by John Philips of The Mamas and Papas, was proclaimed from the rooftops of every commune in the Bay area. The Haight-Ashbury district of San Francisco was the pot-smoking spiritual centre of the movement. No-one really knows why, it being an otherwise rather downmarket collection of run-down homes in the artistic heart of the city. Distantly related to London's Soho, New York's Greenwich Village, Paris's Left Bank and Sydney's Kings Cross, *The Haight*, as it was often referred to, was a riot of bearded love gurus, craft shops, peace signs and at every half dozen paces, roadside stalls offering bead necklaces and exotic shirts. I bought a truck-load! Nothing before or after can match the euphoria of that period. It was a time to be young and fate had kindly seen to it that I still was.

San Francisco! - America's favourite city, and it was easy to see why. Imbued with history from its days as a burgeoning sea-port and favoured rendezvous of the pirating fraternity, the area has developed into the most cosmopolitan of cities with a natural harbour second in magnificence only to Sydney. There is a "spirit" within San Francisco that is totally unique. Friendly, purposeful, un-hurried and dignified, whether one is riding the cable-cars, having a quiet moment in the Golden Gate Park, shopping downtown or taking a harbour-cruise, this is probably as close as one can get to the real America! That may not have been the opinion of the former inmates of Alcatraz, but even The Rock retains an aura all its own.

Renting a Firebird, we scoured the city and nearby Oakland which actually houses over two-thirds of San Francisco's population. Across the Golden Gate which has only pretenders to its title as the world's greatest bridge, we took in Sausalito and the magnificent Redwood forest at Muir Woods some ten minutes further up the highway. With only limited time, we poked around San Rafael and Santa Rosa, some fifty miles or so further north before having to return. Again, I was conscious of just how at home I was on the US freeways, left-hand drive for some reason seeming far more natural to me.

And so, after four years as essentially displaced persons, we finally were headed for our original destination - Vancouver: British Columbia. It had been worth the wait. Here it seemed was the confluence of our needs. An equable climate, unlimited access to America, snow on tap just across the Rockies, commutable distance to Europe and (at that stage) a vibrant and expanding Canadian economy, jobs unlimited and no need for a Green Card! Swiftly making contact with Granny Bailey's relatives and apologising for the forty-six month delay, we retired to the hotel room for a well deserved rest. It was just all too easy.

Awoken from my reverie early next morning by the inconsiderate ringing of the telephone alongside my right ear, the front desk announced, "Sorry to disturb you Mr Bailey, an urgent long-distance call for you."

It was Nanna, with the fully unexpected news that Grandad had suffered a further relapse of some sort and was back in intensive care in Bournemouth hospital. Having left on-forwarding contact numbers at each point of departure, and with Nanna having additionally our intended travel itinerary, our whereabouts had been easily pinpointed.

That mum must return at once was beyond question. This then presented two major hurdles. Firstly, our available finances could extend to only one return ticket and to have her travelling alone was dicey in the extreme, especially in the context of what had happened two years earlier.

"I'll be fine," was all she said but in that tone, I knew she would be. Even had she contracted malaria, bubonic plague and legionnaire's disease en route, she would undoubtedly have still made it!

Having seen her off that afternoon, I was left to contemplate my next move. I had now but a few traveller's cheques left, the balance of an economy ticket valid only in a westerly direction and most likely, a job still in Sydney. As I walked aimlessly around the Vancouver Planetarium a few hours later trying to make sense of an insane situation, I pondered why fate seemed to be earmarking us to live anywhere but Canada. Returning to Sydney additionally would not be without some inherent danger. There was still the possibility of Magistrate Farquhar's Federal Officers waiting to escort me to boot-camp on arrival. Travelling on a UK passport however and having purchased originally one-way tickets, the likelihood of a military reception was negligible I reasoned. I couldn't see a permanent "watch" having been set up at Kingsford Smith Airport on the offchance I may return. With great reluctance then, I made contact with our Canadian relatives and cancelled the impending family reunion that had been set down for the next day.

Making reservations for the next flight to Sydney, via Honolulu and Auckland, which as it happened was scheduled to depart in less than five hours, I cast a final look around at what was so nearly our new homeland and which would now have to wait-out one further Act in this complication-filled drama that appeared to be scripting itself as it went along.

CHAPTER SEVEN

MARQUED FOR DEATH

Touching down at Mascot on a warm Monday morning, I had no need of the false moustache, Beatle wig and accentuated limp. Not a solitary MP in sight! Up and through customs without a hitch, I hopped into the nearest cab before I realised I had nowhere to go! Remembering then, that at least I had a car in storage, I called Ernie Moore, who fortunately was home that morning. I arranged to be there within the hour. The Vauxhall had been well-cared for in our absence and having caught up on recent events across a well-stocked coffee table, followed by some outward bodily improvements courtesy of a shower and razor, I drove across town to my employer. Bruna was seated behind her usual desk in reception and looked stunned to see me.
"Didn't think *you'd* ever be back here," she said, as immaculately turned out as ever.
"I hadn't planned on it myself," I told her, asking then if Colin McCrae, the company's owner and managing director was in. My query was unnecessary, as the man himself emerged from the two-way radio room and seeing me, waved me into his office. Colin and I had always gotten along seamlessly and my job was still intact whenever I could start. I opted for the following Monday. In my absence, Oliver, my co-worker and friend for some years, had filled in for me. He wanted his old job back, and so everyone came up smiling.
For the first day or two, I checked in to the West End hotel in lower Pitt Street in the city. At just $35 a night with full tariff, clean and well appointed suites and a restaurant that was a nostalgic throwback to the thirties. It was only marginally more expensive than a bunk at the YMCA. First thing on my return after lunch I rang Bournemouth. Mum answered. Arriving there well in advance of my own touchdown she had already spent time with her father who she described as "poorly" but out of immediate danger. Evidently some respiratory problem though not emphysema. For her own part, she declared herself to be fine. Her voice and manner appeared to confirm this. She told me she expected to be able to get back to Vancouver early next week. I coughed once or twice and mentioned this may not be a good move since I was back in Sydney.

"You're *where?*" she shrieked, as un-cool as ever I had heard her. "Sydney," I reiterated, "Cash crisis remember?....Air fares?....a job here! Not a lot of choice when you come to think of it?"

She hadn't given the situation any great thought understandably and following a few moments silence, said.

"And just where are we going to live?"

I pointed out that we faced the same position a few days ago in Vancouver when we actually *had* some money! With reserve funds we had banked in Sydney left over from the sale of *South Pacific*, we could surely find somewhere to rent for six months or so until finances were out of the red-zone. Not totally convinced of my logic I suspect, but with no better ideas herself, she agreed to contact Thelma with details of her flight arrival as and when.

Under the impression a smidgeon of "PR" wouldn't go astray, I then rang the Sydney Morning Herald's Editorial Chief of Staff, to sound out their attitude to Joyce's return. It really wasn't necessary.

"She's coming *back?*" he gushed, for all the world a kid who had just won a trip to Disneyland, together with a year's supply of sherbert.

"Thank God for that!" he continued, "We haven't been able to find a replacement for her and the cadets' shorthand skills have all but evaporated. When will she be able to get in?" I volunteered probably the end of the following week. He was a happy man. This then, left the question of finding somewhere to call home.

Unlike four years earlier, when on arrival we hadn't known our way past the baggage carousel, every point of the compass in Sydney town was as familiar to me now as my own fingerprints. Of the five hundred or so suburbs on offer, less than thirty or so were a realistic possibility, either by virtue of distance or demographic acceptability. Besides, the old adage "pay a little more and you get a whole lot more" has considerable merit when you're contemplating your full-time surroundings.

The next few days, I checked out numerous rental properties and found the bargain of the century. That it happened to be in the harbour foreshores in Sydney's most exclusive conclave - Point Piper, was decidedly a plus, but not the prime motivation for taking it. One quarter of an enormous sandstone edifice that by virtue of its ramparts and crenelles, looked from the roadway for all the world like a small european castle, the apartment was so gigantic, no-one wanted it and it had been on the market for months, reduced now to an insultingly low rental. Even the agent showing the property had commented before leaving her office, "I'll show you the place of course, but you won't be interested in it!"

So much for the psychology of sales, not to mention the owner-agent code of ethics.

The "flat" to refer to the Wyuna Road residence, offered almost twice the interior space of a standard three bedroom home, helped not a little by the near thirty-five foot long lounge. Two enormous bathroom suites that could easily have promoted their own beachwear fashion-parades and four bedrooms each of which might have hosted proceedings for "Bob & Carol & Ted & Alice." The stumbling block most likely for most, being that the entire apartment offered simply polished floors requiring for the average tenant, acres of carpet. This was of no detrimental consequence in our case, having carpets on tap in storage.

To the disbelief of my realtor companion I agreed to take it. She just looked at me, lips quivering in shock and repeated mechanically, "You *want* it?......you mean you'll sign a lease?"

"I'll sign a *leash* if that's what it takes?" I replied.

She wasn't big on humour, still she was pretty young, give her time! We drove back to the office in silence, except for her gear-changing that required a real lot of work if the clutch was to have any chance of survival much beyond a fortnight.

The rest of the week was taken up un-crating our possessions once again, made worse by the knowledge that there was yet a further re-pack on the horizon when the eventual move to Canada became a reality.

I was actually working up to my third *Chestnut Teal,* at Thelma's Wycombe Road apartment, when mum's call came through. Grandad was back home, greatly improved and she had herself booked on a Qantas flight, due in at Mascot late Tuesday evening. This would give me ample time to complete final preparations at Point Piper. I also took some well-allocated time out to see *Bonnie and Clyde, Guess Who's Coming to Dinner* and *The Graduate*, starring "newcomer" Dustin Hoffman.

On seeing the colossal apartment, mum simply put her hand luggage on the nearest table and said,

"Couldn't you have found something a little bigger?" I knew though she approved. Quality always transcended practicality in her view.

December of 1967 saw much that was unusual. America launched the first micro- wave oven. December 11th saw the unveiling of the Anglo-French Concorde and on the 18th, Harold Holt the Australian Prime Minister, disappeared in the surf off Cheviot Beach near Portsea in Victoria, believed to have been drowned. It was the biggest news story in Australian history, at least since the end of World War Two. Even

Lyndon B. Johnson, the US President, attended the State Funeral for Sir Harold in Melbourne. For the next twenty or thirty years, in the absence of ever finding his body, theories occasionally were expounded as to the possible "faking" of his death, Government cover-up and the inevitable abduction by UFO. The facts were much simpler. Holt was seen by a friend, diving off a rock into fifteen foot breakers just as a king tide was washing ashore from Bass Strait, creating a very rough swell. The question is why, knowing full-well the dangers and eccentricities of this particular 500 yards of coastline - did he do that? No one is ever going to know.

Life for those first few months at Point Piper was incident free, but given our track record, the most inept of clairvoyants could have predicted a new cycle of disharmony taking up pole position just over the immediate horizon. The onset of this was heralded mid April, just a week after the assassination of Martin Luther King in Memphis, Tennessee. As it happened, I was walking to the corner-store at nearby Rose Bay, and had reached the end of Wyuna Road where it forms a T-junction with the principal eastern route, New South Head Road. A wide crossing there provides the only opportunity for half a kilometre in either direction, for PWG's (Pedestrians with Guts) to gain access to the Rose Bay side, short of tunelling beneath the roadway. Ahead of me was a young girl. Traffic had already ground to a halt and the driver of a truck at the head of the group was smiling at the girl crossing, young enough as she was to have been his daughter but old enough to stir the adrenaline. Without any warning, a small delivery van bypassed the queued traffic in the right hand lane and seeing us, braked....but far too late! Although knocked down myself by some part of the van - perhaps the nearside guard or even the mirror housing - the girl took the major part of the impact. Thrown forward several metres, she lay there now, face down and un-moving. Quite uninjured, I was up before anyone had moved and knelt down beside her. She was groaning and trying to pull herself into a foetal position. Although no readily-obvious broken bones could be seen, she was in a bad way, shivering uncontrollably and her legs, forehead and right hand, bleeding profusely. A small carrybag and handbag lay nearby, their contents strewn across the road. By now the truck driver was beside me while the delivery boy was spewing up his breakfast kerbside. Long before the days of cellular phones, someone had to hasten to a nearby house to summon an ambulance. I asked the truck driver to stay with her while I ran back to our apartment and found a large blanket. I doubt I was four minutes. By the time I returned, the girl was crying softly and in a lot of pain. The blanket however, served the dual purpose of keeping her warm and keeping hidden the skin damage. She then asked me to retrieve her possessions from the roadway which I had nearly completed when the Police arrived.

"Hey, you there, what the fuck do you think you're doing?" I make no apology for the language, simply reporting the event verbatim. I looked up.

A totally obnoxious young Police officer was eyeballing me from his highway patrol Falcon. I told him I was picking up the girl's possessions at her request. He got out, crossed over to where I was crouched and said "The Hell you were, get the fuck out of here right now before I book you for theft."

"Yeah? You do that mate and see how far it gets you!" We both turned around. It was the truckie, some fifty pounds heavier and six inches or so taller than the patrol officer. "Like he said," he was continuing, "The girl there asked him to pick up her stuff - that alright with you?"

The cop, with no ready comeback to hand said nothing, then ambled off and joined his partner just as the ambulance pulled up. I went across to the girl who was being attended-to by a paramedic. They loaded her into the ambulance with my blanket, and I never saw either again! Not hanging around to watch the anguish of the van driver, who doubtless lost his licence, savings and job, in that order, I finally got to cross the road!

I have always loved cars, from my Matchbox days onwards. I am, if you would know it, presently driving my seventy-fifth vehicle! Even during the infamous ball-gum period, I would walk the streets while dad was psychologically undermining his own self-esteem, peering at new releases, old classics, learning to differentiate between the models. A huge range there was too in the fifties. Besides the broad spectrum of British-built vehicles, London was host also to the best of the best from Europe and America - a few of the less salubrious as well. In time, I was as familiar with a '48 Cadillac Fleetwood hardtop, as I was a '59 Facel Vega Excellence, a 50's Citroen, a '49 Armstrong Siddeley Sapphire or a Russian Volga. I knew the slightest grille-change on every Ford, Morris, Rover, Austin and Buick, from the late 30's onwards and collecting new-car catalogues at dealerships was a passion. Why then did my "metal-skinned friends" turn on me? and as you will read, the next decade was a litany of on-going automotive disasters, near-death experiences and straight-up fender-bending on a monumentally grand scale, perhaps unsurpassed in the history of the human experience. And this, having racked up an impressive record by road, sea and air already!

Mid year and mum was laid low by a further respiratory collapse. Bobby Kennedy fared worse however, being assassinated on June 8th in the Ambassador Hotel in Los Angeles after a political rally. Nothing much about this world was making sense right now and perhaps it was apt that the late actor Richard Harris should have such a monstrous hit as the surrealistic seven-minute plus *MacArthur Park* at this time.

At the Scottish Hospital for a change, I recall sitting with Joyce bedside as The Monkees were belting out *Valleri* at the nearby Rushcutters Bay stadium. She was responding slower now to treatment and the duration of the attacks were noticeably longer. For myself, I seemed to be spending more time at the Sydney Morning Herald offices now than at my own job which was by necessity having to be supplemented late nights to keep it together.

On her eventual discharge she was this time, visibly weakened and needing several days recuperation before entertaining any return to work.

With the onset of Spring, mum's condition improved and we resumed our weekends' exploration of the NSW coastline and inland areas. The Hunter Valley and the southern highlands being two areas which provided uniquely Australian scenes of beauty quite unlike their European counterparts. One wonders just how many Sydney born and bred residents have yet to discover the sights and sounds of much of their own home-State like so many in Britain who have never ventured beyond their local, safe and familiar paths.

Late October saw the opening of the Mexico Olympics and the year passed into history when the crew of Apollo 8 became the first astronauts to orbit the Moon. Twenty-three now, a clock somewhere was ticking audibly.

An apartment the size of that in Wyuna Road was ready-made for the Christmas experience. Lofty ceilings permitted the tallest tree on offer, while the half kilometre or so of picture rails extended the creative ability of the most experienced of festive architects. We were up to the challenge and that year was filled with colour, vibrancy and Christmas spirit. Visitors were frequent and included all members of the Bavin family as well as the majority of the reporting staff of the Sydney Morning Herald and Sun newspapers. The star fell from the tree twice, which was nothing more than Colin making his presence known. Last thing each night, the little church shed its hallowed beams, during which the cumulative memories of all former Christmases were loosed upon an appreciative audience of two. More than three decades on now, what recollections that tiny ecclesiastical time-capsule must have captured and stored behind its miniature stained-glass windows....another generation's childhood - there is room yet of course for so much more - the tale is but barely started!

With the Beatle's White album racking up sales like nothing before it, and Barry Gibb's wailing, propelling the Bee Gee's to unimagined success in the US, the last of the sixties kicked in. Looking at the palm of my left hand. along the life- line specifically, I was approaching a series of sharp turns.

Though something less than a "party-animal" by nature, I was occasionally to be found at the odd bash. One such low-key little affair happened to be Oliver's party. (Oliver who you may recall if you haven't been skim-reading, being a work-friend of mine.) By today's standards the night was dull. No ecstasy, spiked drinks, loose women, sidewalk punch-ups, road rage.....I can't recall much worse than the odd broken stiletto heel. Farewelling the surviving revellers at shortly before midnight, I hit a near deserted Parramatta Road, heading for the city and the Eastern suburbs.

Within a few intersections of The Sydney Morning Herald building on Broadway, I noticed far behind me a solitary vehicle approaching rapidly. Stopping at the lights at the next intersection, the newcomer reigned in behind me - a white unmarked Police Rambler complete with fully marked Police officers. Moving off with something less than undue haste - the only option open to a four-cylinder Vauxhall, the Rambler remained glued to my tail. The next set of lights, right at The Herald itself, my companions remained in the car's slipstream. As I moved off, the Rambler accelerated past and some thirty metres further on, braking suddenly, slewed sideways, blocking my path. Pulling up, one of the officers with his gun drawn, was screaming at me to get out of the vehicle. Once again I found myself bundled into the rear of a Police car for no obvious reason. The trip to Police headquarters at city central was but three minutes - my Vauxhall being impounded by the arresting officer and keeping up the rear.

Met at the counter by an older and kindly looking officer, I noticed a look of undisguised repugnance pass between him and the two young turks in uniform. Words were exchanged and I was left in the care of the desk-sergeant. As the others returned to their Rambler, I was somewhat amazed when he looked up at me and said,

"I'm sorry mate - you were just in the wrong place at the wrong time!"

I asked him what he meant and what offence had I supposedly committed?

"They've charged you with Driving under the Influence, exceeding the Speed limit by more than fifty kilometres an hour, and resisting arrest."

I laughed - there was no other option.

"None of this is true," I replied. "They cut me off, I wasn't driving over the limit - they had already followed me for several intersections and I've had less than half a dozen drinks in five hours. Fifty over the limit? the car doesn't *go* that fast! No one even asked me what I'd had to drink! and how did I *resist* arrest when they waved a gun in my face and shoved me in the Police car?"

The sergeant looked rueful, "Look son, these two are from the North Sydney Safety Squad, they have racked up a heap of shonky convictions the last year or so, and the word is they're bad cops but I didn't tell you that and I won't be repeating it...we understand each other? Just go get yourself a good lawyer!"

Following this somewhat remarkable exchange I was by necessity, ID'd, finger-printed and locked up for the night with the usual suspects! There was no point waking mum up until the morning. One of us at least, may as well have had a decent night's sleep. The moth-eaten blanket they threw me was most probably lice-infected and in use since Ned Kelly's capture. But mention must be made of the "toilet," a standard bucket, for communal and open use in one corner of the cell. Several "overnighters" gave me the impression that this was par for their course, having no hesitation in urinating (or worse) at regular intervals during the night. The notorious "Bangkok Hilton" could have taken pointers from this lesson in dehumanising treatment.

At a hastily convened court-hearing next morning, bail was set at $2000. It may as well have been twenty thousand! We simply didn't have it. The desk sergeant however had a word on my behalf, quite unsolicited, and approval was given to use the Vauxhall as collateral. I then rang home.

"Sorry I'm a little late mum, had a slight problem with the Police last night! No, nothing much - just drunk as a skunk, speeding, driving through red lights, stuff like that, Oh yeah, and I ended up having a physical with a highway cop too, wouldn't let him take me in without a bit of a set-to....Where am I now? Central cells but the *good* news is - bail's only two grand."

What I *actually* said was.

"Sorry to wreck your morning - but I'm just on my way out of the Police lock-up now. Don't ask me anything - I'll explain when I get back!" There was then a brief pause, after which she simply said,

"How many are dead?" She had such style!

There was of course no way to explain the preceding night's events without it appearing either fictional delusion or a poor attempt to justify the indefensible. If she believed me - I couldn't be sure! If she didn't, it was never going to be exactly prejudicial to my case. The hearing was actually set down for two months hence, during which time I had the dubious pleasure of having to report weekly to the local police station to comply with the terms of my bail. Represented by a friend of the Bavin family, one Brian Sully, an up and coming barrister whose manner very much recalled to mind the late actor Vincent Price. Methodical and meticulous in his approach to the brief, Brian left no stone unturned in his quest for justice, even obtaining (by whatever source, legal or otherwise) a full dossier on the two vigilante cops.

"My word, these are an interesting duo." he muttered to me in his chambers one afternoon. "Not held in the greatest of esteem by their own peers it seems. I think we may be on to something here."

The NRMA were brought in to independently test the vehicle and the results showed what I already knew.....that the car was incapable of reaching the speeds they had nominated in the original charge-sheet. As Brian said to me, on reading the report I handed him, "Indeed! - you might want to hang on to that one!"

Friends and acquaintances from the party, willing volunteers in my defence, were paraded before Brian.

"I have no wish to educate you all in a particular line of defence," he said, "Just tell the truth and expect the prosecutor to "suggest" you may be mistaken on every point. Let him "suggest" whatever he wishes and keep your answers to a minimum."

Accordingly, we had our day in Court.

The Prosecutor, having outlined the Crown's case called the two arresting officers. Their evidence was identical, word for word, mannerism for mannerism. Unemotional, unconvincing and dead-set perjury!

It was Brian's turn to cross-examine.

"You maintain then, that my client drove at well over one hundred kilometers an hour from Forest Lodge (some five kilometers further back, long before they first appeared in my rear vision mirror!) continuously, towards the city?" They concurred.

Then holding up an enlarged map of the area, affixed to a whiteboard, he continued.

"An examination of that particular section of road shows, as you can see, the placement of seven sets of traffic lights," he pointed out the location of each one, successfully capturing the magistrate's attention. "We have undertaken several independent tests at night, and it is clearly impossible to drive that distance at any speed, without running a red light and yet you maintain my client did not infringe in this manner?"

A lot of squirming in the witness chair! Their only comment. "The defendant drove at more than one hundred kilometres an hour or more, the entire distance....possible or not!"

The NRMA's report was next up. Successfully objected-to by the Prosecution, as admissable evidence, it was nevertheless read by the magistrate prior to his upholding of the objection and thus the facts were tendered to the only person who mattered anyway.

The question next of "Driving under the Influence?" The police were asked how they determined I was "drunk." They had no choice but to admit I had not been asked about any alcoholic intake, as well as confirming that no doctor had been called to undertake a blood-test at the station.

"You simply formed an opinion then, that my client was intoxicated?" Brian suggested with a sardonic edge.

"In my opinion he was blind drunk behind the wheel." said rogue cop 1.

"Yet you say he drove at more than one hundred kilometres an hour through *seven* or eight intersections without running a red light, endangering others, swerving, or even driving in a dangerous manner?" Brian enquired.

"I can't comment on that," was the worst response he could have made.

The case for the defence was a classic of unrehearsed and often laughably conflicting evidence. Half a dozen guests from the party that night took the witness stand. None could agree what time the party started, how many were there or even what alcohol was available. As regards the latter, evidence given under oath, ranged from an AA meeting to what you might expect to find being served at a Russell Crowe Oscar celebration party! At its conclusion, the magistrate shook his head and turning to Brian, said, "Mr Sully, perhaps you would like your client to take the stand and clarify the matter in his own words."

I was up. Fully prepared for the Prosecutor's word-games, no quarter was given and having detailed precisely what did happen that night, during which time the magistrate I noticed, flung many a long glance at the North Sydney boys in blue, I was excused.

In his summing up, the magistrate had plenty to say. He noted the seemingly practised evidence of the Police which he felt was highly "questionable" to say the least. He made specific mention of the "compellingly odd" evidence as presented by Defence witnesses which by virtue of the differing accounts showed at least no collusion and was almost refreshing in content. He found no evidence to support a charge of drink-driving and concluded by saying,

"It is my opinion, the evidence provided by the Police and the circumstances surrounding the Defendant's arrest are highly controversial but not within the jurisdiction of this court to pursue. However, I cannot undermine Police procedure and challenge the validity of the action of these officers and thus find the case technically proved only. No conviction will be recorded against the Defendant and the decision of this Court is that Mr Bailey shall have his license suspended - for just 24 hours. Taking into account his inappropriate incarceration overnight, he is free now to drive. I see fit also to levy no fine on this occasion."

The biggest smile was reserved for the desk-sergeant who looking across at the two constables made clear his approval. They slunk out, obviously close to spraying the bench and courtroom with bullets. He crossed over to me and shook my hand.

"Well done son, just a word of advice - get rid of that car!"

With the possibility that morning of facing a substantial fine and a six or twelve month disqualification, this was as good as it gets. Thanking Brian profusely for a job exceptionally well-handled and for which he would accept no fee, we returned to Double Bay and celebrated with two pepper-steaks at George's Steakhouse, and a bottle of Moet! In 2005, Brian is now a greatly respected senior NSW Chief Justice.

I should have taken heed of the sergeant's advice. In the next two weeks, I was booked for "Changing lanes on the harbour bridge at 7.32.am. (The lane-change restrictions coming into effect at 7.30.am.), "Driving at 62 in a 60 limit," and "Exiting a freeway without correct signalling." The same cops obviously, using various unmarked cars. It was time to trade.

The weekend was spent "on the strip", the hundreds of used car dealerships lining Parramatta Road on the main route west. After test-driving some thirty or so vehicles and feeling no kinship with any, I came across the one place I should never have walked into - a small used-Jaguar dealership. We didn't need one, couldn't afford to buy or run one, let alone insure one! But there it was, an immaculate white '61 auto 3.4 litre saloon with log-books and full history. All her life, mum had just once, wanted to own a Jaguar - and I had it here in my power right now, to make it happen. Even with the more-than reasonable trade-in for the Vauxhall and every last dollar in the bank account, there was still left a balance of $800 which would have to be financed, in those days, the simplest of arrangements for anyone in full-time employment. All was accomplished in an hour and papers were to be drawn up for my signature and the deal set for completion the following afternoon. I merely told mum I hadn't found anything suitable when I got home that evening. From memory, I think she looked at me with some suspicion, but said nothing.

It had been for several months now, a bi-weekly fixture, that Oliver and I spent lunch times at the local outdoor swimming pools - The Leichhardt Aquatic Centre. Whether a fitness drive, an opportunity to flex some youthful muscle, or just simply a case of plain recreational indulgence I really can't recall, but every Monday saw us heading off down Norton Street and this one followed the same script. With a red up ahead at the intersection of William Street we slowed, it changed to green some three or four seconds before we made it and I recall Olly pointing out a group of young girls having themselves a picnic in the Pioneers Memorial Park just across the road. This actually proved to be a case of bad timing as far as his hand was concerned.....it being the first thing to go through the windshield.

Deceleration from sixty to zero in less than four feet, at least in a forward direction.....three times that sidewise! does tend to generate quite some G-force, but there again, semi-trailers often tend to stamp their authority on collisions of this nature. I opened the door which promptly fell into the street as there was nothing left beyond the firewall and the roof had receded some two or three feet from its original alignment. I had now a make-shift sunroof. The truck that had run the red, was stopped some thirty metres further down William Street, the engine and front of the Vauxhall wedged beneath his bull-bars. Just then, a uniformed lady, who it transpired was a nurse on her way to work, ran over to the wreckage.

Are you alright love?" she enquired.

I wasn't quite sure how to answer that, as the instrument panel was wrapped around my chest in a rather intimate embrace and I was having some trouble extricating myself from its clutches. The sun shining through the hole in the roof was pleasant enough though. I looked across at Olly, and wished I hadn't! Exactly where the blood stopped and the upholstery began was not immediately obvious. Some three or four inches of his forehead bore a full-layer gash, seeping copiously a crimson tide, a result of his impacting with the rear vision mirror, itself bent fully out of shape now, the glass but a recent memory. His left knee was wedged securely beneath the dash, while the right was forced back into the seat, the metal lid of the glove compartment having dropped and intruded below the knee, some two inches or so into his leg. Many years before seat belts were made compulsory, this was as good an argument for their installation as any. If there was a positive here, it would have to be that being a front-end collision, there was no leaking fuel and the question of incineration without relevance. Had it been different there would have been no way of freeing him in time. At this juncture the driver of the semi, a dishevelled relic of latin extraction, peered in the passenger's side window, took one look at Olly and collapsed in the roadway himself, muttering an escalating stream of "Mama Mias," complete with anguished hand movements.

"I kill him, I kill him" he sobbed, totally out of it.

Olly was far from dead however and though barely conscious, was moving feebly. The ambulance was there within a few minutes, the nurse meanwhile having performed an exemplary job of stemming the blood flow from his forehead.

They got him out, having to remove the glovebox-lid additionally and whisked him away to hospital.

"He'll be fine," they assured me.

Free myself from the instrument panel by this time, the first of a convoy of vehicles arrived. A second ambulance, the Police, fire truck and the emergency rescue squad. I was doing my bit for the anti-litter campaign by picking up the driver's door, when the traffic cop walked over.

"Did you witness this accident?" he asked.

"Indeed I did," I responded. "Had a really good view actually - I was driving!"

He looked me up and down, peered inside the wreckage where Olly's blood was congealing in several places, glanced at my seat which was bent almost into a "V" and crushed part-way into the rear cabin and muttered,

"You being smart lad?"

"No Officer," I replied, "I *was* driving, we were just on our way to the aquatic centre, when the semi there (I indicated the wreckage down William Street) collected us half-way through the intersection."

He wasn't listening...just staring.

"No-one could get out of that without a scratch - you're probably in deep shock!" he volunteered.

Maybe I was - but I felt just fine. No cuts, bruises....far less shaken even than a James Bond martini. He called his partner over.

"Here mate, have a look at this? This guy was driving - can you believe it?"

They moved over now to the driver of the semi, who was beyond being in shock. Fully unable to walk, the cops had to support him beneath both arms to manoeuvre him to the sidewalk - where his day grew infinitely worse.

Following his distinctly unwise admission that he had been "In a hurry to get to the jeweller down the road and hadn't seen the light," he was booked for "Negligent driving", and "Dangerous Driving occasioning bodily harm."

It was the arrival of the tow-truck that recalled to mind the irony of the moment. Just an hour or so to go, before finalising the paperwork at the car yard and taking home the Jag, the Vauxhall was reduced from an $1800 trade-in to a $100 pile of scrap metal. Insured only for third-party property, it would be months most likely, before anything could be recovered from the other driver. Catching a cab to hospital I waited for an hour or so while they worked on Olly.

Finally admitted to his ward, he looked substantially improved. Cleaned, stitched and in the case of his leg - repaired, he was at least lucid.

"What happened?" he asked.

"A semi-trailer ran over you." I told him, "A big one!"

Peering at me through one eye that was on its way to closing, the other pretty much black already, bandaged hand and right arm in a splint, ahead of God-only knew what body-pains tomorrow, he stared at me.

"How's the car?"

"From the rear seat backwards, it's fine," I said, "Nothing a steam-hammer couldn't fix in a couple of seconds!"

Olly looked at me for a while.

"How come you're not in here with me?...he waved in my direction, "You look like you're not even bloody bruised!"

"I'm suffering Olly, I'm suffering, believe me!" He stared up at me,

"God....you've done the Jag, haven't you?"

"Yep....came within an hour of owning it. Glad I didn't mention anything about it at home. Problem is now, I don't have any car. so we might not be doing too much swimming for a while Ol."

"Swimming?" he replied, "Don't reckon I'll be *walking* for the next month or so...there's thirty-odd stitches in my leg they tell me." He looked up.

"Hey, I've got $600 saved up – it's yours to put towards another car 'till you get his insurance money. I'm not using it, you may as well have it."

Olly was like that, straight-out generous and a true friend in need. I thanked him and moved to shake his hand. He pulled back.

"Just don't *touch* anything!" he mumbled.

Scraping together a couple of hundred dollars of my own the following week, I was back on Parramatta Road, by bus this time, checking out one particular item of interest: 1960 Ford Fairlane 500, US Import. Immaculate. $850. They weren't kidding - cars don't come more immaculate. Cheap, on account of the fact that American "tanks" had never been popular in Australia, it was to me, the ultimate road transport. They took $750 cash. What they *didn't* tell me until later, was that this particular car had previously been a Police highway-pursuit vehicle in Nevada, which accounted for the fact that its "worked" V8 blew everything else off the road, as I soon found out on the way home. Mum strolled out to see it when I pulled into the driveway and ambling around the colossal fins and rear tail-lights said simply "I see!" Within seconds she was back inside, re-emerging with her handbag and front door keys.

"Well, let's go then!" This was right up her alley!

July 20th was kind of a big day when Neil Armstrong and Apollo11 "splashed down" in the Moon's Sea of Tranquility at 4.17. pm. One fifth of the world's population, an estimated 650 million people watched the televised momentous event. Who could have believed that thirty two years later, the actual setting for Kubrick's masterpiece 2001: A Space Odyssey, NASA would still have been unable to effect a manned landing beyond the Moon? In '69 there was talk of planetary colonisation by the new millennium, yet here we are in 2004, still taking infra-red photos of members of our own solar system. About the only speck of current interest being that one of Jupiter's moons - Europa, is now causing a buzz in astronomical circles with the disclosure that it may be covered in ice with flowing water beneath...a notion Arthur C. Clarke expounded decades ago.

Just three weeks after the moon-landing, on August 9th, Charles Manson and his "family" gave the world a new meaning to the word "helter-skelter" when actress Sharon Tate, then the wife of film director Roman Polanski, and four other house-guests, were systematically butchered at Tate's home in Beverly Hills.

Joyce meanwhile was continuing to teach at the Herald, although little more than propped up in a chair for eight hours to conserve energy. For myself, a few complications had set in - I'd met Helen! Having just turned seventeen that week, she had been working as a junior clerk in our office and I had taken her home once or twice, it being pretty much along my own route. From a family with more than their own fair share of troubles, she had four younger siblings - two brothers and two sisters, three of which were either blind or near-blind by virtue of hereditary glaucoma. With her mother too thus afflicted, it was obvious she could use a little help in her life.

My increasing time away from home won me no points with Joyce.

"You're going to see that girl again are you? she would say. Never *Helen*, always "that girl!" It was not wise to get into semantics with her.

"I'll be back as soon as I can," was my invariable reply - and I usually was!

There came the day though that we had all been held up for several hours at the Sydney Eye Hospital where Helen's sister Kerry, had by necessity to undertake a series of tests, ahead of surgery to remove two cataracts. It was late evening when I returned. She was slumped in her chair barely respiring, willing guilt upon me, eyes locked in a "look what you've done to your mother" stare. Basically having to "scrape her up," I was inside St Vincents in record time. By virtue of some cortisone injections and other respiratory wizardy, she was discharged many hours later but with now a permanent new fixture in our home - a steel oxygen cylinder with breathing apparatus! It could not be said with any accuracy that Helen and I were "going out." I simply had now two lives - one at home, while between transporting Joyce to and from work, cooking, washing and every other household chore imaginable, trying to attend to Helen's needs. I'm not sure where my work obligations slotted in there, but they did.

The cost of maintaining the domestic oxygen supply was not inconsequential, and by chance that Spring, I came across an ad for an accounting vacancy at CIG (Commonwealth Industrial Gases), an Australian division of BOC (British Oxygen) for which mum had herself once undertaken some part-time work in the late fifties. Applying with accounting experience, but no formal qualifications, I was staggered to be offered the job. What a position at CIG *did* offer was two highly relevant plusses! Firstly, free oxygen cylinders as a staff member...and down the track, the opportunity to transfer to CANOX (Canadian Oxygen) resident fortuitously in none other but the city of Vancouver! Could this all be coincidence? The one downside? The two evenings at T.A.F.E. studying for the Commerce Certificate.

Shortly before Christmas, the lease on the apartment lapsed and was not offered for renewal. We had therefore to move again - this time to a ground floor flat of slightly smaller, but still huge dimensions, in nearby Bellevue Hill. The Fairlane had passed into history, traded in on a Monaro coupe for twice what I had paid for it. My life was a maelstrom of appointments, social division and late nights, up to my journals in Balance Sheets, Profit and Loss statements, Company Law and Management Ethics, as if in my experience, management *had* any ethics! It came to the point of course that Helen wondered why I couldn't spend more time with her, while mum begged an explanation as to why I should spend *any* time with "a girl obviously not your social equal dear!," not that in her opinion I would ever have found one that was. During all this time she and Helen had never actually met. Then, just two weeks before Christmas that year, I returned home one night to find Helen and Joyce decorating the tree together. Rarely struck dumb in my life, this was as unlikely a scene as Brad Pitt reading the 6.30. News.

Helen looked up - for all intents and purposes, a cat having stumbled across three saucers of warm milk!

"I telephoned earlier, and your mother asked if I would like to come over and help with the decorations."

I heard the words, I saw the evidence...yet still I could not believe it. Did this indicate a change of heart or was it simply an astute fact-finding mission? Whatever, my arrival brought about a near schizophrenic change in attitude and as I drove Helen home just half an hour later, she said to me, "I just don't understand it - she was so nice to me this afternoon, showing me photo albums and telling me about her life. She made me cups of tea and treated me like a daughter....it all changed the moment you came home!"

They were never to meet again and in hindsight now I wonder if Joyce ever regretted her chosen course of action. Was it a case of "competition" or simply a fear of being left alone, as her illness entered new and unchartered waters?

Thus the battle lines were re-drawn, both camps on standby....and me in no-man's land between them. An unresolvable conflict that was taking no prisoners yet neither side could ever claim victory. For a while, everyone just co-existed.

During the early part of 1970 mum and I would take long drives in the Monaro. Melbourne, Brisbane, The Gold Coast, even Adelaide were ticked off the "done that" list. Helen and I took up ten-pin bowling and as part of the Rushcutter's Bay "Eagles," took on and defeated every team in the comp, eventually running out trophy winners. With averages up into the 190-200's we well and truly carved out our ten minutes of fame that year. I don't think mum ever once asked for a progress report or even made reference to the game.

The Monaro, plagued with on-going mechanical problems and remarkably, the only new car I have ever owned, was eventually retired and replaced by an EJ Holden - six years older yet ultimately reliable and never once requiring attention - a burial perhaps, but never mechanical work.

The Beatles broke up that autumn. The Carpenters were coming on strong, but it was another hot year for Creedence Clearwater Revival, with *Bad Moon Rising, Green River* and *Down On The Corner*. Swamp magic!

Late July and as big a deal as the opening of the 2.3 mile Aswan Dam in Egypt was, I faced one that was bigger! Helen dropped the news that she was six weeks pregnant. There probably *could* be worse circumstances in which to start a family but for the moment, they escaped me. There being less than no purpose in relaying the news to mum, it probably achieving no more than to confirm anyway her existing expectations, I remained silent on the issue for now.

Up for my first-year exams, I somehow pulled second in the State, certainly in defiance of all attending circumstances. My employers then vented their obvious appreciation with an inter-departmental promotion and pay-rise. Mum attended the presentation presupposing that Helen then wouldn't That's what it was all about - scoring points!

As the emphysema extended its stranglehold, she was able to do less and less and eventually, a second oxygen cylinder was required to be installed behind her desk in the classroom at the Sydney Morning Herald offices. I often wondered how she held out those eight hours. Her physical deterioration also brought about irrational fears of being rejected and she became a mistress of manipulation, able to bring-on asthmatic attacks whenever I was home later than expected. How Helen managed to hold-up throughout this period, given the physical and emotional changes being wrought upon *her* by the pregnancy is also a good question. The monthly check-ups at St Vincents were by now a mere farce.

"How are you Mrs Bailey?"

"Fine Doctor," The specialist would smile at her.

"*Not* according to our test-readings Mrs Bailey, and your current chest X-Rays would suggest you have been dead for some years."

He would then invite her to exhale into a machine that measured lung capacity. Barely causing the needle to register movement, he would smile again at her.

"That's good Mrs Bailey. Just keep using your oxygen mask and undertake as little exertion as possible. We'll see you next month."

I knew that Vancouver was all but "beyond the infinite" now, the event horizon that we could never cross together, at least in this lifetime. She still made the odd reference to it, I suspect in a last desperate bid to rid herself of Helen's influence.

On October 4th 1970 Janis Joplin sang *Bobby McGhee* for the last time when she died from a drug overdose in Hollywood. Less than a fortnight later, Australia was to experience its worst-ever industrial accident that claimed the lives of forty-four people when Melbourne's Westgate Bridge collapsed mid-construction on October 16.

Later that month, as Helen was getting visibly larger, the contents of our garage got dramatically smaller - someone having relieved us of the old EJ. First I knew of it was when the Police turned up shortly after dawn one Tuesday morning to arrest me for "leaving the scene of an accident" just off Broadway some two hours earlier.

"Where is your car Mr Bailey?" inquired one uniformed officer.

"Last time I saw it, which was around midnight," I replied half awake, "It was downstairs in our garage."

"Perhaps you could show us?" put in his companion.

All that was there as it transpired, was a small pile of broken glass, the remnants, it would seem, of the driver's side quarter-window. This at least convinced my two six-foot plus cohorts that I was not the quarry they were seeking. Witnesses that morning had taken the EJ's number after a pedestrian was knocked down on a crossing in the city.

This of course left me without a car.....but not for long. The next day, shortly before lunch I received a call from the Police Station at Burwood in the south west, telling me to come and remove my car as it was blocking traffic. Having no knowledge that it was even stolen, which said much for their own internal systems, they were more concerned with what sounded like a case of illegal parking. With the street address, I caught a cab there within half an hour. Emerging from the taxi I stared for fully ten minutes at what used to be my car. I then walked to the Police Station. I struck the jackpot immediately.

"Noel Bailey, someone here called and asked me to remove my car?"

"Yes, I did," replied the officer on the front desk. "You got a problem?"

"Why did you not mention that the front end was smashed in, the front tyre missing, boot wrapped around a tree and both rear tyres flat." I asked, "Not to mention the seats slashed, dashboard with holes punched in it and all the wiring pulled out? You knew it couldn't be driven!"

He was a smart bastard.

"Not my problem mate!" he grinned.

"It is *now*," I grinned, "This car was reported stolen this morning – think you'll find it's under Police jurisdiction. Give me a call when you've towed it to the impound!" I turned and walked.

"*Hey,*" he called out.

"And while you're at it," I added from the doorway, "Give the desk sergeant a call at Double Bay, I'm sure he'll be delighted you've "found" it."

I didn't often walk out of a Police Station a winner!

In the next few days, the car was towed from the Police impound where it was recorded, photographed and fingerprinted, to my own smash-repairer. Just *how* they were going to fix this I was curious, but it was the Insurer's decision and they didn't want to write it off. In the meantime, I needed a car and after a couple of hours doing the rounds of Parramatta Road once again, came across a magnificent old 1961 Humber Super Snipe - gun-metal grey, solid steel, leather and walnut interior. The absolute *last* choice of car-seekers across the country, being British, ponderous, heavy on gas, and dated, in that order. It was insanely priced at $420. I sank into the plush driver's seat and motored my way home in luxurious elegance...with $20 left over! The Humber proved a pillar of stability and even after the EJ was returned weeks later, immaculately rebuilt, we held on to it and later parted with the Holden instead.

Between Helen's check-ups, Mum's check-ins and escalating work from night-school with the addition of new subjects, Taxation Law, Office Management and Computer Processing, I was learning to sleep standing-up. Christmas came, but all I remember is having the turkey stolen from the back seat of the car while I was paying for fuel in the service station, last thing on Christmas Eve. I hope it went to someone who really needed it. As for us, we celebrated with a number fifteen chicken instead. I simply made some extra seasoning and used smaller plates.

"*Hot town, summer in the city, back of my neck getting burnt and gritty.*" These lyrics by The Lovin' Spoonful, so typify life in Sydney during January and February. '71 was no exception, with sun-screen and cold beer competing for sales honours. What was unusual was Rolls Royce declaring themselves bankrupt on Feb 4th. For many, a national tragedy signifying the ignominious yet definitive end of the British Empire.

Six days later, Los Angeles was rocked by its biggest earthquake for thirty-eight years. Whilst not the *big-one*, fifty-one people died, a thousand injured and the damage bill topped a billion dollars.

Early March and Helen was "on standby." Fully determined to remain aloof from current proceedings, my telling mum on March 4th that, "I'm taking Helen in to King George hospital now to have your grand-daughter," was met by stony indifference. Given that she was even unaware of the pregnancy until this point, it was some performance.

"Any idea when you'll be back?" was all she said.

It didn't deserve an answer.

Ghinda was born the following afternoon and if I thought my time-utilisation chart was pretty full at this point, I had no idea what was to come. Named of course to commemorate a childhood lifetime's bond of affection with my north London cousin, the word itself derives from a tiny African village substantially bombed during a military offensive during the last war. More than likely, less than half a dozen people carry the name worldwide now.

Such was Joyce's strength of purpose, however misguided one may judge it to have been, she made on my return, no reference to the event. Whilst predictably less than concerned as to Helen's condition, no information was sought as to the baby's health, its size or even current location. For my part, no comment was offered. In order that I might reasonably commute between the two camps, I found Helen a small garden flat at Edgecliff, the next suburb along New South Head Road and marginally less than eight minutes away, but remaining still, a crippling additional expense that in other circumstances would not have been necessary.

Those early months of fatherhood were conducted in something less than ideal conditions. Whilst as proud and inspired as most any new parent, having then to basically dovetail two dissimilar lifestyles, was not without great difficulty. Helen naturally wanting me to spend more time with both herself and my daughter was unable to repel a growing resentment towards my often early departures, while mum was ever ready to bring on an acute respiratory attack in the event of perceived neglect on my part. Taking into account increasing responsibilities at work as well as a heavy study load, I was ageing rapidly!

April 15th and Patton deservedly took out Best Picture and Best Actor for George C. Scott at the Academy Awards. Ten days later - April 25th, saw the establishment by the West Pakistan Government of a new territory, named Bangladesh, home now to thousands of refugees fleeing the violence and political unrest of the Eastern state.

As much for my own sanity as anything else, mum and I planned a weekend in Tasmania offered under an incentive-driven package deal. Needing only to drive to Melbourne, the offer included the car ferry to and from Hobart - a lengthy overnight trip (then) of sixteen hours plus, Bass Strait being fourteen or so times the width of the English Channel. Thus mid May we headed off for Melbourne, which in those days pre-freeway status, was a thirteen hour ordeal, less than 30% of it even dual carriageway. From the Victorian border onwards, mum's breathing seriously deteriorated, having virtually exhausted the contents of one of the oxygen cylinders. Still adamant she could make it, we struck out for Melbourne's CBD arriving close to eleven p.m. Pulling into the hotel car-park I looked across at her. She was in an agony of despair and with tears brimming, she said, "I'm so sorry Noel, I just can't breathe. We have to go back."

Paying the Hotel the courtesy of cancelling our reservation, we returned to the Hume Highway and headed for the NSW border. As the Humber sped through the early morning, the only accompaniment was her dreadful wheezing, the oxygen mask supplying it seemed, her only tenuous life-line. Well into the second cylinder now, the gauge's needle with little consideration for its mistress, was receding with undue haste. Some ninety kilometres from the border still and by necessity, driving at almost double the speed limit, we had reached the outskirts of a forgotten township when a siren announced the arrival of a distinctly unwanted road-user.

"Your licence and registration please sir?"

Clear now of his bike, the cop was wandering around the car. I had the impression he had never seen a Humber before. "Are you aware you were driving at excessive speed?" he added, almost as an afterthought.

"Er, yes officer," I replied, "This *is* somewhat of an emergency."

"Mind telling me *why* sir?" he asked.

"My *mother* officer - you might note she's not all that great. I was actually on my way back to the hospital in Sydney." He bent down and peered across at her through the driver's-side window. He saw the silhouetted form slumped in the front seat gasping, the oxygen cylinders in the rear.

"Jesus Christ!" he muttered.

With that, he leaped back on his bike and motioned me to follow. With his siren blaring, we had a Police escort right the way to the NSW border. I don't know what speed we averaged, but it was certainly straining the boundaries of credibility.

"Good luck son," he said at the border. "Hope your mother is OK - don't worry about the Police, we will advise NSW headquarters of the situation and if they have any spare highway patrol bikes I'm sure they'll be happy to escort you."

I thanked him and floored it. One thing about those cars - they may be sluggish brutes at take-off, but once stoked, they are still cruising at a hundred and fifty. Driving all night, we came across barely another car, let alone a cop. All the while that needle was edging towards the thin-red-line and mum's condition was now critical. Still a hundred and fifty kilometres shy of the Sydney metropolitan area, I was struck with a graphic realisation. Here we were, exactly one quarter of a century on, speeding through the night once more in a Humber Super Snipe of all cars, with another medical emergency. In 1945 it was to *give* life, this time to save it! Could this all be mere coincidence? In 1945 however it paid off, I offered up a silent prayer that the odds were still with us.

As I swung into the emergency bay at St Vincents hospital, mum was now barely conscious. They wheeled her into a private ward and every chest specialist on duty was attending to her within minutes. They sent me home. As I walked back out to the carpark, it hit me...almost twenty-six hours driving with no break. How I got home I don't know but I slept for thirteen hours straight. That evening I returned to the hospital to find her improved, but of deathly pallor and weakened to a pitiful extent. Her doctor took me aside.

"Your mother is resilient to the point of disbelief." he said, "Theoretically, she shouldn't have been able to make it through the night - her remaining lung is, as I presume you know, with but the slightest of functionality left. How she has managed the last twelve months or so defies medical understanding."

This of course was not news to me. He was continuing.

"Whether or not she can recover sufficiently to be discharged I couldn't say."

"Give her three or four days," I said. He smiled and walked off. As it turned out, it was not until the fifth morning that she was able to leave and this time saw her enter a new phase of respiratory hardship. Unable now to manage even the least exertion without discomfort, her mobility around the house was noticeably restricted. The oxygen cylinder was her constant companion now and my ability to leave her alone at home severely restricted. Whilst putting in as much time as circumstance permitted at Edgecliff with Helen and Ghinda, it wasn't enough and for the first time in my life, I regretted probably selfishly, having been an only child.

It was a period of soft rock. David Cassidy and The Partridge Family were huge, John Denver was pleading *Take me Home Country Roads*, Paul McCartney and Wings were strutting their top-selling tripe with *Uncle Albert/Admiral Halsey*. Middle of the Road's *Chirpy Chirpy Cheep Cheep* was everywhere and the greatest of them all, Don Mclean's *American Pie* hit the deserved number one spot. An anthem for the 70's and a classic that will never fade from memory! Other enduring greats around this time were *Hot Love* from T-Rex, Rod Stewart's *Maggie May* and *Brown Sugar* from The Rolling Stones.

Heading into spring and forty-two people died in the Attica prison uprising in New York on September 9th. Two days later former Communist head Nikita Krushchev died in Moscow. Perhaps the most bizarre news at the time was the re-opening of old London Bridge at Lake Havasu - a resort in the middle of the Arizona desert. Shipped across from London, stone by numbered stone, the bridge represented for oil millionaire Robert P McCulloch, a ten million dollar tourist investment. To celebrate the bridge's "re-opening," a banquet for eight hundred including the then Lord Mayor of London, complete with ancient pageantry, duplicated that held for William IV at the bridge's inauguration.

How mum continued to work was a source of mystification. Needing to not only drop her off at the Herald building, but to see her now to her desk - she refused to avail herself of the oxygen cylinder on standby, claiming it was unsightly and inappropriate. I put forward the view that the cadets would find a sudden corpse in their midst, considerably more unsightly and even *less* appropriate!

Through it all there was still no complaint and many were the cadets who remained unaware of the extent of her illness. Her skills with the most basic of make-up were awesome and always dressed in cheery though subtle colours, her demeanour remained one of well-being. In the evenings I would pick her up, cylinder at the ready in the rear seat and she would allow the previous eight hours respiratory torture to run its course, freed at last from her iron will power.

Towards Helen there was to be no relaxing of the strictures she had placed on herself. Not once did she ask about Ghinda. To do so now, would in her mind have been to capitulate and this could simply never be. An option quite without precedence in her view.

That she still yearned to move-on was pointedly evidenced. On one occasion I found her sealing up a letter she had addressed to a relative in

Canada. It wasn't up for discussion evidently and so no reference was made to it. She also kept in close contact with Grandad who I knew would have preferred to see her back in England. Shortly before Christmas that year, she said to me one evening, quite without warning,

"Noel, promise me you'll finish what we started?" Not entirely sure what she was talking about, I agreed that I would. Then she added.

"It doesn't matter where or when you die, simply what you've achieved!"...she looked at me for a moment then carried on reading. I wasn't sure whether her bloodsteam was marginally overstocked with oxygen or that perhaps she was just feeling acutely insightful. Whatever, I simply acknowledged the statement.

Probably another case of being in the wrong place at the wrong time, but the Humber early that summer lost its claim to "magnificence" when a young learner drove directly through a stop sign, to the unutterable horror of her instructor, and collided with my offside passenger door. Unceremoniously dented by the impact, the driving-school's Ford Escort was close to a write-off, as was her chance of retaining that teacher for another lesson. The damage to the Humber was superficial rather than serious and although the school admitted liability and paid promptly, it was time for a change.

About the only thing less popular than British cars in Australia were American missiles. Never having caught on here, it has always been possible to pick up a top example of US automotive creativity for thousands less than your typical Holden or Falcon. Probably if the locals realised that Falcons were of American origin too, sales for *these* would dry up also! In any event, out poking around car yards one weekend, we happened upon a 1965 Pontiac Parisienne, maroon in color with champagne leather upholstery. It was just $1,450 and totally unmarked inside and out.

"This is more like it dear." said Joyce and she had loved the Humber.

Ghinda was almost nine months old now and we had all settled into a totally bizarre life-style of my coming and going, it being the latter which caused the major disharmony understandably. Problems were continuing to compound themselves within Helen's family as her two sisters struggled now with increasing levels of blindness and the difficulties associated with such a cruel handicap. Her youngest brother David whilst similarly afflicted and having partial sightedness then could only look forward to a limited time-span of any quality of vision before the glaucoma lowered the boom-gates forever. It was an experience brought home to me just how much we all take things for granted, sight being one of them.

Following a letter from Auntie Lucy in Doncaster that Reg had died in Pateley, following a lengthy illness, mum was devastated not only by his death but by the news that the farm had apparently been bequeathed at the last moment to his housekeeper who had tended his needs, as his ability to look after himself waned during those final months. Having no materialistic interest in the property, it was rather the lifelong memories of the farm that she found so hard being cut from what had been promised as her ultimate inheritance. She never raised the issue again but the hurt and disappointment were undisguisable.

Mid October and another automotive interlude of the rarely experienced kind.

A normal Saturday morning in seeming respects. Having just turned out of our apartment block, I was navigating the Parisienne steadily along Fairfax Road for some essential shopping in Double Bay. Turning right into Bellevue Road, as I had done many hundreds of times previously, I had three-quarters completed the turn when something, the weight of a Sherman tank to judge by the impact, having failed to give way to its right, struck and partially entered, the rear passenger door.

The Pontiac performed multiple spins that would have pulled a "nine" or "ten" with the judges at any Winter Olympics and came to rest half way up the opposite sidewalk, amazingly avoiding other parked cars, not to mention *people*. Pushed forward in my seat, the lower part of the dash had opened up a deep gash in my leg...ruined my pants. Barely out of the car, two hulking suits with dark shades approached. I looked across at the other vehicle. The Caddy had seen better days, at least from the front-end's viewpoint. Definitely the winner in the encounter though, the Pontiac was completely staved in from the boot to halfway across the nearside front door. I looked closer at the limo. Commonwealth plates, Government flags on either side of the hood and fully blacked-out glass. Of all vehicles, the Australian Prime Minister's car! Whether or not Billy McMahon was aboard I never found out, but now one of the two "agents" was addressing me.

"It will all be taken care of sir, just leave it to us."

I mentioned that by law, I was required to call the Police, simply to comply with legal and Insurance procedures.

"There will be *no* Police report," he replied and looking at him, I was inclined to agree. "As I said," he continued, "It will be taken care of, trust me!"

At his request, I gave him the name and address of my preferred body-shop and at that juncture, an ambulance turned up, called presumably by a concerned onlooker. Although the leg was bleeding profusely, I was far from needing an ambulance but at the coercion of my two companions who assured me it would be better to "be on the safe side and have it checked," I hopped in the back. The last I saw of the Pontiac was of it being pushed off the sidewalk by the two G-men. Pondering just how and why such complexities kept criss-crossing my life and barely having travelled a kilometre, I heard the ambulance sounding its horn wildly, followed by severe braking and then the mother of all collisions. I was thrown to the floor. Exiting from the rear door, outside was bedlam, the ambulance and another vehicle, a van of some sort, were tangled head-on. Steam was rising as were tempers. The ambulance driver was locked in heated dispute with the other driver, amazingly both still mobile and yet both vehicles consummate scrap.

I'd really had enough, and limping noticeably, set off for home.

True to their word, the Pontiac was fixed within ten days. As the repairer said when I picked it up.

"What kind of weird Insurance company do you have mate?....paid me a bank-cheque up front, with a little extra?"

Christmas came and went. At least no-one stole the turkey this year. Mum tried her best to dredge up some seasonal spirit, but barely able to do more than navigate a path between the lounge and her bedroom, left little options for merriment. Thelma came over for Christmas dinner and within the limitations her illness allowed, mum was her old self. Leaving them together I spent the remainder of the afternoon with Helen, it being obviously Ghinda's first Christmas. The little flat was hung with decorations, bells and sprigs of holly we didn't need at home and a small but serviceable little tree sat in a corner, weighed down by tinsel, candy canes, lights and glass ornaments. Beneath, lay Ghinda and Helen's presents, as proud and as enticing as any in the land.

1972 started sadly with the death on January 1st of Maurice Chevalier who died in his beloved Paris at age 83. He had performed on stage up until only a few years previously. The ninth child of a house painter, he was headlining the Folies Bergere at 21 and with trademark songs such as "Sank 'eavens for leetle girls, for leetle girls get bigger every day," he won a Continent's heart.

Scorching hot weather in mid January was the last thing we needed and I was probably CIG's most common visitor to the loading docks that month obtaining re-filled oxygen cylinders. Had they not been free to staff members, we would have been bankrupted. As it was, the emphysema was spreading in what had to be its final quest for supremacy, with accelerated haste and mum's quality of life now reached a chronically abysmal stage. Check-ups at the Hospital were fortnightly and totally without any purpose - even her own doctor was visibly moved by her condition and could offer no constructive words of comfort or support. Invariably he would have his head bowed when I wheeled her back to the car. For her part, there was still no murmur of discontent or any hint of surrender in the face of insurmountable odds - if this thing wanted to take her out, it was going to have to fight right to the last man standing and even then it would need a decent gauge shotgun and probably several rounds of ammunition.

Month after month she fought for life. Propped up at work for eight, six, four hours....whatever she could. I would get her home, virtually carry her in, since by now she would have weighed no more than 40-45 kilos. Unable eventually to even bathe herself or walk to her bedroom unaided - I would lie awake night after night, week after week, listening to that agonised wheezing. I can still hear the hiss of that oxygen cylinder - as clear to me today as it was thirty-three years ago. Was it I often wonder, a friend or foe? - keeping her alive certainly, but for what - one more round of a fight she was always going to lose, even by a tko?

Still, she had me take her to work, if only for an hour or so, and with of course her faithful oxygen cylinder in tow, until finally on Monday 15th May, probably down to that very last functional lung-capillary, I got the call to come and take her to Hospital.

Placed immediately on an external breathing device, there was to be no more miraculous recovery. Already puffy in the face from copious amounts of cortisone, there was nothing anyone could do. Her doctor standing by, was visibly shaken. "Never in my thirty five years of medicine have I ever seen such determination to live," he said to me. "I treated so many young soldiers during the war who died from their wounds - how many I wonder could have lived had they one quarter of your mother's strength of will?"

It was now a matter of time, and leaving her heavily sedated, I returned home. When no call came the next morning I drove back to St Vincents where they admitted me to her ward. Several of the cadets had sent flowers which were set out around the little room - it reminded me for a moment of *Brookside's* finest hour, their scents a gentle tribute to the many young lives her existence had touched in some way. I looked at the wreckage on the bed, for such it was. A broken Stradivarius, an unfinished symphony, a cracked Ming vase. Much like Humpty Dumpty, nothing could put this back together. As I looked at her pained expression, shrivelled chest rising and falling to the "thwack, thwack" of the respirator, wrists the size of a young child and dreadful sunken cheeks, she opened her eyes....and with an effort which tore at my very soul, tried to smile. Unable to speak, she simply wanted me to hold her hand, which I did for some two or three minutes before she lost consciousness again. I wanted so much to take her home then, not to Bellevue Hill but *home,* back to *Brookside.* Back to her old room, where I could put her to bed and go outside to play once more. Dad would be home soon and he would know what to do. I needed him now so desperately!

The specialists returned and consulted charts, notes, each other - nothing that was possibly going to do Joyce any good. An injection was administered.

"You are aware" said one, "that your mother is in the final stages of the disease?" I nodded.

"We have given her further sedation. It might be best if you go home now and we will call you when it is time."

"How clinically detached!" I thought to myself. I wonder how *they* will be viewing things themselves when it is "their" time? I bent over and kissed her cheek then drove home.

The call came at 2.05 am. the next morning. At the nurses' desk they told me that she was slipping away quite peacefully as she was fully sedated now. I asked if I could go in and see her.

"Certainly," said the nurse, "But she will of course not know you're there. Besides the sedation, she has slipped into a deep coma - it will not be long - I'm sorry!"

I entered the room.

If possible, she looked worse. Eyes now sunken themselves, the lids trembling, perhaps in a REM stage. I hoped she was dreaming of Christmases long ago, her childhood at 40 Munden Grove, perhaps her school trip to Belgium in 1937. Maybe she was walking again over the Yorkshire Moors with Louisa, or clinging on to the back of Reg's jacket as the motorcycle sped its way to Pateley Bridge. Maybe nothing more than simply waiting for me to come home from school. I wondered if dad was on his way now to collect her? He had had such a long wait!

I sat in the chair beside her and took her hand. I *wanted* her to die, to rid herself of this torment - there was nothing more to prove. I told her I loved her so much and as God is my witness, I felt pressure on my hand. I stared at her. No movement, eyes quite closed.

"You *know* I'm here don't you?" I said. This time the squeeze was unmistakable.

I leant over her and whispered, "I'm so sorry for all the problems we've had....." I was going to say over Helen and Ghinda, but again, downward pressure. She *knew*...and was just making it right. Her way!"

"Are you going to look in on me from time to time?" I asked. A strong squeeze this time! and with that, she didn't die - she just *left*.

Then for a fraction of a second I saw a miraculous change occur. Gone were the sunken eyes, shrivelled skin, disease-ravaged frame and in their place a Joyce I'd never seen. One in her late teens, full of life and vigour. I think that was when dad must have arrived.

She was only forty nine.

CHAPTER EIGHT

THE LONG AND WINDING ROAD

As I walked from the ward, a small group of specialists and nurses were clustered behind the night desk. They looked-up as I approached, the conversation tapering off as if directed to, by an off-set production assistant.

"You all have a lot to learn about comas," I volunteered in passing, leaving them to ponder this seemingly cryptic comment.

Ringing Grandad was as difficult a phone call as I've ever had to make, but I sensed in his grief, an acceptance that at least there would be no more suffering and he *had* been fully aware of his daughter's condition.

Joyce's funeral ceremony, held in the peaceful grounds of Sydney's Northern Suburbs Crematorium was a standing-room only affair. I mentioned in the last chapter the many young lives she must have touched - I hadn't realised just *how* many! Cadets past and present, journalists, Chiefs of Staff, Editors and Editorial Executives, right the way up to Warwick Fairfax himself, milled about in solemn but strangely, not depressing mood. Everyone, including Australian relatives we didn't even know we had, were there to celebrate her *existence*, not her death! Joyce was as much in control here as she had been in life. At the cremation's conclusion, I took her ashes home with me as she had never expressed any particular wish in that direction and I needed time to consolidate my thoughts on the possibilities.

I was able of course to offer Helen now a more suitable place to live and we moved her few possessions out of the Edgecliff flat. That mum had never seen or held her grand-daughter who was now fifteen months old, remained for me a rather sad realisation, though it had been a decision she alone had the right to make.

I found myself at the crossroads. Able to put in normal working hours at CIG that first week following the funeral, I made enquiries and determined that a transfer to CANOX in Vancouver was a real possibility. Was I after all supposed to make this trip without Joyce? Helen and I talked about it and it would mean leaving her mother and family who were dependent on us in many ways. That Friday, the decision was taken from me when the Herald rang and asked if I would take over mum's job. Given my three years' investment at CIG, not to mention being in my last year now at T.A.F.E. I thanked them, but declined their lucrative offer. Less than half an hour later they called back, with a salary offer that was just this side of insane. Well over double my current wages and with a guaranteed six monthly review which would elevate the position to levels unreachable, in the short term at least, elsewhere. I told them they had a deal and that I would start Monday week.

So much for planning!

With the expectation of being at last able to cement some sort of a future, (Vancouver wasn't canned by any means, merely shelved temporarily) I took the Pontiac down to the local BP service station the next morning for a long overdue "grease and tune-up." I felt this was the least I could do following its overly harsh treatment at the hands of the Prime Ministerial chauffeur recently. After lunch, as I walked back along Bellevue Road, I noticed some frenetic activity in the garage. Hopefully the car was ready.

I rounded the corner and stared......at hell on earth! The Parisienne, at a list of forty-five degrees, was parked astride an E-Type Jaguar and the remains of someone's beloved Beamer. Driven clean through the rear wall, the car was demolished from the front fender to the windshield, its tyre-marks clearly outlined on the crushed bonnet of the Jag. Perched now with its rear wheel on the E-Type's roof, dust was still eddying about, in places floating to the ground. Walking closer I could see the garage's owner on his knees by the bowser, hands to his head in despair obviously. Looking up, he saw me. "We'll fix, we'll fix, you not worry" he muttered in broken Mediterrano-English, waving his arms about in a flurry of continental distress.

I asked him what happened. He explained that his service manager had obviously underestimated the power of the Pontiac and had panicked, driving it into the lube-bay. The collision with the rear brick wall had been such that he had broken one leg, fractured the other and had been taken to hospital. I told him I had an urgent appointment and needed a car *now*. He pointed to a rather splendid looking Holden Torana SLR 5000 show-piece parked nearby.

"My wife's car," he said, "She just been totally re-built, it's yours until we fix the big Parisienne. You like?"

I liked! Thanking him, I climbed in and headed back to the apartment. Not two hundred metres up the road, I pulled up at a crossing whereupon a four-wheel drive piled straight in the back of me, telescoping the Torana up to the rear seat, a total write-off. Walking back to the garage, the proprietor was still slumped to the ground seeking inspiration from somewhere.

"Do you have anything else?" I asked nonchalantly, brushing pieces of safety glass off my shoulders. I had never before actually seen someone have a full-on break down - it was quite interesting.

Having to hand-in my official resignation at CIG, I suppose I had been half-hoping they might make a counter-offer, or at least some inducement to retain my services. How misguided can you be?"

"It's your decision," said my boss, not even looking up from his tea and biscuits, "I'll have the pay-office send out your cheque." He swept a few crumbs into his trash can, indicating that there was nothing further to discuss. Not even a "Good luck," or "Thanks for the memories." Parting was such sweet sorrow.

I stared up at the Herald Building. The sun was shining directly on to the windows of the cadet training room high up on the very corner of the building. I entered the old and battered Wattle Street lift. Looking around the room, one oxygen cylinder was still pushed up against the rear wall. Comforting in some ways - sad in others. All Joyce's registers, text books, reading materials, old exam papers and monthly reports to Heads of Department had their precise spot. Whether in cupboards, filing cabinets or simply stacked on her desk, nothing was out of place or where it shouldn't be. Even the chairs were set out neatly, equidistant around the two huge tables which at a pinch could seat twenty apiece. This was going to be a hard act to follow. I picked up a piece of chalk and commenced a doodle on the left hand side of the great black-board. I could almost hear her beside me, "I don't *think* so dear!"

On my side of course was that I knew every cadet, having filled-in for mum an increasing number of times over the past year or so. An hour before the first of the Herald cadets were due in for their lessons, I decided to have a late breakfast in the enormous work-canteen. Up in the seventh floor "hangar" which due to its size it had been nicknamed, one could order most any entree, grill or roast that might take your fancy.

Providing as much a social environment as an instructive one, the cadets would unburden their weary young souls in the "Shorthand" room, a place where time-out offered an opportunity to seek advice about their current assignment, expostulate against their own Chief-of-Staff's perceived heartlessness, or an editor's rejection of their first story. It was a safe-house, a crying-room. The *Masada* of the 5th floor!

This wasn't to say they didn't have a strict schedule to keep up with me either. Without an achieved minimum speed of one hundred words a minute, no cadet could be graded - an edict of the AJA (Australian

Journalists' Association). Some handled the theory fine, writing copper-plate symbols yet suffering a melt-down when brain and hand became unwilling partners. Others, massacring the rules of Pitman's shorthand and scribbling the most illegible of tripe, were still able to read the piece back by virtue of their near-photographic memories. Then there was the occasional talent that could write so fast anyway, they barely needed shorthand. I grew to love their different idiosynchrasies. The shy new cadets barely out of school, ultimately polite and who would sit nervously chewing a nail or playing with a lock of hair rather than asking for help during an exercise. The non-thinkers, who while reading aloud attempting to transcribe from shorthand to English, would interpret "Towards the end of Spring" as "Trust the night of supper" .and wonder then why I looked at them disparagingly. The timid, the aggressive, the woeful, the impressive. Your normal cross-section of working humanity.

Having to liaise closely with the Editorial Training Executive in terms of assessing an applicant's suitability for a cadetship, we were usually expected to select annually a final sixteen to twenty individuals from a field of some two hundred interviewees, themselves culled from six to eight hundred applications! Within a few weeks one would invariably wonder, surveying the new talent, what mistakes might now be showing themselves to have been made.

Life for now, was markedly easier, for the first time in years my being able to go home and stay home. The Pontiac was finally re-built, having waited many weeks for a replacement hood from California, we having acquired in the meantime a cheap but somewhat rare Vauxhall VX/490 sports to keep us mobile in the interim. An incident not six weeks following the funeral remains prominent in my mind. One friday night late June, an abrupt knock at the front door disturbed my contemplation of the 6.30. news. Answering it, I was confronted by a couple of shambling hulks not fully clued-up as to social niceties.

"Is this the correct address for Mrs Joyce Bailey?" muttered moron number one.

"It *was*," I replied. "Why, what's the problem?"

"We'd prefer to speak with Mrs Bailey thanks." said moron number 2.

"Well, I'm afraid that's not possible," I replied.

"Do you have her forwarding address?" persisted his companion.

"*No-one* has it." I told him, "What's this about? - I'm her son."

"Your mother owes DJ's (a major Sydney department store) over two hundred dollars mate and we're here to collect it - *now!*"

"Then you're in for a long wait - *mate*," I replied.

"Listen here son," said the uglier of the two, "We're not leaving here until we see Mrs Bailey, now do yourself a favour and go get her for me."

It left me no choice.

"You're right," I said, "just hold on a minute."

Fetching her ashes out of the wardrobe I could sense Joyce's appreciation of the moment. Reaching the front door, I thrust the box into his hands.

What's this?" he asked.

It's Mrs Bailey," I said, "Don't be too harsh with her!"

He read the label. "Jesus Christ!" he muttered, "Oh Jesus," He thrust the container back into my hands and the two hightailed it out into the night. I never heard from them again.

1972 saw a booming economy in Australia, in Sydney's property market especially. Home values were soaring month by month. Seeking to get in on the action, and finding money being literally pressed on the buying public by Mortgage lenders getting richer by the day, it appeared that having less than nothing as a deposit, no hindrance whatsoever. What did prove to be tricky, was finding a house at all. Virtual panic-buying saw houses being snapped up within hours of being listed. Thus the day we came upon a most appealing little timber cottage in the far northern suburb of Eastwood, the accompanying property salesman laid it on the line.

"If you like it," he said, "take it - it won't be there by the time we get back to the office."

We signed up then and there, paid a couple of hundred dollars as holding deposit and returned to the Real Estate office, where as he correctly prophesied, two couples were waiting, cheque-books in hand ready to submit offers on the house. I recalled dad's words... "Always look for the cheapest house in the best street!" rather than vice versa. At just $19,250, 22 Gwendale Crescent was "pretty" rather than "vibrant" with the most unusual of rear gardens. Built on the edge of a very old quarry, a dozen steps at the rear of the upper level, descended to a totally secluded grassed area below, which itself backed on to a small land-locked forest beyond the property border. Natural rock, virtual caves in places, jutted from the steep facing, a landscaping feature impossible to duplicate. Though a reasonable sized three bedroom house with a gigantic lounge-room, the apartment at Bellevue Hill was vastly bigger and by the time we had moved in less than half our possessions, the little house was looking seriously smaller. Amazing what you can cram when circumstances dictate though, and eventually we were installed! *"It's My Party"* may have been the last record I played in *Brookside*, but Carly

Simon's *"You're So Vain"* (allegedly dedicated to Warren Beatty for those who may not know it) was the first to reverberate around Eastwood. It was a happy if not carefree period of playing young families. Ross and Helen next door, who moved-in the same day as us, were our own age and about to start the game.

We lived in each other's kitchens, dens, barbecue areas and garages. I had the jacks, he had the tools! Ross and I kicked off many days with a 6.am. swim at nearby Ryde Pools, while the two Helens had occasional girls' nights out during which time Ross and I would quaff more than a few liquid ambers together while watching cricket, footy, whatever. Dinner parties, card and games nights, late late movies, early early mornings, bowling evenings...we did it all. Gwendale had never seen such frenetic entertaining. Some of the older and longer-established residents openly frowned upon the joie-de-vivre being exhibited at the further end of the little cul-de-sac and took to crossing to the opposite footpath when out for their nightly constitutionals. As our respective cranked-up sound-systems belted out *Dead Skunk In the Middle of the Road, Long Cool Woman in a Black Dress, Crocodile Rock, Nights In White Satin* and the best of Neil Diamond during those hot August nights, our sliding popularity plumbed new depths of disapproval.

August 22nd saw the opening ceremony of the 20th Olympiad at Munich which was to witness the highs and lows of human behaviour...seven gold medals to US swimmer Mark Spitz and the massacre of seven Israeli athletes at the hands of Arab extremists. The following week, two White House aides - Howard Hunt and Gordon Liddy, were indicted in Washington on charges connected with the break-in at the Democratic Party Headquarters at the Watergate Hotel complex.

"Twenty-Two" may have been our house number, but in Northern America it proved during September to be anything but lucky. On the 2nd, precisely that number died when a bomb explosion ripped through the Blue-Bird Cafe, a Montreal nightclub, trapping patrons inside. Almost three weeks later (Sept 24), a privately owned jet crashed into an ice-cream parlour in Sacramento, coincidentally also cutting short twenty-two lives.

That December in Australia saw Billy McMahon tipped out of Government and Gough Whitlam, the white-knight of the new Labour movement, moving into the Lodge. Just a fortnight earlier, Richard Nixon won a second term of office in the White House by landslide. His days were at his own hand, to be numbered.

Christmas was once more a child's celebration and naturally, Ghinda cleaned-up at the pillow-case presentation. Thelma as always, shared our yuletide festivity as well as Ernie Moore, his wife Doreen and nine year old son Geoffrey. The old decorations were witnessing a generation's rebirth, the small church - some new parishioners!

1973 - a good year for Thunderbirds and Caddies, a bad one for inflation rates. Ghinda grew, the bank-account dwindled. Cool suburban living reached its zenith when I brought home one night, in a fit of burgeoning domesticity, Shandy - a cross labrador and who knows what else? Not ten months old, it was hit by a car - in what was arguably the quietest street in Sydney, contracted rabies and had to be put down. Par for the course.

Gwendale Crescent that year, became the cadets' home as much as ours. Many was the time we would arrive home late evening and find two or more cars out the front awaiting our return. Young reporters with assignment worries, personal problems or simply wanting to talk things through. It got to the stage that we were forced to take "bookings!" Many of those youngsters are today leading media journalists and entertainment identities, I often wonder what *they* remember of those nights now, some three decades on.

A regular visitor to Eastwood in those days was Helen's mother - Aileen, a woman whose patience and endurance had been tested to the limit over some thirty seven years and who at that stage had yet to meet *me!* Blessed with the driest of wits and whose idea of heaven was a night listening to the late Slim Dusty at the Sydney Opera House, here was a person who could see the funny side no matter what life dished up and in her case, it was barely up to the main course. Having lost her father early in life, her husband by extreme violence and the majority of her sight by glaucoma, she had further to contend with near-destitution, the approaching blindness of three of her own children, life-threatening blood pressure and other severe physical ailments. On a good day, she looked 52. But here stood one of the greatest living examples of Christianity ever to walk this planet. Gracious, selfless and generous beyond any I ever met. Aileen would have cut her own heart out with a rusty can-opener if she thought it might save another! In times to come, Ails would be all I had to hold on to and there was never a more rock-solid pillar.

Early '73 and Helen suffered a miscarriage brought about by complications associated with having AB negative blood. Rarely afflicting the first-born, she was placed under the care of a gynaecologist specialising in this area to monitor any future pregnancies.

Once in a while I still saw Olly. Fully recovered physically from the semi-trailer interlude, he exhibited now an understandable nervousness when in the proximity of either large trucks or green-light intersections, straining forward to satisfy himself that no road-vehicle was bearing down on his right, to finish what the earlier semi had started. That Spring, I met him in town one afternoon for a couple of beers at the Journalist's Club. He appeared to be unusually withdrawn. Following the failure of two schooners and a brandy-chaser to free-up the uncharacteristic silence, I asked him what it was that had him so absorbed. I was not prepared for the reponse. He just sat there, tears filling his eyes, this being the last person on Earth one could perceive as a wimp.

"Ol, whatever *is* it?" I asked. For a full minute, he made no move to answer.

"I'm dying," he said eventually.

What can you say to such a confronting statement?

"Jesus Olly," I muttered. Probably the most inadequate response I could have come up with. I just sat there stunned.

"Talk to me " I said, "What have they told you?"

"I've got leukemia." he responded at last. "It's pretty advanced....they don't think I'll make a year!"

"But surely there are treatments," I replied, "Bone marrow transplants, chemo?"

"The specialist said they can possibly delay its progress, but this type of leukemia they can't cure - it's just a matter of time." He gazed outside resignedly.

Looking back now, he *had* always been very pale and quick to tire. Perhaps had the condition been diagnosed earlier and treatment commenced, the prognosis could have been more positive. As it was, the road ahead was rocky, uphill and fully devoid of exits. We drove to the very end of it.

As the year progressed, inflation worsened, interest rates spiralled and home repayments were increasing on a monthly basis. We weren't so much feeling the pinch as being crushed by a financial anaconda! Something had to give...first-up being the Pontiac, the departure of which left me feeling with a remarkably ugly sense of deja-vu as I recalled standing in dad's bedroom all those years ago, watching the Consul make its way up Danson Lane and out of our lives for the very last time. We at least did own a second car in 1973 - although in keeping with our motoring tradition - not for long! It may have been an old Holden Special but it deserved better...come to that, so did I.

With Ghinda strapped into her car seat we were driving along the Esplanade at Bondi Beach early that Summer, when a family of pigeons took the slow route across the street - by foot rather than by wing and seemingly with an advanced road-sense...they used the services of a marked crossing! Having to brake hard to avoid injury to any of the single-minded flock, the car following, ran straight up our rear. The collision telescoped the Holden and left Ghinda hysterical with laughter crammed up not more than a few inches from the rear of the front seat.

The Police viewed my participation somewhat unreasonably in the wash-up. I was booked for "Dangerous stopping" with the novel addendum in brackets of, "Illegally giving way to a flock of pigeons!" Naturally the other driver also picked up a ticket for "Negligent driving." the Government coffers doing rather nicely out of the incident. For a while I considered a courtroom challenge to the citation but given the cost and difficulty in persuading representatives of the R.S.P.C.A. and W.I.R.E.S. (Wild Life Rescue Service) to give evidence on my behalf, it was vastly cheaper to just pay the ticket.

Barely a month later I again ran foul of the law in extenuatingly bizarre circumstances. Returning from a late night party held for one of the cadets who had been lucky enough to pull down a posting in the London office, several guests including my warped self, had been participating in a domestic roller-derby in a nearby street. Having tied the laces in knots of such pedigree, no-one could undo them, despite the best efforts of several volunteers, I decided to drive the few kilometres home with the skates on intending to cut them off with a knife if needs be. Just past the first set of lights - the familiar siren heralded the most unwelcome of visitors.

"Licence and registration please sir?" I handed them over through the driver's window.

While standing on the sidewalk writing out a speeding ticket for an alleged paltry 65 in a 60 limit, the cop called out "Have a look at your offside front tyre driver, it's just about smooth." This was the last thing I wanted to hear! Leaning across and winding down the passenger's window I replied, "I'll take your word for it officer, I'll have it fixed right away."

"You have a spare?" he asked. "Sure," I answered, "Never been used!"

"Well then, change it now and I won't book you!" he added, tearing the ticket from his well-used pad of motoring souvenirs, walking over and handing it to me.

"Er, right...well actually I don't have my jack with me officer - I'll do it soon as I reach home." I tried a smile.

"If you want to get *home* Mr Bailey. you'll do it *now*...I have a hydraulic jack in the patrol car." So saying, he walked back to his Falcon and retrieved the item in question from the trunk. Tentatively, I climbed out of the driver's seat and stood holding on to the open door. Kerbside with his jack he looked up at me.

"What are you standing there for - you want *me* to do it for you?"

Hesitating, I kicked forward.

"I can explain this!" I said, emerging from behind the front guard. He watched me dumbfounded, glide all the way to the kerb. Looking up from my feet he simply said,

"Are you *on* something mate, or just plain brain-damaged?"

"I told you there's an explanation for this," I started, but he cut me off....

"I don't want to hear it. I can see what the problem is. You're nuts mate!"

No one spoke! He simply filled out and handed me a second ticket. "Driving while not in proper control of a motor vehicle!" I changed the spare in silence.

Turning to me before he eased himself back into his patrol car, he called out.

"Hope you're not planning on skiing in the near future?"

During the Spring of '73, Pablo Picasso died in Southern France aged 92. Resignations from the Nixon administration were becoming passe as fallout from the Watergate break-in embroiled more and more top-level aides. *The Exorcist* was scaring the hell into everyone and for myself, I acquired a '59 Plymouth Belvedere hardtop (a decade later we would have called her *Christine*). OJ Simpson was breaking all pro-football records and the colossal twin-tower 110-floor World Trade Center opened in downtown Manhattan, never dreaming of the catastrophic fate that was to befall her just 28 years later. July 21st and what *would* have been a baby brother for Ghinda was called out prematurely when Helen suffered a further miscarriage at 2.am that morning, shattering so many hopes and plans. A tragedy experienced by countless young women since time immemorial and one which has unavoidably to strike so many more.

On air, you couldn't avoid Stealers Wheel's *Stuck in The Middle With You* or Slade's *Gudbuy T'Jane* whatever your choice of radio station.

In Australia, you couldn't avoid getting poorer either! With inflation now well into double figures - how long we could hang on to the house was anyone's guess! January 1974 wasn't much better, especially in

Queensland where the worst floods of the century caused the Brisbane river to inundate huge areas of the metropolitan area including the city itself where water many feet deep, flowed through the central business district.

By April there was no option but to sell the house and so with great regret, we put up the "For Sale" signs...exactly as it turned out, at the time of the great property-crash in Sydney. From a buoyant market just ten months earlier, you couldn't *give* a house away! Investors and builders were going out backwards across the State. House values plummeted and property buyers were close to being classified as a heritage-protected species.

Eventually a buyer was found. Always some cashed-up fortunate on hand able to exploit a raging-hot investment opportunity! What capital-gains we actually made on the sale were swiftly negated paying off accrued debts. That was the *good* news! Of less celebratory realism….that left insufficient funds in the bank to put down as deposit on even a medium size *garage* in Sydney. Options were thin on the ground. Deciding therefore to relocate some three thousand feet above sea-level, we headed west to herald the start of what was to be an almost decade-long love-affair with Sydney's Blue Mountains.

Number 1 Darley Street, a short walk from the incomparable *Echo Point* in Katoomba, was more than a house. The most charismatic timber home, built in the early part of the century, it offered the loftiest of high ceilings, three enormous bedrooms, a fourth we used as an entertaining area. Three cavernous open fireplaces, solid oak panelling throughout and an arched lounge-room close to thirty feet long, with chandeliers and its own intimate bay window. Add to that a fine dining room and a kitchen that could sleep three at a pinch and you were talking seriously impressive living space! Completing the home's turn-of-the-century appeal, a return verandah looked out upon a tranquil world and just beyond, loomed the cliffs of the Jamieson valley itself.

Such cherished living came at a price though. Having to rouse oneself at five each morning to shave, shower and make the station at 6.10 am to catch the Mount Victoria express to Sydney was a challenge to be mastered. *Four* hours a day of one's life peering out the train window at a world in motion, people fulfilling their pre-ordained destinies. Surely, a defining microcosm of seventies' Australia? It was a period of stability and great happiness. Winter came early that year and as the first snow fell upon our mountain retreat which, with the exception of three days spent at Thredbo Alpine ski resort a few years earlier, was the first I had seen since my childhood. I couldn't imagine life ever changing. For myself I felt that, temporarily at least, I was where I was *supposed* to be. Pity no-one ever handed me the *complete* script (and at this juncture, we were barely ten minutes into the movie!)

One of the reasons the Mountains are so popular with European settlers is that climatically they offer a nostalgic reminder of their homeland. Many was the icy morning I would chatter my way to the ticket office in Katoomba station during mid-winter, while outside a brisk *minus* five degrees greeted other early-risers as they strapped on their thermal underwear and Yak jackets. Such obscenely low temperatures are unknown in the Sydney metropolitan area, not even seventy miles distant! In the summer, even on the hottest days, The Mountains' altitude filters out the draining humidity that invariably blankets Sydney, turning it into one colossal sauna, but with no "off" switch.

Some might say "and not before time," but Helen and I were married that year at a simple but rather beautiful little ceremony at Sydney's Wayside Chapel in the city's east.

And so for a while, life ran at something of a smooth and gentle canter. I was happy in my work, icicles had become a way of life, even the train ran on time. Another new family member had made arrangements for an August check-in and to that end the pregnancy was now being carefully monitored by one of the State's top gynaecologists, in light of Helen's AB-Negative blood grouping. Domesticity was running at an all time high! On August 9th, just twenty four hours after President Nixon resigned the US Presidency ahead of his impeachment over *Watergate,* despite taking every technological precaution, on-going ultrasound scans and the best medical consultancy in the land, at twenty eight weeks Helen went into premature labour knowing what no mother should ever know – that her baby had died. I say "her" baby for despite the role played by the most loving and caring of husbands, it is the female who carries within her that life. No man has ever had to *deliver* death and for all the shared hurt and loss he cannot (being physically detached) experience the absolute decimation of emotion that a girl is left with during those last nine hours or so. I stayed and cried with her.

We had never named him and so rather than bequeath a name simply for posterity, he was loved, honoured and farewelled in the saddest of ceremonies. The tiny casket simply bore the name "Baby Bailey."

Christmas day 1974 will live in the minds of most Australians as the day Darwin was almost totally destroyed by Cyclone Tracy. Although the death toll was remarkably low at sixty five, more than 90% of the city was detroyed when the cyclone struck at 2.00.am Christmas morning, leaving more than twenty five thousand people homeless on what might be regarded as the cruellest morning of the year. Number 1, Darley Street on the other hand experienced the happiest of Christmases that year. A growing three year old's awareness, activities with close friends and copious amounts of yulestide festivity. It was to be several years before such times would again be played out in the season of good cheer.

The year in hindsight belonged to ABBA whose music had dominated the lives of most everyone under eighteen since the release of *Waterloo* early in the year. If you didn't know *Ring Ring*, *Mama Mia* or *Honey Honey,* then you weren't alive! The year passed into recent chronology with Harry Chapin's *Cats in the Cradle*, Suzy Quatro's *Devil Gate Drive* and Elton John's *Lucy in The Sky With Diamonds* keeping the cash-registers running hot well into 1975.

Just into the new year and on January 5th the bulk carrier "Lake Illawarra" slammed into the Tasman Bridge across the Derwent river in Hobart, Tasmania, killing twelve people, as the main span collapsed, plunging cars thirty five metres into the river below and causing traffic chaos that was to last for months, pending repairs to the bridge. Four weeks later, Britons voted a 49-year old Margaret Thatcher as leader of the Conservative Party, still four years before she was able to change her address to No 10 Downing Street, installed then as the country's first female Prime Minister.

Domestically on-track, financially progressive and geographically compatible, was not *this* perfection incarnate? Maybe it was all just too easy for my finely-tuned need for disharmony and social complexity. April came and with it, the surrender of Saigon to the Communists bringing an end to American and Australian involvement in the Vietnam War. *Our* news was different – that of *another* child's intended journey. A young soul perhaps carrying knowledge which all of us have either forgotten or have shed subconsciously. Determined this time to *make* our daughter's acquaintance (*that much* we knew) and with the knowledge that AB-negative research had taken, recently published, giant steps forward, we entered the count-down in as positive a frame of mind as was possible. Ultra-sounds confirmed everything to be normal in coming months and the specialist had all but made the welfare of *this* particular child the focus of his distinguished career. So satisfied was he with the pregnancy's development that in late August we decided (with medical approval) to undertake an overseas holiday – perhaps the last opportunity for many years. Ghirda was four and not yet at pre-school, I had a back-log of holiday due and all pointers were that this was the ideal opportunity to "head off" and show Helen places she had never seen and my daughter at least some of her ancestry. For me of course, the chance once again to touch base with all that was dear to me. Having bought another home in nearby Blackheath, slightly smaller than Darley Street but set on more than 1 acre of beautiful grounds, we moved every possession across to the new house and resolved to lease Darley Street for six months.

Hawaii was as welcoming as always, things having cooled down in more ways than one since the previous month's eruption of resident volcano Mauna Loa after a quarter of a century of inactivity. Waikiki beach and Diamond Head were as beautiful as ever, being surely among the most relaxing places on the planet. Three days of utter bliss, then five hours on and we checked in to the Alexandria Hotel in downtown LA. Originally an art-deco shrine to Hollywood stars and would-be starlets, this once beautiful and atmospheric old hotel is now the haunt of the fast and the furious, having lost its way during the eighties, as I discovered some twenty-one years later. In 1975 however it was still all glitter and film noir. Hotcakes in the breakfast room were like none anywhere, the waiters seemingly all having served their apprenticeship at "Tara." *Disneyland* sat waiting unchanged just down the Santa Ana Freeway at Anaheim – all things to all children and my daughter *was* but a child then. Renting a Rambler Matador, we headed up to San Francisco where I was careful to avoid any clothing boutiques. Holed up at the Cecil Hotel on Suttor, we piled on calories early mornings at breakfast and walked them off during the day in the Golden Gate Park, Muir Woods just across the Golden Gate and in and around Fisherman's Wharf itself. Never in my experience, has San Francisco extended anything but the warmest of welcomes. By popular request we optioned-up one last Disneyland exploratory before flying east to New York. The most beautiful of late summer weather greeted us that year and again I walked the streets of a city willing me to *remember* that which we once meant to each other and which even now in 2003 shows no response when I press the "re-dial" button. To a four year old, Central Park must appear twice the size of The Never Never Land and by the time we had been dragged by an ultimately motivated child from the park's entrance across from the Plaza Hotel, to the lake, the Zoo and then way north past 110th street, it seemed the size of Antarctica. The World Trade Center in those days was but two years old and stood there near the Battery, a gleaming though destined-to-be-short-lived, icon of hope and prosperity.

We flew on to Paris and spent three wonderful days where ten would have been preferable! Just over an hour or so from London now and it seemed almost incongruous to be flying home, with a new generation in tow. Within ninety minutes, the tiny Renault was passing beneath the railway bridge to the north of Welling and negotiating the most familiar of roads, Danson Lane itself. I pulled up barely ten metres from the park gates. How do you show someone memories? How do you instil loss? No more than just a park to an eager four and a half year old, Ghinda did it all. The playground, the forest walks, time on the lake etc, we even put-paid to a few scones and jam at the Mansion House café. Some things can never change! That first evening we stayed over at the Charing Cross Hotel, ostensibly to be able to sample again the delights of the John Betcheman breakfast room. Heaven before you die!

Speaking of which, September 5th I have reason to remember with a high degree of clarity. Having made an appointment to meet a journalistic acquaintance in the lobby of the London Hilton Hotel for lunch and the opportunity to catch up on old times, I was some ten minutes or so late for my appointment as I crossed the road near Park Lane that day. I noticed, as one *is* wont to do, a Police Car parked not far from the entrance, its presence somehow incongruous in such impeccably up-market a locale. I recall glancing at my watch – it was a little after 12.15.pm. Crossing the road not forty metres from the Hotel entrance, I found myself profoundly deafened and sharing the air around me with an assortment of glass slivers, vaporised masonry and the odd artifact that not three seconds earlier had been resident in the hotel lobby. Other than being now prostrate on the roadway, I was shaken but not stirred. Many shops nearby however were in major and immediate need of both a glazier and some tlc. The IRA it was later confirmed, had made their unwelcome presence known once again. Local Police had allegedly been given only ten minutes warning by the bombers and had been unable to even commence evacuation of the building. Two people died that day and over sixty seriously injured in the terrorist blast…the majority in or near the lobby, believed to be the source of the explosion. Due entirely to that lapsed ten minutes, I wasn't one of them. The ultimate irony? My contact had been delayed even longer than I and was still en route to the Hilton when he heard of the blast during an emergency news bulletin. We had a lot to talk about later!

For the next week the little car earned its keep commuting between London, the farm at Wilsill and Scotland where Loch Ness rippled still in its mysterious and charismatic splendour. Returning via Wales, we spent a night as guests of the Clarendon Hotel in historical Blackheath. The next morning we packed the Renault – not greatly more accommodating than the average shopping trolley, and headed off for Bournemouth on England's south west coast. Hard to describe my grandfather's reaction to first holding his great grand-daughter, it not being an opportunity which comes to all of us regrettably. I believe I caught the glint of the odd tear in his eye and Oh, he fussed about with her so. Introductions and emotion aside, it *was* now time to get down to the serious issues – Nanna's bacon and eggs. It had been so long!

After spending three days there, during which time we all visited Exeter, Bath, Bristol, Dartmoor, Torquay, and much of the beautiful Cornish coastline right the way to Land's End, it was time for Phase two. With a long-term booking made weeks before we departed Australia, a berth awaited us on the car-ferry to Belgium. Having in mind to tour Europe by road as far as Greece, we had purchased, with the intention of later re-sale, one of the rarest cars ever built in Britain, a 1963 Vauxhall Friary station wagon of which I believe only a few hundred were ever made. A spacious and extremely luxurious vehicle which at just four hundred and twenty pounds sterling had offered *then* the power, space and comfort needed for such an undertaking. Well large enough for the three of us to sleep in if needs be, the fact that it was additionally in outwardly pristine condition was simply a bonus.

Unless you have ever driven along the Exeter bypass and the tortuous coast road to Dover in England's peak holiday period, you really have *never* experienced gridlock. The trip that day took seventeen hours and we missed the boat by 6 hours and twenty minutes. Fortunately we were able to re-book for the following morning – along with the other thirty or so cars that had also missed their berth. We slept overnight in the boarding queue itself with the tailgate down – '75 being one of the hottest summers ever recorded in Britain, the year the historic Epping Forest burnt out of control during the largest bushfires ever seen in England. The Channel crossing was without incident, beautiful sea breezes blowing off an idyllic swell. Images of the hell-trip that had been *"The Royal Daffodil"* all those years ago but a memory, as hazy then as the far off Belgian coastline. Hours later we disembarked at Zeebrugge near Ostende and had rapidly to acclimatise to left-hand drive conditions. South East to Gent and straight on to Brussels where in those days, sprouts were still the city's main claim to fame rather than Jean-Claude Van Damme who at that stage was still 15. After a way too-brief look at the city we headed south to the pretty Belgian town of Charleroi before crossing over the French border near Givet. Found an appealing little bed and breakfast place for the night a few kilometres shy of Charleville where the proprietors spoke better English than I've heard from some of our British newsreaders. The Vauxhall sped onwards. Villages, beautiful countryside, the Ardennes, this was the *complete* France, not the Thomas Cook travel guide! We were holding out for the "complete *Europe*" when barely half an hour from Reims a heavy vibration from the rear of the car became noticeable – especially on the open highway in de-restricted zones as were still so common throughout France, Germany and Britain then. You wanted to drive at two-hundred plus? No problem! No speeding ticket either, let alone a speed camera.

A mechanical diagnosis was not necessary – I recognised the symptoms of a universal joint in its death agonies. Question was, what to do? That the Euro-dream was over was unquestionably established. Besides the fact available funds did not run to major repairs like this, winging-it in semi rural France was simply *not* the place to expect to pick up a replacement part, where not only would no-one have ever *seen* a Vauxhall most likely, but we were talking here of a vehicle of such rarity there were probably less than fifty still on the road in England and *none* this side of the white cliffs of Dover. There *was* only one half-reasonable solution - to try and cajole the crippled vehicle back to British soil. Take it from me, "cajole" was the precise word-for-the-moment. In the space of twenty kilometres, the whining sound multiplied threefold and the vibration enough now to turn a bottle of cream, if we'd had one in the rear of the car, to cheese. I would have given odds at that juncture of five-hundred to one against us making it even a *quarter* of the way back! The looming scenario of being stranded mid-continent with a mechanised liability and no-way home was rendering my thought-processes *erratic*, to say the least. Within the space of an hour or so, "whining" gave way to "grinding." We came up with then, the perfect combination, I drove, Ghinda slept and Helen prayed! Past sweating, past worrying, pretty much certifiable at this stage, I *willed* the car onwards. Anything much above thirty mph and it seemed the last rites would be imminent. I have little or no memory of that driven nightmare now, merely two vivid recollections. Firstly notification of the French-Belgian border up ahead (I think I was laughing hysterically at this point) and eventually the most welcome sign I had ever seen in my life "Zeebrugge Car Ferry" next left! How many hours straight had it been? How many days, *lifetimes?* They had to prise me off the steering wheel. The "crunching" from beneath the car by now heralded its arrival at the head of the boarding queue.

"Having a spot of bother are we?" offered the immaculately dressed boat-steward, inclining his head towards the driver's side window and listening intently to the car's progress up the ramp.

"Don't do it!" said Helen, helping me to unclench my fist.

Never had the white cliffs been so white *or* such a welcome sight. *Refuge*, normality, my own turf! The rest accorded the Vauxhall during the crossing, had served to quieten down the universal joint somewhat and I figured that if we could struggle *crippled*, across one and a half countries, getting back to Bournemouth would be the least of challenges. And so it proved. Returning the car to where we had bought it, the proprietor was more than happy to refund the money paid as he felt (probably quite correctly) that its condition and rarity had been undervalued at the time of purchase – we departed on a mutual handshake. In the twenty eight years since, I have never seen, either on the road or in "Unique Car" magazines, that particular model automobile.

Needing *some* form of transport, we picked up a Hertz Hillman Avenger rental mega cheaply. The Avenger some might remember, really *was* Britain's answer to the Edsel. It *was* of some major concern when the girl at the desk handed over the keys with a double-edged parting comment "Good luck sir!"

A week later it was time for final farewells to my Grandfather who sadly was destined never to see his great granddaughter again. That they met at least once however in this lifetime, remains a shallow comfort. Heading back to the Charing Cross Hotel in London, we spent our last few days in England in and around Welling and taking in new-release movies including *Live and Let Die,* and Norman Jewison's futuristic social commentary, the acclaimed *Rollerball,* a film destined to be unmercifully trashed in 2002 with the release that year of the John McTiernan insult of a remake.

Purely as a precautionary measure, Helen's by now, well advanced pregnancy had been monitored during this time to ensure all aspects of foetal development were as as they should be. Mid September we returned to Australia by way of a brief stopover in New Zealand, which despite being our second-nearest neighbouring country, neither of us had ever seen.

Returning from a scorching European summer, I again felt the antipodean isolation that invariably accompanied any return to Australia. Somewhere I knew Joyce was reminding me of our pact and that Vancouver's lure still exerted a fascination and calling that was never going to be realistically ignored, however long I stayed here. Sydney well into Spring itself on our return, was little cooler than Britain. Higher temperatures of a different kind however were in store on our return to the Blue mountains. *Normally* when you rent out your home I reasoned, you are entitled to expect to see some rent! This didn't appear to correlate with the agent's way of thinking.

"Don't have anything for you, I'm sorry." He levelled from under his glasses. "We've tried everything. Sent overdue rental notices, even a notice to quit. The tenant doesn't answer the phone or the front door. The neighbour says they only seem to be home at night. Nothing much we can do until we can serve a summons."

"*Yeah?* I said, "You can't *do* anything?...well, I *can.*" I left the office way quicker than I had entered."

Galvanised into action he followed me to the door. "*Hey*, You can't *go* there mate...he can sue you for trespassing." At that precise moment, "trespassing" was the most trivial of criminal activity on my mind. In three minutes I was at Darley Street. It didn't "feel" right! The place was badly neglected and he was correct, no answer to the most resounding of door knocks. By this time the agent had pulled up outside the house, more out of interest I imagine than with any significant interest in my legal well-being. The window to Ghinda's old bedroom window was easily coaxed down – I climbed in! Rarely stunned in my life, I walked through the house. Totally abandoned, I could but stare at the scenes that greeted me. Have any of you ever seen the movie *Pacific Heights,* a film that stars Michael Keaton as the ultimate tenant from hell? *This* was the inspiration for the screenplay I imagine.

Not a solitary room had escaped vandalism! Much of the oak panelling was defaced, split or even torn down. Plumbing damaged, light fittings trashed and the piece de resistance....our very expensive fitted carpets - simply *unfitted* and stolen! So too, all items of furniture that had been left in the house. Subsequent investigations showed the tenant's name and previous addresses all false. It should be admitted, rental id-checks in those days were far less efficient than those today and bond monies demanded, would barely cover a night out at Maccas for the family. It was a very expensive learning curve. Unable to maintain two mortgages, Darley Street was reluctantly put up for sale and sold soon enough. The times she gave us remain fondly ensconced in my higher memory.

October 1st now and the world saw what was probably the greatest sporting event up until that time, perhaps one *still* able to make that claim! The Ali-Frazier "Thrilla in Manila" which saw two obsessed men defy exhaustion, de-hydration and physical damage, which in Ali's case, included even a broken rib, to turn on fourteen rounds of what appeared to be unsustainable boxing courage – even by the end of round three! Ten days later, newcomer Bruce Springsteen crashed into the US Billboard top twenty with his (now deemed to be a classic) *Born to Run.*

November 11th, a day that will forever be remembered in Australian political history when Gough Whitlam became the first Prime Minister since Federation to be ingloriously *sacked* on the steps of Parliament House, fittingly some would say, by the man he himself chose for the position of Governor General. A shell-shocked voting public watched as Malcolm Fraser was then appointed the Liberal caretaker PM, a move vindicated by his party's landslide win in December of that year.

Helen, fully seven months pregnant now was being monitored fortnightly by her specialist and the prognosis remained fully positive throughout the remainder of the nine month waiting period. Life was a canvas, yet we were in no rush to complete the picture. December 11th and late afternoon there were inarguable signs that our latest daughter was ready for the bright lights....literally! Like millions before me, we crossed many dubious orange lights and disregarded the occasional "stop sign" en-route to the hospital. Well into the next morning, Michelle was born completely without complication or difficulty. You would have to say her timing was impressive – Dec 12th, my 30th birthday! Inarguably prejudiced I realise, but was this not at *that* particular moment, the cutest little girl on God's own planet? Specialists, obstetricians and nursing staff weighed, checked and otherwise fussed around the world's latest arrival while Helen cried and I stood there, stunned in the presence of the greatest birthday gift anyone ever received!

With the aura I believe, of a most *aware* infant, Michelle took it all in her stride. Blessed with an abundance of quite thick curly hair, she looked like a really small child rather than a baby. Beautiful features and with strong and active reflexes – her tiny digits were quick to respond to any contact with her palms, upon which she would clench her hands. Definitely no wuss in the making! Leaving mother and daughter together for a while, I returned home to go and pick up Ghinda who I rather imagined at even four years of age, would have had more than a passing interest in her new sister. Barely had I made the hallway when the telephone rang. Helen was hysterical. Michelle had thrown a fit, stopped breathing and had been placed on a foetal respirator but twenty minutes after I had left. Everything that could be done was *being* done and for the moment she was stable and breathing normally once more. There was nothing to indicate the cause of the problem. Little had changed upon my return. All tests had shown nothing wrong and together with Helen, we looked down at her as she lay there in that tiny oxygenated crib, so pure, helpless and angelic. I offered God whatever it would take to let us keep her.

Obviously my bargaining skills were sadly below the skill-level required that day and in defiance of all our attending hopes and dreams, she died later that morning!

What do you say to a four year old when she asks you "Where is my little sister?" I need not I think, dwell on the period which followed.

There are no words! The specialist was a totally broken man and feeling so desperately that he had failed *us* as well as little Michelle, he cried with us and was simply inconsolable. Subsequent testing was unable to find any cause of the problem, the general consensus being that "she just died"…presumably from causes unknown. Looking back now, I can only say that the brief time we had with her was exactly that which we were *supposed* to have. Michelle's spirit would have known this at the point of conception.

No funeral has ever been more distressingly sad and cliché that it is, something died within the two of us that day. The dreadful image of that tiny coffin with her initials emblazoned just above the silver handles is not something you mentally file under "times you want over." The priest's words were echoed replays from a thousand tragic passings but he wasn't talking about Michelle ...he never *knew* my daughter. *I* knew her and I loved her dearly and that afternoon, I said goodbye to her!

For now there was just nothing to do but to look back, seeking answers to questions that were never going to be forthcoming, at least not in *this* life. Exhaustive tests were later run on some of Michelle's tissue samples but no clues emerged as to any physiological abnormalities that could have accounted for so unexpected and untenable an outcome. It occurred to me that perhaps Joyce had now the company of a little girl, an option that she had chosen to forego when presented with the same opportunity during her life and if that were true, Michelle was in fine hands. Christmas '75 was so empty. The tree sat there an unintentional reminder of a family member whose journey to us was cruelly cancelled out at the last minute by unfathomable cosmic will. *Silent Night* took on a new meaning. Our misery however was put in perspective of sorts that yuletide when thirteen people died on Christmas day in the Savoy Hotel fire in Sydney's Kings Cross.

The new year wrought minimal change in our lives. Little reference was made to the tragedy, there seemingly no point, yet in hindsight that was probably quite the wrong emotional and psychological approach to take. Is it *not* so easy though, to make constructive appraisal *after* the event, most relevantly with the benefit of another quarter of a century's living? I continued my tenure as journalist instructor at the newspaper office throughout 1976. We moved to yet another home near *Echo Point* as Blackheath, through no fault of its own, was able to extend only the most wretched of memories. Ghinda started Primary School at the nearby township of Leura and this to some degree, took up both time and focus that may otherwise have been apportioned to less constructive reflection.

The "fish," the 6.10 am. train from Mount Victoria ran as regularly as clockwork. By now I had made that second forward seat in the rear of the third carriage my own. I cherished that little compartment. It remained frequently unoccupied until two stations further on, thus justifying my perceived "squatter's rights!" The bronze luggage-racks that straddled the opposite rear-facing seat. The dusty and worn, one could be veritably uncharitable and call it *tatty* upholstery. The small utility table between the seats, atop which sat the chained (yet always filled) water decanter and its four grimy glass companions. In all those years, I never once saw a solitary passenger avail themselves of the offered refreshment. Screwed irritatingly just off-centre, between the high-back seat and the luggage racks, some old, faded but somehow appropriate, steel-framed black and white photographs of various well known mountain aspects mid winter. Those old scenes were as antiquated as the train itself. At either end of the carriage, centrally positioned and roof high, were two gas heaters that although comparatively diminutive, held their own during those sub-zero mornings. Still I recall the Victorian smell that pervaded that carriage. More than half a century of polish and neglect coexisting in that little world that I inhabited for two hours each morning. The carriage itself was one of eight that although now pulled by a fully unromantic diesel locomotive, had once proudly been at the behest of a mighty steam engine that now most likely existed sadly as a rusting hulk in some lowly patronised railway museum. On the days my alarm clock failed me, I would feel my way still half asleep to the almost opulent rest-room at the rear of the next carriage. There I would shave and attempt to restore some vestige of presentability ahead of the arriving crush. Judging from the looks on some of the girl's faces, I wasn't always successful in that endeavour.

The airwaves were host at this time to Abba's *Fernando*, K C and the Sunshine Band's *Shake Your Booty*, Cliff Richard's first US hit (after 18 years trying) *Devil Woman* and two huge albums: Al Stewart's *Year of the Cat* and the Stone's *Black and Blue*. Sydney author Patrick White handed back his "Order of Australia" in June. Billionaire John Paul Getty died the same month and the Viking 1 space probe landed on Mars three weeks later. July also saw Montreal host the '76 Olympic Games. On the 18th of September, eight hundred million Chinese people stood together in three minutes silence to honour the death of their leader, Mao Tse-tung who died in Peking (Beijing) aged 82, arguably one of the most influential people who had lived in the 20th century.

I was riding the cusp. Didn't know what I wanted or what I *didn't want* for that matter. Something was wrong and I knew it was all slipping.

Nothing definable, but if I had been approaching the Ides of March, it would have been a definite cause for worry! Why was I cursed with this frequent sense of impending disharmony and why did my life forever appear to be one set-up on the most unstable of tectonic plates? Well may I have pondered the situation! Twenty eight years on today and nothing's changed that I can see.

Christmas '76. It all *looked* so right. The house shone, friends came by, a child dreamed of presents yet unopened. I dreamed too. Oh, she was just so *beautiful*, so unreachable but out there…waiting. I knew it! I tried ignoring her, but she *came* to me although never overtly. Just outside my line of vision. Shortly before sleep took hold. I *knew* she'd crossed the road behind me just as I'd made that left hand turn. I'd scan the check-out queues but she had already left. That she lived somewhere at the end of the rainbow was patently obvious….but where was *that* goddammit? - it wasn't even raining!

In terms of beautiful girls, any onlooker might have expressed the view that such daily exposure to rampant (and intelligent) feminine youth must inevitably lead to at the very least, a *contemplation* let us say of "what if?" It *hadn't* let me assure you! There were occasions I freely admit the previous five years or so, that opportunity if not straight-out *proposition* had loomed temptingly, but the score remained unchanged – Mr Reliable 1 : Nightmoves NIL No need for the video ref.

It is said, one's life has distinct 'markers' – a paranormal *signposting* of sorts. Perhaps a time for personal re-affirmation, maybe nothing more than a reminder of the frailty of the human condition. Whatever, one of my *own* was unknowingly imminent with the onset of the new year. Just days back at the newspaper office following the Christmas vacation, January 17th in fact, I had experienced an unusually long and tiring night with late classes and on an unprecedented whim, I decided to stay in Sydney overnight in preference to facing the two hour rail journey that by then, would have gotten me home way past midnight. I rang Helen and told her not to wait-up and that I'd see her the following evening when I got home. The next morning I winged-in to work as normal, simply to be met by astonished stares.

"Something wrong?" I volunteered.

"How the **hell** did you *get* here?" asked one co-worker.

"I drove," I replied, "You can check the car park if you like. Same old car!"

 Much fidgeting and glancing at one another. It began to unnerve me somewhat. Had I perhaps interrupted an audition for an Aussie episode of *The Twilight Zone?*

"Look, someone want to tell me what's going on here?" I looked around hopefully.

"Don't you *know?*" said Ray, one of the sub-editors. "Your train's lying on its side just west of Granville station with the Bold Street railway bridge collapsed across it. The third carriage and half of the fourth are crushed almost flat by five hundred tonnes of concrete and steel. There are *so* many dead."

Sometimes you cannot make any suitable reply. This was one of those times. I felt like crying, also uniquely *chosen*, but one thing I realised then, either I had subconsciously *known* this would happen last night or something *else* did? We travelled in the Press car to Granville in total silence. I will never be able to convey adequately to you, my feelings as I stared down at the broken wreckage not thirty metres away, dust from the collapsed bridge still eddying about the devastated carriages. Someone threaded a film through the projector.

The old man who used to regularly sit opposite me. Always read his paper from the back page to the front. I remember his smart greyish akubra and immaculately pressed trousers. He always smiled up at the incoming passengers, an unsolicited pleasantry so few have to offer these days. The young married couple who generally took up the two seats besides me. Either they had used-up all available conversation before breakfast or neither had anything spontaneous comment to make, as they simply never spoke to each other the entire trip. He would sit there looking twice his age, hunched over the newspaper scanning it word for word – *she* would read a novel. I wondered what page she must have been up to when *their* world cruelly ended. Just across the aisle, a really pretty young girl who I noticed had recently acquired an engagement ring of which she was so proud. Did fate spare her I often wondered? or did a young man somewhere, receive a telephone call that he simply could not fully comprehend that morning? Many others there were. The young exec on the move, the elderly lady who had to be helped aboard each morning at Glenbrook station. The High-School teacher still marking homework submissions even as the train pulled in to Central Station. I saw them every day…I knew them better than some of my own cousins, yet I knew none of their names. Carriage three took the brunt of the collapsed roadway *and* the greater percentage not surprisingly of the ultimate death toll. Eighty three distressingly unlucky persons lost their lives that morning. More than two hundred were injured. In places that third car was crushed to only inches above floor level. With gas leaking from ruptured pipes, rescuers risked explosion and likely incineration as they worked throughout the day and night to extricate critically injured passengers. During the hour or so I stood there watching that dreadful rescue operation I could only wonder what divine intelligence had decreed it necessary that I not share my long-term companion's fate that morning? My fortuitous "escape" made the front page of *The Sydney Morning Herald* that day – *not* the fifteen minutes of fame I had been looking for I hasten to add! In the next 24 hours I even received death threats from the lunatic fringe or more understandably perhaps, relatives of *actual* victims who in their grief, wondered why I should have been spared...a question I have been asking *myself* ever since. It brought to mind however a strangely related occurrence twenty years earlier in 1957 when my father had gotten-up to give a young girl his seat on the evening train-trip home from Charing Cross. Again, he had always sat in exactly the same spot! *That* winter evening saw the occurrence of one of Britain's worst-ever rail crashes just outside Lewisham station, when two trains collided in dense fog beneath an overhead bridge bringing a third train down on top of my father's commuter train when more than 140 people lost their lives. A steel girder that night, tore through the carriage roof killing many passengers, including the girl he had just minutes before, given up his seat to. Dad too returned home that evening miraculously uninjured but wondering "why" him?

It was a long hot summer. As our marriage imperceptibly disintegrated for seemingly no reason, it became somewhat of a two-way recognition of its limited future rather than any identifiable catalyst behind it. We neither argued, showed Ghinda any less love or even lost our sense of humour for that matter. I began to find reasons to stay in the city overnight – usually lodging with Helen's mother with whom I maintained an unwaveringly close relationship. She knew, or at the very least *sensed* the approaching *impasse* and how this recognition must have hurt her. Meanwhile, although I was making no attempt to isolate she who resided still at the rainbow's end, I was more than ever, *aware* of her presence, and curious beyond reason as to her place in my life.

Having nothing better to do mid summer, I stumbled upon a new way to place myself on death row! Following the outbreak of the worst bush-fires seen in the Blue Mountains for a decade, all major townships found themselves encircled by an encroaching wall of flame. Many homes were being lost as conditions became critical. As a mountains resident myself, the choice was easy – I joined the volunteer firefighters' brigade. Just one day's training – in a scout hall at that, was something less than the hands-on experience one might wish for, especially to then find yourself attached to the nearest division the same day. If you have never been in the close proximity of a major bush-fire, let alone expected to *stand up* against one, your life has been all that much safer! To see a tree explode hundreds of yards from the inferno, from the built up pressure of the boiling sap, or to watch a fire race up a gully at a speed that even a cheetah could not outrun (and they can hit eighty mph plus in fifth) is to wish you were back in kindergarden finger-painting. The week in question, the winds had been gusting to almost 100 kph and coupled with a ground temperature of 42 degrees (104-105 Fahrenheit) had ensured that Hell was *really* on site for the duration! An eerie pall of smoke some seventy kilometres in length and which morphed the sun into some brooding and malevolent spectator, had blanketed life from Katoomba to the Harbour Bridge. Burnt and charred undergrowth fell like confetti in suburban back yards and pools, while it was estimated two thirds of the natural wildlife in the area must by necessity have died in the conflagration. Although Katoomba was still relatively safe, only a small area around the lower-mountains township of Woodford was still undamaged, but facing now an eleventh hour crisis. It was to this remaining stronghold that our small band of would-be heroes were despatched. Turning off on to one of the labyrinthine fire trails that ran off the highway at Woodford we could see the inferno raging in the valley below, some kilometre and a half distant, reluctantly penned-in by the high westerly winds. One had the choice of breathing-in a cocktail of superheated air and ash, or not breathing at all, the flimsy gauze mask across our mouths being about as effective as a hand-held fan in a steelworks plant. Instructions from command post had been clear: to protect the homes and properties in the fire's direct path. Accordingly the more experienced volunteers under the control of the full-time Captain on hand, set about their work with axe and chain-saw to create an emergency firebreak. The rest of us were accorded damping-down procedure of all the surrounding bushland, utilising our back-packs that we had filled from the tanker's already depleted water reserves. Less than half an hour later the wind changed direction. In the space of a minute, the fire turned-in on itself and could be seen racing up the gully.

Leaving the houses to whatever fate awaited them, we scurried back to the tanker and headed for the highway. We had travelled less than two hundred metres when with no warning, three enormous gum trees ahead of the truck exploded, followed by a juggernaut of flame that leapt the trail not thirty metres in front of us, laying to waste everything in its path. Orders were shouted to saturate one another with the back packs...but with a ground temperature *here* in the proximity of perhaps fifty-five to sixty degrees we may as well have *spat* upon each other, the water evaporating before it could even take hold. A second arm of the inferno was roaring up the gully behind us with such speed, escape was impossible. Radio contact with base had been lost now and with no clues as to the fire's likely strategy, we were sitting ducks. Having taken up rear position on the tanker by the grab-rail, hanging-on was the only option as we high-tailed it through choking smoke and burning air back down the fire-trail. The gum trees stood like burning sentinels on either side of the road but as we passed between them, an enormous cracking sound could be heard. Too late, I saw the cause! The tree on the right, probably already weakened and unable to sustain the onslaught of fire and wind additionally, was splitting along its entire western aspect. As one tends to do in terms of futile gestures – I raised my arm to fend off what appeared to be rapidly descending death. The enormous timber wedge with sub branches fully aflame fell directly on to the truck. Only the water tank bolted on the back saved me from being crushed outright. Of course that left the less appealing scenario of being burnt to death beneath the flaming mass. My protective hat and top both flared up as I lay on the walkway quite convinced this time my luck had run out. The heat was unimaginable, in fact, looking for any *positives* in the current situation was fraught with difficulty. At that second, two things happened, both of which I had reason to be deeply appreciative of. Dragged clear, albeit unceremoniously by the feet and hosed down by another rescuer's back pack ensured that although less sartorially elegant (and I had a deep affection for that hat) I *was* still alive and except for a searing scorch mark along my left cheek, uninjured. My euphoria was short lived though. The tanker had slewed to a halt as the trail ahead was completely blocked by the raging inferno.

"No way through *that*," muttered the driver. He turned to the Captain expecting perhaps some inspirational advice. None was forthcoming. It was the next comment from one of the older volunteers that really got everyone's attention.

"Oh friggin' hell guys!" He was pointing due east.

A firestorm was racing up the gully directly in our frontal line of vision. Way too wide and mobile to have any hope of outrunning, there was but a solitary option. Using the tanker as a shield we crouched down on the western side – and prayed. Within thirty seconds, the roar of the approaching apocalypse was deafening and the heat indescribable. Searing hot air and flame shrieked overhead. I knew exactly what The Great Fire of London must have been like! Minutes passed and though by now medium-rare, we were still alive – shame about the truck! A cursory examination suggested it had been subjected to an attack by a band of terrorists carrying flame throwers. The cabin was burnt out, the tyres on the eastern side melted and welded to the rims. Blackened and charred, it was never going to be the star exhibit in a fire-fighting museum. I think all of us had near fatal blood-pressure by now and with no radio contact and being a decade ahead of cellphones it was one hell of a long walk to the highway through still-burning embers. By the time we made it, we should have been offered an honorary membership to the national firewalker's union. Later that week the fires burnt themselves out, leaving a 360 degree panorama of devastation as far as the eye could see from the rail line south. In less than a year, natural regrowth sprang up around the black and white vista of charred stumps fully bringing back the mountainous hues and restoring the balance of nature. I considered myself fortunate to see it!

The onset of August that year brought about four unrelated but indelibly etched news items of historical significance. The 16th brought the news of Elvis Presley's death through drug-related complications. The greatest comic of them all, Groucho Marx, died on the 19th, aged 77. August 22nd it was announced to a shocked automotive world that Volkswagen would after more than thirty seven years, be discontinuing production of the beloved "beetle" (The car continued to be built in Mexico however, right up to July 2003.) On the 30th, Police arrested the serial killer David Berkowitz, better known by his more sinister title, "The Son of Sam."

In the run-up to Christmas '77, Bing Crosby died October 14th doing what he loved most – playing on a golf course, just outside Madrid.

CHAPTER NINE

BECALMED

She finally showed her face early that year – and what a face it was. They say that beauty is in the eye of the beholder. I was simply beholding to her beauty! One of the twenty or so cadet-reporters appointed in early '78, Therese invaded my soul, captured my passion and imprisoned that icon of romance set deep in my chest cavity. I loved her of course – I had, since before I knew her. *"Pretty,"* insults the image she presented. To this day, I will sign any affidavit that never in my wanderings have I seen a more vitally attractive girl – and I have been privileged to see a lot. Inarguably, our beautiful daughters *today* could mount a credible challenge to that statement but I think it would still go to the video-ref for a final decision. Eleven years her senior...*and* her teacher, this was not about to make for plain sailing. Possessed of a wife and young child additionally, here was a romantic entanglement the equal of any plotline in *Days of Our Lives*. Having to endure additionally, taunts from my peers at the Herald, such as "cradle snatcher," "opportunist," all the way up (or down) to "damn pervert" I really needed that JD and ice some nights.

As far as life with Helen was concerned, any onlooker would have had to stifle a snigger. Aware of my extra curricular affections and seemingly accepting, if not bizarrely *supportive* of the situation, she would lean over and kiss me at 3 am in the mornings when I would climb out of bed for the eighty-minute drive to Carlingford. (Working for a major newspaper daily *can* put you in line for some bad-ass shiftwork!)

"Give Therese my love," she would mutter, before turning over and going back to sleep. At the time, it all seemed so normal.

That summer of '78 brought to final reality also my sadly misplaced urge to *act,* to be an entertainer, to tread the boards. Following some weeks of intensive night-school acting workshop, I signed on with a mountains-based repertory company for a three week stint of *Twelfth Night*.

What *is* acting? Gesticulating wildly towards yonder balcony in the hope that Juliet will lean forward far enough for you to catch a glimpse of her wonderbra? No, its being told to strip to your undies, lie on a cold wooden floor and improvise being a rose, whose petals are unfurling in the morning sun. If you can do *that* my friends, "King Lear" is but "The Third Rock From the Sun" with just substantially less humour.

Rehearsals are one thing – *first night* another. I delivered, so it was cruelly suggested by one local newspaper critic, an *Antonio* devoid of passion, fire and substance. He *could* have commented on what flair I had shown applying the greasepaint I thought. Took an eternity! Yeah OK, I forgot a few lines, muffed a few words – problem was in retrospect, *Antonio* has so *few* to muff in the first place. My contribution notwithstanding (hell, the rest of them were diehard seasoned Shakespearean actors anyway) we pretty much sold-out the three weeks. Mercifully, Therese, through work commitments, was unable to witness my thespian massacre. Whilst I felt I actually improved with each successive performance…not a view necessarily shared by others, it taught me that realistically Sean Connery's mantle as the quintessential Bond was under no immediate threat. The Theatre Company's producer stuck by her questionably *poor* choice of casting.

"Don't *try* to act Noel, chill out a tad - be yourself! Let *Antonio* out to posture in his own way." Did *she* ever have the patience of Job?

We saved the best for the closing performance however! Traditionally "muck-up night," when theatre companies often take small liberties with the audience. We *buried* the Bard! The following is probably *not* quite verbatim but is as close as memory will allow.

Act 3, Scene 4: A Street, Antonio and Sebastian are talking.

Antonio to Sebastian: "It doth fit me. Hold, sir, here's my purse." To which Sebastian replies, "Why *I* your purse?" and Antonio responds "Haply your eye shall light upon some toy you have desire to purchase……etc etc,"

Come the aforementioned scene, Sebastian and I converge centre stage. Hot night…greasepaint running in rivulets down my neck.

  Me/Antonio: It doth fit me. Hold, sir, here's my purse."
  Sebastian: "Why *I* your purse?"
  Looking Sebastian squarely in the eye, I *had* to do it!
  "Why <u>not</u> my purse??"

Cruelly thrown offguard by this rude divergence from the original script., "Sebastian's" recovery was nothing short of inspirational. Without the slightest change of expression and barely noticeable a hiatus, he replied.

"*Why* thus do I ask? Because sir, your purse is to your person sacred, I would'st not wrest it from your side for fear of its demise at the hands of hotheads."

He thought he *had* me.

"An oath at your ears sir," I ad-libbed, squaring off, centre stage still. "Tis but a *request* and yet thou would'st toss my words back to the lips that uttered them in such generous issue."

He acknowledged the game.....smiling

"If this tongue offends thy virtue fair Antonio, then pluck it out by the root. Render this ill-manner'd acquaintance a rebuke he shall not forget."

We were *hot!* Critics, fellow cast members and audience alike sat there gob-smacked!

"Hurl not such unfavored text at one would pass on his life in the service of his revered companion." I said, bowing low to Sebastian and proffering my dagger.

"Knowest me then to be a man of *violence*?" countered Sebastian, "Come, sheath thy dagger, deposit with me your purse and perchance good fortune shall unite us in unfetter'd good humour."

At which point I, as Antonio was able to regain control of the written word.

After a stunned silence the audience rose and gave us both a standing ovation. Some might deem this to have been the theatrical highlight of the 20th century. That isn't however how Anne our Producer, saw it.

I wasn't offered another role!

Its always fun being in love again. The opportunity to turn on the demonstrative yearnings and childish delight that a decade or two of supposed maturity has taught you to repress. Definite set-back though when the object of your burgeoning desire is just one of twenty students in the classroom, thirty eight pairs of eyes knowing what's going on in their midst, pretending they don't, whilst you, *knowing* that they are so pretending.....are pretending yourself that they *don't* know...which they of course *know* you're doing anyway! The whole intake soon resolved themselves into two camps. The "It's soo romantic, Therese loves her teacher" contingent and the "How dumb is *she* - getting involved with a married man?" set. Factually of course, Therese was aware from day one of our domestic marriage-divergence path and was never placed under any false illusions. Mapping out the game plan to her *parents* however was an understandably different matter! I was for all intents and purposes, their worst nightmare imaginable. Way too *old*, already married (with a daughter), a non-Catholic and quite beyond redemption – *English* as well! The long standing enmity between Australians and the citizens of the "old dart" still festers and to have their eldest daughter actually bring one of the enemy *home* must have caused her father not a little hypertension. How I made it beyond the first interview I have never known! Talk about *Meet the Parents*, this was *Rocky 6!*

May 15th that year, saw the passing of Sir Robert Menzies, the longest-serving and arguably *best* Prime Minister Australia ever produced. Australia's rock-legend Johnny O'Keefe, took his leave on October the 8th after suffering a heart attack at just forty-three. On the musical front, Abba continued to rule supreme with *Chiquitita* and *Take A Chance On Me*. KC and the Sunshine Band scored major league with *Boogie Shoes* and the biggest of them all late in '78, The Village People's *Y.M.C.A.*

Ultimately the travelling and the sheer impracticality of trying to preserve a terminally-ill marriage, even for the sake of posterity, brought about the long overdue six degrees of separation. When your home is no longer your home where do you lodge? Well in my case, probably the last place you would reasonably expect to be made welcome – with my *mother-in-law*. Aileen invited me back to her home as she would have one of her own sons, never once showing anything but understanding and kindness. Though far from well and with her vision all but gone now, she supported me through what was a very draining and emotionally upending period. That she adored Therese also and showed *her* unbiased affection speaks much for this woman's radically unequalled (in my experience at least) Christian kindness and generosity. As I said earlier in the text, she was my *rock* when I so needed it.

November 18th and nine hundred and ten members of Jim Jones "People's Temple" in Guyana were found dead, persuaded to suicide by their cult leader. Many, including young children, were given grape-flavoured softdrink laced with cyanide and liquid valium. It remains one of the greatest and incredible tragedies of modern times.

Except for our first year in Australia, 1978 was the only Christmas not celebrated in my own home, although Therese's parents it must be said, welcomed me and even Ghinda, to their house that year. It was a time of such transition and re-evaluation.

Having proposed marriage early in the new year and even setting a wedding date of September 1st – the first day of Spring in Australia, there remained the not inconsequential detail of already having a legally wedded wife. Helen by this stage had met another man, a friend and member of the same theatre company to whom I had held but temporary membership the previous year. A speedy divorce was in *both* our interests. Way ahead of the "divorce by mail" system now long in existence, we both had to attend a set Court hearing. I recall the magistrate's remarks that day that never had he seen a more contented, cooperative and obviously loving couple in all his days at the bench. "You two *really* need substantial counselling," was his solitary parting comment. He issued the decree notwithstanding, it being almost ten years to the day, that I had first met Helen!

Infinitely greater hardship lay ahead at work. Summoned to the Editor's office that summer, I was lectured at length on how "it had come to Management's notice that I had been 'fraternising' with a young female student cadet and that the situation was not one they would tolerate." I pointed out, some might adjudge *unwisely*, that the situation was not "theirs" to tolerate, but that all the same, the term "fraternising" might not be truly representative of the situation since we were being *married* later in the year. This appeared to cut less than no ice. I was handed the ultimatum – cease the relationship or go visit the pay office. Therese too, so I discovered, was offered much the same deal…..the same day! Years before terms such as "unfair duress," "work-place discrimination" or "employee harassment" would have ensured us both a healthy pay-out in legal-damages, I found myself thrust into a fully untenable situation. Journalism was Therese's chosen *career* she had spent years earning a Communications degree for just this purpose. I was by far the more expendable. It had after all been a happy and satisfying eight years and I really *was* going to miss those film-preview invites, not to mention the Journalists' Club! – I think I *still* hold the record there for quaffing the greatest number of mixed drinks in a thirty minute period!

Our house in the mountains had of course to be sold and as it happened, being unemployed, this yielded-up the hours necessary to repaint and indulge in a little TLC. Late that autumn, I was to be in need of *considerable* TLC myself! Following a weekend's hands-on session with the paintbrush, plaster and filler, coincidentally (or *was* it?) the completion of the house's make-over, I was headed back to Therese's parents' home rather looking forward to a roast dinner. By necessity in those days, returning via the mostly single-laned Great Western Highway, involved the circumnavigation of multiple tight s-bends around the area known as Linden. On this particular day I simply had the misfortune to be at the right place at the wrong time. Negotiating the third such bend, I was somewhat bemused to find myself confronted by a small white car on *my* side of the road perhaps three seconds from a head on collision. Amazing what flashes through your mind in a few nano-seconds. "Hell, I'm *really* gonna die this time, and *here* at Linden.....how trivial!" then, "Well, the good news is, at least they'll know it wasn't my fault," and finally "Hey, why don't I *do* something about this? The options of course being to either swing left or radically to the right. I was reminded of the old Tony Orlando song *Right or Left at Oak Street?*...I think I probably laughed, then I chose left! Striking the bonnet-high steel guard rail at the side of the road close to 80 kph, the hood was never found. The bolted-down seat belt sash restraints were right out of their league too. Tearing loose, they allowed my head to pass clean through the windshield, my body held within the car however by the still-functioning lap belt. My last clear remembrance was of the white car in the rear vision mirror skidding errantly around the bend behind me. By the time my car was airborne, I was sound asleep. What followed was pieced together by witnesses and Police evidence. On an upward incline following the side-swiping of the guard rail, my car crossed to the other side of the road at a decent elevation, right across the face of the next s-bend. At that precise moment an articulated transporter rounded the corner and was confronted by an airborne 1976 Valiant Ranger that struck the cabin some eighteen inches below the driver's windshield. His comments are *not* recorded! My car sheered off at the firewall, (the engine was later found compacted to the size of a fox terrier, some sixty metres yards away in bushland), my half, continuing to fly north west, round about the same time the transporter jack-knifed and snapped its rear axle with the six cars on board disgorged from the carrier right across the Great Western Highway, taking out several other vehicles following up behind. The Valiant itself was brought to heel by a rather large tree the other side of the road, that it struck some four metres off the ground before falling on top of a Toyota Crown. Witnesses said that I crawled from the wreckage, muttered *"That's all folks"* and collapsed on to the roadway. It had taken less than fifteen seconds maybe, to turn the highway at Linden into a wreckers' yard.

    Having no recollection of the collision itself, my only subsequent memories are of unrelated "scenes"...a brief slide-show of sorts. Glancing down at my right wrist and seeing my watch partially embedded there. Dry-cleaning still hanging over the rear window streaked and dripping with blood. A veil of something or other across my right eye. How neat the front of the car looked with no engine! They later estimated the combined collision-speed to have been well over one hundred and fifty kph.

"Someone looked after you son," I remember one of the two cops supporting my arms saying, "Chances of surviving a pile-up like that are less than nil, you're just miraculously lucky! At that point I passed out – big time! The Highway was closed for almost seven hours I learned later, with more than twelve vehicles totalled, including the six on the transporter, all of which were thrown off. Courtesy of a press chopper, we also made the 6.30 p.m. prime-time Eyewitness-News bulletin. I missed it *all* – they said I was "out to it" in a hospital observation room for fifteen hours straight.

When I finally woke – I wished I hadn't! One eye closed, the other on the way. My face just mincemeat from the feel of it. The "veil" over my right eye, so I discovered later, was skin whose former resting place had been my right temple. Therese was there holding my left hand, by the feel of it, the only area undamaged in some way. When she had first rung the hospital asking for information she was told "Oh, he's on the slab!" which wouldn't exactly have been the words of encouragement one's fiancee would be hoping to hear. Her father brought her straight down. Discharged later that day, I suppose people *have* been in worse condition and still been alive but I would have found that hard to believe. One strapped rib with a hairline fracture, cord burns, the majority of my upper torso closely resembling an Afro-American in colour, a noticeable droop to my right eye (a non-too-cute feature remaining to this day) bandaged and stitched body parts and internally – dynamic pain and organic confusion…the cop was right, I got off cheaply! My mind wandered back twenty two years to that Christmas night I telescoped the "New Yorker." I could have so used a hot bath and some of mum's nursing talents…..not that dad, with all *his* extensive skills would ever have been fixing *that* car again!

The ensuing forty eight hours were spent propped up in bed in extreme discomfort as well as arriving at one inescapably gutting conclusion. Not having had the funds to renew the insurance cover on the Valiant a week before the accident, not only did I now possess *no* vehicle, but there were still three years to run on the payment plan. People have suicided for less! I needed to get objective about where I stood and where I was going…quick smart!

I had no idea how I had gotten there, or indeed where "there" was! I just knew I had to remain near the great stone pillar. Mostly in dark shadow, I could sense rather than see the multitudes there. Away to my right was what appeared to be a great carved wooden bench of sorts where impossibly high up, back-lit in some way, although I could see no artificial light source, a row of officious older men sat in sombre discussion. They did not appear to notice my presence and at no stage even, glanced in my direction. I could not tell, nor did I need to know, whether it was day or night, merely that I had to witness this unfolding spectacle, whatever it was. Behind me I was aware of much jostling and whispered conversation all of which was quite unintelligible. For some reason I found a certain measure of comfort in the proximity of that cool pillar.

Quite suddenly, an area between where I stood and the "bench" became the focus of everyone's attention. I can only describe it as being what you would see if someone switched on an ultra high power arc-lamp and then gradually increased the light intensity. I was shocked and somehow disappointed to see Helen standing there. Although her features were not visible, I knew it to be her. I even seemed to know subconsciously why she was there. There were indistinct murmurings. A singular hooded member of "the panel" addressed her but I was not privy to the meaning of the exchange. Then Helen made her reply. Her words were but vitriol, against me, everything I had ever done or stood for. She accused me of the vilest crimes, both as a husband and as a man. I tried to interject but was restrained by those behind me. Helen turned and pointed in my direction and compounded her lies, accusing me of the most heinous behaviour. She laughed as she mocked my predicament and I felt anger and resentment building in the crowd and in those high up on the bench as she continued her tirade, all the time gesturing wildly in my direction. I was to have no right of reply!

Without warning, a bright light appeared high above us – whether at ceiling level or higher I couldn't estimate, after all there was only an impression of gigantic wooden beams high above the assembly and even they were obscured by a type of cloying mist that penetrated every facet of the proceedings at hand. Helen looked up alarmed. The light was growing in brightness and as it did so a sound, quite indescribable filled the air. Not music, not mechanical, it simply gained rapidly in volume in proportion to the oncoming light. I was aware of a general panic but in myself, felt something of a great peace and beauty. Louder grew the tremendous vibration and suddenly from the centre of the light-source shot a single beam. Helen was pole-axed where she stood. The assembly was instantly silenced and retreated from the pulsing brilliance overhead. Now the light became far too bright to look towards, considerably more *radiant even than our sun. I sank slowly down the pillar, crouching at its base and covering my eyes with my hands. It made no difference. Even with my eyes themselves jammed shut I could still see and FEEL the light's dazzling purity.....I knew it was of celestial origin and I heard amongst the utter pandemonium in that place, a fearful cry go up, "It's Jesus himself!" It was then that I felt the awe, the unbelievable and incomprehensible power that was arcing downwards. I knew what was there, why it had come and now in retrospect, how far we all are from remotely understanding anything about our true origins. As I crouched down knowing there was absolutely nothing to fear but everything to respect, I heard clearly whispered right alongside me, the enigmatic words "Now you know what imbibement means." I slowly opened my eyes. The light and everything else was gone.*

I sat up in bed....not moving for at least a minute. It was maybe two am. I was completely drenched, shivering uncontrollably, but not in the least bit *afraid* or even alarmed, simply aware however something had just happened that was majorly outside what you might term a "normal experience." I am no religious convert but you would want to believe me when I tell you that to be made aware of what I *felt* that night, to be exposed to the awesome and incorruptible power that I *was* for so brief a period is to *know* that life isn't for nothing! As for the words *"Now you know what imbibement means,"* I always *did* know the literal meaning at least, of what it meant and thus the statement remains a total paradox, one I have every reason to believe will reveal itself at the appropriate time. Some fourteen months or so later I was to meet a fascinating lady, who being a psychic and having made her life's work a study of the paranormal, expressed the view that what I had experienced was a *vision* – one that represented in my case at least, some sort of closure with life's earlier chapters. All that I know it *wasn't,* is an over-active imagination at work.

The bruising retreated, skin re-grew, the stitches dissolved, at which time I suffered the worst agony of all - a small envelope marked "NSW Police" arriving in the mail containing a $150 fine for allegedly "Negligent driving." *That* eventuality, so I was told at a brief interview weeks earlier which *itself* was declared "just a formality Mr Bailey," was not even a consideration, for as they commented, "We realise you had to take evasive action in this case." Making contact with the issuing Police station I was met with an embarrassed "Sorry about this mix-up Sir! Yes we *did* tell you that, but the accident-investigation squad insist that *someone* has to be held accountable and since you cannot nominate the driver of the "other car" we are left with the fact Sir, that *your* car struck the other vehicle. I'm sorry!"

Only months after this crash, legislation was introduced by Parliament to allow for "no fault" accident occurrences, where neither party incur a traffic citation. Same old story – my timing all shot to hell. Margaret Thatcher's on the other hand had been *excellent*, as on May 3rd that year, she became Britain's first female Prime Minister. Just two months later John Wayne died of cancer in LA. on June 11th.

What a prospective son-in-law I posed? Over the hill, homeless, no car, no money, no job and no immediate employment prospects. Damn it, I was still shaky on my legs even! Rumour has it that Therese was offered parental advice to the effect that "Its not too late to re-think this sweetheart!" I almost shared their sentiments! My first necessity was to secure transport and with the excessively limited funds available, I acquired a well-loved '63 EJ Holden station wagon for just $375. It got me where I needed to go….even if I *did* have to hold it in top gear most of the time. Therese meanwhile was posted to Canberra, the nation's capital, assigned to a political round. Five and a bit hours there and back (as it was then) every weekend is a hell of a time to hold a car in third gear let me tell you! It wasn't a problem for that long. The morning came when despite the "choice" of my soon-to-be Father-in-Law's Mercedes out the front, next door's new Toyota and a host of near new vehicles parked in the street, someone had to rip off *my* $375 workhorse! Found by Police a day later unceremoniously buried nose-deep in garbage at a nearby council tip, having been pushed twenty metres off a cliff, I had to wonder at my life's total disregard for normality and smooth sailing. Retrieved by crane, the EJ was still drivable, though awash with beer, and dented in several panels. I drove her for several months although hints were dropped at the Real Estate Office, with whom I had found gainful employment, that I "get a decent car" and stop lowering the tone of the place! We compromised. I kept the old EJ – and bought an immaculate '66 Ford Falcon which we drove for years.

The house in the mountains was sold eventually and with the proceeds left over, Therese and I were able to put down a deposit on a quaint older residence nearby that at least would qualify as a "home" to go to after the wedding, *now* just a few months away. Quaint, "The Rest" as it was known, may have been, *livable* it wasn't! "We can *do* this," she said as I looked at the torn, stained rags posing as curtains, the grimy and threadbare carpet, cracked plaster, rusted and filthy bath, condemned kitchen and dirt-encrusted woodwork throughout. What she meant of course was, "*You* can do this!" Let's face it, it wasn't on the market for just nineteen thousand dollars for no reason! With a budget available to us, best described diplomatically as being at "the lower end" of the market – it was this or nothing! In truth, and if I do say so myself, this was to be my finest hour on the home-renovation front. The main bedroom was by necessity the first to be "made-over." The logic being that even if nothing else was underway, we would have a "base" to work from and immediately following a *honeymoon* you can well understand the appeal of a smart and homely bedroom. It also set a template for me to follow for the remainder of the house. Beautiful old pressed-metal ceilings came back to life after stripping and repainting. The walls, often after a session with filler, we painted driftwood with a natural wood-colour for the extensive timber skirting and picture rails. I began to see myself as the Picasso of the paint-roller, although recollecting now how the laundry turned out…"Andy Warhol" might be the more appropriate role model! Commuting from the mountains however, being a ninety minute drive either way, was proving majorly impractical…and expensive. Thus ultimately we stayed with Therese's parents during the week and simply returned home Friday nights.

On the most beautiful Spring day, Therese and I were finally married and even allowing for a healthy degree of prejudice, it was the best wedding I ever went to. The bride was just exquisite - a beautiful Dresden doll in white lace. I don't think I noticed anyone else around. Ghinda was there of course but at eight years old and undeservedly caught between two sets of opposing lives, I *felt* her struggle to try and balance loyalty, understanding and grief. The reception was held at Therese's home and smooth and wonderful as it all was, all I wanted her to *do* was to toss that damned garter over her shoulder and let us get the hell out of there. The honeymoon had been booked at the magnificent Jenolan Caves House, the limestone-caves resort two and a quarter hours west of Sydney, just fifty-five minutes from "The Rest." We had several peaceful and utterly relaxing days there – probably the only ones I can remember having, before or since. The urge to get back to our own home though was particularly acute and within a week I was back on the ladder starting on the lounge-room ceiling. Some ceiling too, seeing as the room must have been twenty-four long not including the bay window. The spare bedroom had already been completed and was fitted out as Ghinda's room for her bi-weekly visits. For all the love and attention she was shown, she just never seemed her old self and despite answering all her questions honestly and in as open a manner as possible, there was one I could never address satisfactorily. "If you and mum loved each other daddy, *why* did you split up?" To an eight year old, things are black and white, there *is* no "Well its like this honey." Therese became, through no fault of her own, yet quite understandably - the enemy! Helen remarried and asked, in as unusual a sociological twist as one would ever be likely to encounter, Therese to be her Maid of Honour.

With the laying finally of new carpet throughout, "The Rest" was well able to live up to its name. Complete with the cosiest of libraries and two grand open hearth fires, it became the comfiest and most intimate of homes, one that no visitor ever seemed in a hurry to leave. We also inherited from its former owners the most stately of antique sideboards which engendered memories of its counterpart in Welling all those years ago, being itself of almost identical design. That Christmas, the little church sat in its appointed spot and prepared itself for a new family chapter. *This*, it didn't have long to wait for, given that Therese was pronounced to be extremely pregnant a short time later.

Of course, harmonious and problem-free living was just a mirage, a cruel tease! Unexpectedly in the new year and months after the accident, came the first of a veritable procession of letters of demand from the owners of the car transporter decimated in the accident. Outrageous quotations for repair-work performed, (but never authorised), damages sustained, even as I recall, a bill for the owner's hotel-stay that night in Sydney. This was followed by equally outrageous claims for damage to the other eight or nine vehicles from individuals across the country. In total, well over $220,000, which in today's monetary value, translates to close-on three quarters of a mill plus! *All this*, simply because on a roll of the dice, the Police had decided to give me a $150 traffic citation. I wrote back to each of them, threatening to die!

Christopher was born July 14th 1980 and in an uncomfortable throw-back to earlier and ultimately tragic obstetric experiences, he had to fight desperately for life. With an *Apgard* reading of 3 at birth, his chances of survival were at best 30:70. I couldn't believe it was happening again! Hour by hour, day by day he was monitored but with some *positive* divine intervention this time, on the fourth morning he was pronounced to be in sufficiently good health to go home. The house was now a home!

July 19th, the 22nd Olympiad opened in Moscow, Bjorn Borg took out his fifth Wimbledon crown, just 24 hours after Peter Sellers suffered a fatal heart attack in London. The Electric Light Orchestra (ELO) were riding high with *Telephone Line* and *South of The Border,* while Elvis

Costello was still extolling the virtues of *Oliver's Army*. The biggest news in Australia was from Alice Springs on August 19th when Police were called to a camp site at Ayers Rock, to investigate the disappearance of ten week old Azaria Chamberlain after her mother Lindy, gave evidence that a dingo had taken her infant child.

Having a new baby kinda took precedence over any other distraction and Chris was the most amenable of little people come lately. No big crier, he took his milk, gained weight....did everything right actually. Selling real estate was majorly hard work at that time, not because I lacked the necessary skills but like every other mistimed decision I have ever made, the early 80's saw rising interest rates in Australia, and hardly anyone was selling or buying property...and if they *were* it sure wasn't through our agency! Bottom line – few sales, very spasmodic commission bonuses – not enough income to support a family and a mortgage – never mind the other pressing quarter of a million dollar debt! A decision had to be made and fast. It was never I realised, going to be one acceptable to my in-laws either. I have never been a quitter, loser, or even one to back down from a confrontation, but this was a fight I could never win. Knowing that from a legal viewpoint the creditors predictably would obtain judgement against me and then would inevitably move to bankruptcy, I was not about to lose my home and everything else, to make restitution for an event I had in no way caused or been responsible for. Nor could I subject a new young wife and child to that level of unrest and unendurable gross financial hardship. After talking it through for hours...days in fact, we decided to sell "The Rest," re-locate to Britain and to basically start over. At least it would be a case of regrouping on my own *home turf.* I was in the market for a new job anyway, thus I figured we may just as well re-build in South London somewhere, with a few thousand behind us, as stay here on Social Security for the next two hundred years, paying off a debt I had no right having bequeathed to me! There was the added bonus that given the (relatively economic) renovations carried out to date, the value of the house had virtually doubled. I wasn't about to hand over all that blood sweat and tears just for the privilege of owing a further $200,000 and being bankrupted into the bargain. It was a good plan – in principal. Selling it to her parents was another story.

"We knew you'd do something like this," was one of the tamer comments and hell, I could so understand their bitterness and disappointment. I must have realised their worst fears and more! I think their greatest hurt was that I was planning to remove their daughter and at that stage, *only* grandchild from their midst. That first confrontation ended at *"The Rest"* with Therese and her mom in tears and me requesting Fred (her father) to remove himself from MY house, the *one* place his kingdom and authority did not extend to. In fairness, I must admit that I had not at *that* juncture gone into the financial aspects pressuring us or indeed made any reference to the impending litigation. Round two was initiated the very next weekend. In the light of a majorly calmer disposition all round, the whole of the problems and pressures besetting us were laid on the table. I'm sure it did nothing for my popularity stakes but it left room at least for negotiation. In the following seventy two hours Fred came back to me with a proposition. His legal advisers, being in his opinion at the very top of their profession, had looked over all the relevant paperwork and were of the opinion they would, through various dodgy tactics, be able to obtain a settlement for a minimum figure – as low as one tenth of the amount sought. If therefore we were to sell "The Rest" he would use whatever monies were left over after all legal settlements, as a 50% deposit on a home in Carlingford that he would buy jointly with us on a 50:50 basis. It was more than a "fair" offer although quite candidly I personally would have preferred to take our chances in Britain with *all* of our money. But this wasn't about me….it was a decision had to be made in the best interests of several other people. We accepted the offer.

November the 4th of that year, ex movie star, ex Governor of California and sometime television personality Ronald Reagan, at the staggering age of 69 was elected the 40th US President. Three days later, another acknowledged actor of somewhat *greater* talents – Steve McQueen, died of lately-diagnosed cancer at just 50. December the 8th blew the collective world's consciousness when Beatle John Lennon was shot dead by crazed fan Mark Chapman, right outside his home at "The Dakota" apartment block, right alongside New York's Central Park.

Having been a model child since birth with absolutely no illness to speak of, Christmas was notable for the onset in Christopher of chronic asthma, a condition that still affects him badly twenty two years later but to a substantially less degree. "The Rest" shared with us one last Christmas but was sold very quickly, having multiple highly motivated buyers on hand, it being the pick of properties for sale near Katoomba's Echo Point at that time. It has left me with nothing but fond memories of the most beautiful home one could ever want. I can see it still…..*smell* it even in mid-winter, the two open fires, hot logs blazing, while the heaviest of mists rose from the floor of the nearby Jamieson Valley and blotted out everything much beyond our fenced border. Icy outside…warm as hell indoors after a hot roast dinner, bottle of wine and steaming hot soak in that old antique bath that eventually came up so well. I used to sometimes sit there late nights when everyone was asleep, watching the shadows from the dying embers flickering about the great polished oak fireplace that reached almost to the ceiling and which, with the huge dresser were *still* dwarfed by the dimensions of that magnificent old lounge-room.

Sadly our new home in Carlingford was rather less grand, being at the other end of the scale. A very small and non-descript two bedroom fibro house on a fairly busy road. Offering little in the way of character it was compensated to a degree by having a very large rear garden that was ideal for children. It was also well sited, being opposite the one-track rail terminus, a "spur" off the main Western line, as well as being handy to the area's major shopping mall. Besides the fact there would appear to be no way to cram our possessions into so confined a space there was the soul-destroying reality that the whole renovation process had now to be *recommenced* as every room was in drastic need of attention. The *really* bad news? The entire exterior needed painting too. Fortunate also that we didn't have a Ferrari - there was no garage!

Having bid farewell to a career in real estate, not being able to wait around long enough for the market to pick up, I took a position with American company analyst Dun and Bradstreet, with still at the back of my mind, the hope of making it ultimately to Canada. At least with an International group of such impeccable pedigree and with offices worldwide, the opportunity to work towards an overseas transfer was ever-present. It was the beginning of probably the most stable decade of my life, not that it had had much competition since my early childhood. Promotions came blessedly fast and I was made Reporting and Operations Supervisor within a short time, responsible for the hiring and training of company reporters, not so far removed in job specification and parameters from my years at the Herald.

In world news, a lot happened in '81. Australia sunk to its lowest level in sporting history on February 1st when Trevor Chappell bowled the last ball of an international cricket match *underarm*, to deny New Zealand the chance of victory. March 30th saw the attempted assassination of President Ronald Reagan who was shot in the chest at close range by twenty-five year old John W. Hinckley Jr.

On April 14th NASA launched the world's first reusable space shuttle *Columbia*, the same craft that was to make tragic headlines twenty two years later when its entire crew of seven astronauts died when the shuttle disintegrated on re-entry Feb 1st 2003. On May 13th Pope John Paul II was the subject of a major assassination attempt by Mehmet Ali Agca, an escaped Turkish criminal. Shot twice in the abdomen, the Pope underwent a five hour operation before he was declared "out of critical danger." Steven Spielberg's *"Raiders of the Lost Ark"* was the biggest film of the year. July 18th, two suspended walkways at the Hyatt Regency Hotel in Kansas City collapsed, killing one hundred and eleven people and injuring almost two hundred more. On Wednesday July 19th someone scribbled the words "Just Married" and hung it on the back of the seventy year old coach that was ferrying newlyweds Prince Charles and Lady Diana to their honeymoon. Yet another pairing that was to end in tragedy.

By Christmas I had painted a *new* home into existence. Less than three fifths the size of "The Rest" it was case of making every square centimetre count. Even so, you can't get a gallon of milk into a one litre carton. All we had *left* was a smallish tin-roof verandah at the back of the house. Amazing what creative things you can do with a few cross-beams, the underside of a corrugated iron roof and even some unsightly bare and unpolished floorboards! It was just a matter ultimately of getting used to eating dinner in mid summer in that little room when it was nudging one hundred and twelve degrees Fahrenheit! Shortly before my thirty-sixth birthday, Therese happened to mention, "Oh by the way, I'm pregnant!"

News came early in the new year that Grandad had died in Bournemouth at ninety-one years of age after a full and healthy life. I had desperately wanted him to see Therese and Christopher but this now could never be. He left me a small inheritance of some $10,000 which we decided to use on a trip to England, as in all likelihood with two young children (and whoever else might be planning to sign-up with us) there would be neither the opportunity or funds in the near future to make such a journey.

Thus with everything arranged, we took off for Hawaii on March 19th. For Therese, never having been outside Australia, it was a real awakening. Had one of *those* myself, when Chris' brand new stroller we had bought for the trip, completely fell apart, much to the great amusement of a cluster of co-travellers, as I retrieved it from the baggage carousel at Honolulu. Retraced then, a familiar path to Los Angeles, checking in at the old downtown Alexandria Hotel. Took Chris to Disneyland and although only two, to this day he swears he remembers it well. Drove up to San Francisco for a day and revived some great memories of the old city, from the Golden Gate Park to the beautiful sequoia forest at Muir Woods. On to New York where the Californian warmth was but a memory. Pushing Chris along 34th street in temperatures nudging zero was an experience. The poor little fella, having only ever know an Australian life-style had never been exposed to such icy trauma. He didn't murmur the entire morning until we got him back to the hotel room, then prised his fingers off the stroller whence he threw up from one end of our suite to the other. This was followed by an asthmatic attack that took some hours to stabilise.

Flew on to Frankfurt which was not much warmer but just so modernised and changed from the city I first saw in 1969. Memorable in the upshot, in as far as the airline lost half our luggage at Frankfurt International Airport, having allegedly loaded it mistakenly on a plane bound for some other European destination. Exactly how and why was never explained. We *were* however able to select replacement suitcases infinitely better than those we had lost. As for the original luggage, it was promised to be returned to us in London, and actually was! "Home" again if only temporarily, was everything to me that day. We rented a small Renault, which with Chris strapped in the back and our luggage loaded in, was not far off being overladen. Having partaken of another incomparable John Betcheman breakfast at the Charing Cross Hotel where we were staying that first morning, we headed off for Welling.

No matter how many times I drive down Danson Lane, the clock is wound back for me. I *know* if I willed it hard enough, I could still wake up in my bed again dreading that double English period to kick off the week, being just about here again. Shame too I still haven't finished that Biology project due to be handed in Tuesday first thing.

Walking along the path to the lake that day, the thought of living in Australia, let alone being in my late thirties and having a family of my own, just seemed so impossibly remote. I have never really *left* the lake, the swings, the old English Gardens or the Mansion house – I never *can!*

Pretty cool in Britain in March and this day was no exception. Therese said nothing, but I could see her thinking, "Yeah right, well this is all nice and touristy but where's the beach?" But hey, I *loved* her and it meant a lot to me at the time being able to show her some of *my* turf, shivering though she was. Chris too, even if he never sets foot in England again and he is after all 100% pure Aussie now, has at least *been* there, seen and touched some of his ancestry. It was to be fourteen years before his sisters had the same opportunity.

Friday April 2nd was interesting! More than six thousand Argentinian troops invaded the Falkland Islands and managed to overcome the eighty four British Marines stationed there. Thus, following Britain's one hundred and forty-nine year governing status of the Falklands, it was suddenly on an unprovoked war footing. Unusual to find yourself driving through a country, the image of peace and tranquility one moment, and at war just one news bulletin later. I was wondering if things could *really* turn full circle and I would find myself conscripted overnight. Therese's parents were panicking of course...her being five months pregnant a mitigating factor. We assured them there was no likelihood of a nuclear strike and that life in the UK was not expected to materially suffer at that stage. Had this occurred *post* 9/11 perhaps the prognosis may have been different. The conflict *did* indeed escalate but not before we had left the UK. During the succeeding week, I took Therese back to Wilsill to see the old farm, all over Yorkshire, Scotland and Wales and back for a night at the Charing Cross Hotel. That little Renault was knackered. We returned to Sydney mid April, via Los Angeles and Auckland.

Kate joined us July 14th. The least complicated of recorded births. She simply emerged, stared defiantly at everyone in attendance and after being weighed, washed and wrapped-up, lay in her humidicrib looking out, exuding the attitude, "OK, well *that* was a piece of cake, now where do we go from here?" In 2005, nothing has changed with her!

July that year also recorded two major tragedies. A Pan-Am jetliner went down in New Orleans killing one hundred and forty-nine passengers and on the 23rd, actor Vic Morrow and two Vietnamese children he was carrying on-set, were decapitated when a chopper crashed during the filming of the John Landis directed segment of *The Twilight Zone: The Movie*. Offsetting such grim reading and from the "It could only happen in Britain" file, the biggest security lapse in history allowed Queen Elizabeth to awake early on the morning of Friday July 12th to find a young man sitting at the end of her bed clutching a broken glass and dripping blood over her coverlet. She was said to be unamused.

Continued my tenure at Dun and Bradstreet but although a reasonably well paid and "comfortable" position, the long term prospects were looming as somewhere between slim and "don't count on it!" Additionally, international "transfers" were shown to be an proven *rarity* unless at the level of State Manager or higher. I figured it was a question of laying low for a while and seeing what opportunities might present themselves from whatever source. They usually do, just a question of looking!

Beloved actors Henry Fonda and Ingrid Bergman died within seventeen days of each other in August and just a fortnight later on September 10th the world was further shocked when actress Grace Kelly was killed after her car crashed off a mountain road in Monaco. Not long before Christmas, the Soviet Leader Leonard Brezhnev died and on December 22^{nd,} sixty-one year old retired dentist, Barney B. Clark became the recipient of the world's first artificial heart. On the music front, not since Elvis Presley, had anyone affronted parents and the self-styled uprighteous alike, until newcomer Madonna. *Borderline* sold millions - *Like a Virgin* was to raise the ire of many millions more. Seen as the virtual anti-christ in many eyes, she was to them, single handedly responsible for leading the corruption of the world's female youth! In world movie news, Arnold Schwarzenegger's screen career finally hit its straps with *Conan the Barbarian*, whereas the biggest film of this and most any other year, was Ridley Scott's inarguable sci-fi classic - *Blade Runner*.

Those "opportunities" I had been awaiting, were *still* not presenting themselves and thus for a while, life ran in neutral, not by particular definition, good, bad or indifferent. The new year did not start off too well in Australia when seventy two people died in the calamitous "Ash Wednesday" bushfires in Victoria and South Australia on February 16th, the worst in Aussie history. I received a personal commendation from the Vice President of Dun and Bradstreet in New York for "services rendered"…but *no* pay rise. Matter of fact, I became after that, probably management's most disliked employee in the country..."fraternising with the enemy" I think was the unofficial charge. I could live with that! April brought some highly unoriginal news from Therese's gynaecologist ...."Guess what?"

Jennifer weighed-in just four days up front of my thirty-eighth birthday, barely seventeen months after her sister. That's all we needed - *another* opinionated, egocentric and self-willed Sagittarian! Now three children *really* upsets the family dynamics. You're suddenly talking wall to wall people here. Not good in a two bedroom house! I do have to say though I became an expert at time management. I had all *three* bathed, changed, fed and smiling before I caught the 7.30 am. train to the city….no mean feat! You realise just how *bad* your life has gotten when you hang out that forty-second nappy on the line just after midnight as the temperature is nudging barely three degrees (yeah believe it, Sydney, Australia isn't *all* beach and barbecues my friend!) and you can no longer hold a clothes peg with any guaranteed certainty. It was yet a while before disposable diapers were the preferred way to go here.

Aside from Chris' worsening asthma and the myriad nights spent propping the poor little guy up on my lap every two hours with his life-saving nebuliser mask clamped to his mouth, life wasn't half bad. We were all having *fun* – the fundamental necessity of life. My career was definitely "on hold" having been called into the State Manager's office late that year and being told, "Well Noel, its like this – your own high standards are just not realistically achievable and management feels that you should be more accepting of your staff's finite capability." Translated as roughly, "Hey, what do expect here? Intelligence? ethics? A solid week's work for a full week's pay? Some measure of corporate efficiency? Yeah, I *was* delusional, no doubt about it!

September 27th and Australia pulled-off the greatest sporting upset in history when it took out the America's Cup in Newport Rhode Island, after the New York Yacht Club's 132 year dominance of the race. On November 11th, ownership of *Ayers Rock*, the planet's greatest monolith and one of the country's biggest tourist attractions, was returned to the Aboriginal elders of the area, to be known henceforth simply as *Uluru*.

1984 – A year that had sounded so futuristic when I was a child and in no small part due to George Orwell's novel of the same name, was here. Odd, I didn't *feel* especially futuristic. Hopefully still, 2000 would do it for me…remembering I had all those years ago dwelt on that distant and exciting milestone while still collecting conkers. Well, *hopefully* I'd see it anyway. It was going to take me fifty four years after all to get there – a score neither my dad or paternal grandfather had been able to get past! Shortly after astronauts Bruce McCandlass and Robert L. Stewart recorded man's first space-walk one hundred and seventy miles above the earth on February 7th, one of those well-disguised little opportunities I had been laying in wait for, attempted to sneak past me. I was way too quick for it! A position advertised for a reporting supervisor with College Mercantile, the company that just so happened to be Dun and Bradstreet's major competitor in Australia. Given my experience and intimate working knowledge of "the enemy" how could they not hire me? Fortunately, that was the way *they* saw it too. I recall being a major tourist attraction at the interview that day! "Hey, do you know who *he is*?" was passing along the office grapevine with unchecked vigour. Installed at my new desk within two weeks, this was cool stuff. Treated with considerably more respect and paid vastly better than my previous tenure, working with a slightly smaller and more dedicated team was far more to my liking. Had Dun & Bradstreet known of my intended *defection* I'm sure I would have been asked to remove my good self from their premises earlier – I made sure they didn't. There was however to be the most ironic of sequels to this particular event just three years later.

As luck and coincidence would have it, Steve, a friend of mine, a former top salesman from Dun and Bradstreet no less (this was the first I even knew he'd even *left* the place) was in the throes of setting up a new marketing company within the College group. Maybe he just liked the cut of my suit, whatever, I was offered a departmental transfer, *with* a major pay-rise before I could say "Yeah right, and shortly I'll be waking *up* no doubt!" Opting to decentralise, the group had recently completed a new head office building in Ashfield, an inner western suburb of Sydney. The makeover therefore was rendered complete with a new luxury office, state of the art computerisation and private parking. Hell, we even had a staff *penthouse*.

"My own secretary would be nice?" I mentioned to Steve the day after we moved in. "Sure," he said "You're damn *right,* you need one. Write up the ad, you can interview them next week. Pay her what you think's reasonable." Steve *did* have style!

Thus Sue came on board the following week. Miss Sue *Smith* to be accurate. Never did exist a more complete and able secretary. She may have been the least adept person I ever did see executing a gear change but in her chosen profession she was nothing short of indispensable. One had only to *mention* an upcoming business trip and the plane, car and accommodation was booked and the documentation sitting neatly folded on my desk pad. Speaking of business trips, shame the frequent flyer points scheme wasn't a major inducement in the early 80's in Australia. In the next couple of years, I must have been on a first name basis with half the airport staff in Brisbane, Melbourne, Adelaide and Perth. I went to sleep counting air-bridges. National Data as our company division was known, built and sold business-orientated databases. I discovered an affinity with computers, they were smart, efficient and clean! I was also finding a hitherto unexperienced event – having money left over *after* the weekend. Therese began to find the occasional twenty and fifty dollar note skulking away surreptitiously in her purse that had been conspicuously absent a short time earlier. Steve meanwhile had grandiose plans requiring grandiose investment by College's owners. Unfortunately for him, while he talked-up big – they spent up small and sooner rather than later, Steve found himself on the outer periphery. Either I was to meet my own Waterloo or I could navigate a path between the warring parties that might lead to where I wanted to be led?

Mid '85, and following the death on May 27th of some ten thousand people in a cyclone in Bangladesh and the Bradford football-stadium tragedy in Britain four days later, when forty people burned to death after the grandstand caught fire, it came to be common knowledge that the owners of College had been sourcing offshore funds with a view to a "do or die for the glory" bid to finally trounce Dun and Bradstreet as the market leader in the Australian mercantile arena – some might say an unwise if not foolish aspiration. When the dust settled, the cheques and documentation exchanged, from the owners viewpoint at least, something was definitely rotten in the State of Denmark. It appeared that the 49% of the company they had been floating had somehow been marginally tampered with at boardroom level and what they ultimately signed-over was in fact 51% of the company. Not only did they no longer *own* College they found, they no longer worked there! I now was an employee of the enormous Canadian-founded but international conglomerate – Moore Business Systems Inc whose specialty worldwide was business forms through its Moore Paragon division. This *was* a company the equal of and as financially backed *as*, Dun and Bradstreet. Steve was heaved as being part of the old order and a new Manager for National Data brought in, Leon - a guy I had actually known for some years. I found myself additionally with a pay-rise, Steve's old company car and the opportunity to present myself to the new board in Melbourne to explain *how* our division was going to generate a six figure income in the next 24 months. That proved tricky without echoing the "Steve" factor - being that "you need to *spend* money to make money." In essence though, that *was* my message!

Five people in two bedrooms was becoming a problem. *Any* way you slice that equation you're left with highly undesirable mega-crammed living! With finally an annual income you'd admit to your *least* favourite bank manager, we had a chance now of moving up to somewhat more convivial domestic circumstances. Ever aware of dad's ageless and inarguably good advice – always buy the worst house in the best street, we soon found *that* little beauty. Number 22 Dremeday Street, in nearby Baulkham Hills had been on the market for months.

"I'll show it to you," the agent had said "But, you're *not* going to thank me for it!" I liked it already!

Give the girl her due, it was no "house of the week." Neglected, run down, unloved and at $85,000, the shabbiest and least appealing puppy in the pound. We *had* to have it! What it *did* have was, full-brick construction, four bedrooms, huge eat-in kitchen, lounge, dining room and separate play/entertaining area. Even a servery. OK, the carpet *was* threadbare, rags on some of the windows and floors and needing painting throughout but hey, having just done this three times running, may as well clock up a fourth. With basically *no* room livable, Therese and I spent the first week or so "camped" in the entertaining area with crated possessions packed floor to ceiling. In any event, what could be *more* "entertaining" than that first rainstorm, watching the water cascade down *inside* the wall and through the built-in bookcase? *This* as it eventuated, was on account of the metal roofing having been laid inexpertly, one might say sub-intellectually – wrongside up! Was this to be *The Money Pit 2*? The children's bedrooms were first on the hit list as the "Picasso of the paint-roller" fell back upon his old tried and tested techniques and gradually, a lovely home was returned into being. I would not claim to have the *beginnings* of my father's home-renovation skills, but from a child's viewpoint there were distinct parallels between Dremeday street and Danson lane. At much the same age in their lives, a dark and run-down older home with a huge rear yard, quite the last word in botanical neglect!

Not often you buy a house and you have absolutely no idea how big the grounds actually are! The reason for this apparent enigma was that to the immediate rear of the huge, if not slightly listing old garage, that later we managed to park two cars and a mini-van in quite comfortably, ran a rusted-out chain fence the width of the property. Beyond that was well, *darkness,* I think covers it nicely. An enormous and none-too-healthy tree of elm-like character yet of unknown genus, lorded over the entire area – boundary to boundary, branches encroaching on our three neighbour's properties. So thick were the overhead and intertwined branches that one could stand beneath it anywhere during the heaviest of showers and not feel a drop of rain. At ground level, several decades of rubbish, rotted wood, discarded fridges, washing machines and otherwise dysfunctional electronic items littered the area between which, bushes, bamboo, thistle and wild grasses had staked a claim. For days, we drove the invaders backwards and finally we located the rear fence together with the remains of an enormous yet rotted and dilapidated cubby house that had once been a child's dream sanctuary. Requiring the largest rental truck we could find, the area was emptied of its tyrannical usurpers leaving only the huge tree to be cut down by a team of arborists. With inbound sunlight now, grass gradually returned and before you could say "Damn, is it Kate's birthday again?" we had ourselves a small soccer field. The wheel had completed a full revolution now. I knew that far far away, some children were playing by a lake and wondering just why they were feeling so happy.

They weren't the only ones! Marine scientist Dr Robert D Ballard was smiling too. On September 1st he found the *Titanic*, some seventy-three years after she foundered. The first two weeks of October brought a succession of tragedies as on the 2nd, 10th and 12th respectively, the passing of Rock Hudson, Yul Brynner and Orson Welles left the world a poorer place.

On December 12th I found out what it was like to be forty – remarkably like being thirty nine as far as I could see!

CHAPTER TEN

NOTHING SUCCEEDS LIKE FAILURE

January 31st 1986 and the world watched replay after slow motion replay of the space shuttle *Challenger* as it exploded in a stream of flaming debris just 74 seconds after take-off from Houston. Seven astronauts died that day, a tragedy that was to be repeated (as I mentioned in the last chapter) when *Columbia* disintegrated on re-entry seventeen years later.

Promoted to NSW State Manager after Leon's unheralded exile early February, I knew I had finally *made* it when they handed me the keys to the Penthouse. The money was good - the mini-bar on the roof even better! Most of my time during this period had been spent authoring what was intended to be an upmarket corporate reference work entitled *"The Australian Business Atlas."* An ambitious and pricey leather-bound book that compared and statistically profiled Australia's seven major cities, primarily from a business-density viewpoint at zipcode level. Having gained publishing acceptance from the redoubtable McGraw Hill Book Company, the work was at pre-publishing and final editorial stage, when the Managing Director and half the Australian staff there, found themselves ousted overnight. *"The Australian Business Atlas"* was a flow-on casualty. Many months of writing, fact-finding and diagrammatic statistical analysis for nothing. No other interested publishers could be found short-term and the project was by necessity, shelved. Still, there was always the mini-bar!

Barely had Autumn established its imperceptive grasp on the seasonal calendar that year, when came upon a day like any other, but for the subtlest of variations. State Manager at morning tea - *unemployed* by the lunchbreak! In the tradition of most "faceless" management decisions, it was left to the company's financial accounting team to inform the terminated masses of the "regrettable decision made in the light of continuing economic uncertainty." Retrenchment is always an expensive proposition from a managerial standpoint and that day I figured, the "executions" would have set the company back a cool quarter of a mill plus – hard cash!

"We'd like to thank you Noel for your extreme assistance, patience and diligence during the transitional period following the company take-

over. Unfortunately however due to the Board's decision to cut back on regional staff levels, your position has effectively become redundant."

Put simply.... "Thanks for the memories – the elevator is right behind you!" Hardest to bear was handing the keys to my new company car back. Even as I exited stage right though, I had a plan...you gotta *always* have a plan! To be honest with you, I *did* make one small detour that morning – before handing over the company paraphernalia, I emptied the mini-bar in its entirety.

Just months after taking on a crushing mortgage, finding yourself *unemployed* is not exactly the career move you were looking for. Agreed, the termination pay yielded up a small comfort-zone but that was little better than finding yourself on death-row after being framed for murder in the first! It was time for the corporate dream. Most every underpaid, under-appreciated member of the workforce has at one time mused over starting up their own business. The chance to be your own boss, make your own decisions, your own life! Answerable to no-one, with the possible exception of your bank manager. The historically proven reality is however, that one in five small business undertakings invariably go belly-up within two years. It was my call alright but as I saw it, with no job anyway I had everything to gain and not a hell of a lot to lose. Yeah right! where's a decent clairvoyant when you need one?

In any event, my problems ranked significantly less than those of a real estate salesman living in Kiev in April '86 following the disastrous melt-down on the 26th of the Chernobyl nuclear reactor, not sixty miles distant. The ensuing radioactive cloud heading due west wasn't that great a tourist attraction either.

So what *was* my plan? Simple, I had just spent five or so years in the database industry, building up not just a rudimentary knowledge of information resources and market-place needs but developing a not inconsiderable network of clients and industry contacts. Sure, I was forty grand shy of being able to start up on my own but why let the *little* things hold you back? Where a billion dollar multi-national had failed, I would succeed, I still had the key resource *they* now lacked – me! Evidential of his magnanimous generosity and to my eternal gratitude, Therese's father deposited a considerable percentage of the aforementioned sum into my account shortly after my declared intent to "go it alone" to help get me started. A very successful mechanical engineer who had built up his own toolmaking company over the previous twenty years or so, I had carved out suddenly the smallest niche of unlikely credibility for myself in announcing my business plan. As it happened, David my former IT

252

manager in Melbourne, was also something less than enthused with the Moore Business Systems *modus operendi* and decided he would toss in his lot with me. Partnerships they say, rarely work out! We would see.

Before anything however I was now missing an essential item in my life – a car! Not in any position to blow a dollar more than necessary, I found a twelve year old Toyota Crown that besides being in absolutely mint condition, was to prove the best car I would ever own and amongst the other seventy six I've enjoyed thus far, it has surely faced some stiff competition. These days, whilst currently indisposed through lack of funds, it sits nestled within its own garage, watching the rain fall outside, remembering better days and seeing the once young family it carried daily, grow up. For its 30th birthday next year, I made a promise to have the car roadworthy once more.

On the entertainment front, director James Cameron swept both Ripley and the audience into new realms of cinematic fantasy that summer with the release of *Aliens*, a new benchmark in terms of adrenalin-fuelled sci-fi action and a hugely successful sequel to 79's original *Alien*. Perhaps an even bigger impact was made by the Japanese company *Nintendo* who introduced their computer games to the western world mid '86. Cyndi Lauper had a worldwide hit with *True Colors,* Madonna had a desperate message for her dad with, *Papa Don't Preach.* The Bangles still felt obliged to *Walk Like an Egyptian* and Whitney Houston never was to get over her *Greatest Love of All*.

Shortly before Christmas 1986 we opened for business in smart new serviced offices situated downtown Parramatta – the site of the first Australian Government House. The company, much to the irritation of my former employers was called, (some might say optimistically) *International Data* – so named in essence, to continue and expand my formerly divisionalised *National Data* operation that I had headed-up within the Moore Group and which I heard had since ground to a halt. This was significantly the dawn of the personal computer age. 5 1/4" floppies were high tech but the 20 megabyte hard drives of the day were totally incapable of manipulating databases such that *International Data* was running and which at half a gigabyte plus, needed a full blown Digital-Vax or Tandem Non-Stop system to house and operate them. Our first six months sales exceeded all expectations. Problem *was* however that after deducting the leasing costs of the US hardware we were probably in-front by maybe two cappuccinos? A packet of *TimTams* would have sent us into the red! Thus, a combination of increased billing costs and *more* sales, addressed to some degree our somewhat dodgy bottom line but an early retirement wasn't looking good.

What *was* making money however was the house. With interest rates at an all time low, property values were skyrocketing in Sydney and by the time Pat Cash became the first Australian to take out Wimbledon in 17 years, after trashing Ivan Lendl centre court July '87, our equity was up 50%. Needing more cash for the business was as simple as filling out a loan form. "Ya got a house mate? No probs – how much d'ya want?" The company was at that stage, like most small businesses in their gestation, getting by under the quintessential and age-old methodology of one step forward and two steps back! But as a family we were all having the time of our lives. 22 Dremeday lived its finest hours. Bed-time stories were in big demand, the cam-corder ran hot, preserving for ever, images of beautiful young lives untouched yet by any flecks of the world's darker realities. Little wonder that Lisa looked down upon our remote suburban beacon that year and said to herself *"That's* where I want to be born!" She waited until October the first – well, it *is* warmer then!

On October 19th developments of quite a different kind brought increased blood pressure and heart palpitations to share dealers around the globe, when the New York Street Stock Exchange sold 52 million shares within thirty minutes of its opening for business. The Wall Street madness saw ten billion dollars wiped off the value of the Australian share market alone. It was rumoured that sales of hand-pistols however, hit an all time high that morning.

I still saw Ghinda as often as she was able to make it…sometimes Helen would drop her off at home, othertimes I would meet her in the city for an all too brief coffee and sandwich. Now sixteen incredibly, she maintained the closest bond with Chris for some reason, but I could sense she was "straying" somehow. There were dark clouds forming not that far over the horizon and I sure was no meteorologist. I loved her as much as I loved any of the children…she *knew* that, but I just sensed she was "letting go" and there never *was* going to be any safety net for her.

Christmas '87 – that little church sitting in its customary place on the dresser, glowed so bright. *Four* children now came to wonder at its simple message as it held sway in a darkened room that Christmas Eve, a lit sentinel of hope, love and the stored memories now of three generations. As was the custom throughout the 80's, Santa maintained the tradition of hanging their stockings, each bulging with promise, from the old hallstand which sat in its appointed spot near the front door. There was always a deranged scramble at early light Christmas morning, to be the first to retrieve their own stocking. Even as the ensuing years' manhandling took savage toll on these icons of happiness and childhood remembrance with substantial fraying and ripping of the fabric, all four of them could always recognise their own possession, irrespective of the wrapped contents or the varying order in which they might be hung. Let's be realistic though, this was only ever the entrée – the real deal always *was* piled up under the tree!

January 26th 1988 and one and a half million people crammed the foreshores of Sydney Harbor to participate in the country's elaborate Bicentenery celebrations. Two hundred years down the track and Australians *still* can't enunciate the colour "maroon" properly!

The business was kicking on, barely profitable to be sure, but at least establishing itself in the market place which at that early juncture was all that could reasonably be expected. I had re-hired Sue my long time secretary from Moore Business Systems and without her unequalled efficiency and hard work, those early years would have been very destabilised. As far as INXS was concerned, the title of their then current hit - *Need You Tonight* - could not have been more appropriate! A tad irritating having to fly to Melbourne for Partnership meetings but what else is an American Express card for? Our database was expanding as was our *client* base and it was definitely a case of "so far, so good!" Minor partnership squabbles reared up - mainly along the lines that simply because the business had been of my initiation, based on my own expertise and funded totally by the Sydney connection, I really *wasn't* entitled to decide policy and corporate strategy, despite the fact my business card read *Managing Director*. David invariably slunk back to his mainframe and looked after what he did exquisitely well – the operational software design and maintenance. Clients were showing us loyalty and sales were covering that bottom line, mortgage repayments and God knows how many breakfasts at Ronald McDonalds. There was now a new buzz-word in the market place….CD-ROM. It was however what it could *do,* that interested me. The ability to hold our entire national business database on one disc, allowing a user to interrogate it and then download that which he or she might require. This, in the late 80's was electronic nirvana.

"Wasting your time mate" was David's contribution. "CD-ROM is just a gimmick, won't ever catch on!" Despite my disagreeing and attempts to get him to dig a little deeper into some of the existing US applications, he could not be swayed and the subject was buried with not a little acrimony.

Speaking of acrimony, the American warship *Vincennes* on July 3rd that year, managed to shoot down an Iranian commercial airbus in the Persian Gulf carrying 290 civilians, many of whom were pilgrims. It was *not* the US' finest moment, nor was any plausible explanation immediately forthcoming as to why the airliner was at any stage regarded as being a likely spy-plane. George Harrison had an enormous hit mid-year with *I Got my Mind Set on You* which may have been a coincidental pointer to Republican George Bush being voted-in as US President on November 8th. The Beach Boys hobbled out on their walking frames to do it one more time with *Kokomo* (from the Tom-Cruise-for-teenies flick *Cocktail*) and Brit flavor of the month Billy Ocean, was near desperate, pleading *Get Out of My Dreams and Into My Car!*

With David's on-going disinclination to take an active part in any evaluation and development of a cd-product, we registered a second business entity, *United Directory Systems* (UDS) which later that year, signed a partnership agreement with a major international electronics firm to produce what was to be the country's first business marketing tool – *Australia On Disc*. An interrogatable and retrievable database of all Australia's fifty-five yellow and white (residential) pages. The product launch was successful despite the fact that as at August 1988 there were estimated to be less than two hundred cd-rom drives in the country, 95% of which were in the Government sector. One additional stumbling block being the price of the units – close to $2300 each and *all* external drives. It was to be some time before each and every personal computer in Australia, came with an inbuilt cd. It was not until the following year's upgrade in fact, that interactive cd's for home-use came onto the market - games, encyclopaedias, atlases and similar educational software discs.

Even split 60:40 with the new partner, which was the trade-off for having the discs mastered by an associate company, *Philips Dupont Optical* in South Carolina (*then,* one of only three cd-mastering plants worldwide) early sales were looking comfortably ahead of budget. One slight ripple in the fabric of corporate calm however was David, voluntarily cut adrift from the project, I rather doubted he would remain content in his self-enforced product isolation.

The year was to end in utter tragedy when a terrorist bomb exploded aboard a Pan Am Jetliner over Scotland which crashed in Lockerbie, killing all 259 on board and 11 on the ground. Subsequently unravelled Government cover-ups in both Britain and the US, determined that middle eastern terrorist groups had conspired to bring the plane down in part pay-back for the Iranian incident earlier in the year. This of course would have been of little consolation to discover for the 270 who died on December 21st - my father's birthday.

Unable obviously to fit *four* childrens' seats across the rear of the car now, we were obliged to move up to "people-mover" status. Shortly before Christmas therefore, we acquired an eight-seater Toyota Tarago (*Previa,* in the US) One of the early RV's, this mini-bus was cutting-edge transport in the 80's despite having the acceleration of a lawnmower and front suspension the equal of the average exercise bike. Did someone say "reliable" though? They don't make them tougher. In all its years of duty, the thing never once threw a spaz and we're talking round-the-world mileage two or three times here!

March 23rd that year and the greatest environmental disaster to yet befall the planet, occurred when the oil tanker *Exxon Valdez* grounded itself, with the help of some questionably inattentive navigation, on Bligh Reef in Prince William Sound, Alaska. 10.8 million gallons of crude spilled from the wreck which in fifty two days had covered the entire Alaskan coastline some four hundred and ninety miles south of the reef. Just ten days later on April 2nd British sport was devastated when following the collapse of a barrier at Hillsborough Stadium in Liverpool, ninety six soccer fans died and a further one hundred and seventy two were injured. It was England's worst sporting tragedy. Almost prophetic that Billy Joel should have such a gigantic worldwide hit with *We Didn't Start the Fire,* a song embracing other major world headlines since the fifties.

In terms of pyrotechnics however, things *were* hotting up on the partnership front...*both* partnership fronts as it transpired! Mid-year a trusted client called me and said "Hey, I see you guys have a major competitor in Melbourne?" I enquired as to what he was referring to and he pinpointed an ad which had appeared in the country's leading business tabloid *The Australian Financial Review,* that morning. Advertised on a state by state basis at bargain-basement rates were databases corresponding precisely to those that we held at *International Data,* on behalf of *UDS.* No company point of sale identified, simply a telephone number. Reeling in a couple of favours, I had the number traced. A new connection so it turned out hooked-up not twenty four hours earlier, to none other than yep, *David's* desk! Yeah, this *did* place us on a major war-footing in a hurry! Unable to deny the clear evidence, David sought refuge under the oft tried and tested philosophy – "aggression is the best form of defence." Having evidently seen late the previous year an episode of television's hi-tech program *Beyond 2000,* during which a lengthy segment was devoted to the recently launched *"Australia On Disc"* new business product, he, in his own words, "lost it." Figuring he had been "cut out of the deal," and fully ignoring his own stated preferences to "have nothing to do with CD-ROM," he had erroneously concluded that he was "owed" big-time and that therefore the theft and illegal sale of data which belonged exclusively to *United Directory Systems,* was no more than a means to a end. I think I gave him a *more* than reasonable choice. Buy-out my 50% share in *International Data* or explain his new-found business strategies, involving a clear-cut case of corporate fraud, to the Victorian Police! I was shy one business partner by the end of the week as I recall.

Not exactly a bed of roses over at the other partnership headquarters either. Reconciliations of remaining units held in stock, against partnership revenue *paid,* failed to match-up by the proverbial mile. The company's divisional management was loathe to discuss the issue. My attorneys weren't! Subsequent enforced stocktaking checks yielded up an interesting fact....at least one hundred and fifty boxed copies of *Australia On Disc* mysteriously "having walked out of the warehouse," which at $699 each, was anything but chicken-feed at the time. Inevitable litigation requiring that the company pay-up our contracted share of the missing discs, achieved three things! *No* money, an immediate shut-down of the company's CD-ROM division and inter-departmental transfer or retrenchment of everyone associated with the project. The former head of the division found himself whisked unceremoniously to some remote European outpost where he remained *incommunicado*. "Sue us" was the offer "See what that costs you?" Gotta hand it to them, it was a smart move.

Forming then a secondary partnership with the two expatriot company techos who had been instrumental in building the first disc, and who maintained communicative links with the mastering company in the US, we set ourselves by necessity, a *limited* time-frame in which to produce the '89 upgrade. This was accomplished with minimal heartache and for a while there we were back on track.

On October 17th life in San Francisco was anything but, when a devastating earthquake measuring 7.1 on the Richter scale struck the Bay area. Sixty two people died, more than three thousand seven hundred were injured and twelve thousand rendered homeless by the 'quake that left the city with a damage bill nudging six billion dollars.

1990 – now *that* had a futuristic ring to it! Not that this was to be of any lasting relevance to Russia, once a super-power but with the relinquishing of Communist rule on February 7th becoming merely a collection of States in chaos. Just four days later, Nelson Mandela was freed by South African authorities after spending twenty seven and a half years imprisoned for his political beliefs and visions for an end to the racial injustices in his country. On April 25th the Hubble Space Telescope was launched by the US.

Business lurched ever onwards. With the technical support of Geoff and Dennis, they of the partnership-come-lately, and the evolvement of "Dataware," new mega-powered US data-retrieval software, sales of *Australia On Disc 3* hit warp factor 6. *Here* surely was the turning point? Forty-five years down the track but hey, patience *is* a virtue! Mid year and from way left-field befell the most unlikely of corporate opportunity. A cashed-up London-based marketing company looking to expand their operations to Australia came a-calling! Having in mind to acquire the country's best and most comprehensive database, both business and residential, we came fully accredited! Several zeroes sweetened the deal. A quarter of a million basically to acquire the data and close down UDS, plus retention of my position as Managing Director of the new Australian Operations. One hundred grand retainer per annum, 15% share option and performance incentives. Put it this way, I didn't say "Well hmmm, let me think about it!" Simply said "Come up with the contract, I'll sign it." *That* little formality however was no push-over. Every little thing was checked out and promises made to "complete" inside ten days. The ten days stretched to two weeks...three. Several last minute glitches needed to be ironed out, frequently from teleconferenced and hastily convened meetings. Once even inolving *numero uno* direct, as he sped between meetings in his London cab! All was completed, the nominated day for signing arrived. Shame the contract didn't! At the eleventh hour came that which I had suspected but for reasons I hadn't. "Many apologies! Cannot go through with the deal as the British Company has itself just been acquired by a Canadian conglomerate!" It didn't conclude with "Have a nice life!" but it may as well have! The reason for their stalling was now fatefully evident! Swiftly shelving plans for the tri-level five bedroom mini-mansion we had all but put down a deposit on, it was time for a reality-check! I had the vaguest inkling of "slippage" on the horizon once more and somewhat more than just losing one of the three cars we really didn't need.

Cellphones then, were just about the hottest gimmick around – I had a hands-free model installed in the Crown, which given that I was on the road much of the time in those days, enabled me to retain permanent client contact. Also came in remarkably useful making those "surprise" bookings for the children's special nights out at the local "Black Stump" restaurant. All but Lisa were attending Primary school now and despite the disappointment of the failed "take-over" we were I thought, entering a "golden age." How tragically astray was *that* estimate?

Therese had, a short time earlier, begun attending a series of self-awareness lectures designed principally to enlighten and to broaden not only one's perspective on life but one's *place* in it. She had in the first instance gone there at the urging and insistance of her cousin. By degrees I was noticing subtle changes in her.....and I was worried! Robert Palmer may have been the king of cool at the time with *Simply Irresistible*, but as even *he* found out, the good times rarely last. They most *especially* didn't last for pop group Milli Vanilli who had their Grammy Award for *Girl You Know Its True* rescinded after admitting that they lip-synched their songs, which elevated them into the pop hall of infamy.

Ahead of the groundswell, I was invited to attend a major marketing and hardware expo held in Las Vegas that November, just four days after Margaret Thatcher resigned as British Prime Minister on the 2nd. An Annual event, the expo was a forum, staged in six major hotels on "The Strip" at which the latest computer technology was exhibited and the international marketing fraternity offered the chance to showcase their own products. If it wasn't on display – it didn't exist! Leaving on the 12th November, I spent three days in the desert air before flying on to NYC where amongst other things, I ascended the World Trade Centre for what was to be my last time, as tragic circumstances were to dictate. As always, I stayed at Loewes Summit on 51st and Lexington and if anyone offers a better grilled steak in lower Manhattan, then I have yet to discover it.

Heathrow was on terrorist alert that November and perhaps on account of that fact *and* a scarcity of tourists at this particular time of year, I picked up a weekly car rental for less than I would have paid for a day's hire back home. Driving south east to Welling, it occurred to me as I crossed Blackheath, that this was the first time since the mid sixties that I had returned to my home-town alone. For November it was remarkably temperate. Coolish but sunny and invigorating. Since I had my camcorder with me I filmed a mini-documentary of Welling and Danson Park for the benefit of the children, so many of whose bed-time stories had featured insignificant but recognisably happy places of interest there. I was also fortunate enough to be able to organise a few hours in the park with my cousin Ghinda, she and I having not been there together since we were children, more than 18 months before Joyce and I left England. To say it was an emotional re-union would be the most outlandish of understatements. 85 Danson Lane on the other hand, was by now a sad and pitiful sight. Owned by a trucker who had solved the need to keep edges at the front neat and tidy by concreting the entire yard, not a vestige of "garden" remained. No hedges, front-fencing, gate etc, just a prime-mover, where in another time, the hydrangers and rhododendrens had once proudly sat. The rear garden was gone. Simply a formless pile of uneven ground and neglect. No paths, no lawn, no brick walls, not even an identifiable *flower bed*. Simply some rusted-out steel fencing long since serving any useful purpose and a discarded child's swing-set listing aimlessly close to where "mid-off" might once have been sited upon my old cricket pitch. The two sole icons of beloved memory – the ancient apple tree with its profusion of "Granny Smiths" *still* stood centre garden, little bigger than it had been thirty years earlier but now sadly in need of dad's pruning. While at the northern extremity of the rear yard, right beside where I now stood looking through a gap in the fence, sat the old gnarled tree where Peter and I had built our split-level "tree house" and where even now I could still make out some loose strands of rusted wire that had once been a part of the mesh-roofing, hanging forlornly from the upper forks. It was line-ball as to whether the truckie had even been *born* in those days! For the record however, little else seemed much changed in Welling except that never again will I be able to quaff a Ferrara's ice cream wafer, the beloved parlour having long since passed into obscurity.

Spent a couple more nights at the comfortable old Clarendon Hotel at nearby Blackheath, using this primarily as a base from which to commute to London and whilst reacquainting myself with many favoured old haunts in nearby Kent. When came the time once more to hit the M35 orbital for the drive back to Heathrow, I shed a silent tear not knowing when I might return.

Returned to Sydney via Singapore, then Kuala Lumpur, principally on account of the fact I had never been there. Standing out amongst many other Malaysian attractions is the magnificent domed Sultan Abdul Samad Building, the enormous commercial Dayabumi shopping complex and the wonderful National Museum opposite KL's central railway station. Regrettably for me, it was to be another eight years before the Kuala Lumpur skyline would be dominated by the world's tallest building, the twin Petronas Towers.

January 17th 1991 marked an arguably underwhelming news snippet. The first transatlantic crossing in a hot-air balloon, by none other than eccentric Virgin Records boss Richard Branson, who touched down in Yellowknife Canada, having drifted the 6,700 miles from Miyakonyo Japan, in remarkably quick time.

Under the terms and conditions of the existing business partnership, we operated a joint banking and checking facility (requirement of two signatories) whilst all sales and client information was recorded in a central log to which both partnership entities had equal access 24/7. The day in February thus, when I received a call from a major real estate group in South Australia, asking me technical questions as to the setting up of their national network database application for *Australia On Disc,* I was "concerned" let us say, there being no documentation recorded for either their inclusion as a new user *or* the fate of the S15,000 they paid for the licensed privilege of *becoming* one. This somewhat elevated my festering suspicions. These were shortly after brought home in dramatic, some might say *catastrophic* circumstance, when an enquiry at the bank revealed no trace of the $185,000 resident there not twenty four hours earlier. "You withdrew the balance yesterday morning as you may recall Mr Bailey" I was informed, half expecting it. Amazing just how easy it is to forge a signature. In the next twenty four hours certain other "new" users came to light. Given that our weekly stock-take checks balanced against sales figures there would appear to be only two possibilities. Fudged disc-replication figures or secondary print runs at alternate cd duplicating facilities (which also would have required my signature.) Figuring the element of *surprise* may stand me in better stead when push came to actual shove, I concentrated my resources on determining the actual criminal *modus operendi*. With the co-operation of US authorities it proved to have been my first guess – forged paperwork. As evidence, they forwarded me copies of the original documentation, showing a variation of at least one hundred additional discs manufactured from that we had agreed to replicate. This however was almost a secondary issue, since I was personally indebted to the tune of some $80,000 for work effected on behalf of the original data. Having no option, I reported the matter to the Fraud Squad, together with the supporting documentary evidence obtained. The *immediate* effect of the theft of the partnership funds however was that I was suddenly insolvent to the point of being unable to even make mortgage payments on the house.

It was at this juncture that Therese chose to make clear her intentions that she wanted a re-alignment of her living circumstances and *that,* quite definitely to exclude my own presence. Not since that day I returned home from school at fifteen to find both parents in hospital and on the critical list, had my own life faced such unwanted and unsolicited chaos. Not everyone has had the experience of facing the imminent loss of their wife, house and business, all in the same week. All the more hard to take when seemingly everything was running at optimum trackspeed only weeks earlier.

Just literally *hours* ahead of Geoff's arrest by the Sydney Fraud Squad, he was found stone cold dead, hanging half-out the window of a semi-detached inner city cottage he had financed with my money. Ruled a coronary, I would adjudge it more a case of *karma*. In the next week or so the Police uncovered a trail of gambling debts and shonky business dealings guaranteed to ensure that nothing would ever be recoverable. Besides leaving me stranded between a rock and a hard place, he managed to leave a wife and young daughter in destitute circumstances. His young partner Dennis was ultimately found to have no case to answer, despite the probability of his willing involvement in the scam, as he was a minor partner with no company shareholding as it eventuated, and all documentary evidence bore only Geoff's signature. I recall his unsolicited smirk as, in company with the Police, we left the premises. Also the bitterest of ironies that followed. Dennis had been especially fond of the phrase "At the end of the day mate, what goes around *comes* around." Within twelve months of that last interview, he was diagnosed as having an inoperable brain tumour. Strike two!

The full amount misappropriated, fraudulently obtained….whatever, was never able to be established. That I lost my $90,000 plus share in the partnership bank accounts *was* documented, but the number of sales made over and above those I never knew about, would have resulted in an overall loss well over a quarter of a million dollars in hard cash. How *far* over, only Geoff and Dennis would ever have known. So yeah, I learned the *hard* way the potential downside of a business partnership! Three in two years embarrassingly….*four* if you include a marriage. My immediate problem however was one of survival. As the unpaid (unpay*able*) monthly mortgage accumulated, it would be simply a matter of time before the bank foreclosed. In any event, the only way to repay the business loans taken out, levered up through the house equity, was by disposing of the home. I was able to maintain an income of sorts, reverting to sales of business data, much of which I was now able to generate myself with the latest software becoming available on personal computers. With no disposable cash to hand, Therese's plans to move out were by necessity put on hold for a while. It wasn't until the Spring of '91 that she finally moved into a rented town-house relatively close-by and where she still lives.

In the world of pop music, US band Nirvana, led by the short-term Kurt Cobain, released the *Smells Like Teen Spirit* track from their *Nevermind* album and so was born the international grunge movement

263

that year. Compact Discs were now outselling both vinyl records and cassette tapes.

Although St Nicholas still filled to overflowing the four stockings and the loungeroom sparkled as ever with traditional Christmas decorations while happy children "oohed" and "ahed" as each wrapping was discarded with firm deliberation, there was a dark shadow inveigling proceedings. One of sadness from my viewpoint – uncertainty and disbelief from the children. It was also to be the last Christmas we would ever have at Dremeday Street and the house knew it! As it happened It was *also* the last Christmas ever to be celebrated by the USSR too, which officially suffered complete dissolution on Christmas day with the resignation of President Gorbachev, leaving in its place a new Russia, one known as the Commonwealth of Independent States. An end to the once mighty Soviet Union.

1992 and at that stage the 5.442 billion people living in communal disharmony on the planet were the proud owners of an estimated nine hundred and ten million television sets. Some mad trivia fact you say? Predictably I found myself once again trying to offload a house during a property crash and from a market place valuation of just on $300,000 almost ten months earlier, the best offer inducible was $196,000. With the mortgage and every other business loan paid out, it left enough only to pay rental bond monies and removal costs. Thus we found ourselves with no more than a "get out of jail" card right back on the starting square, albeit in a neat little red-brick three-bedroom home in leafy Baker Crescent, still in Baulkham Hills and barely five minutes from our now lost and desperately missed family home. From the children's viewpoint however one really positive aspect at least…..a tiny but serviceable little park right across the road from our new driveway. In the ensuing years so much fun was to be had there.

Helen rang me that February with news that that filled me with sadness. But for a few phone calls and the very occasional meeting, I had just about lost contact with Ghinda. I knew she and Helen were not cruising in smooth waters and that she had taken herself out of the loop for a while, having by choice no contact with either of us. What I *didn't* know was that she had gotten herself well and truly into the drug scene and was heading down that road traversed by so many before her. That avenue of despair with no side-streets or welcome signs. This news was bad enough. That she had also given birth that week to a little boy who died the following morning from drug complications, just plain shattered me. To know that I had been a grandfather however briefly, yet never to have *seen* the child was sad in the extreme, but just not being able to *be there* for Ghinda was way worse. Since the tragedy, she had checked out of the hospital apparently and gone to convalesce at some location in Queensland which she was not prepared to divulge. She was, so Helen said, so consumed with guilt over the distressing affair that she just wanted to be on her own. The father evidently was a short-term proposition, long since out of her life. Like Helen, I spent a heap of time trying to trace her whereabouts but she had done an exemplary job of covering her tracks. I knew she would eventually make contact with me and it was just a question of waiting.

Chris of course was the first into High School that year and the first to bring home those crippling term fees, which like most Private Catholic Education Colleges in the area, are geared towards eventual parental bankruptcy. Therese and I had divorced without the need for acrimonius court dealings and the question of "access" either way was never an issue. If any positive aspect existed in the situation at all, it was that none of the children were ever exposed to bitter recriminations or even inter-parental confrontation. Nevertheless, for a previously very close-knit family, the resulting split left unavoidably, deep-seated scars and not a little latent unhappiness.

Offsetting such unfathomable ponderances, a nightly tradition at Baker was to patrol the rear garden at dusk, seeking out fairy-life within the confines of the bushes, shrubs and cloistered tree growth that crowded in upon the neat rectangular lawn. You could smell the magic, *hear* the rustling! Remembering so well my own deliberations as I tip-toed round the concrete walkways at *Brookside* peering up into the privet hedges, the expressions on the girls' faces as they would listen intently, before the inevitably breathless *"I see one daddy!"* was to experience utter and unconditional purity. Jenny later constructed a tiny fairy grotto within the front hedgerow, complete with an old biscuit tin which served as a wishing well. In times to come, and at the height of oppressive financial difficulty, I would kneel there myself some nights and believing so wholeheartedly in Jenny's own trust, faith and love within that tiny enclave, I would slip a few coins into the water and pray for help and opportunity. At the most critical of times, something always came up to save us.

Cash flow remained on life-support, having experienced yet another partnership debacle. Honest enough people this time who simply over-estimated their own capability. Commissioned to produce *Australia on Disc 4*, what they finally brought to the market-place was a truckload of cd's that didn't actually work. Not a great demand for small round drink-coasters that year either! Managed to retrieve a couple of former business clients who at least paid hard cash for some database work which in turn just about kept pace with the rent and four school-lunch-boxes daily, Lisa now having made her debut at kindy. The beginning also of years of incalculable time and mileage trekking from one sporting venue to another. Weekends were to become a blur of soccer, cricket, tennis, baseball, and netball comps....frequently within hours of one another. It was those at the *same time* we really had trouble with! Therese would go to one, me to another. Add to all that - swimming, skating and roller-blading (and later on hockey) as the whim took one or several of them and I discovered that driving a V8 Ford Fairlane was about as intelligent as casting Monica Lewinsky as Mother Teresa in *Missions of Mercy*.

November 7th saw Bill Clinton voted into the Presidency and on December 9th actor Anthony Perkins, forever immortalised as *Psycho's* "Norman Bates," died. A little known fact, but Perkins' widow Berry, was to die herself nine years later aboard American Airlines Flight 11 when it slammed into the North Tower of the World Trade Center on that fateful morning in September 2001 – a strange confluence there in terms of numerological coincidence..."nine" and "eleven."

Whilst on the subject of 9/11, just two months into the new year - Feb 23rd 1993, Osama Bin Laden's *Al Queda* terrorist group, undertook their first attempt at bringing down the WTC when an enormous explosion in the underground car park that day, killed six people and injured one thousand and forty eight others. On April 19th seventy two members of the Branch Davidian Religious Cult died in a fiery conflagration when heavily armed authorities stormed the group's compound in Waco Texas after earlier laying siege to the property.

I *could* compound the boredom here and regale the ardent reader with on-going details of intimate family living during this period or better still, the uncompromisingly dull and rarely profitable corporate dealings that kept us afloat, rather than at the forefront of the Sydney social pages. Fact *is* though, it was simply a rare and wonderful privilege watching the children grow and being able to share in that transition. Admittedly I had retained no particular unfulfilled urge at that stage to design and build a miner's hat with working electrical circuits, a diorama of Tutankhaman's tomb, a kite, a space rocket, a medieval castle with turrets, crenelles, drawbridge and armory. A replica soccer stadium, Egyptian mummy and my two *personal* favourites – the working Aztec calendar clock and the mobile mousetrap! My own belief is that the teachers pool ideas and orchestrate the most bizarre projects possible, knowing full well the parents are going to have to spend time with their children helping them if not assuming the role of chief model maker in most instancies! Like, a twelve year old girl is going to be able to figure out how to design and construct a working miner's hat with inbuilt light source? Of course in later years, work-assignments requiring help, knew no limits. Six-minute speeches on varied topics such as "How, as a character during WW1, the war affected me!" "Life under the Pharaohs." A self-written *working* software program complete with code and predictably with the advent of the Internet, a forty-five page website including site-map devoted to "Changing perspectives." I think I learned far more through the children's homework during the next decade than anything I pulled down at Bexley Grammar School.

Speaking of the Internet, whilst mid 1992 saw the actual integration of the world wide web as such (and *this* more than two decades since its early conceptual development) access to it was primarily Governmental and Research-based. It was not, even towards the end of 1993, yet available to the majority of personal computers in Australia.

At 4.20 am. September 24th 1993, came the announcement from Monte Carlo that so many had prayed for – that Sydney had won the right to stage the 2000 Olympic Games. From that day on were erected multiple electronic sight-boards right across the city, counting down the hours to the Opening ceremony, never mind the fact that the site for construction of the Olympic Village and main stadium was yet to be finalised, although Homebush Bay was the front runner.

The big hits in the lead-up to Christmas that year were *Mr Vain* by Culture Beat, *All that She Wants* from Ace of Base and *Please Forgive Me* by Bryan Adams. You couldn't saunter past Chris's room day or night without hearing at least one of them....repeatedly! For the benefit of non-Australian readers, I should mention a time-honored tradition Down Under. Late Christmas Eve, excited little children (and ours remained thus "excited" into their late teens!) ensure that a tray is left out beneath the tree containing three essential items. Some lettuce, a carrot (no discussion will be entered into regarding the dietary preferences of Dasher, Dancer, Donder and Blitzen etc!) and a chilled can of beer for Santa. For the non-believers, not a single Christmas went by that just a substantially gnawed carrot, the remnants of a lettuce leaf and an empty beer can remained on the tray next morning.

January 6th 1994 will remain as a day of infamy in the annals of sports history, when Olympic ice-figure-skating medallist Nancy Kerrigan was savagely clubbed in the right knee with a metal baton by the husband of her US rival Tonya Harding. Together with a third accomplice, both were arrested and charged one week later. May 6th President Bill Clinton faced the first in an extraordinary chain of forthcoming accusations of sexual harrassment, while on June 18, actor and former pro-football champ OJ Simpson was arrested and charged with the murder of his wife Nicole. The latter, defintely not being the inspiration behind the world wide hit of the moment *Love is All Around* by Wet Wet Wet (yeah right…well, moving right along!)

From a corporate viewpoint, having run out of options so far as *Australia On Disc* was concerned, it was time for a re-think. Circumstances appeared on the horizon, such that a Western Australian-based team of programmers offered themselves as prospective partners in a new venture. Following a few days discussions in Perth a fresh partnership came into being and within a few months was launched *The Australian Business Index (ABI)*. A national database of all Australian businesses but with substantially more information than one would find in the yellow pages. Having secured a Government contract to install the disc in every Trade Embassy worldwide and also on behalf of a major retail chain….we experienced a (brief) resurgence of equable living standards. The next few months saw many a happy family weekend spent down at Jenolan Caves House in the Blue Mountains. A certain restaurant – The *Royale Cafe* in nearby Parramatta, had a table for five on permanent standby while we splurged out big-time on a classic Buick Electra hardtop which, courtesy of its 7.3 litre engine, ensured that it was never too far from a gas station. It remains the only car I ever purchased with an American Express card.

So what's with the title of this chapter you wonder? Yeah, well I'll be getting to that later – bear with me!

Considerable unrest and violence dogged 1995. March 20th the *Aum Shinrikyo* "Supreme Truth" Cult were responsible for a sarin gas attack on the Tokyo subway. Although only eight died…thousands were injured. Over two thousand died during the Rwanda massacre on April 22nd while the war in Bosnia was escalating also. Just three days earlier (April 19th) one hundred and sixty eight people including nineteen children lost their lives, when Timothy McVeigh 27, detonated a massive car-bomb outside the block-long Oklahoma City Federal Building, allegedly in pay-back for the raid on the Branch Davidian cult at Waco the previous year. Appropriate perhaps that the Cranberries should have had such a hit with *Zombie* early that year.

With the release of Microsoft Windows '95 we had a problem. Pretty much every PC in the country was now running "Windows" software and the days of MS DOS were dead and buried. Whilst our DOS-based CD software could still be "read" on any computer it was falling behind in terms of competitive applications. Above all else, we needed a Windows-based product and that fact alone was to seal the fate of yet another partnership who promised the world but delivered nothing! In July we brought out an ABI update which found a market of sorts – users principally that already *had* the product and simply needed updated information. New purchasers however were scarce, the catch cry ringing out loud and only too clearly...."Get back to me when you have a Windows product!" Fortuitously, there were still three or four clients who used our data on a Commercial Licence basis so that enough funds were kept flowing to meet outgoings *and* the cost of the lunch-boxes.....by necessity, swelling in bulk content with two of the four now running consumptive teenage appetites. The most popular films of the year? *Braveheart* which went on to win Best Director for Mel Gibson, George Miller's *Babe,* the talking pig that won the hearts of audiences the world over and the critically acclaimed thriller, *The Usual Suspects.*

December 12th and according to every calendar, my timeline had extended to fifty. It *had* to be wrong! Just four years shy of dad's fulltime score? No way! Sure, my hairline was in deep trouble but hell, dad lost his at 28 – I still had some....*if* you caught my profile at the right angle that is! But it wasn't the physical worried me. Inside, I simply was *not* fifty. I neither thought, acted or looked at the world as one of such age should. Maybe my leg-cutter had lost a yard of pace but I could still walk on my hands, outrun the kids in a sprint, name all the states of America...every major pop star of 1995 and even handle teen-speak. "Chill out dude. Wasn't tryin'to diss ya, just want ya to take on board what I'm layin' out here!"

January '96. Hot summer with day after day up into the high thirties - low forties (For non-metric readers, that's as high as 108-109 degrees Fahrenheit.) Biggest song around the country at this time was Coolio's *Gangsta's Paradise* from the Michelle Pfeiffer flick *Dangerous Minds*. A couple of renewed contracts in late February/early March led to the best news Jenny and Kate had heard since birth. The realisation of a (promised) world trip in September...a school holiday and the only time at this stage of their education that they could really afford any time off school at all. The days were counted down on a hastily drawn calendar hung on the wall.

Sunday April 29th[th] and Australians were shocked senseless by the news out of Port Arthur, a sleepy little tourist spot in passive Tasmania of all places. Fruitloop Martin Bryant 28 walked into the Broad Arrow Café, commented aloud *"Lot of wasps around here today – not many Japs though?"* He then pulled a rifle from his sports bag and shot most everyone in the café...continuing his spree outside. His rampage was brought to a halt by Police, after he was trapped in a burning building, by which time however, thirty five were dead and 17 more injured. A local pharmacist lost his wife and two daughters that morning. Further tragedy struck the US on May 11, when a Valujet crashed in the Florida Everglades killing one hundred and ten passengers and crew.

The Buick had been replaced by an eight-seater Rambler Matador Station Wagon which to this day remains Lisa's favorite car. About to apply for her Learner's permit herself now in 2005, she might not see it that way if she had to drive it. Mid July came news that UK scientists Drs. Ian Wilmut and Keith Campbell had cloned the first sheep from adult cells. The lamb was named Dolly.

Friday June 14th and as a small consolation for having to wait some years before her own trip abroad, I took Lisa to New Zealand for the weekend, in company with Chris. She had accompanied me there on a business trip two years earlier and remarkably had retained a clear remembrance of the layout of Auckland being able to guide us to a specific restaurant, neither Chris or I could locate. The Capital of New Zealand is a vibrant, well laid out city with an excellent freeway system and a harbour arguably as impressive as Sydney itself. We picked up a Laser Lynx rental very cheaply and toured the region north to south, gaining full value for the unlimited drive package. Staying overnight at a cosy and most hospitable of bed and breakfast residences within five minutes of Auckland International Airport, the weekend was both relaxing and enjoyable…adjectival features that might permanently describe *any* visit to New Zealand in my experience. The following morning came the tragic news of yet another US air mishap when a 747 airbus plunged into the Atlantic just off Long Island NY, killing all two hundred and thirty people on board.

Just eight and a half weeks later, the excitement at Baker Crescent was at fever pitch. I don't think the two girls slept too much the previous night. Therese kindly drove us to the airport and by the time we heard "United Airlines Flight 7 to Los Angeles, now boarding at Gate 55" I think we were talking serious adrenaline flow. Brief stop-over in Hawaii then on to LA. Rented a compact and headed off to the fine old Alexandria Hotel to renew a nostalgic acquaintance and to stock up big-time on those fabulous hot-cakes once more. I had actually pre-booked a room there for us before leaving Sydney. Dismay turned to unutterable despair as on approaching the hotel it was obvious something drastic had overtaken the area in the intervening thirteen years since last I saw it. In the last stages of dilapidation and decay, some might say in keeping with its immediate surroundings, the grand old hotel was now no more than a flop-house, a refuge for the up-market street bum at $20 a night. Presenting our "booking" slip to the somewhat elderly Negro holed up behind some seriously impenetrable steel bars where once was to be found the hotel check-in, he looked us up and down before saying "You guys got the *wrong* place for sure!" I told him, last time I was on site it was a fine Hotel. He then explained how the area had become the haunt of junkies and flunkies towards the middle of the eighties and just gone from bad to worse. Still we had nowhere else to go that evening, so he let us all stay in what must have been the only decent double room left....for just $20! Where once sat the old art-deco breakfast room, was now a jumble of decrepit old furniture, hosting perhaps forty or fifty inter-racial homeless men, either playing chess or just sitting there staring vacantly into space, their only companions a cigar on its last legs or a pre-used cigarette butt offering maybe a couple more drags. We "ate" that night, courtesy of a food machine on the ground floor, that dispensed some Ritz crackers, a pack of processed cheese and soft drinks. With some security alarm activated at half-hourly intervals and way too close for comfort....it was a long night.

Next morning we set out for Long Beach and spent several hours in and around the *Queen Mary*. Later we lit out south along the Santa Ana Freeway bound for Anaheim and Jenny and Kate were able to indulge their greatest wish - to see Disneyland. It was the souvenir shops *I* was trying so desperately to avoid. As it turned out, we actually rocked-in the day they were presenting a *Lion King* pageant there. It was quite excellent.

Touching down at Kennedy, we had to direct the Indian cab driver to Loewes Summit on 51st who was adamant there *was* no such hotel. Much the same problem tourists experience in Sydney these days apparently. Late September in New York or more specifically Central Park, is a unique and quite wonderful experience. For Kate especially, who had wanted to see it ever since I first described it to her as a little girl...it was the culmination of a dream. Never having seen a squirrel in Australia either, both girls were fascinated by their grace and tameness. Hours were spent additionally poking around the upgraded Central Park Zoo, just across from the Plaza Hotel, which in their short lives has been immortalised by MaCaulay Culkin and Tim Curry in *Home Alone 2*. Standing in the foyer, Jenny asked "Can we stay here dad?" I explained that our available funds would barely cover room service for one night. The following day we walked the fifty odd blocks down to the Battery, pausing at 34th Street to check out Macy's and the Empire State where we joined the queue for the lift to the skywalk. On the ferry out to Liberty

Island that day (five years before the events of 9/11 saw it closed permanently) we looked back at the sunlit twin towers of the World Trade Center never dreaming of the relatively brief life-span left to them. Even at fourteen, Kate had developed a deep and inexplicable affection for all things American and it was no surprise to me to hear her say whilst walking down Fifth Avenue to the subway one morning, "This is *just* how I imagined it all dad!" I knew only too well.

When we landed at Heathrow I had a certain feeling of pride. I had *done* it. I had gotten them to my home and whatever else might happen in the future, nothing could ever take this away! I still have the same obligation to Lisa and by what means *now* I can fulfil it, I have simply no idea....but it *will* happen and then all four will at least have touched some part of their ancestry whatever it might mean to them. Pre-booked into the Charing Cross Hotel (where else??) both girls lived the ultimate forty five minutes – having breakfast at the John Betcheman room there. Mention that locale to them today, their eyes will glaze over.

Having received a brand new Fiat in place of the smaller and way cheaper Fiesta that I had pre-booked but which Budget were clean out of, it afforded us a considerably (free) upgraded level of transportation and in the ensuing ten days, we made the most of the opportunity. Before anything however, I had to go *home!* Parking right outside the park gates, I could scarcely believe that after all these years' bedtime stories, I had them here *with* me, seeing for themselves the lake, the olde English gardens, the manion house, the swings and wrecked though it was....my house. If nothing else, it was worth the enduring image of Jenny trying to row across the lake to the tiny island. I think she performed three total circles before finally semi-controlling the oars. Talk about *Master & Commander: The Far Side of the Lake!* I hope however it meant to them what it did to me. Spent some time in Welling with them, unchanged as it always is, pointing out my old haunts and places of interest.

Back in the city the next day, took them all around London. Piccadilly, St Pauls, Trafalgar Square, The Tower of London, Buckingham Palace etc...the whole touristy box and dice. Based at Charing Cross of course, dad's old building – The Civil Service Stores, was still there, right opposite in The Strand, although now simply a collection of sub-let shops on the ground floor, right at street level. All that remains of the department store days is the exterior clock on the building's southern façade. There was of course another place I had to take them. The farm in Wilsill. Still owned by the couple to whom Reg left the property, they saw us looking over the gate and when I mentioned who I was, I saw the recognition "Oh.....you're *Joyce's* boy are you?"

Obviously unsure as to what I *knew*, nothing was said, in fact they were very hospitable and invited us all in for tea. After that I walked Jenny and Kate all over the farm, right down to the River Nidd and the old swing bridge itself, under which flowed those cool waters of my youth.

Just a twenty-five minute drive to Knaresborough and Mother Shipton's unique petrifying well. Fully built-up and commercialised now, complete with accredited guides even, and such a far cry from the early fifties when the few families who knew about it, would simply walk down to the grotto and leave some article of domesticity for retrieval in years to come – perhaps an old kettle, pair of socks, a memento, whatever....*knowing it would still be there!* Such has life changed!

Replete from a fine meal in Harrogate, we then crossed the Stray and headed north for Scotland. What kind of a visit would this otherwise have been for the girls to miss perhaps the greatest scenery on offer in Great Britain? It's a long haul in one afternoon and evening, up to Edinburgh, across to Glasgow then north-west to Dumbarton, on to Crianlarich and Fort Augustus at the mouth of the enormous Loch Lochy. Sleeping fitfully in the car for a few hours just shy of Fort William, shortly before dawn we re-commenced the drive along Loch Ness, stopping at Urquhart Castle which the girls checked out in such early light that is afforded a dumb-ass tourist at 5.50 am and having additionally to scale two security fences not surprisingly unmanned at that God-forsaken time of day. At least we saved twenty pounds all up in entrance-fees! They had the entire run of the castle, right down to the shoreline – until that is, we noticed a rapidly approaching speedboat on the Loch with ominous Police-like markings. That little tour was by necessity, terminated.

Continued on to Inverness where we had just one need – *breakfast*, and a wash. The small but extremely hospitable Cummings Hotel answered that call very nicely thank you! After a cursory tour of the city we started the long haul back – to Wales. The Fiat by this stage looked like some major loser from *Gone in 60 Seconds*....nothing remotely like the proud new Euro-saloon we had picked up with just twenty six miles on the clock. It was nudging one thousand already! Many miles of motorway flashed past, mostly in torrential rain, as we circumnavigated Carlisle, Penrith, Lancaster and Preston, turning left shortly before Manchester to head-off towards Chester and shortly before nightfall, the seaside resort of Rhyl on the north coast of Wales, some ten miles or so from Colwyn Bay. Blustery doesn't describe the prevailing conditions adequately, these were full-on gale-force winds. Still, it was enough to say they had *been* to Wales lets say! Spending the night at one of those myriad motorway inns that now dot the English countryside, being both economic and very convenient, we slept well and at breakfast - ate up *big-time*. That morning we headed south, to the counties of Somerset, Dorset and Wiltshire.

Bath offered plenty to interest them, the thermal spings especially, ancient Rome being both girls' current period of historical study. *Not* a good locale when one is keenly aware of budgetary limitations however, with souvenirs in that particular part of England – a financial quicksand. Given additionally the relative close proximity of both ancestral *Longleat* and nearby Stonehenge, it is more than likely that *Maccas* remains for many families, the only affordable eatery at the end of the day. We stayed until darkness fell at Stonehenge, watching the shadows thrown up by those ancient sarsens, inexorably lengthen until the light totally faded. We then drove back to the old Clarendon Hotel at Blackheath.

In the ensuing days I showed them everything that time permitted in London, including the British Museum – a day's application in itself to take-in most of it. There remained one last excursion, one I had yet made no mention of. On the pretext of farewelling Danson Park, we returned to my hometown and after a last walk around the lake returned to the car. Then linked back up with the main motorway to the South East where we drove to Dover. There, I booked us on to the first available *Hoverspeed* to the French coast. As Kate said, never having seen such a craft, "Thi*s* is really cool dad!" Spent a few hours in Calais where, amongst other things, we came face to face with the world's most expensive cappuccino – six dollars even, and it wasn't even a winner in the frothy beverage stakes.

Leaving Britain at the end of that week, our send-off was complete. A Police Range Rover pulled me over just yards from the rental car check-in.

"License please Sir?" he muttered impatiently. After gridlock on the M25 orbital to Heathrow and with now less than forty five minutes to boarding ourselves, we were equally impatient.

"A problem officer?" I asked.

"I'm writing you up for speeding Sir and running a red back there." He jerked his head back along the road behind us.

"I don't *think* so Officer," I said. "We have to be on a plane in forty minutes." I flashed my International License, keeping my British equivalent well hidden. Taking it, he examined it minutely.

"So you're *not* English then, don't have a British Licence? Not much I can do is there?' he flashed a smile. "Your lucky day!"

We returned to Sydney via San Francisco. This proved to be Jenny's favorite stop-off. The Bay City turned on the most glorious warm weather that week and aside from Kate throwing-up as our rental car negotiated the twisting turns to the Redwood forest at Muir Woods, it was a fitting location to end the most memorable of vacations. Most popular sights were undoubtedly The Golden Gate, Lombard Street, the cable cars and in Kate's case at least... many of the homes in Sausalito. Caught the late flight out the following day and headed back to Sydney via New Zealand. Not only did they miss a week of school that October, but Lisa's ninth birthday also. Los Del Rio had instigated a worldwide dance craze that year with *La Macarena* which had logged-in at number one in Australia on August 26th and remained there nine weeks straight, until The Spice Girls' *Wannabe* dethroned it for the remainder of the year.

As early as February 1997 the business started foundering. Two major clients who had for many years renewed data-contracts with me, pleaded the fifth and opted out. No warning, just the standard fall-back excuse "Sorry – management budgetary constraints old chap!" Suddenly shy close to twenty five thousand dollars in two phone calls, that's one *hell* of a lot of school lunches down the tube.

Yet another "cult-mass suicide" at Rancho Sante Fe California. On March 27th authorities discovered the bodies of thirty-nine sect members that had self-ingested a cocktail of vodka and phenobarbital. The *Heaven's Gate cult* as they were known and led by one Marshall Applewhite, believed that the inbound comet Hale-Bopp was being trailed by a UFO that would transport their freed souls to a higher plane of existence. The group had recruited its members through its own web-site. For all we know, Applewhite may have been correct.

A fifth partnership with a small Canberra-based software development team had resulted finally, in a windows version of ABI but with its limited speed of operation and the partners' obvious preference (like every computer techo team I ever met) to skew the software functionality along their own ideas of what was needed, rather than what I told them to produce....it was a hard-sell. We were also up against another unexpected competitor – the Internet itself! It had become a "perception" obstacle. "Why should I buy your product when all the information I'll ever need is on the Net?" Factually this was completely erroneous, simply the ingrained belief held by so many that "everything now" *must* be on the Net, so lets not buy anything! Sporadic sales of data were barely keeping place with domestic expenditure and eating *out* was becoming a luxury now, rather than a staple. The Rambler had long since gone, replaced by a sixteen year old Fairlane and a nineteen year old Mazda 929 that became Chris' pride and joy when he obtained his full driving license that year - to the day, on his seventeenth birthday. You know the years are locked into "high-range cruise control" once your children start driving! Chris had then left High School and was employed full-time at the local MacDonalds outlet and was getting like many others his age, a decent grounding in work-experience.

1997 saw the passing of an extraordinary number of well-loved public figures. On June 26th renowned oceanographer Jacques Cousteau died in Paris. The following week (July 2nd) the screen's most beloved actor, Jimmy Stewart died in the US. On the 15th, fashion designer Gianni Versace was shot dead on the steps of his Miama Beach mansion. It was on August 31st however the world *stopped*, when Princess Diana died in still-being-debated circumstances relating to the spectacular car crash in a Parisian road tunnel. The mourning worldwide, but particularly in Britain was unprecedented. Elton John's subsequent tribute to Princess Diana – *Something About the Way You Look Tonight/Candle in The Wind,* was to become the fastest selling single of all time. On the 5th September, Nobel prize-winning missionary Mother Teresa died and on October 10th singer John Denver took a light plane over his beloved Rocky Mountain High for the last time, before crashing to join several of his musical compatriots in an early grave.

The year closed out with Swedish pop newcomers Aqua upsetting the status-quo by "corrupting" the minds of adolescents allegedly with a cutesy but far-from-innocent *Barbie Girl* followed by *Doctor Jones*. Christmas came on with an enforced budget. One less carrot, a smaller piece of lettuce and just a twist-top for Santa.

Late February 1998 and with the loss of virtually my last remaining client of renewable significance (themselves in dire straits) I began to really feel the heat. Having to come up with credible excuses why the rent could not be paid on time took all my literary and imaginative skills. When all is said and done however, the only words *any* creditor ever wants to hear is "When will I get my money?" Small jobs trickled in….for now, just sufficient to stave off eviction but utilities were threatening and the menu-board in the kitchen was down to a single-line entry. "Dinner has been temporarily suspended." The children were aware of "financial difficulties in transit" let's say, but were not on a "need to know" basis as far as looming prospects stood. The paper-run, started years earlier for the children and which I now undertook myself, began to take on awesome significance. That $40 - $50 was often the difference between eating and not…money that once would barely have covered half the bill for a thrice-weekly night out at the Royale Café in Parramatta.

If only my name had been James Cameron! *Titanic* took out Best Film at the Oscars that year (plus ten others) and became also the highest grossing film of all time, which considering the $300 million it cost to make, was a justified outcome in some ways. Not surprisingly, Celine Dion's *My Heart Will Go On* from the film's soundtrack, topped charts around the world for months also. On May 14th, Frank Sinatra died from a heart attack aged 82.

I was dying much slower! I struck rock bottom when the day came I had to call a charitable organisation for food vouchers. Hard to convey the depth of emotions generated that day. They ranged one supposes, from outright embarrassment to self-recrimination. The many years I had *given* to various charitable causes, never in my wildest dreams supposing I would, in *this* lifetime at least, be needing to *call* upon their services. Strangely, I hadn't developed a self-deprecating complex that had been the cornerstone to my Father's sense of self-failure but unlike the predicament *he* found himself in, I had no-one to help me. Actually, if the truth be known, Therese God bless her, *did* help out and frequently sent the girls over with supplies of frozen foods and groceries which must have stretched her own limited budget.

Problem is of course you *need* money to make money in business! Sales lead generation requires intense telephone canvassing – problematic when your phone's about to be disconnected on account of not being able to pay the last bill! Client interviews obligate one to *get* there....fuel helps too! You sure as hell ain't gonna close any deal fronting up to the company reception desk saying "Sorry I'm late, missed the bus!" My nine year old suit was something less than eye candy too at this stage. Was this a case of being sorry for myself? Hell no! just being realistic. Deals still went through notwithstanding...few and far between admittedly but at the last throw of the dice something always came up. We still ate, although I was learning the *hard* way the value of food. Loaves of bread that once would have been heaved overnight were preserved for the next day's toast...if not the day after's. Cuts of meat I would never have insulted the cats with, became gourmet feasts par excellence. A bottle of champagne every second night gave way to a six-pack of soda water, eventually just plain water. Serve it up in a tall wine glass – the effect is amazing. That I had previously lived a life of rude indulgence had never really occurred to me – it was a hard lesson indeed. We saw out the entire year playing shuffleboard with the incoming bills.

Holding off on one to pay another, always just days ahead of either disconnection, cancellation, eviction or starvation.

Late spring, Chris's recently come-by Nissan Bluebird, came off the loser following a close encounter with a rogue truck. Leaving the trunk lid resting up against the wall of a nearby church and the rear passenger door and roof half way across the back seat, the Datsun cut a sad picture of dysfunctional transportation. About the only positive aspect being that one second tops, was the difference between the car's death and his own. Just three days later, my own Falcon station wagon was stolen from the driveway close to midnight and used in a local jewel-store ram raid, before being mechanically if not professionally trashed. Neither were insured! We really didn't need that!

Really didn't need the last quarter of '98 either! As if on cue, most every client I still had, found some reason not to buy anything. "Too near Christmas," "We'll do it next year," "Funds are a bit tight right now," "Yeah, it's a great deal, give us a week to think about it!" I've yet, in almost thirty years to have someone come *back* to me after "thinking" about anything, and saying "Right, now lets do it!" It's the equivalent of the failed job-application and the inevitably condescending "But hey, we'll keep your name on file should anything come up?" Like, *does* it ever? By Christmas then, we were sitting atop a financial Mount Versuvius ...actually, *Krakatoa* might be a better analogy for those with any knowledge of vulcanology. The rent was substantially in arrears, phone and power bills pressing, hell, we were even out of milk! As the Offspring were singing at the time, *Pretty Fly (For a White Guy)*. Santa *came* still, but it was readily obvious the elves had been scraping for product that year. Takes way more than an empty wallet to rain on *our* Christmas parade though, and the tree stood proud as a symbol of tradition and indestructible family unity. Maybe prouder than *ever* that year.

Despite a couple of unexpected sales early in the new year, it was just a matter of time until our luck finally ran out. By early March I was bereft of funds to the point of desperation. I don't think one has truly tasted failure or known true debasement until you are forced to ask your own children for money for such as a loaf of bread or even $10 of fuel. I was usually able to repay them, but that does nothing to assuage one's plummeting self- esteem at such a defining moment. To compound the misery, having exhausted all avenues of further deferred rental deadlines, we were finally issued with a fourteen day eviction notice to quit our home of the past seven years. That same day remarkably, I had a phone call from Ghinda who wanted to meet with me in the city after her long yet self-imposed exile. She was in pretty poor shape but just seeing her again was at least a start. Brought her home to meet the other children, the only time I think I have *ever* had the five of them together. With just four days remaining before being booted out of Dodge by the Sheriff, we managed to find an old home in nearby, though rather less salubrious Northmead. The good news was, the rent was insanely cheap, almost half what we had been paying. The *bad* news? It was due to be pulled down in six months for redevelopment!

A once grand old timber home, though shabby now, It was clean and very spacious. The huge rumpus area was one third the size of Baker Crescent alone and served as the entertainment area *and* my office having a separate nook for the computer gear. Lisa and Kate shared a large room while Chris picked up the master bedroom. For Jenny, we converted what was once a substantial lounge room complete with open hearth fire – the envy of everyone all through winter. That still left an additional decent size dining room in the centre of the house. At the rear of the property, a huge wooden deck led down to a very private semi-tropical garden, which in the coming tenancy period, provided many happy hours of cricket and soccer. The downside was that the home was on Windsor Road – busiest thoroughfare in the northwest of Sydney. Pretty much impossible to exit the property without major difficulty during peak periods, but we learned to live with that. Kate had left college and was working in the city in a legal firm. Jenny was in year ten at High School and Lisa now completing her last year of Primary and showing already an early aptitude for soccer.

Mid March and little more than a week after the death of master director, Stanley Kubrick, war erupted in Kosovo after Yugoslavia's President Milosevoc ordered the massacre of ethnic Albanians there. US President Clinton countered with massive air-strikes which bombarded Belgrade for seventy-eight days straight. Newcomer Britney Spears also conquered the world during March and April finding herself topping worldwide charts with *Baby One More Time*.

We finally got hooked to the Internet that year (with the other one hundred million plus worldwide) and this alone was instrumental to my finding some new business which was a life-saver. Had managed to replace my stolen Falcon but until now had been unable to help Chris replace his. A 1980 Toyota Corona for $950 may not be the car of choice for the average young street-racer, but it sure as hell is a glamour vehicle when you don't have your own transport.

The six months came and went and news filtered through that the owners would not be "developing" to well into the new year so we were handed somewhat of a respite in terms of imminent uprooting. Pulled in a substantial order mid year that made it possible to bring all financial arrears up to date and to fill the gas tank…a luxury I had not been able to indulge in for many months. We even had cable TV installed which was pretty much left switched on to MTV 24/7 which is probably why we saw TLC's chart topping *No scrubs* ten times a day. They were eventually displaced at number one in December by Eiffel 65's *Blue*.

During the run-up to Christmas and of course the new millennium, the one subject on everyone's lips and in news articles pretty much daily was the YK2 bug. A panic identified two decades earlier when shortsighted Microsoft techos had created worldwide, computer chips unable to read beyond 1999. The fear was based on the premise "What if all computers believe at the stroke of midnight December 31st it is now 1900, that being the year to which they would default having no recognition of the figure "2" at the front of a string of year numbers?" Theories ranged from a collapse of the banking system, the failure of domestic utilites worldwide, to total global communication melt-down and social anarchy! Billions of dollars were spent internationally ensuring new software programs were YK2 compliant as well as protecting the corporate world from what was perceived as possible catastrophe. Laughably, scientific and technological opinion when all was said and done was simply "We just don't know what will happen?" I took the easy route, simply resetting my computer clock to 1998 at Christmas.

And so it was that new year's eve, Jenny and I, celebratory drink in hand, sat watching TV alone with not a little interest it must be said, as in company with a billion others, we watched the millennium countdown live from Auckland – the first major city in the world by virtue of its close proximity to the International meridian, to breach the deadline. Whatever was to happen, would happen there first, right in front of a worldwide audience. Many were expecting at the very least a total city-wide blackout, TV shutdown and hopefully some frenetic screaming to jazz up the event! Nothing…absolutely nothing happened. Biggest fizzer in the history of globally anticipated armageddons!

The year 2000 was rather like turning 50 – nothing noticeably different from being 49! For the first time however, the world's population topped six billion, virtually triple what it was when mum's water broke, or at least, when *I* broke it, somewhere along the Welsh border that night back in '45. Little wonder traffic is at gridlock now.

It was a return to the hard times soon enough. Bills 1 v Income NIL That paper round was beginning to loom as a veritable font of riches in a dearth of corporate opportunity. I had the perfect counter – I would write a book. Having reneged on my self-promise at fifteen to keep a diary all my life, this would make up for my failure to do so. Even should it never see the light of day as a published work and the likelihood was that it never would, *still* it would remain a record of a life, one perhaps that a great-grand-child may one day come across in a dusty attic, bring downstairs to his or her parents and say "What's this mum?"

So little time to worry about the financial aspects, with Jenny's almost weekly now, modern and ancient history assignments to help out with, Lisa's first year at High school and housekeeping duties running the redline. An opportune moment perhaps, to pay my respects to a shattering death in the family – our beloved Simpson minimatic. Bought during our honeymoon in 1979 for $429, this simplest of little washing machines gave of its all for twenty- one years straight without a breakdown, service call or even hiccup. It had even outlasted the dryer by seven years. The *bad* news though – now having to wash everything by hand in the bath. My parents had hand-washed all my childhood, so I figured *I* may as well. Besides, with no funds to replace the Minimatic, it was that or go find the nearest river.

On March 14, Stephen King became the first major author to publish a novel electronically when *Riding the Bullet* was released on the Internet as an e-book with no download capability. You wanted to read it? You paid $4.50! Over five hundred thousand *did* just that - in three days!

With the landlord having developmental problems (lack of ready cash I imagine) our tenancy was extended at six monthly intervals which allowed us to see out another full year in the house. For Jenny that meant another cosy winter with her roaring fireplace and for me, countless hours between May and September collecting firewood. Ghinda came over a couple of times during that period and we had a few card evenings together – in Jenny's room. It was the warmest! On July 25th a horrific Concorde crash near Paris killed one hundred and thirteen people. As a result of unsustainable annual flight losses, the entire Concorde fleet was de-commissioned in November 2003.

Kate passed her driving test at the first attempt and was soon motoring proudly along in the car she had always wanted, a white 1986 VL Commodore Berlina. Meanwhile, it was a case of one step forward - two back, as far as finances were concerned. Through unusual circumstances, I had been introduced to Richard, a Perth-based architectural planning consultant and obviously knowledgable computer programmer, able to see the potential for a product such as ABI. Older than me even, it was most gratifying to suddenly be able to exchange ideas with an intelligent person. Over the ensuing months, the framework of a closer business relationship came into being.

Winter that year was an audio mix of *Bye Bye Bye* from *Nsync, Destiny's Child's vocal gymnastics with *Say My Name*, Britney Spears sexy little turn *Oops!...I Did It Again*, *Freestyler* from Bomfunk MC's and Kylie Minogue's *Spinning Around,* not to mention white chick gone black, Anastacia and *I'm Outta Love* which she was arguably, never able to equal, let alone top.

On September 15th the eyes of the world were on Homebush Bay NSW, watching the stunning opening ceremony of the 2000 Sydney Olympic Games, arguably the most flamboyant and successful ever staged. More than ten thousand athletes from 200 countries competed against one another during the two week festivities. In 2004, the games returned to their spiritual home in Athens.

George Bush was ruled by the Supreme Court to have won the US Presidency December 9th after ordering a halt to a Florida re-count. The closest US election in decades. An incredible number of entertainers died in 2000, including Victor Borge, Hedy Lamarr, Sir Alec Guinness, Jason Robards, Walter Matthau, Steve Allen and Sir John Gielgud. Not sure if former Canadian Prime Minister Pierre Trudeau should be listed as an "entertainer"….many would say he should.

With a very small Insurance policy maturing that Christmas, my having turned 55 (and thereby beating both my father and my paternal grandfather) we actually had a January with a few spare dollars. This eventuality had proven somewhat timely as I was presented with a vet's bill for Binkie, one of our cats that had come off the worse for wear with a speeding car, for a coronary-inducing $870, making him one chronically expensive feline. Incredibly, my second Falcon was stolen also, from the garage where it was awaiting repair and simply to be mobile over the holiday period, I acquired a small Toyota Corona for just $800, hoping for a life-expectancy of six months tops. At much the same as it would cost to *hire* a car for three to four weeks, we were talking realistically, disposable car value here!

Our second and last Christmas at the old house. The place resounded with good cheer and from what I can recall – pretty good wine too! Hell, by the tenth time you heard *Teenage Dirtbag* from Wheatus, you needed a stiff drink.

2001 and the year of Kubrick's/Arthur C. Clarke's great Space Odyssey and yet we are no nearer to space travel now than the day the film was released. Hard to credit that it was considered likely, following the moon landing in '69, that man would be looking to deep space exploration, if not planetary *colonisation* by the year 2000 with a generally accepted consensus that the earth would be at least orbited by manned space stations by then. Certainly communications have seen huge advances in such as the Internet and audiovisual cellphones but interterrestrially, we're going nowhere! What *has* propogated itself unchecked is AIDS, racial hatred and bland automobile design.

Jenny headed off to Cairo that January for three weeks with the school. Having, like myself, a long-time interest in Egyptology, she was hoping desperately to get high enough marks in her final exams that year to gain a place at MacQuarie, the only University in Australia that offers Egyptology as a course. Internationally, the faculty there garnered enormous respect and acclaim later in 2001, consequent upon its findings at major archaelogical digs in and around the Valley of the Kings. In 2003 the same team identified what they believe to be the lost tomb of Queen Nefertiti.

March 5th and Ghinda turned 30. It was not a day of any great celebration, as in order to take her out for a coffee (Helen came too) we had to sign responsibility for her at the drying-out clinic where she had been placed for a fortnight, so I discovered. Still coming down from her last drug binge she was in a sad way and beyond spending time with her and telling her we loved her, there wasn't a great deal else to be done. She has steadfastly refused to live with either one of us and even now, believes she can overcome her addiction herself. Historically, her actions do not back this up!

We had to vacate late March, just ahead of the demolition team and graders rolling on to the site. There is something inherently sad about seeing an old home demolished. Years if not generations of memories being bulldozed and for what? Some jerry-built quick-frame town houses with shonky brickwork and cheapskate roofing – maximum profit, minimum quality! I like to think that we shared two particularly happy Christmases with the old home at the very end of its allotted timespan. Some houses lock on to an existential wavelength with people, they tap into an emotional rut that is inexplicable. Such was the case of 95 Windsor Road with me. Call me untreatably sentimental but I visited that old house after we moved...every day. I would walk through the empty, silent rooms feeling the pulse slowing up. The over-run and now sad garden, a throw-back to another time. I just wanted to *be* with her right to the last, until they put her down for good. I didn't have long to wait!

Our next home was just six minutes away, in Railway Street Baulkham Hills. Barely a three minute walk to the old rail station. Only problem for commuters is that the last train actually departed platform one, seventy five years earlier on January 28th 1928, after which the entire Parramatta to Castle Hill line was pulled up. A Bowling Club now sits astride the land where once stood Baulkham Hills station. Just two streets away from our old home in Baker Crescent, the new house was big, which given the need to put a thousand books and almost four thousand videos somewhere, was just as well.

Gladiator deservedly cleaned up at the Oscars but Pat Rafter failed to hold out a rampant Goran Ivanisevic at Wimbledon. The two biggest songs of the moment? LeAnn Rimes *Can't Fight The Moonlight* (from the God-awful teen flick *Coyote Ugly*) and Eminem's *Stan*.

Richard and I were knocking some sort of partnership structure into shape but income was slowing to the direst trickle. Had not Dick lent a hand some months with pressing utility bills, we would have been knackered. As it was, I was still relying on the kids to help when they could and making increased demands on the St Vincent de Paul charity who were stoically carting over food parcels by the car load! The occasional small sale brought the barest relief but this really was *not* the way to be living in your fifties. Dad had been there, done that, and look what happened to him? I *was* sporadically putting together chapters for the book – no shortage of items to write about. Just needed to *live* long enough to finish it, well at the rate I was going!

Chris celebrated his twenty first in July (God, how old *am* I??) and he was more than good humored about the fact my upper limit for any type of gift was up around the $10 mark. I'll make it up to him when he's 31 maybe.

At 6.45 am September 10th (remember we are a day *ahead* of the US) Kate rang, sounding shocked as all hell. *"Turn the TV on dad...quickly. Something terrible is happening in America!"* I sat watching that screen all day. I didn't move. Like so many others around the world, I was as stunned as ever I have been by anything! The sight of those planes in multiple replay, bringing unthinkable carnage and horror into the proximity of so many innocent lives and of those great towers plummeting to the ground, was mesmerising in its improbability. As poignant and heartbreaking as anything, was to watch those poor workers trapped above the inferno beneath them, forced by the insufferable heat to seek refuge on the outer window ledge or in many cases to jump. That day I really looked at *myself*, my priorities, my "acceptance" of all that was going wrong in my own life and I knew I owed it to all those victims to do something concrete! I could never *know* them obviously but I knew I owed their lives a debt somehow and that in getting myself back on

284

track eventually, and by whatever means, would mean in some small way that their deaths had not been for nothing. I like to imagine that many people had a similar reaction. Far from what you might call an *epiphany*, it was rather, a cranial re-boot!

November 29th and Beatle George Harrison died from inoperable cancer. He had survived a multiple stabbing at his home eighteen months earlier. Only Paul and Ringo left now to carry the flame.

It was to be a memorable Christmas for Jenny. Mid December and together with just about every NSW student with access to a computer, she logged in to the exam results web-site! With an average mark way into the eighties, she had done it! I was just so proud of her but happier still *for* her! No one ever worked harder towards a goal than Jenny had those last two years. The results were a fair and just outcome. In Australia, final year students have what is known as "Schoolies" week. Usually held on the Queensland Gold Coast, thousands of students from across the State congregate on the "strip" for a weeks relaxing and partying. An unwinding of sorts after twelve years unrelenting schoolwork. Jen also became a legal adult while she was away that December. That Christmas was all Kylie Minogue and *Can't Get You Out Of My Head* as well as *Smooth Criminal* from Alien Ant Farm. Biggest worldwide film release at the time was *Harry Potter and the Sorcerer's Stone* which despite lukewarm reviews took a world record $93.5 million dollars in the US on its opening weekend. The unexpectedly bad news to top off the year? The house was sold and we were given sixty days to move on. Now that really wasn't very nice!

January 2002, and it was time to put our corporate heads together and work out strategy and a product time-line. For this purpose, I flew to Perth for a few days and we mapped out how the partnership was to operate. A new company, Australian Business Information Pty Limited was formed with a third Director, Peter Edmonds, a long time associate of Dick and with *his* financial input the plan was to work towards the creation of two main products. A new and re-written ABI and a windows version of *"The Australian Movie Disc,"* a DOS version of which I had formerly published back in 1995. Neither would be a quick-fix as it were, but would need to be developed slowly and carefully. My input principally would be to bring to the partnership, updated and complete data, which in the case of the movie disc would present itself as a time-consuming and on-going task, with still considerable research needed. The Perth connection would be responsible for the software functionality which also was not going to be an overnight tweak. But at least we had a *plan* now and that is something that had been sadly lacking since the mid nineties! Pink couldn't have had a more appropriately titled hit right at that moment, *Get the Party Started*.

Time once more to move. Damn, the houses just kept getting bigger! 17 Whitling Avenue in Castle Hill was a class act. Utilising a near thirty foot long (spare) lounge room as a bedroom for Chris, all five of us had our own quarters. Jenny this time, a *suite* of rooms in her own downstairs "wing." Wide enough in the driveway to park five cars abreast at a pinch, one could quite easily accommodate thirteen vehicles in the front yard. Not that we ever *had* to.

President Bush's State of the Union address on Jan 29th was his first reference to Iraq, Iran and North Korea as being the "Axis of Evil" so far as the war on terrorism was concerned. A new name in the pop world, South American lass Shakira, was coming on strong with *Whenever, Wherever* a song she followed up with the somewhat suggestive *Underneath Your Clothes*.

With some direction now, I was spending most every day at the computer, researching pertinent information for both products. Entailing a considerable amount of data-entry, three hours straight would usually be more than enough. For "relaxation" there was always the next chapter of the book! Katie had decided to return to college at this juncture to complete her years 11 and 12 and she would frequently be around to help me Tuesdays with the paper-run, which was *still* my only regular income as such.

The stand-off between Israel and Palestine, itself no nearer a solution than the day Moses came down off Mount Ararat, flared up again over March and April. Israeli tanks attacked the West Bank in retaliation for the hundreds of dead and injured civilians resulting from fourteen suicide attacks since Christmas. Fact *is*, Palestine is going to run out of suicide bombers long before Israel runs out of people! Speaking of areas in conflict, East Timor became the first new nation of the millennium on May 20th when Jose Aexandre Gusmao was elected the Republic's first President. Australia has led an International peace-keeping force in East Timor since Indonesia's withdrawal in September 1999.

Without Me from Eminem became Marshall Mather's biggest seller to date but even more staggering, twenty-five years since his death, and Elvis Presley hit number one again, the last week of June with *A Little Less Conversation*. Now *that's* show business!

Our beautiful Lisa, whom I have unintentionally written-of but little, was now a genuine soccer star in the girls' league and in big demand with various clubs. The guiding light of her school teams, both indoor and outdoor (as with cricket) there were now barely any evenings left in the week she wasn't training or playing somewhere. All three girls have shown a great aptitude for sport, Kate also winning a premiership with her soccer team that year. Chris, I have to mention was no slouch either, be it baseball, soccer, roller-blading or tennis, at which he was at one stage pressing for a junior grading. Had he pursued cricket, I have no doubt he would have ended up opening the bowling for his State.

The worst act of terrorism since 9/11 struck Bali on October 12th. A massive car bomb exploded in Kuta, the principal tourist nightclub area of Bali. Two hundred and two people died including eighty-eight Australians. A further two hundred were badly injured. On October 26th Chechen rebels pulled off a front-page first, seizing seven hundred and sixty three hostages in a Moscow theatre. Russian authorities were none too shy about retaliation. They released lethal gas into the building which took out the rebels quite effectively, but also one hundred and sixteen hostages in the process. In hindsight it was designated a "successful operation." One would however wonder how relatives of the dead hostages viewed it?

Biggest selling cd's come Christmas, were *The Ketchup Song* from Las Ketchup (I'm serious!), *I'm with you* by Avril Lavigne and local girl (least, she lives barely ten minutes away) Delta Goodrem's *Born To Try*. I say "biggest selling" cd's, perhaps it would be more a truism to say biggest *downloaded* songs! To be honest, I can't recall when we last actually "bought" a disc.....pretty much everything is downloaded from *"Kazaa"* these days. Well might these "kids" have been pushing the boundaries of childhood to the nth, but that tray with the carrots, lettuce and beer *still* was the last task ticked off the "to do" list Christmas Eve.

Perhaps in a blaze of unheralded motivation, I completed two further chapters of this book during the January vacation period, possibly on account of the fact it is the one time of the year I am left to my own devices whilst the other four follow their various social and sporting pursuits. Many hours were still being expended researching and incorporating data for the benefit of our joint business enterprises, one or both products hopefully to be in store by mid 2005. Preliminary trial software sent over for evaluation was looking positive, though not yet running at simplistic "user" level.

Late March, early April, the world watched as coalition forces launched the War on Iraq, ostensibly because Iraq had thwarted repeated requests by the US to disclose the location of its alleged weapons of mass destruction. Backed by British and to a lesser extent Australian troops, the war was ultimately successful only in dismantling the Saddam Hussein dictatorship. The governments of all three countries lost substantial ground in the electorate over their handling of the war effort. Hussein meanwhile remained seemingly no nearer to capture than Osama bin Laden. Might have had something to do with the three billion dollar booty he managed to wheel out of the Palace, long before the first Tomahawk took flight! *His* luck however finally ran out in December 2003 when he was dragged dishevelled and alone from a rotting home-made bunker in rural Tikrit to face what might be termed an interesting Q & A session by his American captors.

Another family member became a licensed driver when Jenny scored her "P" Plates that winter. My having acquired yet another Falcon, the old Toyota, still running after three years and that which she had learned on, became Jenny's pride and joy. It may have been somewhat less stylish than her sibling's "wheels," but at least she wasn't paying hers off! Able to commute to Uni now without having to rely on (virtually non existent) public transport or other family members, her life took a definite turn for the better.

Kate obtained her twenty-first birthday key mid July and enters now a golden period of her young life, one she is indupitably in the Director's chair of.

From a viewpoint of constructive financial betterment, the last few months have contributed neither hope nor hindrance. Sure, completely unexpected news that our lovely home was to be bulldozed and redeveloped as a town-house site at the end of January 2004 was an eventuality we could have done without, but hey, these are small potatoes.

And so as I sat there on December 12th - my 58th birthday, I reflected on the passage of exactly forty years to the day since mum and I landed in Australia. For all the complexity, hurt and difficulty of those forty years, I wouldn't have done anything differently. The good times cancel out the negatives twenty to one! But for a blocked gall bladder in 1982, I have never been ill, I'm not susceptible to colds. Never needed glasses and will be requesting my last rites before I need a scrip for *Viagra!* OK, so what *physically* do I have to show for those two-score years? Roughly $27 in the bank (less the imminent monthly fees) and a truck-load of books, videos and dvd's? Wrong! I have five children...*best* investment I ever made!

Speaking of which, we all had especial cause to feel pride in Lisa's soccer achievements just up-front of Christmas that year, when she not only gained selection to the Australian girls' soccer team to tour Fiji, but was also instrumental in the team's successes. Typical, was her *own* critical assessment? *"I played crap dad!"*

With the wrecking ball but a few hours distant, February 2004 saw us move yet again to a rather magnificent home in Baulkham Hills – pretty much back where we started. Product development is showing a green light now and maybe, just maybe.....2005 will deliver what we have waited for the past decade and beyond.

Australia racked up an all-time best gold-medal tally at the Athens Olympics in August, with seventeen gold amongst their total of forty-six medals, thus topping their performance in Sydney 2000. Only Russia, the US and China managed better.

September 2004 and Madonna was once again re-inventing herself while Cher began spruiking her "farewell" concert. Iraq continues to pose greater image problems for the US than pre-Hussein. North Korea has nukes and Al Queda is waiting to take out the Empire State Building. Islamic-based terrorism in fact plumbed new depths of infamy with the Chechen school-hostage drama at Belsan late August, that saw more than three hundred and ninety people die, more than half of them young children.

Following the detonation of a two hundred kilogram fertiliser bomb outside the Australian Embassy in Jakarta on September 8th, it would now seem the network of terror has reached even the Antipodean doorstep.

It would have been preferable to close both this chapter and the year itself with a few balancing words of festive good cheer. Regrettably, the world was to witness at precisely 11.59 a.m. Boxing Day, what must be regarded now as the greatest natural disaster of modern times.

Following the collision of two tectonic plates ten kilometres below the ocean-floor, and barely sixty-five kilometres off the shores of Sumatra, an earthquake measuring 9.0 on the Richter scale created a subterranean faultline one thousand kilometres long and which forced up the ocean floor in places by more than eight metres. As the waves radiated outwards from the epicentre, tsunamis up to twelve metres high swept inland devastating the populated coasts of Thailand, Indonesia, The Maldives and Sri Lanka.

By mid January 2005, the death toll had reached a barely credible two hundred and forty thousand, seven hundred people, made worse by the fact that well over one-third were young children. In Sri Lanka the largest of the waves washed away an entire train, uprooting tracks and tossing the carriages back into the jungle. The *Queen of the Sea* as she was fatefully known was carrying more than seventeen hundred people. None survived. It enters the history books now as the greatest train disaster of all time.

Hundreds of thousands were injured, millions rendered homeless and the economic damage to the countries themselves in the multi-billions. Australia (who themselves confirmed thirty lives lost and up to twenty-five still missing) led the world in terms of immediate aid with a billion-dollar rescue package. Re-building of the affected areas will take many years.

For the remaining 6.4 billion of us left on the planet though, tomorrow will be just another day at the office – as it has always been. Despite the last Ice-Age, Pompeii, The Black Plague, Hitler, 9/11 etc, there's always the hope that next week might be better.

EPILOGUE

REF'S CALL

I have a recurring dream.

Of late we have taken as a family, to playing cards. Perhaps some innate group therapy....but we like it. Gives us all an opportunity to launch mini-vendettas against other members who may be viewed as having it coming to them. It's all in good fun - at least until someone throws their cards in their partner's face and stomps off to bed, blaming the cards, the other player's stupidity or just bad luck for their losing streak.

Tonight it is Rummy and the five of us are seated on the carpet in our regular spots watching Lisa deal. We snigger as Chris is dealt that worn old card with the slight tear at the corner...the rest of us all know it is the Jack of Diamonds. Doesn't help anyone particularly but it's fun knowing anyway!

Lisa as usual is creaming everyone. Jennifer sits there frowning with indecision and stroking Binkie, an overfed tabby of decidedly regal bearing, who is lying patiently on the lounge waiting for an end to the annoying contact. Kate, about to lay down the exact card Lisa needs to go out probably and Chris, one finger up his nose in customary profile, staring vacantly at what is probably the one pristine spot left on the carpet. It is my turn and I pick up the eight of clubs - the precise card I needed to lay down my hand and land them with a major counting job. Unheralded, an agonising pain grips my chest - hot steel is constricting me, I cannot breath, or even speak.

Words back-up in my larynx. I have no way to get them out and I drop the cards. The pain surely cannot get worse than this but it does. I grip my chest uselessly, the look of horror on the children's faces devastating in the extreme. Jenny moves to help me and Kate almost wrenches the phone from the wall-socket to dial 000.

Chris seeking to provide some support, pulls me towards the sofa, so unaware of its significance. The same one that bore dad's last seconds of consciousness all those years ago. Despite the jolting agonies, I smile at the irony. Vision is becoming unfocused though I can still hear their voices.

I cannot succumb...not now, not like this!

Someone is messing about with the brightness control. Everything is fading to black. I open my eyes, no wonder it was so dark - odd time to have closed them when you think about it. Very gradually the volume returns and the cacophany of sound is all about me. Jenny is hysterical as she holds on to my hand, which strangely I cannot feel. I am aware too of a complete cessation of pain now as I look down. Oh Christ, no..no...

I'm staring at my *own* body. So much smaller than I'd imagined myself to be and looking nothing remotely like the reflection, a lifetime of mirrors had led me to believe. Slumped there against the sofa, the scant hair appears whiter than I can recall and so sadly raked forward in places, in that time-honoured male fashion, trying forlornly to cover the bald patches. One strand aspiring to do the work of hundreds. As if it mattered! I look so *old.* the clothes are crumpled and worn and such that even in their heyday were clearly lacking a mainstream fashion sense. I look at each in turn. Jenny, only too aware of the unfolding tragedy in her midst, clinging to some vestige of hope. Lisa, my beautiful link with childhood, on the very fringes of maturity, facing an unexpected situation she is fighting to come to grips with. Katie - looking on with seeming calm but inside, her emotions tearing her apart and my only son Christopher, having to grow into a man with each passing second, as once did I. I cannot bear their distress and impending separation and I am filled with a sudden hatred of God, his empty promises and meaningless words of would-be gentility. *"Suffer the little children?"* His son died at thirty three, in agony yes, but not in the presence of his own offspring.

"Give us our daily bread and forgive us our trespasses?" Who is to forgive God for his trespassing here in my life....*our* lives? I cannot, *will not*, permit this! By enormous will and concerted effort I somehow regain control of my damaged body. The pain is beyond belief. Jenny sees the momentary flicker of my eyelids and grasps my hands ever tighter. Her expression is misery incarnate. I am aware suddenly of another presence, over to the left side of the room. I know it to be Joyce although the rippling in the very fabric of the air alongside, betrays no recognisable feature. Binks stares unconcernedly at a point where the wall meets the cornice.

"You must let go Noel, there is nothing further for you here. You will understand."

The words are not spoken, but I hear them nevertheless. As I look towards the source, I see her. The proud bearing, kindly expression, features restored to the peak of her youth, untouched by sickness or the taint of any life sufferance. She is not dressed as such, but appears swathed in some form of opaque apparel. Looking upon her, I am a child again. I wonder where Colin is and immediately become aware of a response. "He is waiting for you - it is time now to go."

I seem suddenly to be looking down at proceedings, the last scene of a play being enacted on a small stage. I try to hold out my hands, but I have none, I can see no part of myself, I am still rising imperceptibly. I *will* them to see me, to look up and know I am alright. Kate gets up suddenly and runs to the front door.

Two men in white uniform enter the room below. I watch as the paramedics perform CPR, desperately trying to regain control of a battle already lost. The children are lined up either side now and I feel their desperation, loss and anxiety. It is uniquely unbearable, being far worse than the pain of the heart attack itself. Now I discover one last facility denied to me - I can no longer cry and with no outlet for the all-consuming emotion building to a shattering climax, I emote in an agony of torment.

Kate looks up. It is a long glance and for the fleetingest of moments I see replacing the panic and horror, a look of questioning intensity. It lasts but a second, yet I cling to the notion that deep inside her subconscious - she *knows* and remembers. As I now remember. Even as the Humber ploughed its way towards the approaching Welsh dusk that cold day in December 1945, I knew *then* that this day was to come. Both it's exact date and time. I have always known! I look in Joyce's direction and she merely inclines her head, pleased that I have construed, at least in part, the truth.

Now she smiles, an expression of such overwhelming compassion. I look now upon my children. But they are *not* mine or even children, simply souls like myself dwelling in young bodies currently but with their own paths to find and walk down.

That I will be permitted to return and watch over them intermittently is beyond question, as I know now Joyce has done with me down through the years. I love them all dearly and realise at last the privilege it has been to know them in this incarnation and that the bond of familiarity can never be broken.....merely interrupted, as it has been. It is all such a very small segment of the maturing process.

They and the room fade from view as we rise ever higher. Whether through will or simply the granting of an unspoken request, I am suddenly aware of a shift in reality. Seemingly but seconds since the room passed from view, I appear to be descending through what seem to be cloud layers but are not, being of no earthly origin.

A panorama unfolds, one that is timeless, yet for me even now, brings full circle the events of a recent lifetime - one blessed with so much, but such that I could not see during its unwavering countdown, being distracted by the negatives brought to bear at times - both critical and less so. I was the luckiest of them all!

The grass undulates slightly beneath a summer breeze, its surface changing like brushed velvet, unsure of which side looks the better. Towards the centre of the green expanse, the most familiar of shapes. Small ripples disturb the surface of the water and from my vantage point I look down as the Lake relishes contentedly in its role as guardian of the great park. I see the railway engine as it ploughs its way alongside the shoreline once more and I can hear the children's cries of delight, a recurring echo from the past. Further up on the hill, the Mansion stands proudly, a lone white sentinel, watching over its charges, while to the east, the fairground appears to have more than it's fair share of customers. I strain to hear a well remembered melody. The Everly Brothers are still having trouble waking-up "little Susie" by the sound of it.

But there is one more thing, one last port of call. Moving ever westwards, the Lake narrows and becomes a stream. Eventually there looms a dense forest over which I pass silently, seeing clearly through the canopy of overhanging foliage, the main trail which snakes its way north. I arrive soon after, at that which I seek.

The garden shimmers with colour. Neat lawns and pathways bear witness to a family's pride in their home there, at the very edge of the park. I sense the great love in this place, such that will stand until the end of time itself.

Below, it is approaching dusk on a warm summer's night. A young boy tosses his cricket ball up a few times then runs in and bowls to his father. Words are exchanged, trajectories suggested and the boy bowls again, faster this time. The father looks down at his missing middle stump then looks back towards his son - he smiles!

By the same author.

IMAGINE FOR A MOMENT

Eight short stories:

"Greetings Y'all, I come in peace. The Lord is my Shepherd, Don't be Cruel....and puh'lease, don't step on ma blue-suede boots!" uttered the newcomer in a failed mastery of a southern accent.

"You mean 'shoes' don't you?" said Kevin, not entirely convinced he was fronting the genuine article.

"Shoes...boots, what difference?" added the figure, strumming a few notes as if to engender a feeling of bonhommie, "I'm back, that's all that matters."

"So you're Elvis?" mused Kevin, "What was your biggest hit?"

"It's now or Never," replied the other. "Satisfied?"

"What was on the flip-side of '*His Latest Flame?*'" Kevin probed further.

"Lordy, how can I remember?" retorted the newcomer running his fingers through his hair. Kevin noticed that his scalp didn't look quite right and rippled oddly around his forehead, directly beneath the jet-black kiss-curl.

"Little Sister,' he added, "that's it, *'Little Sister'*.....anything else?"

Kevin thought hard for a moment.

"What was your twin brother's name then?"

"Twin brother?" said the other. "Hell I never *had* no twin brother."

"Yeah? so who and what are you then?" demanded Kevin, hunched almost imperiously over some fallen masonry.

The other stared back at him quizzically.

"You mean he *did* have a twin brother?" the figure looked crestfallen, "Our databank does not record that information!"

Kevin noticed that the fake accent had been replaced by a flat nasal Aussie twang now.

"So why are you decked out like that?" he enquired.

"We like to set the local inhabitants at ease," replied the being, "Taking on the appearance of a well-known planetary identity usually works," he added, "Would you rather this?" Again he pressed various quadrants on the touch-screen of his 'form adaptor' returning instantly to the transluscent shape Kevin saw emerge from the craft earlier.

"Mmsgghth Ynllan shrrk imdo hrtunnsum yygh" emanated from the being's "head."

"Could you re-phrase that?" said Kevin dryly.

The figure tapped in a few commands, reconstituting himself as a Parking Police Officer.

"Sorry, that's the problem with our moleculiser," the visitor continued. "If we do not adopt human form, we cannot communicate in your language. You're wondering why we came?"

"It *had* occurred to me," said Kevin. "You just destroyed several buildings, a high-rise and a sports complex. You probably killed more than ten thousand people!"

"But there are *millions* on this planet," said the Officer, "does it really matter?"

Kevin thought for a moment. He was probably right. Certainly none of them were his friends - what *did* it matter when you came to think of it?

He noticed that the other was beginning to scribble on what looked like a small pad.

"What are you doing there?" he asked.

"Writing out a ticket," said the other, "Your vehicle is unregistered and parked on a public street - just doing my job y'know!"

Kevin was outraged. "Yeah? and what about *your* heap of intergalactic junk - illegally parked across the entire street? You going to book that too?"

"No need to be *aggressive* human," said the visitor. "I think if you knew the fire-power of that craft, you'd show a little more respect. Choose your words a little more carefully. Maybe even *apologise* for your inappropriate attitude here?" He handed Kevin the ticket, "Now, where were we?"

Extract from **CUBITUS DROPPED BY** © 2002

Coming in mid 2005

KIMLAN

A magical adventure for believers.

Lulu Publishing Inc, Morrisville NC
http://www.lulu.com/noel

© United Directory Systems (Aust) 2005

Printed in Great Britain
by Amazon